THE
LAST
LONG
RIFLE

DAN PARKINSON

The Paperback Trade
843-2947

ZEBRA BOOKS
KENSINGTON PUBLISHING CORP.

ZEBRA BOOKS are published by

Kensington Publishing Corp.
850 Third Avenue
New York, NY 10022

First Printing: July, 1995

Printed in the United States of America

For Carol,
forever

Prologue

The Shambles of War

Long Knob, Missouri, June, 1865

He was out of his head for a time, drifting in fogs so that sometimes he thought he was still in the war, while other times it seemed he was at home. Mary and little Tip were there, and Pa was helping them build a house. He couldn't quite see the house, but it was just right. Pa had built houses before, and he knew how to make it right.

But those were only dreams, and when they drifted away he knew that. He was in a house, with a roof over his head, but it wasn't his house or his roof. There were people there with him, and they came and went—a man, a woman, a wide-eyed little girl and . . . who else? Just them, it seemed. Them, and a dog named Biscuit. The only one that didn't keep drifting away, like the dreams that came and went—was the dog.

He wasn't sure the others—the three people—were real at all.

He slept, and he dreamed, but the dreams were all confusion. Pain like thunder in his head almost blinded him sometimes, and only made the confusion worse because when the pain swept over him he couldn't think at all. He simply endured it, because there was nothing else to do . . . and then he would sleep again.

Sometimes the people were there with him, and sometimes not. Sometimes he knew that they were feeding him, tending him, caring for him, and other times they simply existed . . . not people at all, but just patterns among the patterns, that moved around and blended with the light and the shadows.

For a long time, he was sick out of his head. But then things began to make sense, little by little, and he could recognize a face, or a voice, or the smell of bread baking in an iron oven.

The woman was young, with a face that might have been pretty given a chance. Little wisps of blond hair sometimes escaped from the severe austerity of her bonnet, and it was like sunshine. She had eyes that might have glowed like morning sky, had she let them, but it was not her way to glow. The little girl was like her mother must have been a long time ago. Of them all, he liked her best. She was too young yet to bind her soul with moral shackles. She was a free spirit. Like Biscuit, she was just what she was.

The man came in, as he did each evening, smelling of sweat and woodsmoke and fresh-turned soil. He came across to the narrow bed and looked down, his eyes concerned. He was bearded, but clean-shaven down to his chin. He had no mustache, and a word came to mind and hung there. Mennonites. These people were Mennonites. Or were they Quakers?

"How is our guest today?" the man asked, then leaned closer, peering. "Ah, thee can hear me, then?"

He tried to speak, but it was a rasp in his throat. All he managed was, "Who . . . ?"

"Good!" the man beamed. "Did you hear, Placid? He is awake." He sat on the edge of the cot, sighing as a man does who has spent a long day in the fields. "Jacob

Langenkamp," he said. "Yonder is my wife, Placid, and our daughter, Greta. Can thee say thine own name?"

"C-Caleb," he tried. "Uh . . . Sergeant. Sergeant Caleb . . . ah . . ." It wouldn't come. For an instant he had almost known, but then the instant was gone. He didn't know who he was.

"Poor soul," Placid murmured. "The injury to his head has cost him his memory."

Jacob Langenkamp patted his shoulder with a large, gentle hand. "All in God's time," he said quietly. "Thee has a head wound, Caleb. And other wounds as well. Thy arm was broken, but it is set and will mend. We believe ruffians beat thee and stole thy coat and boots. It was our Greta who found thee overhill. We brought thee home to tend."

"And Biscuit," he rasped.

The man's smile was almost a grin. "And Biscuit," he amended. "It was truly the old dog who found thee first, and led Greta to thee."

"I was . . . walking," Caleb struggled. "I was on a train, as far as it went, then I . . . I hitched, and I walked. I'm going home."

"Where is thy home?" Jacob asked.

"It's . . . I don't know. Mary is there, and Tip. And Pa, he's helping us build. He knows how to set a roof beam. It's . . . God, I don't know where! I don't know who I am!"

"Ease thyself," Jacob's calm voice soothed him. The woman— Placid— was there, too, with a cool cloth for his aching brow. "It will come," she said. "Rest thyself, and mend. God will let thee see, when it is time."

He slept, because there was nothing else he could do. The days passed, and he was stronger with each sun. He got himself up and about, and dressed himself though the pain in his left arm made that task excruciating. He had nothing but an old shirt and stockings, and a pair of nondescript britches that came from no uniform. But in the waist seam was a little pocket, and in the pocket was a metal tool. Placid had found it when she washed and mended his things. It was of brass, in the shape of a cross, and each of its little arms held a steel bit— a screw driver, a slender little spike like a steel needle that folded out on a hinge, a little open-end wrench and a stubby steel-wire brush. The whole thing was no wider than a dollar, and exquisitely crafted. At the center of the cross was a tiny design stamped into the brass— three letters: A-K-V.

He took it out into the sunlight to see it better. Warm breeze drifted through the little valley, rustling the leaves of big trees. For a time he sat in the sun, looking absently around at the rugged hills that were a close horizon in all directions. He felt at ease among the hills, and the trees were like trees he might remember, but there were no memories in this place. Home was somewhere else.

Again he got out the little brass-and-steel tool, studying it with eyes that sought answers. It might be a gun-cleaning tool, he supposed. Wrench, screwdriver, drum brush, and nipple pick . . . it probably was. But what did it mean? Why did he have it?

Who was he?

He sat on a stump, gazing around at the only world he seemed to know, the tidy little world of the Langen-kamps. The house was rustic, but sturdy. Skill had gone into the dressing and setting of its logs, the leveling of windows and doorframe, the careful pitch of its center-beam roof. A house built lovingly, and kept with care. Like the tidy gardens around it, the wide barn and assorted sheds behind and the cleared fields nearby, the homestead was not ostentatious or pretentious, but it was solid. It was an honest house, in honest surroundings, the home of honest people.

Decent people, he thought. Strange, but not so different from us, my Mary and little Tip. . . .

He hadn't heard Greta approach, but now she stood before him, her blue eyes dark with concern. "Are thee weeping?" she asked.

His vision seemed misty, and he wiped impatient fingers across his eyes. They were moist. "I was just . . . thinking," he muttered, then managed a smile. "I miss my home."

"Mama says thy head is cracked," Greta said. "But thee will mend. She says God knows thee for a good man."

"Then I wish he'd tell me who the . . . who I am," he shook his head. "I want to go home, child, but I don't know how." At his feet, Biscuit yawned and sprawled in the sun. He envied the dog. Biscuit was where he belonged, here. It would be good to be where one belonged.

Greta was looking at the trinket in his hand, curiously. "Does thee have a little girl like me, at home?"

"No, but I have a little boy. I call him Tip, though his name is . . . it's Thomas, like his grandfather. Tip would be about your size now, I think. Eleven or twelve."

"Do thee not know?"

"I've been away," he said. "I've . . . I know I've been to war. Do you want to look at this?" he handed her the little brass tool. "Be careful, that point folds out and it's sharp."

"What is it?" she held it in the sunlight, curious eyes probing it for secrets.

"A cleaning tool, I believe. It seems like I've had it a long time. But I don't know why."

He stood, stretching his lanky frame, noticing that the constant pain in his arm had diminished a bit. The break was healing itself. He felt the need to be doing something, and noticed a woodpile beside a flat-top stump.

He strolled over to it, and Greta and Biscuit followed along.

The axe was awkward for one hand, but he managed to split a chunk with it, then set it up and split it again. Greta bustled about, gathering the pieces. He had split a wood-box full before Placid Langenkamp came from the house with a pitcher of cool honey-water. "Rest thyself now, Caleb," she ordered. "Too much effort too soon will bind thee sore."

Summer breeze drifted in from the west field, where Jacob Langenkamp was working with a team of mules, turning dark soil around the edges of a ripening grain field.

"Wheat," Caleb said. "He's raising wheat there. Is that durum or hard red?"

"You know the wheats?" Placid noted. "Yon is hard red. They say the mills will open soon. We've not had a cash crop since the fighting. But Brother Lawrence has gone about and seen the mills at Cold Creek and Hays. He says they'll grind this year."

"Flour mills," he muttered, trying to grasp hidden memories that taunted him and then ran and hid. "The Osage started with durum, but then they sowed bread wheat. They needed milling. Pa built a mill for them. Then another . . ."

Placid hovered near, waiting, but there was nothing more. He sighed and shook his head.

"All in God's good time," Placid shrugged.

When he had rested, he walked around the place, seeing the barn, the carefully tended stalls, the hanging tackle. There wasn't much he could do with only one good arm, but he found things to do and he did them. And then he found others. It was good to work. It seemed like home.

When Placid called Greta in, the girl came to give back his brass tool, but he waved it away. "You keep that,

Greta," he said. "It is a pretty thing, and was built for an honest purpose. Maybe it will bring luck one day."

Except for the clothes on his back, it was the one thing in this world that he was sure was his. It seemed right that a little girl with bright eyes should have it.

Caleb stayed on. He helped with the harvest and he helped with the baling, and by first frost he had regained some use of his left arm.

He had a bed in the barn now, and Jacob had put up walls to give him a cubicle that was his own, with lamps and bedding, a wash basin and a bucket to bring water from the pump by the door. He had offered to drive for Jacob, hauling separated wheat to Cold Creek, but Jacob had been adamant about that. "Thee . . . uh, *you* cannot even say your name, friend," he said, "much less prove it. Those who robbed th— robbed you, took away thy identity. You were in the war, but on which side? They say the war has ended, but in these hills it goes on. When Mr. Lincoln was killed, it became worse. There are Jayhawkers on all the roads, who will hang any man they believe a rebel. And there are others who prey upon those the Jayhawkers pass."

These were unsettled times, he said— not safe for any man, but worse for a stranger who went in public. There had been . . . numerous incidents. Caleb would be safe enough here for the time being, until the brethren had a better plan or until he himself knew where he was bound.

"Why?" Caleb wondered. "I'm a stranger to you, too."

"We know what it is to be fugitives in our own land," Jacob said, sadly.

"Who are the brethren?" he asked. "You've spoken of them before."

"Friends," Jacob shrugged. "And neighbors. We keep

to ourselves, Caleb. Some of our people have been persecuted for their beliefs."

The tone of it was clear. He would say no more. So Caleb stayed close, and found what work he could to make himself useful. One season became another, and his host came and went and told him little.

Then on a bright, cold day, other men came. By twos and threes they arrived, and Jacob made them welcome at the house.

In the evening the lamps were lit and there were a dozen or more men gathered in Placid's parlor. Jacob came to the barn and knocked at Caleb's door.

"Thy . . . ah, *your* curiosity is evident," he said. "The men visiting are our brethren, Our meeting is private, but it concerns thy situation. I can tell you little more than that, Caleb, but Brother Lawrence bids me say to thee . . . to *you,* that we mean you no harm. We know you have been a soldier, and that you have lost your memory. We know that you were attacked and robbed. There are many who might do such a thing, but they are no friends of ours. We will help you if we can."

There were things they had not told him. He knew that. He had the feeling the "dangers" Jacob mentioned were far more than just dangers to himself. They were in danger, too. Yet they were concerned for him. He trusted them, and when Jacob returned in the midnight hour, with a quiet, stern man he introduced as Brother Lawrence, Caleb trusted him, too.

He would have to leave here, they said. The "bluecoat marshals" were being withdrawn to Springfield, and leaving these parts to the "Home Guards." They explained little, but there was an ominous sound to it.

The Home Guards would have no such constraints as the marshals. There were those who would use the new situation to their own ends. Many had old scores to settle, old grievances that festered in them, and there would be bad times.

But there were remote places, places where those caught up in the storm might wait it out, and Caleb had shown himself a decent man. He would be welcomed if he chose to go to sanctuary. Men were ready to spirit him away, to a place more safe than this, where he could rest and work and continue to mend.

"Your memory will return in God's good time, friend," Brother Lawrence assured him. "We offer a shelter until that time comes."

"What do you want from me?" Caleb asked. "I'm not of your faith. I don't even know what your faith is."

"No matter," Brother Lawrence said. "We each assist the needy as we can, for who can say when we may need assistance in return?"

He left the Langenkamps' that same night, hidden in the bed of a cart, and was given breakfast in a haybarn. Then he was hidden again, in a tiny space among hay bales in a tall wagon, and once again he was on the move.

Twice the wagon was stopped, by men who were only muffled voices beyond the hay, and once the hay was prodded with poles. But he wasn't found, and the journey continued.

He spent a night in a deep cleft among brushy peaks, surrounded by men he didn't know, and another night hidden in a dark loft. Then he and four other men— two of them Negroes— were taken by wagon up a steep, curling trail that led deep into high, rugged hills, a wilderness of daunting cliffs, vertical drops into shadowed little canyons, and eroded stone slopes.

When the sun was high, they came out of the forest on a ridge top from which all directions seemed to be down. In the shadowed distance ahead and below was a little settlement, and a precarious trail wound down toward it.

"This place is called Culver's Hole," the mule-driver told them. "All through the war, it's been a refuge."

"For whom?" Caleb asked.

"In war, them as chooses sides has little patience with them that don't," the driver said. "But some folks think there's better ways to solve problems than with armies."

A word appeared in Caleb's mind. "Shirkers?" he asked. "Been called that," the driver nodded. "That, an' worse. Anybody doesn't like it here can leave. Kansas is that way," he pointed westward. "An' the Territories yonder, southwest. Closest civilization is over there, though." He turned to point east. "Hays, it's called. Anybody want to take his chances with Judge Tolliver an' his bunch, that's where they be."

The little valley at the bottom of Culver's Hole was a strikingly pretty place. Dozens of little farmsteads crowded the rich bottomland, ringed by vertiginous slopes on all sides. "Y'all are welcome to stay here," the driver told them. "There's work enough for all, and roofs to sleep under. An' we got people out scoutin' ways to help you past the patrols when you're ready to go on your way."

"I'd settle for a place on one of them wagon trains goin' to the west," a scarred young man said.

"Me for Texas," another spat. "Just as soon as this leg will hold me."

The two Negroes said nothing, but Caleb knew what they were— freed slaves with warrants against them. There were those who balked at losing their Negroes, and used the law to hold them. Any bounty collector who found them would be a few dollars the richer.

"I just want to get home," Caleb muttered.

Get home. Everything would be all right if he could just get home. Mary would be there, and Tip. And Pa would be there. Pa could help him sort things out. Pa . . . he squinted, trying to remember Pa's name, because it was his name, too. But like always when he tried to concentrate, the thoughts just slipped away. Pa's name was Thomas . . . Thomas *what*?

The name would not come, and the harder he tried the fuzzier the images became. Now he couldn't even see Pa's face clearly. The last thing clear was the thing Pa held in his hand. An old long rifle, ornate and graceful in the style of an earlier time— brass trim embellishing a sleek maple stock, which couched a long, businesslike octagon barrel.

Caleb shook his head in frustration. The only name he could grasp was the rifle's name. She was called Lady Justice.

Springfield, Missouri, April, 1866

The mail coach from Jefferson City arrived at Springfield in mid-afternoon of a gray, soggy day. Three days on the road, it was spattered and muddy as it pulled up at an overhung platform in front of a two-story stone-and-brick building where the Stars and Stripes hung sodden on a whitewashed pole. Four soldiers with muskets stood disinterested guard at the platform, then snapped to form as a sergeant appeared at the door behind them.

Federal marshals riding coach escort tied their mounts and stepped up on the wooden platform to hand their documents to the sergeant. "United States mail," one of them said. "And two passengers."

A soldier stepped out, opened the coach and set a step-bench under its hatch. The two who emerged were an old man and a young boy, both seeming tired but fit.

The sergeant scanned papers in the marshal's packet, then looked at the arriving man. "Woodson?" he asked.

"Woodson," the man nodded. He was fairly tall, slim, and muscular of build, with a calm vitality about him that belied the iron-gray color of his hair. "Thomas Paine Woodson. And the boy is my grandson."

"His name?" the sergeant asked.

"Thomas Woodson, same as mine," the man said.

"You're a long way from Topeka," the sergeant noted. "Business trip?"

"We have family here," Woodson said.

The sergeant shrugged, closed his packet and stepped aside. "Yes, sir," he said. "Sorry for the formalities, but these are unsettled times."

"So I hear," Woodson nodded. "Has there been trouble?"

"There's always trouble. But just lately it's that murderer, Devil Luke. There's word he's around here these days."

Their luggage was being unloaded, and the boy stood watching, counting the pieces as they came off the coach—two valises, a pack like a sailor's duffle, but of leather instead of canvas, a small, bound trunk and a long, slim form in a soft leather sheath. When that was handed down, he took it, holding it protectively. It was as long as he was tall, and the soldiers glanced at it curiously, then turned their attention to the offloading of mail. It wasn't uncommon for travelers to carry guns, it was just that this gun's fine casing, soft suede with beaded patterns, made a man curious to see the rifle inside.

The unloading was almost complete when a closed carriage pulled up on the muddy street and a woman's voice called, "Thomas! Over here!"

Thomas Woodson waved at her. "Emily? Ah, girl, it has been a long time."

At the carriage, Woodson reached up and swung the young woman down, hugging her as her feet found the ground. "Emily," he grinned. "You are as beautiful as ever, child. There's someone here you haven't met . . ."

"Tommy?" she turned to the boy. "Of course you're Tommy!"

"Well, don't just stand there, Tip," Woodson said. "Say hello to your aunt Emily. Emily Dean."

"Hello, Thomas Speer Woodson," she said. "My, you're almost a grown man."

"Hello," Tip said. Wise eyes in a solemn young face studied her. "You look like my grandmother's picture," he said.

An hour later they sat in easy chairs in a small, pleasant parlor, and Emily poured coffee. "John was detained at the shops," she said. "So I came. I'm sorry the children aren't here to meet you, but John's sister has them at Jefferson City for the month. Has your journey been difficult, Thomas? Your wire was from Topeka . . ."

"Your letter found us there," Woodson said. "It must have been months on its way. We've been traveling."

"So I gathered," she nodded. "Looking for Caleb. And Mary . . . ?"

Woodson glanced at Tip. "It was the miscarriage," he said. "She became ill after Caleb left, and got worse. We found a doctor at Leavenworth with experience in such ailments. He said she had never healed properly. Then last summer she developed blood poisoning. It was a close thing."

"We weren't sure. The post has been so erratic."

"She'll be all right," Woodson assured her. "They caught it in time. She'll be in the sanitorium at Topeka for at least another month, but she's feeling well. She'll be good as new when we take her home. Tip has been traveling with me, taking care of me until his mother's well."

"What have you learned?" she leaned toward him, concerned.

"About Caleb? Well, we know he was mustered out at Jacksburg the past June, and took passage on the railroad as far as Chapel Hill. That's where the line ended then, though they're pushing it further west now. From there he hitched a ride to Brent's Crossing, then set out on foot. Said he didn't want to wait for a coach. Somewhere west of there he just disappeared."

"We'll find him," Tip said, emphatically.

"Yes, we will, son," his grandfather nodded. "We'll find him."

Woodson sipped his coffee, then fixed Emily with searching eyes. Like her sister, Rachel, Emily had become a beautiful young woman. Auburn hair caught the light from the window, and her eyes were the deep blue of morning sky. So like her mother, he noted, and a hard, tight pain lodged itself in his throat. So much like Martha. My love, I miss you so. . . . He blinked to clear the sudden mist in his eyes. "You said there was news of Caleb?"

"Nothing definite," she shrugged. "But there's this." From a bureau drawer she took an enameled box and opened it. Inside was a small, cross-shaped tool of brass and steel. Woodson lifted it out, looked at it closely, and sighed. "It's his," he said. "This is Albert Voigt's mark— the gunsmith who made it. Where did you find it?"

"Some people John knows. The Langenkamps. They have a little farm down by Cold Creek. They didn't say very much."

The old man stood, took the doeskin case from the boy and pulled out the rifle. Long and slim, sleek and elegant, Lady Justice seemed to glow in the muted light, a fine work of art in maple, brass, and steel. He opened the ornamented patch-box in its stock and took out a small utility tool. It was the twin of the one in his hand.

"We'll go to Cold Creek, then," he said.

"We don't even know if he's alive," Emily pointed out. "It has been so long . . ."

"My Dad is alive," Tip declared. It was the second

time he had spoken since they arrived at the Deans' house. "We just have to find him, that's all."

She nodded, understanding. "We're all searching, Tommy. We'll find him. Why don't you both rest now. John will take you out there tomorrow."

Tip retrieved the rifle, slid it back into its case, and set it by the hearth. "Grandad has had this a long time," he told Emily.

Thomas Paine Woodson leaned back in an easy chair, gazing at the beaded suede of the old case, still seeing the rich metals and sleek wood beneath, and remembering.

A long time. So very long ago, it seemed, but only yesterday. He had been about Tip's age then, and there had been an old man . . . a fierce old man he cherished just as Tip cherished him now.

Memories, he mused. A man lives in his memories. Without memories, a man is no one at all.

Memories and old stories that filled the gaps of memory . . . gazing at the old rifle standing by the hearth, and at the little brass-and-steel tool he held in his hand, Thomas Paine Woodson let his mind drift back over the years, remembering.

I

The Foundling

Western Kentucky, 1805

The cabin was fairly new, but poorly built and drafty. Its single door hung askew on cracked leather hinges, and the shutters of its windows were broken. Chill autumn winds crept through the chinks, and the place stank of illness and death. But the woman lying on filthy quilts by the cold hearth no longer smelled it. Dimly, she knew that she had been worried . . . some time in the past. But she didn't remember why. It seemed as though she had lain there, drifting and alone, since time began.

A day had passed, and a night. Or maybe it was many days and nights. Several times, the boy had come to the door, but she had ordered him away. Now she didn't know where he was. Through timeless interludes she had clung to life, praying that someone would come. Then she had stopped clinging, because it seemed that no one would.

Yet now, abruptly, there were sounds and voices, creak of hinges and the presence of people in the gloomy space around her. She tried to speak, but could not. Then someone— a solid, husky man in fine, dark garb— was kneeling beside her, cradling her head, giving her water. Beyond him, seen dimly, were others. It seemed as though they had always been there.

She tried to speak then, remembering what must be said. Her voice sounded like far away wind, and she tried again. "The child," she whispered. "See to the child. His name is Thomas."

The man above her turned slightly aside. Light from the door limned a strong, solemn face with pronounced brows and dark, shadowed eyes. Distantly, she heard his voice and the voices of others, but she couldn't tell what they were saying. It seemed, though, that she heard a name spoken. Her husband's name.

Then the dark eyes were upon her again and a deep, soft voice asked, "Madam, where is your husband?"

"Gone," she whispered. "He said he'd be back soon. But he didn't come back. He was wary, sir. Some don't care for him, because he has dealt with the heathen. But it was only a bit of trade." Her voice faded to a faint, rustling sound. She was very weak. "The boy . . ."

Other voices murmured in the background.

"The child is safe," the man said. "What of your friends . . . your neighbors?"

"No one." Her words were barely audible. "Most of them gone, I guess. Men came. Burned barns. Tore down fences." She tried to see him more clearly, but he was only a shadow. "Somethin' in the water. It went bad. Some taken sick. We were the last ones here." Summoning strength with an effort, she panted, then continued. "You are a Christian gentleman, sir. I can see that by your clothing. See to the boy. He's a good child. His name is Thomas. Thomas . . . ah, Thomas Paine . . . Thomas Paine Woodson."

"Try to be still," the man said. "Just rest. The child will be all right."

"Promise me," she whispered, urgently. "Don't let the heathen find him . . . or them that burns barns. Take care of him."

For a moment, the man hesitated. Then he nodded. "I promise," he said. He turned to snap a command to others there, then stopped. The woman was not breathing. Gently, he let her head down and pulled the old quilt over her.

"Wash the child and wrap him warmly," he told others around him. "Give him food . . . only a little at first." The language he spoke to them was not the precise English the woman had heard. It was not English at all. It was rhythmic speech— oddly clipped-sounding, yet musical, like the midday sounds of deep forest.

The man looked down at the dead woman, only his eyes betraying any emotion. They narrowed slightly, pity tinged with anger. "They take everything," he muttered, once again in English. "From us. From one another. Then they only destroy what they take, some move on . . . some stay and die. They do not even take care of their own."

At his shoulder, another muttered, "The dead man we found . . . this was his home?"

"It was," the first nodded. "His own people killed him . . . and left these to die."

Moments later smoke drifted from the chinks and cracks of the little cabin, smoke that thickened and rolled and was followed by climbing flames. Within an hour, the cabin would be a smoldering ruin, its burned timbers fallen in upon themselves. By day's end it would be nothing but stubs and ashes.

But there was no one there to see the smoke, or the flames. The dark-cloaked men were gone. It was as though they had never been there.

Indiana Territory, Two weeks later

Cold mist crept across the fields and up the narrow road— low, insinuating mist that shrouded the darkening forest and made Louis Champon's dooryard a bleak, small island in a void of deepening gray.

Beads of moisture formed on the Frenchman's leather hat as he set a copper lamp on his gatepost and opened its little port. The yellowish glow would tell those who were coming that he was alone and they were welcome. Turning his back on the dim light, he leaned against his gate, letting his eyes adjust to the fading gloom. They would be here soon.

Beads of moisture dripped from the stained old tricorn hat he wore, and misted about the wide shoulders of a dark woolen coat with its wide lapels and brass buttons. His slightly-bowed legs were encased in slick-worn buckskin, and the moccasins on his feet were high-laced and finely beaded. Though short of stature, the Frenchman was by no calculation a small man. Broad and sturdy, Louis Champon had proven himself in the sporting rings, back in the days when there was no silver in his hair. As a boxer and wrestler, he was a match for any Scotch-Irish brawler and most Shawnee.

As the lantern hissed and glowed on its post, he raised his head. In the tiny sounds of the forest, something had changed. Ears attuned to the language of the wilderness told him of a moving presence nearby, and his eyes narrowed in speculation. The sound— or absence of sound— was south of him, off the trace. Those he awaited would come from the north, of course, but it would be like them to circle around and come in from another quarter. Once masters of this land, they had always been skilled at furtive movement. And bitter experience had taught them how to be cautious.

On impulse, Champon drew a long, oiled buckskin

sheath from his coat, unrolled it and picked up the bright rifle leaning against his fence. With gentle hands he slid the rifle into the case, hiding the luster of exquisite dark steel, maple, and brass.

Let there be no misunderstanding, he thought. The rifle is pledged. It is not for trade.

Some of Tanecot's young men had hungry eyes.

He heard no further movement. Specter shrouds of drifting vapor muted the forest's furtive sounds, swallowing them as fogs swallowed the last light of evening. Near at hand, leafless limbs were dim traceries against a darkening background of gray. Champon felt a deep sadness as he gazed along the road— *his* road, that in better times had seen the coming and going of trading parties almost daily. This place had been remote then, distant and isolated, deep in the broad forest which was a buffer between the then-distant Anglo settlements to the south and east and the Indian lands north and west. Here Champon had come, to build his cabin and open his road. He had offered a sanctuary. In a time of ceaseless conflict he had made for them a neutral ground. And they had come. From all directions they had come, to meet without paint, without stealth or challenge, in a place of truce.

And because of Champon— or simply because even the most violent of men need respite sometimes— they had kept their peace in this place. For a time they set aside their memories and stifled their hatreds. Here was a place where a man might pretend that he did not smell the powder stench in the air or see the bloodstains on the ground.

There had been too much war. Generations of war. British and French had shed one another's blood on this land. Then royalists and rebels, and after that British and French again. And for the nameless ones— the restless Americans and the roving bands of Indians— the conflict had been constant. By the hundreds and by the thousands they killed each other, without cease.

More often than not, Champon felt, the warfare between frontiersman and Indian was orchestrated by other powers. Gauntlets flung down in the stone houses of Europe and the American east had demanded their price in the wilderness to the west. European enmities— white men's enmities— had blossomed on American ground, and always the red man was drawn into it.

And always, it seemed, it was the red man who paid the price.

But through those years, even in the midst of bloodshed, there had been commerce. Each combatant in each conflict had a taste for what the other produced. And so they met to trade, and Louis Champon's outpost remained a neutral place. And some among them— the red and the white alike— blessed the respite. They came with their wares, and paused there to rest— to smoke their pipes and warm their ale, to haggle over prices, to exchange news and share the bread from Louis Champon's ovens.

Here they had shared sanctuary for a time, each from the others.

Now the proud road was only a narrow gash, a fading trail crowded by encroaching brush. *C'est la vie,* Champon thought. Times change. Yet his cheeks tightened in a sad smile at the irony of it. Only a few seasons past, Ville Champon— or Fort Champon as the Anglos called it— had been a reclusive haven, remote and isolated by distance from all neighbors. Yet it had been a haven of good company. Always there were visitors, in those days. Now the place was no longer remote. The tide of settlement unleashed by the Americans' rebellion— a formidable outpouring of displaced humanity controlled by no crown, no congress, no pact or treaty— had washed across this land and engulfed it. The British had withdrawn beyond the lakes, and the Indians north of the Ohio were left alone to face the "Kaintucks," as some called the relentless, formidable white immigrants who poured in from the south and east.

At Fallen Timbers the heart had been torn from the Shawnee people. In seasons since, the "peace chiefs" had ceded land— valley after valley and league after league. The immigrants came by the score and by the thousands, marking the land, claiming it as their own. And what the immigrants demanded, Governor Harrison took from the Indians. Tens of millions of acres of land— Indian territory by treaty— had become farmsteads. And still the "Kaintucks" came, always demanding more.

Now Ville Champon was surrounded by neighbors. From the top of his hill, on a clear morning, Louis Champon could see the smokes of dozens of breakfast fires in the hearths of cabins so new that sap still ran from their shorn logs. Now there were people everywhere.

And now the place was lonely.

Cold and thick with suspended rain, the mist seemed to soften the land— defeated remnants of forest encircling wide barren grounds where gaping wounds of fire and axe were scars that would never go away. Here the land would never again be as it once was. An age had ended, and new seasons' suns would shine on a different kind of world. As though appalled by what it touched, the fog crept in, as soft and melancholy as cold kindness, drawing its tattered blanket over the ravaged land. In dim autumn evening the mist drifted, obscuring everything. Beyond Louis Champon's gate now were only the dim ghosts of nearby, barren tree tops. They stood in silence, like ancient warriors grieving over the graves of their fallen dead.

Louis Champon knelt to inspect once more the stack

of bundles beside the gate. Expert eyes traced the folds and laps of the sailcloth parcels. Expert fingers ran along their bindings, pausing to test a buckle here and tighten a hitch there. Six packs were there, each weighing forty pounds.

Copper pots and bleached soap, he mused. Darning needles and skeins of combed wool. Little pots of vermilion, indigo, whale oil, and camphor. Dried spices and children's sweets. Tobacco and flints. And ranked alongside the packs were a half-dozen bound kegs of rum. His consignment for the village of Tanecot. Such small baggage, Champon thought, to contain the little comforts and civilized niceties of more than a hundred dispossessed people venturing from a wilderness gone to a new wilderness not yet tarnished.

One-eye could be right, he mused. The Shawnee's worst enemy is his taste for white-man luxuries. Louis Champon had never met Tenskwatawa, who was called "the Prophet," but he had heard of him. The one-eyed warrior had become a power among those Shawnee who followed the great war chief, Tecumseh. As Tecumseh's brother, the Prophet's station among the Shawnee was one of respect. But the spell-binding power he could exercise over his people was his alone. There are plenty of young warriors, Champon told himself, who would gladly follow Tenskwatawa to hell if he decided to go there.

Tecumseh, they said, was somewhere in the south, meeting with leaders of other tribes. In his heart, Champon hoped that the "chief of the Lovely River" would return soon. Left alone among the Shawnee, the Prophet might do anything. The man had a reputation for fierce unpredictability.

And yet, there was a seed of wisdom among his commandments to the Shawnee. Abandon the ways of the white man, the one-eyed man told them. Abstain from their perversions, and we will defeat them. He had been taken up to the spirit world, he said, and had returned with revelations from the Master of Life.

By abandoning all white ways, the red man could become strong again— strong enough to rise up against the white invaders and crush them once and for all.

"A madman," Louis Champon muttered to himself. "Still, in a world full of Bonapartes and Hanovers, of Calhouns and Tammanends, of Darwins and L'Ouvertures, who's to say where madness begins?" Just in the few months Tecumseh had been away, Tenskwatawa had become a power among the malcontents of the Shawnee people. If Tenskwatawa the Prophet had possessed the stability, the constance, the sheer force of presence of his brother Tecumseh, Tenskwatawa might rule a mighty nation one day. But Tenskwatawa was not Tecumseh.

A sudden stillness fell upon the mists of evening, and Louis Champon raised his head. There. Just beyond his gate, riders sat in silent silhouette, a dozen dark forms shrouded by the mist. Broad hats and high boots, wide belts and tailored cloaks . . . they did not seem, in the mist, to be Indians. But Champon knew they were. It was the way of the Shawnee, to seem not to have arrived, but to just be there.

As though they had always been there.

Champon glanced along the rank of them, surprised and wary. These were Shawnee, but not the ones he had expected. These were not the men of Tanecot's village. He squinted, studying them one by one in the fading light. Then his gaze found a familiar figure there— a quiet, broad-shouldered form in a dark traveling cloak that revealed white linen and a sleek cravat at its parted lapels. At first glance, even in good light, the man might have been a colonial gentleman out for a canter in the rain. Resting easily in the English saddle of a fine, dark horse, with his dark hair pulled back in a queue and the brim of a fine hat shadowing his eyes, he might have seemed a Virginia squire or a Pennsylvania merchant, just as those flanking him might have seemed young provincial gentry, carrying their rifles and pouches, out for a casual adventure.

But only at first glance. The leader gazed down at Champon, a shadowed gaze that seemed to go right through him. His deep-set, brooding eyes were like bright agate beneath his hatbrim. They were not the eyes of any colonial, and the strong jaw and wide, pensive mouth were those of no European.

"I see you, Frenchman," the man said quietly, with the precise diction of one to whom English was a second— but well-learned— language. Champon raised his hand slowly, a hesitant welcome, a gesture of respect. "I see you, Chief Tecumseh," he said. "It has been a long season."

"We have been far in the lands of the white *gentry,*" Tecumseh said, putting a slight, ironic emphasis on the word.

And passed among them without their notice, I warrant, Champon thought. He suspected that, sometime in the far past, the Shawnee had learned the secrets of camouflage from their old enemies, the Cherokee. It was said that a Cherokee could become invisible when he wished. But wherever the Shawnee had acquired the skills, they had acquired them well. A Shawnee warrior could be a wolf among wolves, a deer among deer, or the very leaves of the forest. He could go anywhere and hide anywhere— as many a white settler had learned, the hard way.

But such thoughts were not to be spoken. "My door is open and my hearth is warm," the trader invited. "Chief Tecumseh and his followers are welcome to rest."

"There is no time," the chief shrugged. He gestured

at the packs and bales by the gate. "These are for Tanecot?"

"Such as they are," Champon shrugged. "One does one's best."

"Then we will take them," Tecumseh nodded. At his gesture, several of those around him dismounted and led forward spare horses. Expertly, working in misty half-light, they began collecting green limbs and wrist-thick poles, assembling these into pack saddles and travois. Tecumseh stepped down from his saddle. Handing its reins to another man, he came around the gate to stand beside Champon, counting and classifying the packed goods. "You know the meaning of this?" he asked, quietly.

"More Shawnee are leaving this land," the trader said. "Tanecot will go."

Tecumseh nodded, bleakly. "Before snow, most of the Lovely River people will be in Canada. The British do not love us, but they have not betrayed us. So they are our allies," he said. "Others will join us there."

"I hate to see your people go," Champon said.

"We cannot stay here, Frenchman. We must leave. At least, for now." His gaze reached the slim buckskin case standing against the fence. "And this?" he pointed.

"It is my own," Champon said. "A new rifle I got from a Hessian immigrant. Built by his brother, he claimed. It was his best work. I have promised it to a friend, so it is not for trade."

"Of course not," Tecumseh chuckled. "But is it also not for sight?"

With an apologetic grin, Champon picked up the rifle and shucked off its case. He had hesitated to show it—such a handsome implement, with its bright metalwork so appealing to the Indian eye. But Tecumseh was no thief. Champon raised the rifle in both hands, holding it under the lantern's open port. "The Hessian charged me dearly for this," he said. "He claimed his brother had built the 'perfect rifle' in this piece. Maybe it *was* his best work. It was his last. He died the very week it was completed."

"Perfect?" Tecumseh tilted his head. "A gun is a tool. Tools do not have perfection, only function."

"The Hessian held that the 'perfect rifle' is a rifle capable of one perfect shot," Champon shrugged.

"One perfect shot?"

"So he said, though I'm not sure what that means. It is a good rifle. It shoots truly if one aims truly. But so do most rifles."

"Pretty work," the Shawnee noted, extending a hand. Then he withdrew it abruptly, as though the rifle had burned his fingers. He turned aside abruptly, away from the light. "Put it away," he growled. "I have seen it."

You act as though you'd seen a ghost, Champon thought, but said nothing. Quickly, he slid the rifle into its sheath and secured it.

Beyond the fence, men worked— silent men whose elegant cloaks, waxed boots, and wide, English hats almost hid the fact that beneath the fine fabrics and elegant manners were Shawnee warriors. Tecumseh said something in the quick, clipped syllables of Shawnee speech, and one of the men came from shadows, carrying an awkward bundle. It squirmed, and small, stifled sounds came from it. At the gate he handed it to Tecumseh, who cradled it gently in one strong arm while he flipped aside a corner of its wool wrapping. Within the bundle, large, blue eyes blinked and peered out at the Frenchman— wide eyes in a small, frightened face.

"We found this waif south of the river," Tecumseh explained. "It has no one to care for it." Without ceremony he thrust the blanket-wrapped child into the arms of the trader. A fold of blanket fell away, and Champon found himself gawking into the frightened eyes of a skinny, tow-headed urchin— forty pounds of trembling life wrapped in a plain, dark blanket. "You attend to it," the Shawnee said.

"This is a child!" Champon blurted. "I have no use for a child! I can't care for it."

"Then give it to someone who can," Tecumseh shrugged.

"Take it with you," the Frenchman insisted. "Let your women take care of it."

"A white child raised by Indians?" Tecumseh asked ironically, agate eyes fixing on the trader. "In times like these? Attend to the child, Frenchman. If you don't, who will?" From his coat he drew an oilcloth pouch. "Claim papers," he said. "White man's claims. This is the boy's. Do with it as you will." Pressing the packet into Champon's hand, he reached into his belt pouch, then extended his hand. "This is his, too," he said. "I made a promise." The thing he held was a small, beaded ornament on a thong, the sort of amulet a Shawnee might wear.

Champon took the trinket, and Tecumseh nodded. As though there were nothing further to say, he turned away.

Louis Champon was still standing beneath his lantern, holding the trembling urchin in his arms, when the Indians mounted their horses and took up their pack leads. Tecumseh reined around, then paused, looking down at Champon across the fence.

"Leave this place, *mon ami,*" the Shawnee said. "Go to Quebec or the Louisiana lands. The trouble between England and France is flaring again, and the Americans will be provoked to join in. When they do, they will find us waiting. Our friends will not be your friends, Louis. Find a place where war cannot seek you out."

"The child!" Champon blurted. "Does it have a name?"

"Its name— *his* name . . . is Thomas Paine Woodson. Ask him yourself. He can speak." Tecumseh raised a casual hand. "Go in peace, trader."

"And you as well, Tecumseh," Champon sighed, knowing that there could never be peace for the leader of the free Shawnee. "Go in peace."

Yet the last was said to no one but himself and the waif shivering in his arms. The Indians were gone. The mist and the darkness swallowed them, and they were no longer there.

It was as though they had never been there.

II

The Warriors

Southeastern Michigan Territory, 1813

Perry's flotilla held Lake Erie in that angry, gray season. Gunboats off Pelee relayed the message with their bombards. American guns commanded the waters from Put-In-Bay to Grosse Ile, and they had snapped the British supply lines as a man might snap a twig. Now Detroit lay open, empty of the British soldiers who had patrolled there from Fort Malden, and Harrison's regulars were on the march. The British garrison at Fort Malden, commanded by Henry Proctor, was without support. In a matter of a few months, Proctor had gone from tyrannical overlord of a vast region, to the besieged commandant of a threatened garrison.

Proctor knew that he could hold for a time. He had the advantage of a land base on narrow waters, and of a fortified position against land attack. But it was only a matter of time. Malden was a cul-de-sac, vulnerable from every side and a long way from the nearest British headquarters. Perry's navy would come at him, and Harrison's troops . . . and, the most feared, the horde of American "citizen soldiers" gathering now by the hundreds and thousands. Fort Malden's stores were low, and the converging American ranks were swelling by the day. As civilian militias hurried to join them. Resistance would be futile, without supplies or reinforcements.

The Crown's Indian allies were ready for an all-out fight. They were ready to make a stand. Tecumseh had gone so far as to demand it, drumming his fingers on Proctor's desk as he spelled out the logic of a sweep attack against the Americans— a drive in force across the river and a two-pronged attack. The Newfoundland Brigade could sweep down from Detroit, he said, while the 45th crossed at Bois Blanc to hit their flank. The approaching Americans were not Harrison's entire army— only an advance brigade, and a company of cavalry under Conroy. A few hundred soldiers and some militia.

Such an attack might drive them back into the wilderness. Scatter the attackers, Tecumseh urged. Push them into the forests. Give us that much, then withdraw behind your walls if you like. Only scatter them, so we can meet them our way, on our terms.

Another commander might have been tempted. They had all seen what the Indians could do in a strike-and-run conflict, on wooded terrain. But Proctor was a deliberate and methodical soldier. He was not an imaginative man, nor given to any sort of innovation. Such tactics as Tecumseh proposed were no more than theatrics, in his opinion. To Proctor, the situation was clear and simple. His supply lines were broken. There would be no reinforcements, and the Americans were at his doorstep. Fort Malden had become untenable.

A show of resistance, here on this side of the river— on ground claimed by the Americans— would be only a show. Worse, it could be embarrassing to the Crown. It was obvious that the only prudent course was to retreat. And the only sanctuary lay far to the east, deeper into Ontario. Calkin was at York, the garrison some now called Toronto. Once there, Proctor's little force would be part of a much larger force.

The commander climbed to his gate tower. There lay the river, and there— to his left— the waters of Lake Erie With American gunboats on the lake, Fort Malden had become almost an island. So far, no enemy had attacked him here. No soldiers had crossed the river, and no shelling had reached his wharfs. The Thames road was open, with no obstacles. But from the lake had come the sound of cannon, and his patrols had seen the smoke of Conroy's forward unit, as well as other smoke . . . militias moving in support. Time was running out.

Perry was on the lake and Harrison on the land, and between them, at the mouth of the Detroit River, lay Fort Malden, only a few miles from the village of Detroit and ripe for the taking. And now the frontier militias were on the march. Like a dark tide, they flowed through and beyond the advance units of William Henry Harrison's army, without the hindrance of central command to slow their march. The militias were nominally attached to the army. But in fact they were free agents, each with its own command. Some chose to join the ranks of the Butternut Brigades. Others did not. Many had their own ideas of what this war was about and how to pursue it.

From New York and Pennsylvania they came, from the Appalachian settlements, from Snowy Point and Albany, from Chesterton and Vincennes, from the wilderness of Indiana Territory and the new settlements along the Ohio. And from Kentucky's bloody meadowlands streamed companies of mounted riflemen. Some of them were old enough to recall the howling Red Knife times, thirty years before. All of them knew of the massacre at the Raisin. Among them lived a hatred of Indians— especially of the Shawnee— that burned as bright and cold as when the scalps taken in past times were still fresh with blood.

A generation past, the colonies had freed themselves from a preoccupied British crown, to begin the building of a separate nation. But now, again, British interference had become a nuisance. King George plied his war against Napoleon's France, and meddled with American trade in the process. British warships hounded free American traders on the high seas. West of the frontal mountains, Indians still pursued their harassment of American settlers, while British outposts gave sanctuary to the savages and openly encouraged them. Atrocities were a daily occurrence in some areas.

Conscription of sailors from American vessels at sea was not the final insult between governments, but it was the pivotal one. The United States declared war.

England was far away, but the English were not. They were near at hand, along the border and in Canada. Some even remained in the new American territories, occupying posts they had refused to abandon. And many of the Indians— those who had refused to trade with Americans— were with them, a dark presence constantly threatening those frontiersmen who spilled ever further westward across the land. Untold numbers of red warriors were aligned now with the Crown's Canadian troops. There were Peoria, Miami, and Illini. There were Sauk and Fox, Menominee, Kickapoo, Ojibwa, and Pottawatomie. There were remnants of the proud Ottawa, refugee warriors of the once-mighty Pequot and even a smattering of silent, deadly Cherokee and formidable, mystic Lenape, scattered here and there among them.

Each tribe, in its way and in its turn, had tried first to placate the Americans, then had fought to stem the tide of American invasion. Now the best and fiercest of the survivors, the renegade remnants of many great tribes, were banded together, allied to the British, an army within an army. At the center of this force were the free Shawnee, and at the head of the Shawnee stood Chief Tecumseh.

Now in his forty-sixth year, the man named Tecumseh had nearly succeeded in his dream of an intertribal alliance reaching from Canada to the Gulf of Mexico. Classically educated and as fluent in English and French as he was in several Indian languages, Tecumseh had traveled the country for more than a decade, forging alliances. He knew the customs and ways of the whites, and he knew their weaknesses as well as he knew the weaknesses of his own reclusive cousins. Tecumseh had dreamed of all the tribes becoming a single Indian nation, a vast confederacy strong enough to meet the new American nation on its own terms, through diplomacy and statesmanship.

The plan had almost worked. But then, just as the powerful southern tribes were listening favorably to Tecumseh's words, disaster had come at a place called Tippecanoe. Tenskwatawa the Prophet had grown impatient with his brother's slow, careful diplomacy. Convinced of his own infallibility as a messenger of God, the man sometimes called One Eye had recruited his own band of fanatic followers. Among them were the fiercest of the Shawnee— seasoned warriors obsessed with revenge for old wrongs, hard-eyed young bloods impatient for a fight, and some who— like Tenskwatawa— had been touched by the spirits and were no longer ordinary men.

Acting on his own, at a time when Tecumseh was away, the Prophet led his zealots in a series of raids to provoke a military response. When an expeditionary force led by General Harrison— that same William Henry Harrison whose "treaties" had cost the Shawnee half their lands—

marched from Cincinnati, Tenskwatawa was waiting to attack.

Tenskwatawa had been wrong. He and his followers were defeated at Tippecanoe. William Henry Harrison became a hero among the white people, and Tenskwatawa's name, drenched with defeat, was without honor. With his survivors, he fled. It was a humiliation. And as Tecumseh's brother, the humiliation reflected upon Tecumseh. The episode put an end to his dream of alliance. Many of the tribes turned their faces from him, and the free Shawnee fled again to Canada.

But still they were a formidable force, and still there were those who chose to join them because their own tribal leaders had no better answers to white expansion than Tecumseh. Tecumseh had lost prestige, but they knew of no other way to face the white tide, than to follow him.

The "Kaintucks" and the Shawnee knew each other very well. Since the first white men crossed through Cumberland Gap, they had been mortal enemies. Each had shed too much of the other's blood for the memories to fade. Old grudges remained, like glowing embers ready to flare . . . old grudges and fallen dreams.

So, while American warhawks ranted in the reeking, unfinished corridors of the new capital at Washington, while swift American merchantmen joined their privateer cousins at sea, while the roving little armies of the United States moved against the border armies of the Crown, the citizen militias of the western frontiers charged their flash-pans and went in search of old enemies. It was a time for the settling of grudges.

It was autumn now, of the year 1813, and the War of North America was in its second year.

Thomas Paine Woodson had heard the guns— like distant thunder— as he rubbed down the captain's horse by leaden twilight, within sight of the mouth of the little

Huron River. The echoes of cannons' muted drumming clung to his mind as he ate his portion of salt meat and hard bread, and set the tempo of his dreams as he slept beside a guttering fire beneath a dark, spitting sky. The new century was in its thirteenth year, and Thomas Paine Woodson was in his twelfth. Large for his age, awkward sometimes and uncertain of his place in the world, he was still only a boy. But like the men who slept around him in this travel camp, he had been weaned on strife.

With morning the guns signaled again, distant rumbles of sound from the east that seemed to dance among the barren trunks and deadfall thickets of the gray forest.

Wolfing down a few morsels of cold food by first light, the boy rolled his blankets, strapped on his wide belt with its slung axe, and struggled into his old groggin coat. It was too tight through the shoulders, and its sleeves— like the stained and tattered legs of his loose breeches— were too short. It seemed to him, sometimes, that his arms and his ankles had always been cold. As he secured his coat, one of its buttons fell loose in his hand. "Devil take it!" he muttered, grimacing as his voice danced between unaccustomed baritone and a falsetto tenor. It sometimes did that, these days. With another muttered oath, he picked up his belongings, hoisted Captain Cadmont's heavy saddle and hurried toward the pole corrals where nearly a hundred horses awaited their riders.

All around the camp, men were coming awake, rolling out of their bedding to stretch, yawn, and make ready for another day. There was activity around Captain Cadmont's tent, and from the south pickets the boy could clearly hear the strident voice of Captain Stanton— raised in complaint, as usual. As First Company's liaison with the Army of the Northwest, Hall Stanton had seldom been present on the march northward. He and his sons preferred the company of General Harrison's staff to that of his own neighbors from Louisville District.

But when he did show up, it seemed he never missed an opportunity to criticize. Stanton was a cold, arrogant man, and the men of Louisville Company sneered behind his back. "High an' mighty popinjay," they called him. The Stantons had a bad name around Louisville. Even a twelve-year-old knew that. Thomas had ears, and heard the talk. He didn't really know why, but most home folks didn't care for the Stantons. Maybe— as Mistress Merry had said one time— it was because the Stantons were originally Massachusetts people. Most of the families around Louisville hailed from Virginia or the Carolinas, and the peculiar ways of Massachusetts people didn't set well with them.

Maybe it *was* because of being from Massachusetts that Hall Stanton and his sons behaved as they did. Then again, maybe it was because of certain lands Stanton held as receiver— lands that others had cleared, then lost to night riders or to federal warrant.

Whatever the reason, Hall Stanton was not a liked man. Thomas knew the man only by sight, but he had worn the bruises of a brawl with Stanton's twin sons. The two of them had been too much for him, and the beating he took was brutal. Thomas had been "laid up" for nearly six weeks.

Thomas wasn't the only victim of the twins, so he heard. Word was that they had broken the arms of another younger boy a year before, and that they had blinded an old man— someone's indentured servant— just for the sport of it. Still, these things had never been proven, and nothing had come of them.

Thomas had dreams sometimes of catching the Stanton twins apart, one at a time, and somehow evening the score. But the opportunity had not presented itself so far. Mistress Merry had taken ill. For a time both she and Thomas required a doctor's care. Thomas had recovered, but Mistress Merry remained bedridden, and her care became the primary concern of the entire household.

Salem Cadmont had become hollow-eyed and drawn. He haunted the upper rooms, ignoring the world outside. Thomas recalled vividly the day Mistress Merry said, "You must go, Salem. You can do nothing here, but they need you out there. It is war. And take the boy with you, Salem. This is no place for him now."

It seemed only days later that the militia had been mustered, and Thomas found himself— as Captain Salem Cadmont's ward— drafted into service as the captain's "fetch." The title turned out to mean valet, porter, clerk, horse-holder, and general servant. The timing of it meant his personal grudges must wait. He had not seen Jason and Jubal Stanton since the day the militia formed on River Road.

Hurrying now on awkward, sleepy legs, Thomas skirted around a cluster of men gathering up their blankets, and almost fell over a fallen log. As he staggered aside, recovering his balance, his axe handle swatted the shoulder of a burly man just rising from his bed.

"Here, boy!" The man dodged aside, then came to his feet with the easy grace of a large bear. "Mind where you dance!" he growled. "You're clumsy as a possum shoat."

A few feet away, Nathan Horne turned and grinned at them. "Mind your tongue, Horatio," he chuckled. "Yon scamp may grow to be a man one day. Then he'll offer ye a drubbing."

"Beg pardon, Mister King," the boy bowed slightly, backing away. "I was hurrying to get the captain's mount. He'll be wanting an early start this day."

"Oh, he will, will he?" Despite Horatio King's glare, his dark whiskers parted in a grin of ironic humor. "And

is Old Catamount reviewing strategies with his fetch
these days?"

"No, sir," Thomas admitted. "But I heard the guns,
just as we all did. They're on the lake, and Fort Malden
is besieged. If we make haste, we can be at Detroit in
time to catch some British before there are none left
there for us to fight."

"At Detroit?" King squinted at him. "The British are
at Malden."

"But Malden is on a peninsula," Thomas pointed out.
"If we cross at Detroit we can trap them there." With
another slight, awkward bow, the boy turned and scurried away. Behind him, Horatio King shook his head,
grinning. He exchanged amused glances with Horne,
then gazed across the way, toward the only rigged tent
in the encampment. The tent flap was open, and Captain
Salem Cadmont stood before it, his mane of snowy hair
whipping in the breeze. "It's the nature of things," King
muttered. "The old Catamount adopts an orphan cub,
an' the cub takes up the tiger's ways. That boy's been
studyin' the charts."

Across the camp, Hall Stanton's voice was raised again.
The man was making his way toward Captain Cadmont's
billet, complaining as he went.

"Th' popinjay is back," Nathan Horne growled.
"Prob'ly come to tell th' captain how to plan his day."

"Pray Cadmont ignores whatever helpful suggestions
that one's got," Horatio King shook his head. "We've
British to meet, and no time for parade ground pos-
turin'."

"It isna' th' British I fret about in these woods," Horne
said, darkly. "It's them that's with 'em."

"They say Tecumseh himself is with 'em," King
agreed. "If Perry has cut their supply lines, as th' salutes
say, I've no doubt our Butternuts can persuade th' British

to go about their business. But th' Shawnee won't like retreating. It's them we'll meet first, I wager."

The men, and others around them, glanced toward Cadmont's tent. Hall Stanton and his escorts were there now. Stanton cut a smart figure in his bright blue coat with its rows of polished brass buttons. He was waving his arms and pointing eastward, while Captain Cadmont stood stolidly, just listening.

"Popinjay's explainin' strategy," Horatio King muttered. "He's been hobnobbin' with th' book soldiers, an' now he'll be tellin' Old Catamount how to fight Shawnee."

"Hall Stanton wouldn't know a Shawnee if one stepped up an' scalped him," Horne said, sagely.

Nearby, a slouch-hatted woodsman cursed abruptly and pointed. In heavy brush a hundred yards away, there was a hint of movement, gone as quickly as it was glimpsed. "Did ye see him?" the man hissed. "Brazen as a wolverine. Right out in the open."

"Shawnee?" another man asked.

"I reckon. No tellin' how long he's been watchin'. Didn't see him 'til he moved."

Horatio King shaded his eyes, looking around. "Prob'ly a lot more about," he growled. "They been pacin' us for two-three days now, most likely. Where's Christy an' his scouts?"

"Cap'n sent them ahead yesterday."

King shook his head, like a large bear clearing its ears. "Beggars wouldn't get so close if Christy was about," he muttered. "That'n's more injun than the bloody heathen sometimes."

Horne swore under his breath as a shiver ran up his spine. Older than most of the men around him, he knew the Shawnee from other times. They could strike like devils, then disappear like ghosts, and where they had been bright blood painted the ground.

Those who studied on such matters claimed that scalping was a recent practice among the redmen. Their wars among themselves, before the white men came, had been mostly brief, erratic clashes, usually over hunting grounds and usually lasting only a few minutes. Certainly there had been trophy-taking, but the trophies were usually bits of clothing and personal trinkets . . . or the occasional ear or finger.

It was Dutch traders who taught the heathen how to scalp their enemies, the scholars said. And it took an Englishman— General Henry Hamilton— to develop scalping into a big business. In the time of rebellion, Hamilton had bought scalps. And the Indians, especially the Shawnee, were enthusiastic in supplying the new market.

Nathan Horne had seen the results, in the wilds of Kentucky. He had also seen the Shawnee scalps which Jack Christy used as fringe on his possible pouch.

Thomas Woodson carried Captain Cadmont's saddle across the camp to the corral. "Captain's mount, please, Mr. Collett," he told a gaunt woodsman on guard there.

Collett scratched his chin, leveled a searching glare at the boy, then shrugged. "I'll fetch th' brute," he said. "Will he want the bay today?"

Thomas started to nod, then changed his mind. Yesterday's march had brought them across the Raisan to the little Huron River, through intermittent forest and dunes. Just beyond the near, misty groves to the east was open water. Detroit was only a few miles away, and today the First Louisville would arrive there. The enemy was at Malden, just down the river on the Canadian side. "The white," he said, pointing. Across the corral a magnificent pure-white gelding tossed its head, warning away other animals that had crowded close in the bustle of the morning wrangle.

Collett frowned. "Cap'n's been ridin' the bay," he pointed out.

"He'll want the white," Thomas insisted. "If I take him the bay he'll send me back for the white. It's his engagement horse."

Collett shrugged. If the lad said Cap'n would want the white, then most likely Cap'n would want the white. The Cadmonts had no children of their own, and the orphaned boy they had taken in was like a son to them . . . or maybe a grandson. The Old Catamount, as his men called him privately, was at least sixty— a proud, stern old warrior and thoroughly set in his ways. Yet it seemed sometimes that this half-grown boy knew him better than he knew himself.

If anyone present could talk sense to the old man, it was this boy. "You ought to persuade him," Collett urged. "That horse is a target," Collett muttered. "Like that brass-button coat with th' epaulets, that Hall Stanton wears to strut. Was I a redskin— or even a blueback— I might just test my sights on a man as looked like that. But I wager Stanton won't be wearin' his fine feathers when we meet the enemy. An' the Cap'n shouldn't ride his white horse."

"I told him that," Thomas said. "Everybody's told him that. But he's made it clear, he intends to encounter the British on his white. It's his pride, he says. Besides, he says the ball hasn't been cast that can pierce his hide."

"Arrogant ol' fart," Collett scowled, shaking his head. "An' just ornery enough to get by with it." He went to get the captain's horse. The animal had not been ridden lately. It was fresh and feisty, full of the enthusiasm of the morning, but between them they got it haltered, hobbled, and saddled. While Collett held its bit in strong hands, the boy climbed aboard and rode out its constrained pitching. Limited by its hobble, the horse hunched itself and tried to buck, but settled for a crab-like dance around the enclosure.

Thomas clung like a leech, cooing and stroking the animal's neck, working the mischief out of it. From the side he heard loud, derisive laughter, and glanced around. Jubal and Jason Stanton were there, posturing and cackling, mocking him. Both of them wore new military-style coats, but without insignia.

"Sing it a lullaby, boy!" one of them shouted. "Maybe it'll go to sleep!"

"I'd break that animal, was I on it," the other bragged. "I'd take off those hobbles and let the brute get the taste of a spike bit on its tongue."

Thomas ignored them, though the derision rankled him.

When the horse was satisfied, Thomas adjusted the stirrups and led it across the camp. Behind him, he heard the Stantons crowing their insults.

Beyond the center of the camp, there were challenges. Scouts were coming in. Thomas tethered the white horse behind Captain Cadmont's tent, then walked around and ducked inside. Ignoring the babble of voices outside, he spread and rolled the captain's bedding, lashing it into a tight roll covered with oilcloth. He straightened and closed the captain's travel chest, and wiped down the two hanging lamps, securing their plugs.

Across a pack frame lay a long, slim bundle, laced into oiled leather. Thomas picked it up carefully, untied the laces and drew out a honey-colored long rifle. Its polished escutcheons and plates glinted, even in the shadow of the tent. He drew back the hammer and tested the knap of its flint. Satisfied, he opened the pan and wiped it carefully with a bit of dry wool. Then, setting the rifle's brass-capped butt on the floor, the boy put the muzzle of the long barrel to his lips and blew into it.

Under the open flash pan, a tiny hiss came from the touch-hole. The rifle was empty and clear.

Thomas sat on the edge of the captain's cot and methodically cleaned and polished the rifle. "Lady Justice," the captain called the implement. He always referred to it as "she," and to Thomas the designation seemed appropriate. Lady Justice was a beautiful thing, a fine tool from the hands of a master craftsman. She seemed to glow with a lovely light all her own, even in the dimmest surroundings.

"I got her the same place I got you, boy," the old man had told him one time. "From a Frenchman who'd been too long in the woods. He said she was 'the perfect rifle,' and held within her one perfect shot. He didn't say anything of the kind about you."

Outside the tent, men's voices were raised in irritation, and Hall Stanton's fluting voice was the loudest of them. The man was almost shouting. "One day late!" he snapped. "You should have pushed your dolts harder, Squire. I had a chance at fame, and you let it pass!"

"Fame?" someone else growled. "Where's the fame in this? We came to drive the British out of Michigan Territory. Well, they're driven, by God!"

"Fame!" Stanton raged. "A jaunt through the countryside is not fame. A victory is fame! General Harrison is a rising star among the politicians, and . . ."

"An' you want us to get you a piece of that glory," someone growled nearby, not trying to muffle his anger. Other voices joined in.

Salem Cadmont didn't raise his voice, but its baritone rumble cut through the angry drone like a knife through butter. "Be quiet, all of you," he ordered. "Captain Stanton, you may be here to gain prestige among the eastern gentry, but the rest of us have a campaign to conduct."

"Will we cross the river, sir?" someone asked. "We

could catch them, easy enough. We could cross at Bois Blanc and . . ."

"That's up to the army," Cadmont pointed out. "We aren't the army. Whether to pursue the enemy is up to them."

"To blazes with the army," a man shouted. "Let's go after them ourselves!"

"Like a howling mob?" Cadmont asked quietly. "Or a gaggle of politicians? I'll speak with military command. Break camp and prepare to march. We'll proceed to Detroit."

"Then what?" Hall Stanton demanded. "Conroy's a day behind us, but he has only a small contingent."

"Then," Cadmont growled, "we shall proceed as circumstances dictate."

Inside the tent, Thomas had cleaned Lady Justice and was breaking out the captain's powder flask and pouch when Salem Cadmont appeared in the opening. Husky and broad-bellied, his sturdy bulk seemed to fill the space there.

"Stow that, boy," he said. "Then take the white horse back to the handlers and bring me the bay. We won't be engaging the enemy today. Fort Malden has been abandoned. The British have fled eastward, toward York."

III

The Invaders

Village of Detroit, Michigan Territory

The Louisville First Militia Company was mostly Kentuckians, one of more than thirty such companies hastily assembled following the January massacre of militias—mostly Kentuckians— on the Raisan River in Michigan. The men of Louisville Company were farmers and settlers, storekeepers and foresters, tinkers and peddlers. Most came from the rich lands below the falls of the Ohio. A few had claims across the river in Indiana Territory.

Among them were scholars and frontiersmen, landed gentry and drifters, hunters and hawkers, healers and thieves. But they were all alike in two ways. They were riders who appreciated a good horse, and they were crack shots with a rifle. And many of them counted relatives and friends among those left butchered on a frozen riverbank by Indians supplied and encouraged by the British command at Fort Malden, Michigan Territory.

Fast riders spread the word, and the companies gathered. Once assembled under R.M. Johnson, they would become the Kentucky Cavalry. But the call to assembly arrived too late to reach many of them. First Louisville and a dozen other local companies were already on their

way north. With the remainder of his regiment, Johnson
followed. He would make for French Town, receive dis-
patches there, then join General Harrison somewhere
near Detroit.

His missing companies— several hundred men who had
gone ahead under individual commands— would show up
soon enough. They were all heading for the same place.
The regiment could be assembled in the field.

Others were heading north as well. The massacre on
the Raisin River had fired the fighting rage of American
frontiersmen as nothing else could have done. By the
time Oliver Hazard Perry's message, "We have met the
enemy and they are ours" spread, thousands of seething
Americans, armed and angry, were well on their way toward the Detroit River region.

Assembled at Louisville Settlement under the command of Captain Salem Cadmont, the First Louisville
were the first to take saddle and the first to arrive at
the village of Detroit. Within hours, their ranks were
swelled by the arrival of small companies from Lac Qui
Parle, Loganstown, and Rampart. Some of these had
been on the march for weeks. The smokes of still other
units were visible in the distance. Beyond them, somewhere, were the smokes of William Henry Harrison's
Army of the Northwest.

News of the British retreat had reached Harrison, and
his main units now were deployed for a sweep eastward,
directly toward Fort Malden. Lurking Indians, like shadows in the forest, had dogged their march for days, and
there had been bloody skirmishes at a dozen points. The
collapse of Malden was an opportunity for a show of force,
to drive the watchers back, to bolster the supply lines while
pack trains caught up. Only Colonel Conroy's horse brigade pressed forward, along the river, making for Detroit.
In the meantime, militia had already arrived there.

As senior commander of civilian forces present, and

in the absence of a military officer, Salem Cadmont became *pro tempore* leader of occupation forces at Detroit. Acting on a directive from Conroy— carried by dispatch riders and delivered by a glowering Hall Stanton— Cadmont established headquarters at the old, half-destroyed stockade called Lernaoult. Leave it to others, he said, to stage victorious parades and take formal possession of the village. But, in the meantime, someone had to keep order in the place.

In the streets of the village and along the waterfront, militiamen patrolled, and for once many of them shared Stanton's impatience. They had come a long way, and they had come to fight Englishmen and heathens, not to stand guard over an ugly little town.

Old charred timbers still stood here and there among the trimmings of new construction. Scant few seasons had passed since wildfire— fire which some maintained had been set deliberately— had raged through Detroit, burning almost everything that stood. And here and there were more recent vandalisms, committed by British soldiers and the roving bands of unaffiliated Indians who followed them around— Indians of many tribal backgrounds, who answered to no chief.

Again and again, the town had been virtually destroyed, but its reasons for being there remained. For a time there had been Colonial troops, stationed there after the earlier defeat of the British. Then there had been British again, roving out of Fort Malden to drive out the American forces.

Blood had been shed many times on Detroit's little streets, and the interval of peace since the last conflict had been a reign of terror for some. Colonel Proctor's protection of this border region was, as even his officers admitted, decidedly partial. Settlers of Canadian extract were relatively safe from the hordes of savages. But Americans were not. The ransom of captives became a daily business in the territory. The going rate for Canadian civilians who happened to fall into Indian hands was eighty dollars. But the ransom paid for American captives was limited to five dollars, by order of Colonel Proctor. Few Americans were presented for ransom. Their scalps were worth more than their lives.

Still, business was business. The British presence was a sort of stability, despite the routine atrocities it condoned. Fort Malden, at the toe of the Ontario peninsula, regulated the commerce of the border. And commerce proceeded whether or not nations were at war. The narrow bend between Lake Erie and Lake St. Clair was the best crossing on the Detroit River, reliable in most seasons. So residents had been rebuilding, and a town stood again on the north shore of the Detroit River, barely a stone's throw from the Province of Ontario on the other bank.·

The town bustled now with the activities of autumn. Forges flared and anvils rang. Skid-teams labored along the waterfront. Foresters and teamsters, sawyers and stonemasons came and went about their trade, and trappers haggled with furriers at the docks, ignoring the war which swept toward them. Foundations were in place for a dozen buildings of stone and mortar, but as yet the little town was mostly a collection of cabins and barns, warehouses and sheds. There wasn't much there to hold the attention of hundreds of impatient volunteer militiamen looking for a fight.

The raising of the Cadmont's flag over Lernaoult brought a few cheers from citizens— mostly from those recently arrived from other places. For the more established townspeople, it made little difference what colors flew there. British or American, they all spoke the same language and would trade for the same wares. There had always been flags at Detroit . . . flags and soldiers, of one persuasion or another. *Someone* would always occupy the territory, and their soldiers would frequent the taverns and pay coin for their comforts.

Some, indeed, were unhappy with the change. Word of Perry's capture of the British fleet on Lake Erie had spread quickly. Everyone knew that it spelled the end of the present regime, and there were those in Detroit who would lose fortunes because of it. And now the people had seen the boats going up the river from Malden, and had seen the soldiers passing in the distance, across the water. Now columns of smoke standing like sentinels above the horizons said that full-scale war had come again to Michigan Territory. Even more obvious was the stillness directly across the river. The "civilized" Indians, Tecumseh's Shawnee and their cousins, were gone.

Despite the ravages of raiders in the surrounding countryside, Tecumseh's organized people had remained passive enough, in the shadow of the Union Jack. They had remained aloof from the raiding and butchery, so far as anyone knew, and they had been good customers. Now they were gone, as though they had never been there. Their villages, some within sight of the town, were deserted. And even if they returned it would not be as friends. They had chosen their side in this war. The fight at Tippecanoe had made that clear.

William Henry Harrison was no friend to the Indians, and President Madison— at least in this respect— agreed with Harrison. Both knew that Tecumseh's "nation," despite its quiet civility, would be formidable if aroused. What might follow would make the random atrocities of the wild bands look like child's play. Beneath his educated manners, Tecumseh was Tecumseh, the greatest of the war chiefs.

To Harrison— and to Madison— Tecumseh was the real threat. There would be no second chance for peace where Tecumseh's followers were concerned.

As the First Louisville approached Detroit, Captain

Cadmont had sent scouts across the river at Bois Blanc. Jack Christy and four volunteers had gone, holding their rifles high as they led their mounts into the turgid waters, using the little island as a screen. All five were woodsmen, buckskin-clad and experienced in wilderness ways. Even from the west bank opposite the upstream end of the island, the marchers could see distant smoke arising in the south . . . more smoke than any cook fire would produce.

Late in the afternoon, the scouts came in, crossing the narrows at Detroit. Cadmont met them at the shore. "They're gone," Christy reported. "The whole command. They burned the fort and moved out, just in the past few days. Came this way as far as the river, then turned east, up th' peninsula. We tracked them a few miles, then turned back and came here. They're makin' for York, but not fast. Proctor's got horses, but he's also got maybe several hundred foot soldiers, an' there's plenty of rim-print. Ordinance wagons, an' some field artillery. Six-pounders, looks like."

"And Indians?" Cadmont raised a bushy eyebrow.

"Lot of Indians," Christy nodded. "Hard to count, y'know. Not like Georgie soldiers. Our best guess is there's at least a thousand redskin bucks with 'em, though. Maybe more than that. Track looks like they sent their women an' children on ahead, some time back, with their livestock. Their trail's cold, but the soldiers ain't that far yet."

"Lot of them Injuns have muskets," another scout offered. "Not just bows. Some have rifles, too."

"They know we're here, obviously."

Christy chuckled. "Those're Shawnee, Cap'n. They don't miss much. They prob'ly know what you had for breakfast, an' who's got rips in their britches." He pointed a large, languid finger at the far side of the river. A wide area directly across was cleared and open.

It had served as a staging ground for the traders working between Detroit and the fort. Beyond were the deserted cabins and lean-tos of an Indian village. "Right yonder, just above the bank . . . there was an even dozen Indians sittin' there 'til about an hour ago. They been there all day, just watchin' you folks over here."

"You saw them?"

"Dang right," Christy spat. "That's why we took so long comin' in. We was watchin' them watchin' you. They pulled out just a bit ago, headin' east. Looks like they've gone with the rest. Rear guard, prob'ly, in case you boys decided to go chargin' across there before the Georgies got clear."

"And Proctor burned Fort Malden." Cadmont shook his head. "Well, I guess if it had been me, I would have, too."

"He didn't want to leave it for us," Christy shrugged.

A crowd had gathered to hear the report. "Let's go after 'em!" someone shouted, and others took up the cry.

"Any man ready to leave right now can follow me!" Hall Stanton shouted. "I'm ready to face the enemy!"

Cadmont raised his hand for silence, glaring at the man in the brass-button coat. "You aren't in command here, Stanton," he growled. "I am. So shut your mouth."

Nearby, a horn blared, and faces in the crowd turned. Approaching along the waterfront were mounted soldiers, butternut-clad riders of the Third Ohio. At their head was Captain Mason Conroy. In high collar and parade cap, the colonel looked more like a schoolboy than a veteran of Tippecanoe and several other engagements. But in his bearing was a barely controlled energy that reflected in his eyes. They were the eyes of a fighter.

Halting his unit with a hand signal, Conroy rode directly to the crowd on the ways, dismounted and paced through the throng, which opened before him. Ignoring the outstretched hand of Hall Stanton, he went directly to Cadmont and presented himself. "General Harrison's respects, sir," he said. "What is your situation here?"

"We have secured Detroit, as requested," Cadmont said. "We're supposed to meet up with Rab Johnson and his cavalry, but they aren't here. I reckon they'll be along. The British seem to be in retreat to the east." He glanced at Jack Christy. "How far, Mister Christy?"

"Couple days out," the woodsman drawled. "Half that wi' horses."

"Have you taken formal possession of this town?" Conroy asked.

Cadmont's gray eyes seemed to pierce the young officer. "We didn't come here to be policemen," he said. "Now that the army's here, you can have this place. Johnson will be along soon, an' we'll join him. But right now we're left to our own Ps and Qs. So unless you have any other suggestions, we intend to pursue Proctor and his army."

"To what purpose?"

"To beat the vinegar out of the beggars!" Cadmont growled. "That's why we came, isn't it?"

Conroy turned slowly, gazing past the crowd. His gaze stopped at the militia flag on its pole, above the old stockade. "Detroit seems thoroughly secured," he nodded. "And I'm sure General Harrison will appreciate the opportunity to take formal possession when he arrives. My orders are as open as yours, Captain. I was simply to proceed to Detroit, assess the situation, and counsel with the civilian militias present. Which is you. So I guess I've done that."

"I'd say so," Jack Christy drawled.

"Beyond that, I am to exercise my own judgment," Conroy added. His stern young face broke in a boyish grin. "In my judgment we should pursue the beggars and, as you say, beat the vinegar out of them. Or at least keep them busy until the troops catch up." The grin disappeared as quickly as it had come. "I have a hundred and thirty men. What are our odds?"

"Proctor has at least six hundred, and more than a thousand Indian warriors under Tecumseh. Our combined militias total about four hundred and fifty by latest count."

"Make that five hundred," Christy offered. "There's a bunch from the midden hills just comin' in."

"More than two of them to each of us," Conroy nodded. "But by the smokes we saw this morning, those odds will improve soon enough. Harrison has sent out riders, to all the units they can find south of the Raisan. They're to converge on his command."

"Then he'll be joining us?"

"He and Colonel Johnson know where we are," the cavalryman said. "They'll get orders to us when we need them."

"There's smoke a few miles off," Jack Christy offered. "I make it three to four little outfits already past the Raisan. We can pull 'em in by sunup."

"Sunup, then," Conroy said. Evening shadows were lengthening. A flock of swallows flickered overhead, darting dark specks against a deepening sky. Rising mists stood above the lakes. "We'll cross the river at first light."

Within the hour, parties of woodsmen were heading out to meet the dozen or more little militia companies converging toward Detroit. Lamps were lofted above the Lernaoult gate to guide them in.

Thomas hung around the old fort for a time, to be nearby should Captain Cadmont call him. But the captain was busy. He and Colonel Conroy, along with several other soldiers and a long dozen buckskinned militiamen, were huddled over charts in a dingy cubicle inside the gate. It sounded as though they would be there for a while.

At a fire near the waterfront, men were roasting ducks and frying pan-jack. Thomas drifted in that direction, helped himself to supper, then remembered the captain's white horse. Most of the stock had been herded into livery corrals beyond the settlement— these and the tannery were located where they would be downwind from the town in most seasons. But a small, stacked-pole enclosure near the fort had been repaired, and some of the cavalry mounts were there. It occurred to Thomas that Captain Cadmont's mount should be there, too, for saddling at first light.

Deep dusk was settling as he made his way out to the town stables to get the white horse. The guards there were soldiers of the Third Ohio, and they were reluctant to release any stock to a half-grown boy they didn't know. But when Thomas identified himself and demanded the horse, they stood aside.

He didn't try to saddle the animal. He would do that in the morning. For now, he simply wrestled a headstall onto it, took up its reins and led it back toward the stockade. He was crossing a vacant stretch where a new cabin stood half-built when a shadow moved among the stacked logs and a slouching figure stepped out in front of him.

"Been lookin' for you, boy," Jubal Stanton snapped.

Wide-eyed and wary, Thomas backed a step, hauling the white horse to a stop. "What do you want?" he demanded. He tried to sound stern, but his voice betrayed him. As it sometimes did, it jumped from a raspy baritone to a squeaky soprano and back. He scowled in the dusk, hearing his own words, hating his voice for making him sound ridiculous. A fury rose within him— the same cold fury that always came now when he so much as thought about the Stantons. But he fought it down.

"You got my brother and me cussed by the horse guards, you little bastard," Jubal taunted. "So now I want to ride that white horse. And you can polish my boots. It's all you're good for."

"Polish your own boots," Thomas hissed. "I'm busy."

Beside him, the white horse jerked its head, and there was a quick, scuffling sound. Before Thomas could react, hard hands were on him. From behind, Jason Stanton's corded arm drew tight across his throat. Hard knuckles dug into his scalp, behind his ear, and a knee thudded into the base of his spine. Choking and almost blind with pain, he saw Jubal Stanton coming at him, grinning. "Hold him, Jason," Jubal purred. "I want to hit him some."

"Let's cut off his ears," Jason giggled, tightening his hold on the younger boy's neck. Again the knee jarred him, and a brutal fist thudded into the small of Thomas's back. Bright starbursts of pain lanced upward through him.

Thomas couldn't breath. He could barely see. In desperation he kicked out, as hard as he could, and heard Jubal howl when his boot caught him in the knee. The twin fell and rolled, cursing. With his free hand, Thomas stabbed backward, trying to find a hold on his tormentor. For an instant, his fingers touched Jason's face, and he scrabbled for his eyes. But Jason jerked away, hitting him again as they parted. The hard knuckles just below his arm pit sent a numbing pain down his arm. Distantly, he felt something tugging at his hand, as though to pull it from his wrist. The captain's horse, he thought dimly. I still have its reins. Through his pain a fury lanced, bright and cold, and suddenly it was very important not to turn loose of the reins. Again the horse backed away, tossing its head. Thomas clung, stumbled and fell. Something thumped against the hard ground an inch from his head.

"Jump on him!" one of the twins shouted. "Hold him down!"

Thomas rolled aside, and again something thudded into the ground beside him. It was a builder's adze, eight pounds of sharpened steel on a three-foot handle. Jason swung the thing wildly, barely missing his own brother, then raised it to swing again. "Hold him!" he snarled. "I'll open his damned skull, by— "

Suddenly there was light, and the harsh voices of men. Gasping for breath, Thomas saw the Stantons being dragged back, away from him.

"Two on one don't hardly seem right, boys," a deep voice growled.

Thomas tried to sit up, but flopped back again when the white horse tugged its reins. He tried again, groggy with pain. He heard a moan, and realized it was himself moaning.

Lantern light was in his face, and a large man squatted beside him. Like a large bear investigating a cub, Horatio King peered into the boy's eyes. "Are you hurt, lad?" he asked.

"I'm all right," Thomas managed. "But Cap'n's horse . . . ?"

"The horse is fine," King assured him. "Though he might be bridle-shy for a while. Why didn't you turn loose an' use both hands against those hellions?"

"I don't know," Thomas muttered. Sitting now, dazed. Thomas raised his free hand to his aching throat. His fingers fumbled with the old Indian trinket he wore there— a small, beaded amulet he had owned as long as he could remember. He stuffed it inside his collar.

"You could have reached your belt-axe, had you dropped them reins," a man suggested.

"I know," Thomas whispered. "But if I'd reached it, I'd have used it."

Aside, someone was questioning the Stantons, who stood silent, half-surrounded by militiamen. Sullen glares were their only response.

"You should have used it," King said, glancing at the dropped adze. "I don't see those bullies shyin' from weapons."

Thomas shook his head, confused but suddenly realizing why he had kept his grip on the horse's reins. It was because he was afraid to draw his axe— not afraid of the Stantons, but afraid of himself. "I wouldn't have stopped," he whispered, as much to himself as to King. "I wouldn't have quit 'til they were dead."

Hall Stanton appeared in the lantern-light, glaring and blustering. "What's going on here?" he demanded.

"Boys havin' a tussle," someone said casually. "We busted it up."

"Get your hands off my sons!" Stanton snapped. "Who the devil do you people think you are?"

Horatio King rose to his feet, turned and faced Stanton, seeming to tower over him. "We know who we are," he growled. "If you don't put a leash on these animals of yours, we're the ones who'll do it for you."

By the time Thomas got his wobbly legs under him, the Stantons were gone. Hall Stanton's curses wafted back on the chill evening breeze.

Thomas gritted his teeth against the pain of his bruises, and spent a moment with the white horse, stroking its muzzle, cooing reassurance to it. Then, still holding the reins, he started toward the old fort.

"Where you off to, boy?" King rasped. "We better see if you're busted up."

"I'm all right," Thomas said, not stopping. "I got to go put this horse in the closed corral."

"I'll take you to the Cap'n, then. He'll want to know . . ."

"Leave him alone!" Thomas rasped, turning. "He's got enough on his mind." He tugged the reins and trudged off toward the stockade.

Behind him, rough men in buckskins glanced at one another.

"That'n's got sand," Jack Christy allowed, to no one in particular.

"You heard what he said," King asked, "about his axe?"

"Heard him," Christy nodded. "Boy sounds dang near Injun sometimes. Shawnee'd say he knows the temper of the spirits."

"More likely he knows himself," King mused.

Nineteen miles east, below the windward bend of Lake St. Clair, little fires dotted the forest for half a mile. Here Henry Proctor had called a halt for rest. At the east end of the encampment were the neat cook fires of British troops, a precise circle around a lighted clearing where wagons and field pieces were ranked. Here Proctor and his officers had their trail tents, surrounded by the bivouac of his soldiers. West of them were the scattered fires of the Shawnee and their allies, a random pattern of small glows here and there in forest clearings, each located to take advantage of the terrain.

As dusk deepened to night and mists rose from the lake, Tecumseh came to the command tent. As he bent to enter, leaving his escort outside, lamplight outlined the fan of owl feathers drooping over his left cheek and glinted on the black paint which covered the right side of his face. The great chief had been in council with his sub-chiefs, and was dressed for the occasion. In fringed buckskins and high, beaded moccasins, no trace remained of the country gentleman he sometimes appeared to be among whites. Now he looked like exactly what he was— a Shawnee warrior-chief in his prime, lithe as a cat and as fit as any younger man. Yet when he spoke, it was in English— the cultivated English of a provincial scholar, with only the slightest soft trace of Algonquian inflection.

"They will pursue," he told the officers present. "Cavalry and mounted militia. They are at Detroit." Eyes as cold as dark agate fixed on Colonel Proctor and held his gaze. On the painted face was a hint of contempt. "Now you will have to fight, Proctor. You can either choose your ground, or fight them where they catch you. There is no other choice."

Proctor returned the steady gaze for a moment, scowling, then sighed. The Indian had been demanding, all along, that he stand and fight. Now the Indian would have his way. "How many are they?" he asked.

"A company of cavalry," Tecumseh said. "More than a hundred men. And who knows how many militia? 'Kaintucks' with horses. They gather like autumn leaves on the wind. More of them with each hour that passes."

"It will take them two days, at least, to overtake us," a young lieutenant behind Proctor mused. "On horse, they can march forty miles to our twenty. But they'll keep their distance. We outnumber them."

"They'll hardly be fit for field combat after a forced march," someone else said.

"Neither will we," Proctor muttered. "But they will harry us if they can. And given the chance, they might attack."

"Or we might," Tecumseh suggested.

Proctor shook his head, glancing sourly at the painted savage in his tent. "There's no advantage to sudden assault without surprise. Better to choose our field, as Chief Tecumseh has so, ah . . . *astutely* . . . pointed out." He turned to a chart spread out in lamplight, studied it a moment, then pointed. "The Thames," he said. "Tomorrow we cross to the north side, here at Chatham. My barges should be there by now." He ran his finger along the map a few inches. "Beyond that is wilderness. The fens along the Thames. Marshes on one side, heavy forest on the other. Difficult to flank us there. Short march from Chatham to Arnold's Mill. Only one other settlement. Ah . . . Bywell, I think. We'll burn it. Then there is Moravian Town . . ."

"That's quite a long way," someone muttered. "We'll have been engaged well before that."

"We shall proceed ahead of them," Proctor snapped. "The wilderness below Moravian Town should be our best choice of ground. And we have artillery on the barges . . ."

As the soldiers gathered around their map, Tecumseh eased back into shadows. The Englishmen could plot their position and plan their strategies— with themselves in mind, as always, never with their red allies in mind. Still, when the fight came, he— Tecumseh— would have the final plans. He knew as well as the soldiers did what task would be assigned to him and his warriors. The first defense, to soften the brunt of the Americans' attack, would be by Indians. In his mind he could see the field of battle, and could hear the directives which had not yet been spoken.

"Take position in our fore," Proctor would say. "Hold them as long as you can, then fall back to the forest. Defend our flank, red man. Defend our path of retreat." Let the Indians be first to meet the enemy, the Englishman would decide. Let the Americans spend their force against Indians. Indians were only Indians. They are expendable. Just for a moment, he let his thoughts drift backward, to the words of his brother Tenskwatawa and the fine dream the Prophet had offered: drive the "Americans" from the land. Drive them into the sea.

If only it could have been so, Tecumseh mused. And after the Americans, the British. He blinked, chasing away the fantasy. Those were thoughts for the past. Dreams that would never become reality. What mattered now was now.

He would want to see for himself what kind of enemy was in pursuit. It would be his warriors who must meet that enemy first.

All along, Proctor had been reluctant to stand and

fight, while Tecumseh had demanded it. To the soldier, this land was only a strategic position. To the Indian, it was the last stand, the place where dreams would live or die. It was all that was left of home, and of hope.

The irony of it did not escape Tecumseh. He had fought the white men many times, with arrow and toma-hawk, with knife and musket. But always he had pre-ferred to negotiate. Far more could be accomplished with words than with tomahawks. This time, though, it was he who demanded that they stand and fight. Well, he would have his fight. Proctor would have no choice, but the price of it would be Shawnee blood.

A tendril of mist drifted through the tent flap, a tiny fog barely visible in lamplight. Those around the chart table were unaware of it, but Tecumseh saw it, and he stiffened as a chill grew inside him.

In the mist, his mind's eyes saw a form . . . an object. Long and slender, it wavered as the mist wavered, then coalesced into the shape of a sleek, long-barreled rifle, with brass "star-and-cloud" ornaments. As clearly as though it were hanging in the air before him, Tecumseh saw that same bright rifle he had seen before, years ago— the rifle the French trader, Champon, had shown him. Honey-dark maple, exquisitely shaped and embellished with bright brass, cradled a deadly octagon barrel of dark iron.

For an instant, the spirit rifle seemed to speak to him. "I have waited for you," it whispered, in a language all its own. "You knew I would." Then it was gone, and only a nameless dread remained. Tecumseh closed his eyes and shook his head slowly, from side to side. Then he turned, eased through the tent flap and was gone in the darkness . . . gone as a Shawnee goes, as though he had never been there.

IV

McGregor's Mill

Thames River Crossing, lower Ontario Province, Late September, 1813

The place had been McGregor's Mill, though many now called it Chatham. It had been a busy little settlement on the river once called Tranch but now called Thames. But it was no longer a village. Now it was only ashes, rubble, and charred timbers. No building was left standing, not even the outhouses. The granaries were destroyed, their contents burned and scattered. All the livestock had been driven off. Even an old flatboat tied at water's edge was scuttled, and a dozen canoes along the shores had been breached. Most were ruined.

Colonel Proctor was methodical in his determination to leave nothing behind that might aid and comfort his enemies. The British regulars had systematically looted the place. They took what they wanted and destroyed what was left, and the swarms of Indians following them had picked the remains clean. Not so much as a sack of flour or loaf of bread remained. Even the ovens had been wrecked.

Proctor's forces had crossed the Thames here, turning eastward again along the north side of the river.

"There were barges tied here earlier, an' some on the bank," Jack Christy said, reading the traces as one might read a book.

Astride his white horse, Salem Cadmont raised himself high in his saddle, peering around as Mason Conroy reined in beside him. "That would be ordnance and supplies from Fort MaIden," he said, "and the colonel's artillery."

Mason Conroy had reined in alongside. "Artillery?" he spat. "They brought cannons from Malden?"

Cadmont nodded. "Mr. Pace has questioned the civilians here. Some of their people were put to work loading materials, when the boats arrived. Proctor pressed some local keels into service, to join them. There were several cannons aboard the arriving barges, and regimental colors. A flotilla like that was reported at Detroit, but we assumed they were trying to get through to Lake Huron."

"They didn't divert," Conroy shook his head. "There was nothing to divert them. They're on the Thames, which means this is where Proctor sent them. This is where he intended to go, all along."

"Toward York," Nathan Horne squinted. "But that's still better'n a hundred miles, an' nobody to help him this side of it. Don't he know he's bein' chased?"

"He's going to make a stand," Mason Conroy suggested. "He knows he'll be overtaken, and he wants those guns handy when he does."

"The Englishman's nearest relief is York?" Hall Stanton muttered, gazing eastward. "Why, then he's all alone out here."

"He wants his artillery," Cadmont said to Conroy, ignoring Stanton. "He plans to dig in somewhere and defend himself, where he can defend his flanks . . . and where he has a course of retreat. Proctor's not a field strategist. He's shown that. He's best at ambush."

"Then let's give him no chance for ambush," Conroy frowned.

"When the men are fed, we can move out." Cadmont turned toward Nathan Horne, but the man was already gone. He had spread the word, and cooking fires were already being built at a dozen points around the devastated settlement. Men were working around the pack animals, breaking out trail fare. The soldiers had brought only field rations, and the militia's stock of stores—mostly hard bread, jerky, and pemmican—was running low.

"Have a care with those rations," Cadmont told those around him. "There'll be scant forage ahead, obviously."

Horatio King, carrying the saddle from his tired horse, had paused nearby. He gestured toward the outskirts of the ruined settlement, where a little group of people sat, huddled together and surrounded by curious Kentuckians, "What about them, sir?" King asked. "They've had no food since day before yesterday."

The civilians were a sorry-looking lot. Most of the residents of McGregor's Mill, or Chatham, had fled into the forest at the approach of the militia. Those remaining— a one-armed old man, three women, and a gaggle of children— huddled together now, wide-eyed and terrified, staring around them at the soldiers and the boisterous militiamen who were the latest invaders of their ruined little world,

"Feed them," Cadmont shrugged. "Maybe the boys can patch up a couple of canoes and start them back toward Detroit."

"They're Canadians," a woodsman scowled. "The Englishman should have provided for 'em."

"Well, he didn't," Cadmont sighed. "And we can't just let them starve."

"Riders coming!" someone called. On the far bank of

the river, brush parted and a pair of horsemen appeared, butternut-coated men on lathered horses.

Conroy got out his glass and peered through it. "Riders from Harrison's command," he said. "Now maybe we'll find out what's going on behind us."

By the time the cooking-fires began to produce food, the newcomers had delivered their packets. There were letters that had followed the units from as far away as Louisville and Raymonton, and dispatch orders from Harrison's command and from Colonel Richard Johnson— Rab Johnson to the Kentuckians. The Kentucky Cavalry had made rendezvous with General Harrison at French Town. The combined forces, more than two thousand strong, had met Perry's little flotilla at the mouth of the Huron River. They were being ferried across the lower Detroit to Amherstburg. They were assembling on the scorched grounds of what was left of Fort Malden.

Both Cadmont and Conroy had orders now, from Harrison and Johnson: observe and harry the enemy. Delay him if possible. Prevent him by all prudent means from establishing an entrenched position.

"Observe and harry?" Hall Stanton objected, when Cadmont had read Johnson's dispatch. "It's that bumpkin Johnson! He's persuaded General Harrison to hold us back . . . telling us to avoid contact with the enemy! He wants the victory for himself!"

Cadmont studied the ranting New Englander, hardly believing what he heard. "It doesn't matter whose victory it is, as long as we win," he said.

"My orders are the same as Captain Cadmont's," Conroy offered, startled at the attache's outburst. He knew the man only as a courier— a regular visitor in army bivouacs along the line of march. "It makes sense. We're one mounted company and militia. Proctor and his Indians outnumber us. Also, we know he has artillery. And he has Tecumseh. The best course is to harry them and let our main forces catch up."

"And have *them* take credit for securing Canada?" Stanton scowled. "I know what Johnson is doing. He wants to be a hero! He's after glory. He wants to be a great name in politics! Well, I won't have it! I say we attack Proctor ourselves. Catch him and hit him before he knows we're there . . . !"

"And wind up crow-bait," Horatio King muttered. "Like those poor lads on the Raisan." He raised his voice so that Stanton could hear him. "Those Indians are Shawnee, mister. Tecumseh's Shawnee. God's grace, a few of us might get within sight of them, before they see us. But not within rifle-shot. They'd be waitin' for us."

"Cowards!" Stanton hissed, then back-stepped and almost fell as a dozen Kentucky rifles came to bear on him.

"That's a mighty harsh word, mister," Jack Christy's voice was as cold as winter wind. "We're not cowards here. And we're not fools, either."

Stanton glared at those around him, then turned and stalked away. Mason Conroy stared after him. "That man is what sailors would call a 'loose cannon,' " he muttered. "Is he a fanatic?"

"He's wild with ambition," Salem Cadmont shrugged. "What he said about Rab Johnson . . . well, it's my experience that a buffoon reveals himself in his accusations of others. Hall Stanton flies his ambitions like a flag, for all to see, and right now he's rarin' to impress the politicians. But he's harmless enough. He's none too bright."

"He'll wise up sudden and considerable if he doesn't mind his mouth," Doyle Pace growled, to himself and those close around him.

Conroy shook his head. "Well, Mr. Stanton is your

problem, sir, not mine. But were he in my command, I'd get rid of him."

"He isn't in my command," Cadmont sighed. "He has friends in the territorial offices. When he wasn't elected to head the militia, he got himself appointed as liaison. I'm saddled with him."

With a shrug of disgust, Cadmont swung down stiffly from his horse and went to find a place to sit and to read his mail.

"Let that poppinjay call good men cowards one more time," Jack Christy muttered. "I wager then the Cap'n would be relieved of his burden." Abruptly Christy straightened. He raised his head, turning slowly, his eyes narrowed like a feral animal's, his nose crinkling. "Hush!" he growled, raising a hand.

All around him, men straightened, peering this way and that. The sun was high and silver-bright in a hazy sky. Christy shaded his eyes, squinting at distance, then pointed eastward. Beyond the outskirts of the destroyed village were cleared lands, stripped of their timber. In the hazed distance beyond the clearings were the yellows and crimsons of woodland. Trees, which deepened into forest. A hundred pairs of sharp eyes, trained where the scout pointed, saw no movement, but among them were those who noticed a stillness there, more than the stillness of wilderness. There, in the distant mist of autumn treetops, no birds darted among the branches, no furtive animals scurried about.

"Injuns," Christy said.

"Comin' at us?" King growled, his thumb on his rifle-striker.

"Naw, we wouldn' have spotted them so soon, had they been stalkin' us. Shawnee knows as well as we do about critters goin' still." Christy scratched his jaw, hard fingers ruffling the whiskers there. "Naw, I'd say right now they're just countin' us."

"Counting the scalps they intend to take," Pace muttered.

Salem Cadmont looked up from his reading. His face was bleak and tired, as though he had just aged several years. He thrust a letter away in his coat and stood, studying the eastern distance. Hazy sunlight obscured detail, but he could sense the presence of unseen eyes in the forest over there, and he felt the impact of them— dark-agate eyes in paint-camouflaged faces, eyes that saw everything and told nothing. As though she had a mind of her own, Lady Justice tilted upward slightly, her long, octagonal muzzle swinging eastward. The rifle felt warm in his grip.

Tecumseh . . . the thought came unbidden, and in Cadmont's mind a face shaped itself— a strong, handsome face, agate eyes wide-set and thoughtful above clean, sloping cheeks tanned apple-bronze by birth and by the sun. The face in his mind was serious, intent, and unreadable. An Indian face— equally suited to savage hatred or to gentle laughter. White linen and dark lapels set it off, and the words it spoke were words of reason. Words in precise, slightly accented English . . . words of a fine orator, with a power almost poetic.

But he knew that no satin lapels or fine linens adorned those features now. Now that face would be painted in subtle tints and patterns, matching the woodlands around it— a face with no laughter in it, a face to be seen in death, but not before.

Tecumseh, he thought. Tecumseh is there, waiting for me. He felt a chill deeper than that of the autumn breeze, but there was a strange comfort in it. Life was a big circle, the Indians said. It began, it grew, and it expanded with each day's sun. But like all circles, it must finally close. The letter in his coat— a letter from home— was a closing. It lacked only the finality of death.

It seemed appropriate now that Tecumseh should be waiting for him, somewhere ahead on the York road.

With a slight shake of his white-maned head, Salem Cadmont turned from the invisible enemy beyond the clearings, and peered around the ruins of McGregor's Mill. There was still a campaign to conduct. He took Jack Christy aside, and spoke quietly. "Mr. Christy, those Indians yonder in the woods are the enemy's eyes. It would be better for our purposes if he were blind for a time."

Christy gazed into the distance, his eyes narrowed to dark slits. Absently, his hand brushed the fringe of his wolfskin pouch. The dark scalps there swayed like festoons of raven floss. "Aye," he murmured. "I'll need volunteers, Cap'n. An' maybe a half hour's start."

"Select your men," Cadmont nodded. "We'll have our meal before we proceed."

When the woodsman was gone, Cadmont beckoned another man. "Mr. Pace, find Thomas for me, please," he said. "I'll want a word with the boy before we move out."

Thomas went with Horatio King to feed the huddled little group of Canadians remaining at McGregor's Mill. They carried a pail of Nathan Horne's "stew," along with a few pans and spoons they had found among the wreckage, and some pieces of hardtack. The stew was a foul-looking pottage of boiled meat, barley, and pickled greens, bolstered by whatever Horne had found along the trail and added to it. Thomas knew for a fact that there were several rabbits in the on-going pot, as well as any number of squirrels, pigeons, and at least three raccoons. There also were pine nuts, acorns, various savory roots, and select cuts from a goat that had strayed from its pen at Detroit.

The stew was never quite the same from meal to meal, and was the subject of constant complaint among the men who shared Nathan Horne's fire. Complain as they might, though, the Kentuckians seemed to thrive on the stuff. Whatever else it might be, it was nourishing.

The Canadians had been questioned, briefly, then consigned to a small area where they could be contained. They were not prisoners, and neither the soldiers nor the militiamen bore them ill will. They were simply people caught up in war. They were, though, Canadians, and nobody wanted them wandering unescorted around the camp.

While the cooks worked, some militiamen had erected a sailcloth lean-to for the refugees, and brought them wood for a fire. The wind was chill, and most of them were women and children. It was here they gathered to receive their rations. Thomas handed out utensils and hardtack while Horatio King ladled stew.

The old, one-armed man was named Speer. Of the women, one was his wife and the other two his daughters.

"Cap'n says we can patch a pair of those busted-in canoes," King told them. "We'll leave you them an' a bit of food. I guess you can make Detroit all right."

"It's better'n what His Majesty's officer left us," Speer grunted. His eyes glistened with what in a younger man might have been anger. In him, though, it was only sadness and defeat. "Had us a good place here. I tended the dock. All the buildin's were provincial property, but we paid our rent. Now it's all gone."

"It's war," King shrugged. "Armies don't leave much behind them."

"They didn't have to let their savages ransack our private belongings, though. The only clothes we have left are what we're wearin', and the only blankets are the ones we're wrapped in. If they'd left us what's ours, I'd have told 'em about their planking."

Seated cross-legged on the ground, he set a pan of stew between his knees and began spooning the stuff into his whiskers. He was obviously famished, but he ate slowly, savoring the food.

"What planking?" King asked.

"On the barges they took," Speer looked up. "Those keels were spelled out for repair. The hull seams been split from ice, the past winter. They were just floatin' on their timbers."

"You mean they'll leak?"

"I mean they'll sink," the man said. "The way them soldiers loaded them, they'll not go twenty miles before they scuttle."

"Cap'n'll want to know that," King nodded. "I thank you for mentionin' it."

"If they'd left us even our blankets, I wouldn't have."

King nodded and turned. "Thomas . . ."

To one side, Thomas knelt like a boy frozen in place. He had been passing out hardtack, and one of the hooded heads before him had turned upward, in curiosity. Beneath the blanket-cowl were ringlets of auburn hair and as stunning a face as Thomas had ever seen. He stared in slack-jawed wonder, his eyes wide, memorizing each curve of cheek, each delicate feature. He felt paralyzed, as though he were looking at an angel.

King tried again, raising his gruff voice, "Thomas!"

The boy blinked, and looked around. "Sir?"

"You still have that pretty knife of mine, lad?"

Thomas dug into his pouch and handed over a small, finely crafted knife. Its grip was tortoise shell, carved and filigreed with silver. King glanced at it, then handed it to Mr. Speer. "Keep this," he said. "I won it at dice. It'll bring you something for possibles when you get to Detroit."

Thomas had resumed his gawking. Thunderstruck young eyes gaped in wonder at the girl. But she only glanced at him, then past him, with curious eyes as blue as evening sky. "What are they looking at?" she asked, addressing no one in particular.

"Indians, miss," Horatio King said. "Off yonder, in th' woods. We're bein' scouted."

"Are you men going to kill those heathen savages?"

Beside the girl a woman hissed, "Martha! Mind your tongue!"

"Wouldn't be surprised," King chuckled. "Them and some Englishmen, just as soon as we can. Lot of us had kin at th' Raisan."

"Remember the Raisan," a militiaman nearby growled. Another grinned darkly and repeated it, making a chant of it.

Martha frowned, and glanced again at Thomas, who looked as though he might melt. "What does he mean about the Raisan?"

"The . . . the river," Thomas stuttered. "The Raisan . . . it's a river."

"I know it's a river." She arched a lovely young brow, and Thomas sighed. "What's the matter with you?" the girl whispered. "Are you daft?"

"I don't know," he admitted.

"Thomas!"

A large hand was on his shoulder, shaking him. He shook his head and looked around, at Doyle Pace. "Cap'n wants you, lad," the man said.

"Oh! Yes, sir." Thomas got his feet under him and turned away. His knees felt like jelly. He started toward the center of camp, then turned back, feeling silly. She had asked him a question. He hadn't answered. "They ambushed them on the Raisan!" he shouted at the girl. "They killed 'most everybody! Nine hundred . . . maybe more! Only a couple dozen escaped! *That's* what about the Raisan!"

His adolescent voice betrayed him, breaking on every

few syllables. He sounded, he thought, as though he were yodeling. All around, curious faces turned toward him. Some of the men grinned. Turning beet-red, Thomas scurried off to find the captain.

The old, one-armed man chuckled and Horatio King glanced at him curiously.

" 'Tisn't our war," Mr. Speer grinned, "But it 'pears to me my granddaughter has just taken a prisoner."

"The perfect rifle," Salem Cadmont mused, turning Lady Justice over in his calloused hands. "That's what the Frenchman said. 'One perfect shot,' he said." For a moment more he studied the rifle, then laid it across his knees. He sat on a lash-crate, while the travel camp jostled and roiled around him. Errant winds tousled his thick, white hair, and sunlight seemed to capture itself in each flowing lock. To Thomas, standing before him, the captain seemed to have a halo.

"The Frenchman brought me this rifle," Cadmont looked up at his ward. "Same time he brought you to my care. Do you recall any of that, lad?"

"Only a little," Thomas shrugged. "I remember fog and fire, and there were dark men on horses, and one of them said my name. I think I remember his face." He fingered the beaded talisman hanging at his breast. "It was a . . . a strong kind of face. He gave me this."

"Those men would be the ones as gave you to Champon," Cadmont nodded. "He never said who they were, and I never asked. What matters is, the Frenchman brought you to me. To Merry and me. You've been like a son to me, Thomas. And I made a promise. I said I'd see to your future."

"Yes, sir. You've told me . . . ."

Cadmont waved him silent. "And I've told you about the patent, as well. I saw to its recording, in your name.

It's in the Louisiana lands." The man drew an oilskin pouch from his coat and handed it to the boy. "My holdings are encumbered," he said. "When I'm gone . . . well, but this is a secure claim. It's your heritage, Thomas. I meant to give it to you following this campaign. You have education now, as much as the scholars I've hired can give you. This patent is the rest of my promise.

"I had thought we'd journey down to St. Louis, you and me . . . and Mistress Merry. By keel from Louisville, she . . . she would enjoy an outing like that. In St. Louis there are land offices, with maps and routes. Then you'd know what's yours, so one day you might go there and claim it." His voice sounded distant, and somehow old.

"I'd like that, sir," Thomas nodded. "Seeing St. Louis, and all. But you needn't give me this now. There's no hurry, is there?"

"You keep the pouch," Cadmont said. "Put it away with your gear. Maybe you and I will go to St. Louis, maybe not. There are no certainties in this life. But *you'll* go there, boy. And from there you'll go on with your life."

Though the captain was looking directly at him, Thomas felt as though the man were not seeing him at all—as though he were seeing something beyond . . . something bleak and cold. Abruptly, the boy felt a deep concern. He wanted to comfort this man—this stern old warrior who had been almost a father to him for as long as he could remember. But there were no words. "I don't want to go to St. Louis alone, sir," he said, hesitantly. "Not without you. We can go home first, to see Mistress Merry. Then later we can go to St. Louis."

Cadmont sighed, looking away. "Mistress Merry won't be there to greet us, Thomas. Not ever again. I've a letter . . ." With an effort he dragged his thoughts back to matters at hand. "Of course you don't want to go alone, Thomas. But should the time come, you will. And it's for the best." He gazed at the little, beaded trinket dangling from the boy's neck. "There are some who'd say you have the Indian sign on you, Thomas Woodson. I don't rightly know what that means, but sometimes I believe they're right."

The muse left him as abruptly as it had come, and he stood, checking the pan on Lady Justice. Her load was fresh and ready. "Get my horse, lad," the captain ordered. "We're off to harry the enemy."

By threes and fives, Jack Christy's volunteers wandered casually down to the river. Some carried clusters of canteens and waterbags, others armloads of coiled rope, tar buckets and various other things . . . anything that, from a distance, might misdirect a spy. Only when they were hidden from view by the screening foliage of the riverbank did they drop their burdens and assemble as a group. There they loosened the thongs on their tomahawks and knives, daubed themselves with ash and dark mud, tested the loads in their rifles, and headed eastward along the river. The moved swiftly, but in silence, moccasin-clad feet testing each step as keen ears and sharp eyes tested the thickets around them. With no more commotion than a casual breeze through the brush, sixty veteran Indian-fighters— lean, lethal men who had learned their skills from those they now hunted— headed for the deep woods east of Chatham.

For the task at hand, Jack Christy had selected men like himself. Many of them carried dried scalps as trophies— some on their pouches, some as dark fringe on their buckskin shirts, some adorning rifles and sheaths. Several wore their hair unshorn, as long and flowing as a woman's hair . . . or an Indian's. The long hair was a dare, and a taunt. I have taken scalps, it said. Here is mine, if you dare try for it.

"More Injun than any Injun," neighbors in the Kentucky backlands said of some of these men. Most of them, like Christy, were quiet, reclusive men— men with scars too deep to be shared, men with memories they could not erase. Mostly, they preferred solitude and the deep woods to the structures— and the strictures— of society.

And among them were others, sinister young men of a subtly different mold. There was Joel Creed and David Holmes. There was Jonathan Malifant, who seemed always in trouble with the law, and the silent, sinister Ezekial Dunn. Of most of these, people spoke not at all . . . except in times like this, when they were needed.

They were dangerous and unpredictable. They were outlaws among their own people. But they shared one great value. They liked to kill Indians and they were very good at it.

In those woods just ahead now, Shawnee scouts lurked, camouflaged warriors as stealthy as ghosts. And it was ghosts— men as savage, each in his way, as any red heathen— that Jack Christy led to find them.

Through a thousand yards of dense, riverbank growth, the sixty wound their silent way. Then Christy raised a hand and they stopped, melting into the tangles and the shadows. Again Christy signaled, and several of them spread and moved forward, past him. Even his eyes barely saw them as they passed. In an instant they were gone, and the rest waited. A minute passed, then two more, and Joel Creed appeared. A quick gesture, and he was gone, but the message was clear. Christy led the main party forward again. Fifty yards on, an Indian lay sprawled in the brush, face down. A tomahawk cut, blade-deep, gaped between his shoulder blades, and the top of his head was a six-inch circle of crimson gore.

Just beyond lay two more. One's throat was sliced open, the other had been stabbed at the "V" of his ribs. Both were scalped.

There were probably twenty more braves within earshot, Christy knew, but there had been nothing to hear. Methodically, the woodsmen pressed forward, spreading and moving up from the river, to flank the Indians and fall on them from behind.

V

The Harriers

The Upper Road, Southwest of Moravian Town

As in many of the early encounters of the War of North America, the first blood spilled in the invasion of Canada was Indian blood. For rear guard reconnaissance, Proctor relied on his red allies, and it was among them that Jack Christy's woodsmen struck.

For a time, Shawnee warriors had lurked along the upper road past McGregor's Mill, watching the activity of the pursuers behind them. In the midday hours Tecumseh himself had been among them, his agate eyes seeing everything as he assessed the situation. It was in his mind to ambush the pursuers in the forest between McGregor's Mill and Arnold's Mill.

Obviously the pursuers were a small advance party, he reasoned. A decisive encounter now might deter the main forces of Harrison's army at a crucial time. Studying the terrain, Tecumseh picked out the places where camouflaged warriors might lie unseen, ready to strike. To the north, the land was increasingly swampy. Natural traps abounded in the deep forests as yet untouched by saws and axes. A sudden, coordinated attack, seeming to come from nowhere, could stun and bloody the white savages.

Many of them would die, but the strategy would be more to maim than to kill. Any Shawnee warrior knew a dozen ways of crippling a man— of leaving him screaming in agony from severed hamstrings or broken knees, blinded or disemboweled but still alive and conscious. General Harrison would be close behind with his army. A few score injured men to care for would slow him, maybe cost him several days' march.

But Colonel Proctor flatly refused to allow a diversion at this point. The Englishman had his own plans, and would not change them in the slightest. He had mapped a defense strategy, based upon a stonewall stand at a place further east where the swamps and streambeds narrowed the line of march to less than two hundred yards in width. This was his plan, and he would consider no others. Despite past errors, Proctor had faith only in his own strategies, and no interest in anyone else's.

In disgust, Tecumseh led his best warriors— his Shawnee "ghostmen"— eastward to flank Proctor's line of march. In the rear, a gaggle of young Chippewa were left as observers. It was these the Kentucky woodsmen found when they pressed forward to clear a path for Salem Cadmont's cavalry.

Most of the Chippewa never saw those who killed them. Only a handful escaped, drifting through the forest like leaping shadows, to tell what had happened. By the time Proctor learned how close his enemies truly were— fairly dogging his tracks— the Kentuckians were abreast of him, on both banks of the Thames, their deadly rifles harassing the line of keel barges that carried Proctor's ordnance.

Two of the raftlike keels were taking water visibly, slogging as Canadian boatmen poled them close ashore. Again and again, sniping from the forested banks cleared their decks. Finally, midway between Chatham and Moravian Town, the barges crept to a complete stop. While musketeers of the 41st Regiment raked the river-banks with steady fire, British soldiers salvaged what they could— bales of provisions, a pair of field cannons and ammunition, several crates of woolens, and the colonel's personal wardrobe. With Proctor himself supervising, they unloaded heavy stacks of goods. Some of the ord-nance was transferred to other keels, but most of it was brought ashore on the northern bank. The crippled ves-sels were scuttled.

By sunset, the landed goods were assembled. The can-nons were harness-rigged, the bales and crates loaded aboard wagons. Proctor's personal goods— along with the records and reports from Malden— were lashed into a high-wheeled carriage confiscated at McGregor's Mill. The conqueror of Michigan was ready to continue his retreat.

But the delay had given Cadmont's Kentuckians time to again flank the British. As long shadows settled over the peninsula, nearly a hundred buckskin-clad men lashed their stirrups and muffled their harness in the shadow of forest groves, then moved out. Eastward they crept, leading their mounts along the very edge of the swamps. Behind them, a mile southwest, Mason Conroy's regulars broke cover at a gallop. They loosed a hail of musket-ball at the British rear guards, then veered away while the redcoats braced for a charge that never came.

Here and there a man fell, but only a few. Yet the diversion did its job. Pipes shrilled, and the disciplined redcoats— many of whom wore coats of blue or gray now, as a result of French blockades and convoy raids which had cut off England's supply of crimson dyes— formed defensive lines. Within moments hundreds of Indians, those of Tecumseh's scattered bands who were within sound of the gunfire and the pipes, were hurrying toward the sounds.

Working far out ahead of the covert "Kaintuck" raiders on the far flank, Jack Christy's scouts found only four lurking Indians where there had been scores. These four fell where they stood, without a shot being fired.

In deepening dusk, the buckskin-clad harriers moved on, bearing eastward. And leading the main party, astride a dark sorrel mount, was Salem Cadmont. Having made his plans, he had changed horses and drawn a dark wool cap over his silver mane. To Thomas's puzzlement he responded only, "This is no proper meeting of the enemy, boy. This time the task is only to bleed him, to wear him down and delay him. The real engagement will come later.

"It's then I'll want the white horse," he had added in a murmur that the boy barely heard. It was as though the old man had forgotten he was there. For a moment his fierce blue eyes went soft and remote. He seemed to be looking at something far away.

"She enjoyed seeing me ride the white horse," he murmured. "She said it made a handsome sight."

Forbidden from following the raiders, Thomas was put to tending stock and standing guard on the stores, along with a few other boys and some of the older men. Distracted by his duties, and by watching Conroy's cavalry form for action, it was a time before he noticed that Jubal and Jason Stanton were nowhere in sight. Hall Stanton was there, strutting about the clearing in his brass-button coat, trying to direct Conroy in alignment of his troops and generally making a nuisance of himself. But his sons had gone off somewhere.

The bivouac was on a low, cleared knoll just off the Detroit road. At Nathan Horne's signal, fires were lit—little, smoky fires laden with tree-bark and fallen leaves.

Their smoke rose on the chill air, and drifted away on high breezes moving down from Lake Huron.

"Give 'em somethin' to think about," Horne said, watching the smoke.

From the knoll they could see distant movement where the British troops were spreading among brush and deadfall at the edge of a dark, swampy sump north of the road. There was no sign of Indians, but that was no surprise. Most of the redmen with Proctor now were Shawnee. They would not be seen unless they chose to be.

It was just at sundown that Mason Conroy and his soldiers swung into line facing east, and a bugle sounded. At a trot, Conroy led his riders eastward, toward the enemy. Even spread as it was, the cavalry detachment looked very small. Thomas pictured a valiant David advancing upon Goliath. With each second they drew closer to the musketry awaiting them in the brush. Within a hundred yards now they would be in rifle range. Two hundred yards and musket balls would find them. "Look plain out of place, don't they?" Nathan Horne chuckled. "Yonder they go, right out in th' open, an' maybe ten Englishmen takin' a bead sight on each one of 'em."

"Don't the British *see* that?" Thomas pointed. "It's too plain a trick."

"We'll see," Horne shrugged, unconcerned. "Was the Injuns in charge, they'd smell a rat right off. But Henry Proctor's a book soldier. Soldiers an' wild boars attack head on. It's hunters an' panthers that go for the blind side. Ol' Catamount is as much a panther as the cat he's called after. Just watch now, boy. This is how th' cap'n wants it."

Two hundred yards from the entrenched British, Conroy signaled and his cavalry unit broke right and left, their horses surging into a gallop. Muzzles flared and little smokes erupted all along the British line, as deadly balls sang through the gap where the line's center had been. In a heartbeat, both sections of cavalry had veered at a run, directly at the British from two quarters. Now their weapons spoke, raking the screen of brush. A ragged volley, and they wheeled again, angling in, using their pistols now to pick out targets. Musketry returned the fire, and here and there a butternut rider crumpled in his saddle. The Americans hesitated, then wheeled and withdrew, just beyond musket range.

It was precisely what British officers might have expected of a small pursuing force using its resources for effect— a dashing charge, well executed, to be followed by another charge. As the butternut horsemen reloaded their weapons the British saw to their own loads and dug in more securely.

Moments passed, and a bugle sounded again. But instead of forming for a charge, the American horsemen spread wide and dismounted— a long, thin line of deadly silhouettes just beyond musket range, with the gold of sundown behind them.

On the right flank of the British line a savage figure emerged from brush and waved his arms. Even from the American line the pattern of bright paint on his face was plain— paint that blended with the forest colors of his buckskin garb and the owl feathers woven into his long, black hair. His voice carried across the intervening distance, a deep, angry voice speaking perfect English, "It is a trick! Where are the Kaintucks?"

As though in answer, the whip-crack rattle of rifle fire erupted beyond the British entrenchments— a ragged volley of aimed fire, that seemed to go on and on. Here a red-coated soldier plunged from cover, screaming and bleeding. There an Indian flopped into the open, dead even as he fell.

Suddenly, then, the swampy forest behind the British was alive with thundering hooves, blazing rifles and the chilling war-cries of Kentucky fighting men. Like the dark hand of fate, the Louisville First Militia fell on Proctor's army from behind and bored through, leaving a wake of dead and dying men, flying mud, and billowing rifle smoke.

The Indian in the open whirled, leveled a musket and fired. A Kentuckian toppled from his saddle. The Indian dodged aside as a horse pounded past, then dodged again as a rider lunged at him with a wide-bladed sword. He whirled like a dancer, raised his empty musket and swung it, taking still another rider out of his saddle. Lithe as a cat he spun and side-stepped, dodging blades. Then he fell face-down as a horsemen thundered over him. As the militiaman passed, the Indian surged to his feet, drew a tomahawk and threw it. It buried its blade in the rider's back, between his shoulder blades.

Leading the militia charge, Salem Cadmont broke through the British barricade. Just past the brush he reined in and turned, waving his men past him. His saber flashed red and silver in the sunset's rays. He saw the lone Indian cavorting in the rush of horsemen, and saw the tomahawk that struck down Mr. Dall.

With an oath, Cadmont sheathed his saber and raised Lady Justice. But the Indian had disappeared.

The last few militiamen were clearing the brush then, thundering past him, and behind them were British soldiers and Indians. Like deadly shadows, Shawnee warriors streamed from the forest. Here and there, arrows flitted among the retreating militiamen, and now Proctor's troops, regrouped and reloaded, added musket fire to the fusillade. Cadmont ducked his head, spurred his mount and headed west. A hundred yards, and he was through the thin line of Conroy's troops. As he passed, the soldiers fired a smart volley, every second man firing as others stepped into place to aim. Sprinting Indians, pursuing the militia riders, suddenly found themselves between two firing lines. They hesitated, milled and turned away. The Shawnee had learned long ago that only a fool faces ranked musketeers on open ground.

Cadmont drew rein and swung around in his saddle as Ned Dall's terrified horse raced past. Men surrounded the animal, caught its reins and controlled it. Strong hands pried Ned Dall's fingers from his saddle-hood and lifted him gently from his perch. Except for his claw-stiff fingers, the man lay limp, his head lolling, sightless eyes open wide. The tomahawk still stood in his back as they eased him to the ground.

"No use," one of the men said. "He's dead. It was naught but his will that held him astride."

Salem Cadmont looked down from his tall sorrel, and pulled off his wool cap. Snowy hair danced in the breeze. Ned Dall had been a neighbor and a friend. With eyes as cold as Michigan winter, the man called "Old Catamount" gazed back across the empty clearing. Conroy's defense line still knelt there, a bristling fence of ready muskets. But the British troops remained hidden in the darkening brush to the east, and the Indians had gone to cover. There was no one in sight out there now. "Did you see him?" the old man rasped. "That Indian . . . did you all see him?"

Some of them nodded. They had seen hundreds of Indians only moments before, but they knew which one the captain meant. "I saw him, right enough," Horatio King growled. "That's no man, that's the very devil!"

"Mark him well, then," Cadmont said. "You'll see him again before we're through. That was Tecumseh himself."

Through a moonlit night they held their ground, the First Louisville Militia and the little cavalry detachment under Captain Mason Conroy. Vastly outnumbered by

Proctor's British and even more so by the Indians allied with the Crown, the American task force might have withdrawn then to await reinforcements. They had cost Proctor at least two days' worth of retreat, and had made a shambles of his provisioning.

But they stood their ground, taunting the adversary by their presence. Having no orders to the contrary, Conroy yielded to the Kentuckians when it came to strategy. And it was Salem Cadmont's decision to spend the night there, in the clearings west of the swamp.

Gray and cold-eyed, Cadmont outlined his intentions. The Englishman would be expecting his outnumbered attackers to fall back with darkness, to leave the field and seek refuge in distance. Even now, he would be telling out-raiding parties— Indian night-marauders led by British juniors— to fall on the flanks of the fleeing Americans.

But those night fighters would not find retreating backsides here, the Catamount said. Instead of a fleeing defense, they would meet headlong attack. When Hall Stanton started to object, Cadmont fixed him with a glare so daunting that Stanton stuttered, fumbled for words, then backed away, muttering to himself.

Camp assignments completed, Cadmont and his lieutenants huddled with Jack Christy for a time. Then Christy moved away, making the rounds of the little encampment, and others joined him quietly.

With his men organized and assigned, Cadmont rolled up in blankets and lay down to rest. Thomas Woodson, hovering near as always, noted that the old man did not seem to sleep, but instead only to retreat within his own thoughts.

In the early hours of darkness, perimeter fires and patrolling guards gave the American camp some security. But deeper into the night these fires burned low, and those who went to fuel them faced arrows coming from the surrounding darkness.

To Stanton, it seemed the old Kentuckian was abandoning them all to the mercy of their enemies. But those near Cadmont knew better, and ignored the Massachusetts man.

As the perimeter fires dimmed, darkness closed around the camp, and sentries crouched low with rifles at the ready, their eyes straining for a sign of movement. They could feel the presence of hundreds of Shawnee warriors— and men of a dozen other tribes among them— creeping silently closer, ready to strike. The moon crept down a darkening night sky, and just beyond vision the shadows shifted and flowed, moving closer.

Just as it seemed the attack was imminent, though, flashes of bright fire danced in the night, nearly a mile east on the upper road, and the rattle of rifle fire drifted back on night breezes. Here and there in the darkness around the militia camp a lurker turned toward the sound and, in turning, became visible for an instant. That instant was all the Kentucky sharpshooters standing guard needed. Rifles cracked, deadly little lancets of bright fire erupting from their muzzles. In the darkness stricken men tumbled and scattered, drawing more fire from the camp.

Two engagements were under way within seconds, one at the Americans' camp, the other at the bivouac of Colonel Henry Proctor two thousand yards away. In the space of a heart's beat a stealth attack on a sleeping camp had become a trap, with scores of Indian raiders and a half dozen Englishmen— junior officers and noncommissioned officers— caught between those behind them and the deadly fire of a hundred Kentucky long rifles backed by military muskets.

Methodically, as a man awakening to a peaceful morn-

ing, Salem Cadmont sat up, stretched the cramps from
his shoulders, and rolled back his bedding. Firelight
haloed his snowy mane and cast leonine shadows across
his wide, fierce features.

He stood and looked to the east. Bonfires were rising
at the British bivouac, and lanterns moved about over
there in erratic pattern. "Mr. Christy will return soon,"
he said. "Prepare to move out."

With the field cleared of spying eyes for a time, the
Americans packed their gear and faded westward, into
the darkness. Night-eyed woodsmen led, a spear point
of riflemen ghosting through the night on soft moccasins. Behind them marched the bulk of the militia,
eighty men afoot, their rifles carried in both hands,
ready to aim and fire. At their head rode Salem Cadmont.

Behind these came the portage stock laden with packs,
and two dozen horse-handlers, afoot and leading six
horses to the man, the cavalry detachment brought up
the rear.

For a half mile they proceeded westward, back the way
they had come, following the upper road with the river
to their left. Then at a signal from Cadmont the scouts
in the lead peeled off to both sides, and footmen followed them. By fives and tens, the Kentucky riflemen
drifted off the road and into cover, disappearing there,
as their supplies and their mounts passed by.

Within a hundred yards, the only movement on the
dark road was from pack animals, lead horses, and Conroy's soldiers. Salem Cadmont eased back until he rode
alongside Conroy. "Give them a mile of easy trail," he
said quietly. "Then make them work for their trace. Harrison and Johnson should be at Arnold's by now. Report
the situation and bring them to us at the double."

"Keep your head down and your powder dry, Salem,"
Conroy nodded. "Don't do anything foolish."

"Just hurry back," Cadmont snapped. He stepped down from his saddle, slung a light pack over his shoulder, and handed his reins to one of the soldiers. "We'll need our horses, and soon. Proctor will try to move further east. He'll want to fortify himself, and Moravian Town is near. We can't hold him long a'foot."

A shadow against indigo sky, Mason Conroy lifted his reins, but Cadmont stopped him. "Take my boy Thomas with you," he said. He turned and raised a hand to beckon. "Thomas . . . boy, where are you?"

But the boy was not behind him. Sensing what the old man had in mind, Thomas had made himself scarce. Mason Conroy grinned in the darkness— just a touch of wry grin that tugged at his cheeks. The Old Catamount would be a bit more careful, he thought, knowing he still had the boy with him. Conroy knew of Cadmont's letter, regarding his wife, and he had seen the reckless audacity of the old man during the surprise attack on Proctor. He had seen how Cadmont halted his mount just past the barricades, seeming almost to invite British musketry as he waved the last of his men past.

The cavalryman touched his hat in salute and snapped his reins. Just a brief salute, but it was for more than the Kentuckian. It was also for the boy hiding somewhere nearby in the darkness . . . a boy who would do what he could to keep this old warrior alive for another day.

When the horsemen and stock were gone into the darkness, silence hung over the upper road— a silence unbroken by the silent tread of men drifting off to both sides of it, all heading back east, toward the enemy. By first light they would be in position to deal some misery to any Britisher who might try to march toward Moravian Town.

Circling wide around the clearings where they had been camped a few hours before, Cadmont led his men eastward along the edge of the forest. He noticed that

Thomas was present again, tagging along behind him as usual, carrying an old musket and a roll of bedding. But there was nothing to be done about it now, so Cadmont accepted his presence in silence.

In the dark hours of morning, they gathered on a tiny knoll hidden by old timber, and burrowed in to get what rest they could. Jonathan Malifant, one of Christy's woodsmen, came on silent moccasins to report that Horatio King and his company were in place southward, along the river.

Only then did Salem Cadmont speak to Thomas, as the boy handed him bedding. "When our stock is returned, I'll want the white horse," he said. "And I'll want my parade coat, with epaulets."

She never saw me face an enemy in the field, the old man thought, his eyes as bleak as winter starlight in the faint glow of shielded candles. Maybe she can see me now, though.

He tilted his head, gazing upward, his eyes roving the empty sky. "Do you see me, Merry?" he breathed. "Are you watching over me now?"

Maybe she is, he told himself. If there is a God in heaven, then maybe she is. Maybe she's there, waiting for me . . . waiting patiently, as she has done so many times.

"If you're watching this day, Merry," he murmured, "then I should be suited to make you proud."

VI

"Remember the Raisan"

Thames River, three miles southwest of Moravian Town, October 5, 1838

Twice within an hour, as pink dawn grew in the eastern sky, Henry Proctor gave orders to break camp and resume the journey eastward. Twice the marching banner of the Newfoundland Regiment flew— with the colors of the 41st and 10th Regiments ranked behind— and twice Tecumseh's warriors spread to flank a line of march. Both times, the march began and was halted by sniper fire from the marshes along the Thames. The long rifles spoke and men fell, and the retreat was stopped.

Among the Indians, Tecumseh and his "ghostmen" were everywhere. No longer did the Shawnee hold back, awaiting commands from the white soldier chief. The woodlands and the marshes were their natural ground, and Tecumseh took command there as hordes of paint-camouflaged warriors drifted into the brush, seeking their tormentors.

In the tangled growth just south of the road, Ezekiel

Dunn crawled from log to shadowed thicket, as silent as a stalking wolf. His long rifle was still warm at the pan from its latest shot, and not far away a British dragoon lay face down in leaf mold, blood seeping from the gaping wound that had been his throat a minute before. A fifty-four caliber ball left little but wreckage where it struck.

Only a few seasons earlier, Ezekiel Dunn had cut a handsome figure at cotillions from Louisville to Richmond. His lean frame had lent itself well to the attentions of Virginia tailors, and his thick, sandy hair had seemed meant for the combing and queuing which was the style of the time.

But that was before Clay's expedition, before the slaughter on the upper Sandusky and the massacre at the Raisan. Ezekiel Dunn had been one of four brothers of good family. But his brothers were dead now, and his estate dispersed. Now only Ezekiel remained . . . alone with his memories and his grim determination. A few Virginia gentry— and a score of Virginia ladies— who might recall Ezekiel Dunn from soirées at Richmond would hardly have known him now. His buckskins dark with wear and streaked with mud, his sandy hair wild and unshorn, month-old beard bristling on his cheeks and daubs of soot on his forehead and beneath his eyes, Ezekiel Dunn was a creature of the wilderness now, and a dozen raven-tressed scalps hung at his belt.

In the wilds of the backlands, in the hideous visage of war, he had found his element and his purpose.

Blending with the forest shadows, Ezekiel eased himself into new cover behind a growth of gray sedge, and raised himself on his elbows, looking for a new target.

Gray-blue eyes alert in the dawn light, he scanned the forest around him, peering for a glimpse of the clearings beyond— clearings which flanked the Thames River Road, where Henry Proctor's soldiers had gone to cover.

Faint movement caught his eye, and he watched as two Indians crept past, fifty yards to his left. His rifle was ready, and his belt axe, but he waited. Just beyond the Indians were others of his own company, as alert as he was. They would deal with the savages. Dunn wanted Englishmen in his sights this morning.

He shifted his gaze and froze for an instant. Twenty feet away, dark eyes gazed at him— eyes that seemed to have no face around them until they moved an inch, and the painted features of a face distinguished themselves from the brush behind them.

It was a face he had seen before. Despite the paint and the camouflage, Dunn recognized the stern, solemn features that were almost European in their cut unless— as now— one saw them in their natural surroundings. The face— this face, but as seen before— was that of a young, dark-haired man with linen collar and cuffs, a man recalled slightly from some chance meeting in some fine house in . . . where? Philadelphia?

The instant of recognition— that instant of hesitation— cost Ezekiel Dunn his life. A banded bare arm as hard and sleek as corded copper slashed forward and a thrown tomahawk whisked through the brush. In an instant it buried its narrow, razorlike edge in Ezekiel's skull, just above his nose.

For a moment nothing moved. Then the Shawnee slithered across, as silent as a snake, to retrieve his tomahawk. He wiped its head on Dunn's buckskin shirt, returned it to its shoulder sling, and resumed his stalk.

His name was Pascotateh, but had Ezekiel Dunn recalled a name to match the face, in that last instant of his life, the name might have been William Miles . . . or maybe Jean Lecomte.

Pascotateh was one of Tecumseh's chosen escorts, the silent band that had accompanied the great chief in his travels from Canada to the Gulf of Mexico, from the

long houses of the Ojibwa and Chippewa to the fine
houses of Philadelphia. Like Tecumseh himself, Pascotateh had lived among the white men. He had studied
their ways, their languages, and their cultures. By dem-
onstrating his interest, he had received the best education their teachers could provide— far better, probably,
than the teachers ever realized they had provided.

Pascotateh was one of the "ghostmen" of the free
Shawnee.

For long moments, as woodsmen of two worlds hunted
each other and silent deaths multiplied in the dawn shadows, it seemed the scattered American riflemen along
the river were doomed. Man for man, in these woods,
their best were barely a match for the Shawnee. And the
Shawnee outnumbered them three times over. But then
the Indians found the tables turned. From both flanks,
darting bands of Kentuckians swept through them, clearing the forest as they came.

It had been Horatio King's idea to set a trap, using
his own snipers as bait, and it was the grim determination of Kentuckians out to avenge the victims on the
Raisan that sprung it.

For most of the men of First Louisville, this was far
more than a military campaign. This was retribution. By
twos and fives, by tens and fifties, the Indians fell back
before the onslaught, only to be met at the cleared road
by howling foresters crossing from the north, led by
Salem Cadmont. It was another harrying attack on the
blue and white soldiers of the Newfoundland Regiment,
and the retreating Shawnee took the brunt of it.

Still, the Americans were vastly outnumbered. Their
only strength lay in such slash-and-run assaults, and they
knew it. For several minutes the smokes of pitched battle
rose above the road, then silence settled. The British and
their red allies had regrouped to fight . . . and found
nothing to shoot at. The Americans simply faded away

into the forests, turned west, and headed for the knoll where they had camped the night before.

As full dawn bathed the landscape, the British worked furiously to reorganize their retreat. Tecumseh watched for a time, then walked along the perimeters of the battleground, followed by several of his ghost-men. British sentries wandered everywhere, nervous and jumpy, but Tecumseh knew there was no immediate danger. The Kentuckians had struck again, and disappeared again.

Like Shawnee, he thought. In fighting them, we have taught them our ways. Now we face ourselves in battle.

Only a few casualties had been suffered, as the roll-takers were finding. Eight of Proctor's soldiers lay dead, and a dozen more had injuries. Six dead Kaintucks were found, and a few more never would be. No one counted the Indian casualties. In all, a small loss. But it was enough. The British retreat was halted just where it had been. They had not moved a hundred yards. The Kentuckians were holding them here, waiting for Harrison's army to arrive.

They came out of nowhere, they struck with ferocity to match any Shawnee's, and then they were gone again. As though they had never been there at all.

Tecumseh shivered, as though a cold wind had found him. He stopped, looking around. This is the place, something told him. Here is where the spirits have led us, and they lead no further. Here it begins . . . or ends.

What had occurred here, yesterday and this morning, seemed inconsequential. Only skirmishes. Yet Proctor's forces were stalled here, and the brightening woods around the clearings seemed to whisper a melancholy chant as breezes touched their boughs.

Down by the river, more shots rang out. The British commander had sent a detail there to burn the boats. Without seeing it, Tecumseh knew what had happened.

The Kaintuck snipers held the river. They had driven the burners away. Now they had the boats and all they carried.

With a sigh, Tecumseh turned. His own main camp was just north of the road, only a shout from the British position, yet isolated from it.

"Send the headmen to me," the chief said. Without question, several of his escort hurried off toward the various little camps of the Shawnee bands and their ally tribes.

When they met, he would tell them. Then those who chose could stay and fight. There would be those who would not choose this as their day, and that was their right. The women and children must be moved eastward, out of the range of battle. The sick and wounded also. Proctor had promised transport for all noncombatants to Moravian Town. But Tecumseh knew the promise was worthless. With injured soldiers to account for, Proctor would not bother himself about details.

The safety of the Indians' noncombatants was up to the Indians.

Many men would go with them, he knew. And if Proctor knew of their departure, he would consider it desertion. But who was going to tell him about it? Henry Proctor had promised to defend Malden, and the Indians had depended upon his word. Then he had abandoned Malden. He had promised to make a stand at Chatham, and the Indians had believed him. But at Chatham there was not even the pretense of a stand. Again the British had retreated, and again it was the Indians who were left betrayed and exposed, with no choice but to either follow or fade away.

Tecumseh was not interested in any further English promises. He had made a promise of his own— to ally with the British and fight at their side. He would keep his promise, but he would hold no one else to it.

By mid-morning, when Proctor's troops were again assembled for a march, fully half of his Indian allies were gone. Tecumseh remained, as did most of his loyal Shawnee. But where there had been more than a thousand warriors, now there were only a few hundred. Many of the Indians watched with ironic interest as the Englishmen formed their marching ranks, and some joked among themselves. Finally, when the futility of it was no longer amusing, Shawnee scouts went to Colonel Proctor and gravely made their report: The American army— General Harrison's regulars and the main body of militias— was less than two miles away. Even now they were advancing to attack.

There would be no further retreat. Under Proctor's pale, angry supervision the British made hasty plans for a line of battle, and dug in.

The army of General William Henry Harrison, fully assembled at Detroit as scattered detachments and militia companies converged there, numbered more than 3,500 fighting men. Of these, fewer than 200 wore the butternut of regular troops. The remainder were citizen soldiers, militiamen from settlements up and down the Ohio River and along the lakes. By far the largest contingent was the Kentucky Militia, commanded by Colonel R.M. Johnson. Militia units of a dozen major settlements made up Johnson's regiment, reinforced by several hundred Kentucky free volunteers assigned by Governor Shelby.

For every man massacred at the Raisan a few months earlier, three now marched from Michigan Territory into the Province of Ontario. To William Henry Harrison and the War Department, the campaign's purpose was to recover all of the territory surrendered the previous year. But for those who marched with Harrison, it was revenge. The Kaintucks came in search of those who had shed so much Kentucky blood— in search of Indians, in search of Canadian soldiers, in search of British expeditionaries . . . and in search of General Henry Proctor, the man they called "the Colonel."

In the king's name, Proctor had invaded Michigan Territory. That alone would not have damned the man in the eyes of the "Kaintucks." Children of a violent time, born of invaders themselves, they were fighters from birth and seldom gave quarter, but they did recognize and respect an act of war. Men of finer cloth, couched in gentler surroundings, said of the Kaintucks that they were a breed unto themselves— as wild as the woodlands they fought to tame and as hard as the rock ridges that sprouted their roots. But there was a code of honor that permeated them. It was a time of war, and war to most of them was a condition of life. Had Proctor waged war honorably, they could have held him in respect even as they fought him.

But "the Colonel" had conquered clumsily and to excess. His "campaigns" were often ill-planned and then— of necessity— brutally completed. Instead of swift strikes and clean victories, Proctor's career was marked with the thoughtless cruelties of one who campaigns unwisely and kills poorly. The blood his troops had let on Michigan soil was slow, agonizing blood.

Further, the officer had practiced tyranny at Detroit and condoned atrocity at the Raisan. And he had allowed— he had even encouraged— the return of the red terror.

For all the hostility that existed between the Americans and England, for all the unredressed claims of the Crown over loss of its investments, and the grievances of the recent colonists over unapologized tyrannies, still they were people of the same cloth. They shared a language, and right or wrong they shared a heritage. Down through the generations they had fought, as oppressor and oppressed on English soil, as master and rebellious serf, as Royalist and Revisionist, as Cavalier and Roundhead, as lord and varlet. Those hostilities, transported to American shores, had resulted finally— inevitably— in revolution.

But through it all there remained a perverse bond between combatants. The Crown sought dominance, the insurgents freedom. But it was a clear-cut, two-sided conflict, until "outsiders" were brought into it. The Indians were neither Norman nor Saxon, neither Royalist nor Roundhead. They were not of the cloth. They were an invaded, displaced people who fought for their own reasons and by their own rules. They were, by their very differences, savages.

The unleashing of Indians in such a private matter as war was a breech of ethics. It was an outrage not to be endured, and those who perpetrated it— notably the "red-knife general," Henry Hamilton, and now "the Colonel," Henry Proctor— provoked a fury that went far beyond the ancient angers of Britanic conflict. Like his predecessor Hamilton in the earlier woodland wars along the Ohio, Proctor's campaign in Michigan gave the Americans a name upon which to focus their anger.

The war between the United States and England was a distant, abstract thing to these inland people. It was an exercise in patriotism and free will. But there was nothing abstract about the mute, shallow graves of a thousand Kentucky volunteers beside a little river called Raisan, or the lingering savagery of the British occupation of Detroit.

For many months, British expeditionaries and American militias had converged upon the Michigan Territory, unleashed by the outbreak of war. And there also, thanks to Proctor's promises, was the last great gathering of the woodland tribes. Led by the free Shawnee who followed Tecumseh, the Indians became part of the conflict.

The fine line between soldier and noncombatant had dissolved, with approval of the Crown's officer. In Michigan, there were no civilians.

For the atrocities that had occurred in a year of cruel war in Michigan, Henry Proctor was the man who must bear responsibility.

William Henry Harrison understood the men in his command. Around them, men and horses were everywhere. Harrison's uniformed regulars, with their parade-drill efficiency, gave a semblance of discipline to the gathering, but they were far outnumbered by the various rowdy, raucous units of independent militia who wandered among them, waiting for direction.

"They're rarin'," Horatio King told Thomas Woodson as several men dodged aside to avoid an impromptu horse-race through the camp. A dozen young Kaintucks of different units were testing their mounts, while others wagered on them. "The enemy's close enough to smell," King growled. "An' these yayhoos can't wait to get at 'em."

Thomas's eyes darted here and there, trying to see everything at once. The excitement was contagious. Across the way he had a glimpse of the Stanton brothers, amidst a crowd of young woodsmen. The Stantons seemed to be bragging about something, and one of them held up something bright, showing it off. But the crowd shifted then, and Thomas lost sight of them. Salem Cadmont strode past, heading for the top of the knoll, and Thomas hastened to follow.

Well within sight of the British line, General Harrison gathered his officers around him. "The redcoats will center on the road," he pointed. "Such artillery as they have will be there. Proctor will position his best muskets there, spreading toward the river. He will place the 41st

just beyond, I think. At musket range, with his reserves
to their right. His cavalry will be just past that patch of
woods over there."

"That's just a little sump," a scout offered. "Maybe a
hundred yards across. Clear beyond, over to the creek.
That's where the real woods start."

"I'll concentrate my regulars along the road," Harrison nodded. "Colonel Johnson's horsemen will move
with us until we engage, then sweep to the left, directly
across that 'sump.' " He turned. "With luck, Rab, you'll
catch his cavalry there, just forming up."

"And the rest?" Salem Cadmont's voice sounded thin
in the sun-bright air. At his side, Thomas Paine Woodson
frowned. "Old Catamount" seemed very tired. His shoulders were hunched, and his cheeks— normally rosy— were
pale beneath the tan of sun and wind. Still, his old blue
eyes fairly blazed with feral energy.

"All the rest of it is yours, Salem," Harrison said.
"First Louisville has given me my enemy. You made him
stop and fight. Now I'll give your enemy to you. The
Indians will be on Proctor's right, I think, in those woods
along the creek. All the volunteers are itching for a fight.
They can join you. Those woods are yours."

"Tecumseh is there," Horatio King muttered. "Our
boys saw him."

"Remember the Raisan," someone said.

Others around him nodded grimly. Some removed
their hats. "Remember the Raisan," several said, and it
became a chant that grew into a war-cry.

"Remember the Raisan!"

Salem Cadmont glanced at the boy standing beside
him. "I'll want the white, now, Thomas," he said. "Please
brush out my dress coat, as well, and see to Lady Justice.
A fresh load . . . the driest powder and the best ball,
with a fine linen patch."

VII

Shawnee Sundown

October 5, 1813

Thomas saw to the gentling of the white horse, then left it with Mr. Collett for saddling. With a stiff brush, the boy dressed out Captain Cadmont's greatcoat until not a trace of dust or lint remained on the indigo velvet of the garment. With resin and sand he polished its brass buttons, and with a scrap of moist doeskin he rubbed the coat's crimson lapels and piped cuffs until they fairly glowed.

He cleaned and oiled the old man's best boots and buckler, then got out Lady Justice. As carefully as he could, he cleaned the rifle, tested its flint and the set of its triggers, and measured fine, triple-ground powder into its breech. He selected a ball, seated it with a linen patch and rammed it home. Then he primed the pan and closed the striker. Lady Justice was alive now, ready to cock and fire. When he took the long rifle, with its leather sling-pouch and charged horn, to Cadmont, he found the captain ready to ride. Seated astride his white charger, with the high sun haloing both manes— the man's and the horse's— "Old Catamount" was more than a striking figure. He was magnificent.

Thomas stood back, pale with dread. They spoke sometimes of men who dressed to kill, but the boy's intuition said otherwise now.

He had not seen the letter about Mistress Merry, but he guessed at its content. Mistress Merry was gone. And without her, the captain had one great thing left to do. Captain Salem Cadmont was dressed to die.

Before Thomas could speak, though, the old man looked down at him, his warrior's eyes as stern and distant as ever he had seen them. "Stay close by Mr. King now, boy" The captain's words were a command and a dismissal. "Attend him, and do as he says."

Without waiting for an answer, Cadmont touched heels to the white and reined hard about. "First Louisville, to saddle!" he shouted.

A hundred yards away, to the right, General Harrison's brigade was moving out— three hundred butternut-clad figures marching ten abreast, a solid mass of fighting men bristling with ready muskets and bayonets. Among them were several dozen armed sailors, led by a young officer in naval uniform. With the British fleet taken and Lake Erie firmly in American hands, Oliver Hazard Perry had led a party ashore to join Harrison.

At the army's flanks rode three companies of uniformed cavalry, one of them Mason Conroy's unit. As the soldiers marched eastward, down the little knoll, hundreds of horsemen fell in behind them with the precision of disciplined cavalry.

Rab Johnson's mounted militia, the largest white force in the field on this day, wore no military uniforms, but they had drilled for months toward this moment. Ahead was the enemy, digging in and waiting. Along the road, where the brush was sparse, red coats and white crossbelts were flowing bits of color against the somber forest beyond.

Nearer at hand, saddles creaked and hooves thudded

as the First Louisville formed itself behind Salem Cadmont. Other volunteer militia units crowded around, upraised rifles sprouting like dark stalks from a swarming field of motley riders.

Thomas found oiled reins pressed into his hand and turned. Mr. Collett had brought him a horse . . . Cadmont's own sorrel. As the boy swung into the saddle, Horatio King reined close. In furs and rolled cap, the man looked like a great, burly bear mounted on a short-coupled dun.

He thrust a handful of folded leather at Thomas. "Take this, boy," he said. "And follow me close."

It was a buckler, with a heavy pistol in its sling. Without testing it, Thomas knew the gun was loaded and primed. He slung the buckler across his shoulder.

Some distance away, he saw the Stantons. The boys were with their father now, all three mounted but hanging back, away from the press of militia. Horatio King saw them too, and pointed as Nathan Horne rode up beside him. "Told ye that popinjay wouldn't brag himself in a fight," the big man growled. "All along the way, he's strutted his brass buttons. Now he's wearin' drab."

"But standoffish as ever," Horne noted. "Prob'ly layin' back to see who wins today. Then he'll decide which side he's on."

Cadmont held his command in check until the soldiers and Johnson's riders were halfway across the clear ground. Then a bugle sounded, and the hundreds of riders began to move. High afternoon sun, quartering behind them, danced on the subtle shades of buckskins and homespun fabrics, of slouch hats and fur caps, of woolen cloaks, wooden stocks, and oxhorn flasks. A widening juggernaut of lethal men astride blooded mounts, they cast dark shadows on the cold ground, and went where the shadows led.

And out ahead of them rode a white-maned man on

a tall, white horse. Cadmont led them forward at a trot, bearing a few degrees left from the path taken by the army. He set course for the north edge of the little patch of woods in the distance, and for the deeper forest beyond. Fifty yards out he signaled, and the riders split into two groups. To a man, the Kaintucks knew what was wanted of them. And they knew where their old enemy waited, in forest shadows just ahead. First Louisville followed the Old Catamount, spreading as they went so that no man was impeded by anyone in front of him. The other combined militias— Shelby's volunteers— fanned further northward, toward the brushy creek there and the woods beyond.

For eternal minutes, the only sound in the land was the muted drumroll of advancing hooves. Then from the right, sounding far away at first, there were little thunders— a gunshot, then several more, then the rolling crash of volleys answering volleys. Harrison's regulars had met the English line.

From his saddle, Thomas saw the rising smokes of battle. He saw musketeers advancing, rank by rank, and he saw Rab Johnson's cavalry charging down on the silent brush of the sump. Like a dark tidal wave the riders hit the brush and disappeared into it, and the sharp, ringing song of rifles was added to the thunder of musketry beyond.

Here and there, darting figures erupted from the brush, into the open. Feathers and warpaint, the camouflage of the forests, glistened in the sunlight like bright banners. At the right of Cadmont's line, some riders veered off, going to meet the Indians. But barked commands brought them back.

"Decoys!" Horatio King shouted. "Hold your fire, boys! The real fight's just ahead!"

Several running Indians paused to discharge their weapons, and Thomas could see where they were aiming.

Out ahead of the militia, Salem Cadmont's snowy mane and white horse, his brilliant blue coat and glinting leathers, were too vivid a target for the savages to ignore. Thomas could almost see the whining balls of death that whistled around him, and in his mind he heard again the gravelly old voice of the man: "The ball's not yet molded that can find me, boy."

To the south, the rattle of musketry became a roar as armies closed. Rising white smokes drifted everywhere, like little clouds gathering in storm. But now Thomas had no time to watch. Sweeping into view around the wooded sump was a gaggle of uniformed riders in full flight.

"Johnson's found their cavalry!" Nathan Horne whooped. "Look at 'em scatter."

For a full fifty yards, the two dozen English horsemen came onward, looking back over their shoulders as though the devil were behind them. Straight toward First Louisville they galloped, then abruptly they saw the men ahead of them. Horses skidded into rump-down turns as the soldiers tried to veer away. Two of three went down, losing their riders. Then they were turned and racing away, angling toward the forests beyond the creek.

All along the line of militia, not a shot had been fired. Their presence had been enough to rout the panicked riders.

The open field ahead was alive with fleeing figures now, dozens of Indians racing for cover with several uniformed Britishers among them.

Again some turned and fired, and again their fire was aimed at Salem Cadmont.

"The Old Catamount's a madman," Horatio King announced, to no one in particular. "He's drawin' fire like flowers draws bees."

Impervious to it all, Cadmont raised an arm and swept it forward, touching spurs to the white. The big horse gathered itself and ran, and those behind followed in step. Thomas clenched his teeth, clung to his saddle and concentrated on staying close to Horatio King. Twenty yards, and the run became an all-out charge, closing on the brush of the little creek.

Now shots rang in the boy's ears, and there was the sound of passing ball— an angry, whining shrill like hornets disturbed. Five yards to Thomas's left a man lurched upright in his saddle, then slid from it. His horse shied slightly, then resumed its gallop, coming abreast of Thomas's horse.

His ears ringing, his heart pounding, Thomas tightened sturdy, gangly legs in his stirrups and braced himself. Brush flew past and the creek was just ahead. Everywhere now there was thunder, and a fierce howl rose above it. All along the line, Kaintucks added their voices. "Remember the Raisan!" they shouted. "Remember the Raisan!"

The sorrel surged, Thomas clung, and they were across the creek, thundering into opening forest alive with painted warriors. All around, everywhere, the woodlands flowed and shifted and became fighting men, men festooned with feathers and daubed with fierce colors . . . men with weapons raised, racing to meet them.

A kaleidoscope of colors and sounds enveloped him, and Thomas drew his heavy pistol. But through it all, underlying the chaos of the moment, an odd, distracted realization formed itself in his mind and presented itself to him.

Out there on the field, when a bullet had found that nearby rider, there had been a sound among all the louder sounds. He had *heard* the ball strike, he realized. Amidst a chaos of clashing noises, one small sound had stood clear . . . the little thump of a half-inch lead ball finding its target in human flesh.

The militia's charge hit the Shawnee line like an avalanche. A storm of rifle balls sang through the forest, and Indians fell by the dozens, no longer hidden by their paint, no longer crouched in their shelters. Like scythes through wheat, the long rifles sang their crackling song and warriors fell before them. By the dozens they fell, but by the hundreds they appeared and swarmed toward their tormentors, adding their own howls to the din of battle. A burly warrior with tomahawks in both hands appeared suddenly beside Thomas, and Horatio King's shot nearly deafened the boy as the big man fired almost at his ear. The Indian was swatted backward . . . and where he had been were three others.

Trembling violently, struggling to control his horse, Thomas raised his pistol . . . but the Indians dodged aside. One of them came up directly under the head of Nathan Horne's horse, swinging a bloody tomahawk. Fresh blood flew as the little axe buried itself in the animal's neck. The horse shrilled, pitched forward and Horne tumbled into thick leaf fall. The warrior wrenched his blade free and turned, and Thomas fired. The Indian sprawled across the scrambling Horne, the top of his head blown away.

Another Indian sprinted past, and Thomas threw the empty pistol at him. It hit him in the back and fell away.

For long moments, all was turmoil. The rifles had spoken, but now it was man to man and hand to hand, a myriad of violences that seemed to fill the woodlands. Abruptly, then, there was shrill birdcall that echoed back and forth along the line. At sound of it, the Indians whirled and ran, scurrying into cover. Within seconds there wasn't a live Indian in sight, as mounted Kaintucks— and some now on foot— swept here and there, searching.

"They're not done, boys!" Salem Cadmont called. "Keep your eyes . . ."

Abruptly, Jack Christy's voice shouted, "Arrows! Defend!" A second later there were flitting shafts everywhere— deadly little spears driven by stout bows, that danced among the horsemen, seeking them out.

"Dismount!" someone shouted. "Shelter an' reload!"

Wave after wave, the arrows came, fletched messengers of bloodshed darting from a hundred bows concealed in the brush. Less devastating than a rifle ball, with its instant shock of impact, the shafts were still deadly when they struck a vital spot . . . and the Shawnee archers were expert. All along the milling ranks of Kaintucks, men staggered and fell, horses shrilled and reared in pain. But only for a moment. The Kentuckians had known there would be arrows. Now they scurried for cover, using every stump and bush as a shield, disappearing from sight as magically as any Indian might.

In heavy brush, surrounded by his ghostmen, Tecumseh studied the terrain with agate eyes as bleak as winter sky.

We have no chance now, he mused. The spirits have led us here, and gone on without us.

The arrows had been his best offense. But the Kaintucks were not broken. A few heartbeats had been gained, a moment's turning of the tide. But it was not turned. Here and there he saw the slight movements— the shifting of hidden men for better position, the flick of ramrods as they reloaded their rifles.

Some of them were even now moving forward to renew the attack. And among them, some were still mounted on their tall horses. They are like the rain that falls, Tecumseh thought. One might avoid the raindrops, but not the storm.

We never had a chance, his inner voice conceded. We are not enough like them to defeat them. We understand battle . . . but they understand war.

Even as he thought it, brush was parting in a hundred places and Kaintucks were appearing again— crouched, scurrying men with long knives and long rifles, coming to seek the Shawnee. And here and there, among them, were riders. Tecumseh caught his breath as thickets shivered and a man rode forth— a tall, proud, old man in a coat of deepest blue, with crimson lapels and gleaming brass buttons. A great mane of snowy hair danced in the patterned sunlight, hair as white as the tall horse he rode.

Tecumseh had seen the man earlier, and had felt a deep respect for him. Here was a man who knew how to fight, and how to die. But now he noticed the long rifle the man carried, and spirit voices told him that he had seen this rifle before. As though in a dream, the rifle spoke to his spirits, and his spirits did not answer. The spirits had gone on alone, and Tecumseh was saddened. For spirits, nothing ever ended. But for every man, there was an end. Deep down, Tecumseh knew . . . it ended here.

At his side, sturdy Pascotateh was reading his thoughts. "Then let it end," the warrior muttered. In a single, fluid motion he stood, threw off his coat and raised his head. The yipping, trilling war-cry that came from him was the same cry that had chilled the blood of a thousand white intruders in a hundred secluded forests— the death-taunt of the free Shawnee.

Instantly, a dozen Kaintuck rifles spoke, and balls sang around Pascotateh as he sprinted, ducking and dodging, into open ground a dozen yards away. Bodies lay there, friend and foe, scattered about like storm fall. Droplets of blood sprayed from the warrior's shoulder as he dived and rolled, defying the white marksmen. His hand found a fallen rifle, and he came up with it, cocking and aiming even as more bullets found him. He touched the trigger and the gun bucked against his shoulder, then wavered and fell.

Pascotateh tried to shout again, to sing his defiance,

but no sound came from him . . . only a gout of bright blood from his punctured lungs. He toppled and lay still.

"It is the best way," Tecumseh muttered. With a growl, he shrugged off his constraining coat and shirt, picked up a rifle and sprinted into the clear, toward the advancing Kaintucks. A hundred warriors followed him, bursting from the brush with howls of anger.

Tecumseh raised the rifle, seeking the white-maned man on the white horse. But even as he found him, the man slumped forward in his saddle, clung for an instant, then slid to the ground.

Pascotateh's final shot had found Salem Cadmont.

His unbound hair whipping around his shoulders, bare chest rippling with the dancing patterns of sunlight and twig-shadows, Tecumseh shifted his aim, found another Kaintuck in his sights and fired.

The sorrel had fallen. For a moment, Thomas lay dazed, trapped between a dead horse and a stump. Then he struggled free, pulled himself upright and ducked back into cover as an arrow buried half its length in the ribs of the dead animal.

All around him, men were diving into makeshift shelter as arrows flew among them. A thump, and Horatio King was there beside him, belly-down in the grass behind the dead horse. For an instant the big man studied him, then he nodded. "You're all right," he said. "Keep your head down!"

Even as he spoke, King's hands flew from pouch to muzzle, pressing a fresh load into his rifle. Another arrow flickered past, and King rolled to the side, glanced around, and came to his feet. As lithe as a panther, despite his bulk, he sprinted forward, beckoning to others as he went. Thomas freed himself again from his cocoon between horse and stump, and followed.

A silence had descended on the forest, but now it was broken. From somewhere near, a voice was raised in a high-pitched shout, a yipping, trilling call that echoed among the somber shadows and seemed to go on and on.

Around him, Thomas heard men curse, and saw some raise their rifles. He scampered past a thicket, and stopped. Out there in a little clearing, an Indian was running, dodging this way and that. Rifles blazed and the red man seemed to dance among the shots. He dived, rolled across a fallen militiaman, and came up with a rifle.

Thomas saw the puff of smoke at its breech, the spearpoint flare at its muzzle, then it sagged and the warrior fell backward. Now there were more Indians out there, dozens and hundreds it seemed, but Thomas ignored them. He had heard a sound that made his blood run cold, and even before he looked, he knew where it came from. King barked at him and he dodged behind a tree trunk as more rifles spoke. Then he looked around.

To his left, only a few yards away, Salem Cadmont sat astride his big white horse. But there was something odd in his posture— something stiff and unnatural. Only for an instant he sat so, then he slumped forward. Lady Justice wavered in his grasp and fell. Cadmont clung for a moment, his lips forming a word. "Merry," he breathed. Then he slid from his horse. He hit the ground shoulders-first, sprawled there and did not move.

King's bull voice rang in Thomas's ears, "It's th' captain! He's been shot!"

Out in the clearing, thirty yards away, a tall Indian held a raised rifle, and King snapped a shot at him. The Indian stepped aside, turned slightly and fired. King grunted as the ball tore through his buckskins and into his chest. With a growled oath he stumbled to Cadmont's side, grabbed up Lady Justice, turned and fired.

The tall Indian staggered back a step, then paused, looking down at the gaping hole in his chest as though it were the most interesting thing he had ever seen. Then slowly, he went to his knees, raised his face to the sky one last time, and fell.

Voices— Indian voices— shouted, "Tecumseh! *Kana'ki Tecumseh!*" The cries blended and became a dirge. It was answered by fierce howls as the Kaintucks left their cover and charged.

Salem Cadmont and Horatio King lay side by side on the cold ground, a winter-bare sycamore tree caressing them with its quiltwork shadows. Thomas Paine crouched between them, looking from one to the other, trying to understand what had happened. At a hand on his shoulder he looked up, into the tired, sad eyes of Nathan Horne. As though reading his thoughts, the man asked, "How old be ye now, son?"

Thomas blinked. "Th-thirteen, sir," he whispered.

"Well, lad," Horne nodded, "I believe today ye've come of age."

In the evening, men wandered through the forest, collecting their dead, assessing their losses, trading news.

The British were defeated. Prisoners would be taken back to Detroit. There were many English prisoners, but few Indian captives. At Harrison's command, the British were to be dealt with according to the customs of war. But no such mercies applied to the savages. Many a fresh scalp now adorned the trappings of battle-hardened Kaintucks.

Of "the Colonel," Major General Henry Proctor, there was no sign. In the height of battle, he had escaped, driving a carriage laden with his personal goods. But patrols were out, looking for him. He would be over-taken, the army assured them, somewhere on the road toward York.

Just off the road, the army had made its bivouac, and most of the activity centered there as afternoon became evening. The collection of reports, review of tactics, the listing of dead, wounded, and missing . . . these things would go on all through the night.

Fanning out from the central bivouac were dozens of smaller camps, where various militia units sought their rest. At some of these fires there was grumbling, as always after a battle. Among the First Louisville survivors, the primary complaint was the strident presence of Hall Stanton, imperiously gathering militia reports and carrying them off to the central camp for presentation to Harrison, Johnson, and their officers.

It was as though the man had declared himself leader, somehow, and no one seemed to know what to do about that.

Feeling lost and lonely, Thomas wandered around the militia camp as evening shadows lengthened. Here and there a new fire was burning, and at one of them Nathan Horne's immortal stew bubbled in its pot. For a time the boy lingered there, but the men were busy and he was only in the way.

At the corrals he spent a time with Captain Cadmont's white horse. The animal had come through the battle without a scratch, and had been gently tended by the hostlers. But in Thomas's mind it seemed the horse must be as lonely as he was. "Old Catamount" was gone, and with him all meaning for boy and horse alike.

At home, Thomas had been Cadmont's ward. With the militia, he had been the captain's "fetch." Now Cadmont was gone, and Mr. King as well. Thomas had no idea where to go now, or what to do. And there was no one to tell him.

He was alone at the corrals when the Stanton boys came. At first it seemed they did not see him. Creeping through the holding fences, they made straight for the white horse.

They were almost on it when Thomas arose from the shadows to block their way. "Get away from that horse," he demanded. "It isn't yours."

For a moment they stared at him in the gloom, then they exchanged grins. "Well, well," one of them crooned. "It's that ol' fart's fetch. Looks like we've got us some business to finish here."

"The kid can wait, Jason," the other said. "I'll get us that nag. Then I'll show you how to break a critter."

With a chuckle, Jubal Stanton walked past Thomas, shuffling a jig-step to taunt the smaller boy. He raised the hood of a little oil lamp on a post for better light, and drew a knife, gazing at the horse's hobbles. As he raised it, Thomas could see the knife clearly. It was a small blade, ornately worked, with silver filigree on its tortoise-shell hilt.

It was the knife Horatio King had given to the old Canadian refugee, Albert Speer, back at Chatham.

"Where did you get that?" Thomas snapped.

"This?" Jubal sneered. "I taken it off some old Canuck that somebody left runnin' loose . . . him an' some women. We taken whatever we wanted. Nothin' they could do about it."

In an instant, all the confusion in Thomas's mind resolved itself—all the loneliness, the fear, and the grief. In that instant they all became something else—a pure, hot fury that blazed within him. Shifting his stance, he raised Lady Justice, holding the rifle by its barrel, and swung it like a club. Ten pounds of steel and rock maple thudded into the small of Jubal's back, driven by blind rage. He gasped, pitched forward, and sprawled face-down.

Without hesitation, Thomas turned and swung again. This time the driving stock took Jason across his knees. The larger boy whimpered and fell. Thomas hit him again.

Cursing, Jubal raised himself, got his feet under him and crouched, holding the knife outthrust. "You little bastard!" he hissed. "I'm goin' to gut you like a . . ."

The swinging rifle hit him again, driving him back, then Thomas was on him. Dropping Lady Justice, he pummeled the bully with wild fists, kicking and clawing at him when he tried to back away.

Frantically, Jubal stabbed and slashed with the little knife, drawing blood. But Thomas was relentless. With a desperate growl, Jubal heaved him away and drew his belt knife. Now he had a blade in each hand and the boy was off balance, struggling to his feet.

Jubal didn't even see Thomas draw his belt axe, but when he charged again, stabbing, the axe was there. It was the last thing Jubal Stanton ever saw.

Mr. Collett found him, standing over Jubal's body. Nearby, Jason lay unconscious. Collett took Thomas's axe from nerveless fingers, then hurried him away from the scene.

Through the early hours of darkness there was furtive, whispered conversation around the First Louisville cook fire. "Gonna be hell to pay," they muttered. "With th' Ol' Catamount gone, who's to stand up for what's right?"

"That popinjay Stanton's got th' general's ear," they said. "Don't matter who's at fault, they'll hang the boy."

Thomas heard the words, but they seemed to have no meaning. Everything that had meaning now was gone. Beyond the firelight, the night was cold and dark. Only in the firelight was there any warmth. The flames, just above their fuel— just in that little span between glowing coals and flickering amber flags— were the color of sunlight on a girl's hair. Thomas simply sat, staring into the fire.

Then someone was beside him, pulling him upright. "You come with me, lad," Jack Christy said. "We got places to go."

"Her name was Martha," Thomas whispered, to no one but himself.

In the twilight, other men waited with saddled horses— Christy's favored gray and the captain's white. Both had packs lashed behind their saddles. In hushed voices, men urged Thomas into the saddle of the white and handed Lady Justice up to him. Jack Christy mounted his own beast and reined alongside, taking the white's leads.

"You ever seen real big woods, boy?" he asked gently. "Plenty of places a man can just lose himself for a while. Come on, I'll show you."

VIII

The Commerce-makers

Central Platte River, Spring, 1836

The Sinclair brothers were dead. From his perch on the east rampart, Louis Champon could see Luke's ravaged corpse lying on the riverbank fifty yards away, sprawled in mute company with two of the Platte River men and at least three of their "hiders," renegade Shoshone lured by the white man's whiskey. From this distance, they were all just a tangle of bodies, and the blood that drenched them— that drenched the mud around them and made the lapping waters more pink than tan— was blood that flowed from all of them.

In life they had been so many separate men— all alike but each unique, some red and some white and each as stubborn as the others, as proud and vital. Reckless young men they were, reckless and restless . . . men full of raging life and robust laughter and rock-bound intolerances. But now, in death, they were like the buffalo whose hides they had collected— just so much meat, bleeding together where they fell.

Ironic, the old familiar voice in the back of Champon's mind reflected. As long as he had known him, Luke Sinclair had despised the Shoshone. Something, somewhere in his past, had given the man cause to hate so. And the Shoshone hiders, it seemed, returned the hatred in kind. Yet because of business, because these Shoshone came with the hide hunters who brought their goods to Fort Sinclair, Luke had tolerated them. He had worked side by side with them to stack and bind the pelts and load them aboard the barges.

And when it came time to die, Luke and those three Shoshone had died together, the first to fall when the Pawnee raiders attacked. Their sprawled bodies fairly bristled now with arrows.

Nearer at hand, the younger Sinclair— Rene— lay in the gap between the broken portals of the half-closed main gate. He and several men of the fort had mounted a hasty defense there, and had driven back two howling rushes. They had defended the gate with their Hawken rifles, and bought a few precious minutes for those inside. But they had paid an awful price. Rene was dead, and at least four others with him. One of them was Rene's Indian wife Ticoba, a woman from one of the sand hill tribes.

Ticoba, Champon mused, peering out between stockade uprights to scan the monotonous, rolling horizon. Ticoba, a creature of warm, dark eyes and shy smiles. In her own tongue, the name meant "tomorrow."

The Sinclairs had drifted down from Quebec . . . when, ten years ago? Champon recalled them vividly from the first time he had set eyes on them— Luke as sturdy as a mountain oak, a young man full of dreams and visions . . . a young man as bulletproof and immortal as any young man with a pretty little bride and a baby. Martha had been a little vision of fresh motherhood, with a tiny, toddling daughter clinging to her skirt. The little family had been sunshine itself. It had seemed that nothing could ever stand in their way.

With Luke's younger brother and some hired men,

with the backing of John Jacob Astor's American Fur Company and an ox-cart full of supplies, they had crossed the winter plains to reach this place. And here they had built a home and a business.

Fort Sinclair's walls were made of logs that had floated down from the mountains. Its soul was that of the Sinclairs. The place had become an island of civility in a raging wilderness, based on a simple notion—the idea that conflicts could be set aside for the sake of mutual profit. Here all men, white and red alike, could gather to trade their wares, to sell their goods to the buyers who came up the river to meet them—buyers like Louis Champon.

It reminded Champon of another place at another time, where he himself had created just such a haven.

The power of dreams, he mused. They grow and become reality, and for a time they give meaning to everything around them.

And then they end, abruptly. Back there, in the valley of the Tahnessay, it had been a foreign war that had ended it. Here it was painted Pawnee.

My whiskers were dark then, he thought. Now they are white, but nothing else has changed.

For the moment, the world beyond the little fort seemed empty. There had been dozens of mounted Pawnee out there just minutes before. They had seemed a hundred, though such a number was unlikely. The Pawnee were a fierce, nomadic people, constantly on the move from one locale to another. In a land where every man is either friend or enemy, the Pawnee rarely had friends. By their own design they were haughty, solitary people, and in this harsh land of rolling prairies, sand hills, and precious water, solitary meant few.

Still, this latest hide party had come from the south, and there had been trouble to the south. Only they knew who they had encountered there, or what adventures they might have had that would bring Pawnee raiders this far into Arapaho-Shoshone country, to seek them out at Fort Sinclair.

Of one thing the Frenchman was certain. Whatever might have so aroused the Pawnee, they were here now, and they would not be satisfied with a brief onslaught. Twice they had rushed the fort, despite the rifles here. They would come again, when they were ready.

On the little, rolling hilltops above the river, grasses waved in the prairie breeze. Here and there a lark darted from crest to crest, and far overhead a hawk rode the endless sky on wide, graceful wings. The only Pawnee within sight were the half-dozen dead ones out there in the grass. Three of them were near enough that Champon could see the paint on their faces and the roached crests of their bound hair. And he knew there were that many more further out, dark sprawled forms hidden by the grass where they had fallen when the Hawken rifles spoke.

The big Hawkens had formidable range. Their voices had brought silence to the land, but Champon knew the silence would not last. The somber land out there was deceptive. Flat and featureless, it seemed, a vista of waving grass receding into the distance. But that was only how it seemed. The little trading fort was well situated for visibility. It offered as sure a view of the lands around as any point might, along this river. But even here, within a few hundred yards in three directions there were countless hiding places— draws and gullies, folds in the land where whole armies could lurk unseen.

The Pawnee understood such land. They could use it to their advantage. They were out there, nearby, and they would be back.

In the river, just past the mud bank where Luke Sinclair and the others lay, three pole barges waited, their shallow keels bobbing slightly as little waves rippled

about them. A ton of buffalo hides was already aboard
the vessels, lashed and bound for transport down-river.
Several canoes and a pirogue rested on mud shoals, and
more bales of hides lined the bank, ready for loading.

Raw wealth, Champon thought grimly. In St. Louis,
such hides were currency. Even as trapping began to decline, the market for flint-hides had grown. More than
a hundred thousand buffalo skins had been shipped
from St. Louis just in the past year. Champon knew this,
just as he knew what boats had carried them and for
whom. For eight years now, it had been his business to
know such things.

Buffalo hides and lead. On these commodities fortunes were built at St. Louis. But here, on this remote
prairie, those green hides out there at the water were
once again what they had been before, when the hide-
hunters' knives were collecting them. They were simply
the leavings of sudden death.

With a sigh, Louis Champon forced such thoughts
from his mind. I am an old man, he reminded himself.
Something like a sardonic grin tugging at his grizzled
cheeks. Young men don't waste time thinking about
things. Young men do what their hearts and their bellies
tell them to do, and think about it later. Old men pay
the price. They have no "later" to lean on.

Andy Blain came across the sod roofs from the west
wall, scurrying half-crouched as he ducked from shelter
to shelter, stopping every few steps to peer out at the
waving grass. His knife-scarred face and jutting front
teeth, accented by fierce dark brows and a stringy beard,
gave him the look of a cornered badger. The likeness
was even more pronounced now, his flat little eyes flashing with the fear and excitement of battle.

As he neared, Champon heard boots scraping on a
ladder, and one of the Platte River hunters heaved him-

self up to the rampart beside him. It was Kruger, the leader of the hide-hunters.

"Now what?" the hunter growled.

"Now they'll come again," Champon shrugged. "They're in no hurry." For the first time he noticed a pair of fairly recent scalps hanging from the man's horn-strap. Pawnee scalps, judging from the strands of downy owl-feathers woven into the hair. Pawnee, but not the scalps of warriors. No Pawnee warrior wore his hair loose and wide. These were women's scalps. The skin caps beneath the raven hair were still putrefying. They were only a week old, or not much more. The Frenchman's eyes narrowed, but he held his tongue. Nothing would be gained by accusing the hunter. The Pawnee were here, and whatever had been done could not be undone now.

Andy Blain was there, then, peering out at the mute prairie. "Both Sinclairs are dead," he said. "An' that gate yonder ain't gonna shut again. What do we do, Frenchman?"

"Maybe we die," Champon shrugged. "That's what those Pawnee have in mind." *Why do they ask me?* he mused. *Because I'm old? I know no more than they do.*

"Maybe they want them hides," Blain suggested. "We could give up some of them. Maybe they'd settle for some hides."

"The hides are mine!" the hunter snapped. "There's women yonder in the blockhouse," he pointed. "Give 'em the women."

"They'll want the hides," Champon agreed. "And I'm sure they'll want the women. And those children, too. But that isn't all they want."

"What else, then?" the Platte man demanded.

"Scalps," Champon said flatly. Again he glanced at the scalps on Kruger's horn-strap. "They want revenge."

"I'll see them savages in hell," the hunter snarled.

"I'm sure you will." With a sigh, Champon eased away from the rampart wall and started down the ladder. His legs and shoulders ached from having squatted too long in a cramped position. The years spoke to him now, in many ways. "How many men are left?" he asked, from the bottom.

"Eight of us," Blain said, "That's countin' the Mex cook. An' there's mebbe five or six hide Injuns."

"Six," Kruger agreed. "We had eleven, but three of 'em's dead an' a couple of 'em run away. Injun trash, ever' one of 'em."

Fourteen men, Champon thought. Seven white men, a Mexican and six renegade Shoshone.

One of the sullen "hiders" trotted by, carrying a pair of rifles. From the parapet the Platte man snapped, "You! Frog! Where'n hell do you think you're goin'?"

The Indian glared up at the man, then went on his way, ignoring him. Champon looked after the Indian. He had assumed all of the hiders were renegade Shoshone. Most such outcasts in this land were. But this one looked slightly different. Maybe he had been of another tribe. Would the hiders fight? Not for the white men certainly, but maybe to save themselves. And maybe because they hated the Pawnee. Then again, maybe not. Champon shrugged and strode away, across the little compound. Fourteen men, three women, and four children, with nothing but some guns and some flimsy stockade walls between them and a Pawnee war party.

If anyone in this fort lives to see the sun set, he told himself, it will be only because the Pawnee are in no hurry.

If there was any hope at all, it must be the river.

Rifle muzzles projected from every portal and chink of the little blockhouse in the middle of the stockade. Champon saw some of them move as he approached, felt them pointing at him. Those inside knew what had hap-

pened, and they were ready. The Pawnee might swarm
the fort, but they would pay dearly for the blockhouse.

Cold leather hinges whispered as the main door
opened, just a bit. Champon ducked inside, and the
door was closed behind him. In the dimness, his eyes
could barely make out the figures around him. But he
knew who they were.

"Luke is dead," he said quietly.

"We saw," a female voice answered him. There was no
emotion in Martha Sinclair's words. Maybe that would
come later.

"That's a war party out there," Champon said.
"They'll come again."

Near the far wall, bright teeth glinted in a sun-dark
face. Miguel Santos had turned from a rifle-slot. "Can
we stop them?"

"No," Champon shrugged. "No, they are too many."

"Then we must leave," the Mexican hissed. "Can we
escape from here, Señor *Lui?*"

Champon looked around at them— dim, huddled figures in a tiny, dark cabin. Martha was kneeling on a
bench by the front wall. Four heavy Hawken rifles rested
in chinks there, muzzles outward, cocked and ready. Her
two girls huddled close to her, one on each side. They
were assembling "cartouches"— rifle loads rolled in
waxed paper. The littlest one gazed up at the Frenchman
with large, frightened eyes. Just beyond, Serafina Santos
tended two guns while her little boy, a child barely four
years old, tended two more. The Arapaho girl and her
baby were in the far corner, half-hidden by flour barrels.
"There are canoes at the bank," Champon said.

Martha Sinclair glanced around at him. "Not anymore. They holed the canoes. We saw them through
the . . . through the gate."

Through the gate. Champon shook his head slightly.
Beyond the gate was her husband's body. Of course she

had seen the savages at the river bank. Where else would she have been looking?

"There are the barges then," he said.

Outside, somewhere, rifles barked. The Pawnee were showing off now—individual warriors on quick horses appearing suddenly here and there, skylining themselves in challenge or making swift feints toward the stockade to taunt those inside. Champon didn't have to see outside to know what they were doing. He knew. Tall, fierce warriors on ornamented ponies—magnificent savages gaudy with paint and feathers—they made enticing targets. And in motion they were hard to hit.

In the blockhouse, Santos came from the far wall. He drew back a rifle and peered outward. "It is a long way from the gate to the river, Señor."

"It's the only way there is," Champon shrugged.

Martha Sinclair eased down from her firing bench. Methodically, she began collecting rifles, checking their loads and stacking them by the door. The two little girls moved with her, clinging to her skirts like chicks to a hen.

Out in the compound again, Champon glanced around the little fort, then called some of the men down from the walls. "Those horses in the farrier's stall," he pointed. "I want them hitched to a hide wagon."

While the horses—two old dray beasts with stone-worn hooves—were being hitched, Champon and Miguel Santos cleared the gate. One by one, they dragged the bodies there inside and loaded them into the wagon, bracing them upright so that they almost seemed alive. Men gathered around—some to help, some just to watch. Serafina Santos, coming from the blockhouse, whimpered at sight of Rene Sinclair and his Ticoba sitting side by side on the high bench. Sticks and rope held them there, and they seemed to be huddled together, looking ahead at something only they could see.

Miguel touched Serafina's face with a hard, gentle hand. "It is not them, Corazon," he murmured. "These are only bodies. Their souls are with God, now."

"It ain't gonna work," Kruger sneered. "Them ol' horses won't run a hundred yards without a live hand on their reins."

Champon considered this, and nodded. "Then someone must drive them," he said. Turning to Andy Blain, he gestured outward, toward the barges. "You must move quickly," he said. "Get the women and children on that light barge. The men can cover from the river bank. Then the rest can follow."

"Hell with that!" Kruger snapped. "We ain't leavin' all them hides here for Injuns to take."

"The loaded barges will never make it," Champon said, quietly. "But it's up to you. Go or stay, as you like. Just get the women and children started down river."

"We'll get 'em on," Andy Blain assured him.

Champon turned toward the wagon with its load of death. He had his foot on the step-board when a hard hand pulled him back. The Indian called Frog was there, barring his way. Glaring past Champon, he pointed an imperious finger at Kruger. "You go!" he ordered. "You drive wagon."

Kruger glared back at the man, then looked away. "You're crazy as hell," he rumbled.

"You afraid?" the Indian drawled. Then with a contemptuous wave he turned and swung aboard the wagon. "I not afraid, *skala-shona*. I drive."

Before anyone could stop him, he raised the reins, snapped them down on the rumps of the dray horses, and the old wagon bounded through the gate, turning west. The Indian shouted, lashing the horses, and the corpses with him bobbed and bounced as though they were alive. Somewhere beyond the walls a yipping shout arose, followed by another and another.

"Get the women and children!" Champon snapped. "To the gate, now!"

As people scurried toward the half-open gate, keeping low behind its walls, a dozen mounted Indians thundered past outside, howling in pursuit of the wagon. Mud from their passing was still flying when Andy Blain slipped outside, glanced around, and headed for the river. Martha Sinclair shooed her girls after him, and pushed Serafina to a run, dragging her child after her. For an instant the Arapaho girl paused at the gate, clutching her baby. With sharp words and firm hands, Martha urged them along with the others. Miguel Santos was right behind them, carrying an armload of rifles.

Champon grabbed up as many guns as he could carry, and hurried after them. Behind him, other men poured from the opening.

The mud flats were twenty yards across, and beyond was a broad expanse of shallow water, deepening gradually. As Champon struggled forward, waist-deep, the rough prow of the old pirogue edged past him. In its hollowed-out shell was a jumble of rifles, kegs, and packs, and a dozen long, sturdy wooden poles. Andy Blain and two other men were pushing it toward the barges.

Rifle fire crackled behind them, but Champon didn't look back. Reaching the nearest barge, he dumped his load on its rough deck and turned to hoist the Arapaho girl aboard. With the baby in her arms, she had been unable to climb.

Then hands were on the Frenchman's arms, dragging him up onto the barge. It was little more than a flat raft, but it did have a spray rail and he rolled behind that as an arrow imbedded itself in timbers beside him.

One of the men from the fort splashed alongside, tying the pirogue's mooring line to the barge. Boots thumped on planking as a trader scurried astern to cut the barge's cable. He swung at it with an axe, swung again, and the barge shuddered as the cable began to part. The man raised the axe again, then screamed and dropped it. An arrow protruded from his armpit. Screaming and thrashing, he toppled over the far rail, into the sluggish current.

Miguel Santos retrieved the axe and completed the cut, and the barge swung free. Ignoring the arrows from shore, Champon struggled upright, grabbed a pole and began working the craft into the deeper current.

On the mud bank, fifty yards away, Pawnee warriors whooped and splashed their mounts into the river. Erratic rifle fire from the stockade scattered some of them, but others came on, clinging and yipping as their horses bounded onward. With each leap they seemed to climb above the water, then splash back— a few feet closer— to climb again.

Champon pushed on his pole until he felt his bones would snap. The barge shuddered, nudging a submerged bar, then swung outward as Miguel Santos dipped a pole and added his weight to it.

The nearest painted warriors were only yards away when a rifle barked, then another. One Indian went down, flipping backward off his horse. Another was flung half-around, blood spraying from his shoulder.

Beside Champon, Martha Sinclair tossed aside a spent rifle and picked up another one. Beyond her, Andy Blain cut loose with a double-barreled fowling piece.

The crisis was past as abruptly as it had begun. The barge rode a slow current, gliding serenely away from the Pawnee. An arrow followed it, whispering across the open deck to lodge itself in a buffalo hide. Two rifles answered it, and an Indian hit the water as his horse went crazy beneath him.

Feeling dizzy, Champon pulled in his pole and looked around. With Martha Sinclair and the man from the fort shooting, Santos adding an occasional shot and the three children— Emily and Rachel Sinclair and the little Santos boy— loading, the barge had become a floating fortress.

There was blood on the afterdeck, where the other man from the fort had been hit— his body now floated face-down a few yards away, drifting with the same slow current that carried the barge— but no one else had been hurt. Champon sat on a short bale of hides, waiting for the dizziness of exertion to pass. I am an old man, he told himself wryly. I am far too old for such as this.

Several Indians followed them at least a mile, a line of formidable silhouettes atop the low north bank. But then they were gone, and the barge drifted lazily eastward, following its own murky shadow as sunlight slanted from behind.

An hour passed, then another, and Santos sprang to his feet, peering ahead. On the south bank, brush parted and a lone figure appeared. He waded into the water, which rose to his chest, then he shucked off his heavy coat and swam. In midstream he met the barge and pulled himself aboard, dripping and sagging with exhaustion.

It was the Indian from the fort, the one Kruger had called "Frog." With an expressionless glance at those around him, he fished his soaked coat out of the river, then curled up on deck, using the coat as a cover. When Martha Sinclair and the Arapaho girl came with blankets from the tackle bin, to cover him, the Indian was already asleep.

In twilight that evening, a tiny tendril of smoke rose above the horizon far behind them. Gazing at it, Louis Champon pulled off his hat.

Fort Sinclair was gone now. And those who had stayed were dead . . . Kruger and his hunters, the renegade Indians who were his hiders, all dead. They died for a few bales of buffalo hides, he mused. Are buffalo hides worth dying for? It was a question without an answer. He had seen men die for far less.

oted, hit the man in the armpit, hauled his imprisoned arm around behind his back, and kicked his feet out from under him. The miner crashed to the floor, and Thomas's knee descended on his back, pinning the twisted arm between his shoulders.

"Now stay down!" Thomas hissed. "You're one too many."

A yard away, the miner with the knife lunged again and Jack Christy kicked him in the knee. The man howled, the knife clattered to the floor and the man tried to retreat, but Christy was on him like a panther on a bear. With tooth, claw, and fist, he pummeled the man, then broke loose. The miner backpedaled, tripped over his retching companion, and landed on his back.

Christy stood glaring down at him for a moment, then kicked his knife away. As though nothing had happened, he found his pouch and horn, slung them over his shoulder, put on his hat and picked up his rifle.

The knifer was sitting half-upright, cursing in a monotone. Blood ran down the side of his head, soaking his grimy shirt. As though discovering something unexpected, he opened his right hand and stared into it. Then his furious eyes fixed on Christy. "You bastard!" he shrieked. "You bit my ear off!"

Christy glanced down at him, indifferently. "Serves you right," he growled. "Pullin' that knife, now . . . that was just plain bad manners, mister."

"I'll see you dead!" the man shouted. With a shrug, Christy stepped forward and kicked him in the face, then strode out the door. The big knife at his belt— the knife he had chosen not to draw— glinted in the sunlight beyond.

Behind him, Thomas gave this miner one last thump with his knee, then stood, glancing around. "Show's over, gentlemen," he said. "Let's leave it that way."

Thomas retrieved his good coat, his hat, and Lady Jus-

tice. A block away he found Christy, cleaning his face at
a horse trough. Together they strolled down toward the
river, where the John S. Amos belched clouds of smoke
and steam as it sidled toward the Platte and Southern
docks. More than twenty of these "floating volcanos"
with their great, dripping wheels and their plumes of
smoke called at St. Louis each month now, except in
winter when the rivers iced over. But each arrival was
still a grand entertainment, and it seemed half the town
usually turned out to watch.

"What was that all about?" Thomas asked casually,
after they had walked a way.

Christy shook his head. "Nothin' much," he said.
"Short fuses, mostly." He rolled his shoulders and tilted
back his head, the way he often did when his rheumatism
was acting up. Sunlight off the water crept beneath his
hat brim to display a seamed, scarred face so molded by
the elements that it had become one with them. Sunlight
and firelight were recorded there, in crease-framed eyes
as sharp as a hunting hawk's. Blunt of nose and wide of
mouth, as lean and seasoned as whang leather, Jack
Christy reminded Thomas of fire, water, wind, and
earth.

His long, bushy mustache was still dark, though the
stubble on his cheeks and chin had gone gray somewhere
along the line.

A rank of pole barns opened out upon the loading
flats, where dray teams came and went, and just beyond
were the docks. The John S. was putting out gangplanks
there, while teams of longshoremen swarmed around
her cargo nets. Block and tackle rattled as crewmen
swung out the gantries. Gangs of Negro laborers waited
for their overseers' commands to take up the hoist lines.
And all up and down the waterfront were people. Hundreds of people. Gentlefolk strolled here and there, a
kaleidoscope of top hats and parasols flanked by their

servants. Liveried carriages with polished brass escutcheons rolled along each street, through motley crowds of tradesmen and craftsmen, workmen and idlers.

The John S.'s steam whistle was a strident, raucous screech that echoed up and down the waterfront, a discordant counterpoint to the shouts and babble that were the song of the docks. Just past the breaker pier, a band was playing, and crowds of boisterous men flowed around it, waving banners and flags. And all along the dock little groups of beaver hats bobbed as the buyers and sellers gathered to vie for incoming cargo and outgoing space.

Jack Christy slowed, then stopped, gazing around him with sad, angry eyes. "This is what it was about, lad," he muttered. "Nothin' but this."

Thomas stood beside him, slim and tailored, taller by inches than the man who had been his best friend all through the years, and didn't respond. Christy would explain or not, as suited him.

"Too dang many people," Christy growled. "Like ants on a heap. I don't belong here, Tommy. Sometimes I can't even breath, seems like."

Thomas simply nodded, understanding. How many things had this fierce, gentle man taught him, through the years? Everything he knew, things like how to move silently in the forest, how to build a cabin and find water, how to fish with a sharp stick, how to set a snare, how to read the stars, find honey, trail a deer, how to kindle a fire from punkwood, how to fashion a shirt from doeskin, and to know what is food and what isn't . . . how to make do on just what God's earth had to offer, and how to stay alive.

Through all those years, as Thomas grew from boy to man, it was Jack Christy who had guided him. But things had changed, somehow. Thomas had gone on learning, past Christy's teaching. They had spent time in settlements, and he had learned the ways of propriety and the ways of industry. They had ridden the river, and Thomas had learned the ways of finance . . . and the fragile, complex codes of competition that governed trade. He adapted to civilized ways. He was at ease in grand theater, dress ball, or drawing room, and could step a fair cotillion when called upon.

And there had been the young ladies— lovely creatures who always caught his eye and sometimes touched his heart . . . except for that part of it that remained so veiled that only a suggestion of memory revealed it. The memory was always there, though— memory of bright ringlets of auburn hair, and of eyes as blue as evening sky. Because of that memory, and because nothing else quite compared, Thomas Paine Woodson's liaisons with young ladies had been few and brief. Between his own reservation and Jack Christy's fiddle-footedness, there had been little opportunity for any courtship.

Yet now, more and more, it seemed that their roles— his and Jack's— were often reversed. For several years now, it had been Thomas who determined where they went. He had sought schooling in Springfield, and Jack had followed along. Thomas had taken employment at Canfield and later at Cairo, building mills and Jack had always been nearby. For the past three years, Thomas had been in and around St. Louis, learning business, doing business, and setting aside a bit of money each month for an idea he had.

West and a little south of here, between forested slopes, a pretty little valley rested among the solitary hills. Part of that valley belonged to him, a legacy from long ago. He had been there several times, setting his corners, making his mark, dreaming his dreams. But those dreams would require capital, and the city was the place to accumulate it.

Christy understood— after a fashion— what the young

man was doing. He heartily approved. But the process of it was taking its toll on him. Jack Christy was a creature of wild places, not of cities. The woodsman was most at home where trails led honestly from one place to another, where life's comforts were birdsong and a warm breeze, where a friend was a friend and an enemy clearly an enemy. The maneuverings and artifices of urban existence were slow poison to him. In the teeming, squalid places he became restless. In St. Louis he was completely out of his element.

Thomas gazed out at the river, his eyes tracing the sweeping lines of the John S. The steamboat lay at rest now, her fires banked, and passengers gathered at her rail, waiting to debark.

"How come you're wearin' your fancy rig?" Christy asked, indicating the topcoat and beaver hat.

"Had business this morning."

"You got business with that boat?"

"Lead," Thomas said, watching the bustle of activity with faint amusement. "I have a one-fifth interest in twelve tons, for delivery at New Orleans."

"That'll make you some money," Christy allowed.

"Six hundred to the ton, last report. I'll see near $1,500, on a $500 investment. Some of it's yours."

"Good money, I reckon," Christy said absently. It meant little to him. It was only money. He glanced at Lady Justice, resting across the younger man's shoulder. Sleek and delicately crafted, the old rifle was as graceful as it had always been. The years had given it a patina that only added to its luster.

"How come you're totin' the lady, then?" he asked.

"There's a German gunsmith in town." Thomas shifted the rifle, gazed at it absently for a moment in the sunlight, then returned it to his shoulder. "Thought I'd get him to look at it."

Below, passengers were debarking from the John S. "I need to sign the lading before they load," Thomas said.

Jack was gazing downstream, where the band had struck up a new tune. Floating up the breeze, it sounded like a marching song. He started toward the sound, then changed his mind. As Thomas strode toward the docks, Christy followed a few steps behind.

The main dock was alive with activity— people everywhere, their voices a constant chorus of sound as crowd after crowd flowed and wound this way and that. It was like a fantastic dance, in a way, Thomas thought— hundreds of people all seeming to move mindlessly, yet navigating their own press with fine skill. A constrained chaos that went on and on. The air was heady with the odors of hemp and pitch, of animal sweat and rich perfumes, of dead fish and live people. He found it exhilarating, but only in brief doses. He could understand how such a press of humanity might drive Jack to distraction.

At the fore gangway a ruckus erupted. Thomas turned that way out of curiosity, pushing through the crowd for a better view.

Among the debarking passengers— a random mix of people of all stripe— was an Indian. Indians were not uncommon along the river, and were seldom noticed as they came and went, minding their own business. Generally, they were careful not to call attention to themselves. But this one was different. This one neither sidled away nor averted his eyes. There was neither apology nor submissiveness about him. He was Indian and he *looked* like an Indian. He was dressed in beaded buckskins and breechclout, his legs bare above high moccasins. His long hair was swept aside and held in place by a bone clip embellished with owl feathers, and he carried a Hawken rifle.

The ruckus was a gang of young rowdies that had gathered at the foot of the gangway to block the Indian's path. They crowed and strutted there, taunting him, showing off for the crowd. A step away was a bonneted woman, and as Thomas arrived she raised a valise and swung it at one of the rowdies, who dodged aside, laughing.

"Leave him alone!" she shouted. "All of you, go away!"

"Injun's got hisself a friend," one of the taunters chirped. "Oh, my!" Disdainfully he swung a backhand slap at the woman—a slap that never arrived. A heavy rifle barrel speared out of nowhere, thudded against his wrist, and his laughter became a howl of pain. He went to his knees, holding his injured arm.

The man who stepped forward to stand over him, glaring at his cronies, was tall and well-dressed—a slim, almost dapper man in his prime. A spotless beaver hat sat slightly aslant on a head of thick, dark hair, and the rifle in his hand was an ornate old flintlock with polished brass furnishings.

"You boys heard the lady," he said, evenly. "Now go about your business. The fun's over."

"You broke my arm!" the one at his feet whimpered. "You son of a . . ."

The rifle shifted, its butt thumped against the rowdy's skull, and he sprawled face-down.

"Mind your mouth in the future," the man suggested.

The other toughs started to press forward, and stopped when their leader found himself staring into the flintlock's dark bore. Its hammer clicked sharply as it was cocked.

In confusion, they hesitated. Then another hammer clicked and Jack Christy's icy voice came from the side. "I'd do like he says, boys," the woodsman drawled. "He gets mean sometimes, an' you fellers wouldn't like that at all."

It was too much for the rowdies. Leaving their fallen

companion to sleep off his bruises, they turned and bolted.

The Indian had not moved. But now he glanced at Thomas and nodded, then paused as his eyes lit on the little beaded talisman hanging below his cravat. *"L'sawana,"* he muttered, and raised agate eyes to stare into Thomas's. *"Sawa'naki Jalacoma,"* he said slowly. *"Lade'qui Tacomthe."* With another lingering glance at Thomas, as though memorizing him, the red man turned away. A young Indian woman carrying a child followed him as he disappeared into the crowd.

"My daddy would roll over in his grave," Jack Christy whined, lowering his rifle. "Sidin' with a heathen!"

"Just an Indian," Thomas shrugged. "He wasn't looking for trouble."

"Just an Indian?" Christy's hiss was a scathing curse. "Bless God, Tommy, that was a damned Shawnee, sure as I'm standin' here!"

Thomas felt a tug at his sleeve and turned. The woman in the bonnet was there, and the blue eyes looking up at him were the color of evening sky. Old memories rushed in on him like a storm tide. "Thank you, sir," she said. "You've been very gracious."

Thomas was vaguely aware of a pair of young girls crowding in beside her, and of the sturdy, white-haired man hurrying down the gangway to join them. He was aware that the crowd around them was dispersing, people moving on now that the entertainment was over. But all of that seemed distant and unreal as he gazed, speechless and wide-eyed, at the face that had haunted his memories for so long. Auburn ringlets peeped from her bonnet, framing the face of an angel, and those blue eyes . . . *those eyes* . . .

With fumbling fingers he removed his hat, and the eyes looking up at him narrowed with suspicious concern. "Are you all right?" she asked. "What's the matter with you?"

The white-haired man was there then, beaming at him over wire-frame eyeglasses perched halfway down his nose. "Well done, *m'sieur!*" he said. "Those idlers deserved what they got." Just for a second his eyes rested on the rifle in Thomas's hand, and he looked surprised. But it passed in an instant. He cocked his head, realizing that Thomas hadn't heard a word he had said. Then he turned to Jack Christy. "Your friend is bemused," he grinned. *"La belle femme,* perhaps. Our thanks to you both. Little Axe has been a friend to us and we value him." He scribbled on a pad of paper and handed the note to Jack. "I am in your debt," he said.

With a further nod and wave, he turned to the woman. "Come, Martha," he urged. "There is much to do." He gathered up the woman and the two girls and hustled them away. A mustached Mexican followed, trailed by a Mexican woman and a boy.

Thomas stared after them in slack-jawed wonder.

"Put on your hat!" Jack snapped. "You look like you been sun-struck."

Thomas seemed not to hear him. Disgusted, Christy turned away. "See you 'bout supper time," he growled, and disappeared into the crowd, muttering. "Knothead!" he grumbled to no one but himself. "Takin' up for a heathen Shawnee! An' him 'thout even a load in his gun!" Pushing through the crowds along the dock, Jack Christy was half tempted to start a fight with somebody— anybody— just to blow off steam.

Long after he was alone, Thomas still stood on the teeming dock, looking where the immigrants had gone.

Martha, he told himself, over and over. Her name is Martha.

* * *

Albert Voigt cleaned his glasses with a soiled cloth, then carried the long rifle over to the window, where afternoon sunlight lent a shaft of radiance to the smoky little shop. Carefully he ran a rod into its barrel, making sure it was empty. Then he turned it this way and that in the light, muttering to himself. With calipers he measured the distances from plate to escutcheon, from hammer lug to pan, from pan to forebolt, and from barrel flat to trigger stage. Each measurement he tested against a brass rule, and jotted on a piece of paper. Below the numbers he drew a diagram— an elongated diamond shape superimposed on a tracing of the rifle's lock plate.

At length he lay the rifle on a workbench and turned to the man waiting by the door. "Why?" he demanded.

"I've heard the percussion lock is better," Thomas shrugged.

"Percussion is better," Voigt repeated, slowly. His speech was clipped and harsh, with traces of Germanic origin. "Well, it is newer, anyway. Do you think it will make the rifle shoot better?"

Thomas thought about this for a moment, then shook his head. "No, not the rifle. But maybe it will make me shoot better. The flintlock has its hesitation. A heart can beat, and a sight can waver, in the time it takes the pan to fire the charge."

"Good!" Voigt nodded. "An honest answer. But the man who built this gun, he was a fine craftsman. He deserves respect. Do you think he would approve of a percussion lock?"

"I think if he'd had percussion in his time, he'd have used it," Thomas said. "A rifle is made to shoot, not just to admire."

"Again, a fair answer," Voigt admitted. He picked up the rifle again, this time holding it in both hands, at arm's length. "The symmetry will change, you know.

This rifle is a fine lady, tall and handsome. She will have less character, to the eye. Do you know who built her?"

"Only what I was told a long time ago . . . that he was Hessian, and that he said this was a 'perfect rifle.' I've never known what that meant."

Voigt cocked a bushy brow at him. "Perfect rifle means she can make a perfect shot," he said. "Maybe only one, but that is enough. Has she made a perfect shot, then?"

"Not that I know of," Thomas admitted. "She shoots as well as I do, that's all." He paused, then added, "Once . . . a long time ago . . . she made a shot that was historic."

Voigt waited, but the young man had no more to say.

"It isn't the same," the gunsmith shrugged. "Ah, but no matter. Yes, I can convert your rifle for you. Come back on Wednesday."

As Thomas opened the door, the man called after him, "What is her name?"

"Lady Justice," Thomas said. "Her name is Lady Justice."

"I don't hold with it," Jack Christy fussed. Firelight danced on his seamed face as he lit his pipe with a sulphur match. "If God had meant for rifles to pop caps, he'd never had invented rocks."

"Your Betsy is percussion," Thomas pointed out, gazing off into the starry sky above the wide river. Supper was over, and the two sat in rocking chairs on Mistress Oakes's porch, soaking in the evening.

"It ain't the same at all," Christy explained. "Betsy always was percussion. The Carlson brothers up at Springfield made her that way." He inspected his pipe, tamped down its glowing coals with a finger as tough as boot leather, and lit it again. "Don't matter to me, though. I'm thinkin' about goin' to Texas."

Thomas turned, startled out of his reveries. "Where?"

"To Texas. Things is doin' down there, I hear."

"Is that what the boostering was all about today? The band and all?"

"Dang right," Christy puffed. "There's some Mescan down there, name of Santa Anna, puttin' the boot to Americans. They need men to come an' fight, an' by jing, I believe I just might."

You're just spoiling for a brawl, Jack, Thomas thought. Peace just doesn't suit you, does it? Aloud he said, "Those people aren't Americans, Jack. They're Mexicans. Texas is part of Mexico."

"Not for long, by dang!" Jack snorted and stoked his pipe. Clouds of pungent smoke drifted around him. "Some of them fellers have been there. They say there's good land just for the takin', once the Mediterraneans is kicked out, an' somebody's offerin' forty dollars and a good horse to anybody with gumption enough to come and do it. You heard about Sam Houston, didn't you?"

"What about him?"

"Why, he's there, that's what. An' Tip Bell, he was with us up at Detroit, though I never run across him there. He was a Shelby man, I reckon. An' Britt Bailey, that was fightin' Creeks while we was fightin' Shawnee. Even that loud-mouthed Davey Crockett's gone down there. Prob'ly figures if he can't outshoot the Mescans he can out-politic 'em."

"What about your rheumatism?" Thomas asked mildly.

"I'll leave it here, by God!" Christy snapped. He leaned forward, squinting at Thomas in the twilight. "What's ailin' you, youngster? You ought to be doin' your best to talk me out of goin' to Texas, an' there you set, like you was a thousand miles away."

"Could I talk you out of it if I tried?"

"Hell, no!"

"You said you'd help me build my mill."

"I don't want to build a dang mill! I want to fight Mescans!"

Thomas shrugged and shut up. After a time he asked, "What was his name?"

"Who?"

"That old Frenchman at the dock."

"So that's what's ailin' you," Christy muttered. "Well, sir, the gentleman's name is Shampo, or like that. Here." He drew a scrap of paper from his coat and handed it across. "He wrote it down, so I could tell you when you got around to askin'."

Thomas leaned back, looking at the paper in the lamplight from Mistress Oakes's parlor window. "Champon," he muttered. "Louis Champon, Great Western Fur Company."

"Fine lookin' woman with him," Christy drawled. "I just happened to ask around. Her name's Martha Sinclair. She's a widow."

X

Angel Found

"Luke Sinclair was a good man," Louis Champon said. He stepped aside, touched the ebony brim of his new hat and bowed slightly as a group of parasoled ladies passed. For a moment he looked after them, then he resumed his stroll. Even with the tall silk hat perched squarely on his head, he was shorter by inches than his companion. Still, he carried his old frame with a sturdy grace that made him seem taller and younger than he was. There was an elegance about them as he and Thomas Woodson strolled along Bluff Street, enjoying the morning sun. Andy Blain trailed along, a few steps behind, his flat little eyes aglow with the excitement of the city.

"He was a dreamer, of course," the Frenchman continued, "but is any good man not a dreamer? Luke Sinclair had vision. He might have made a difference, out there on that wild prairie."

A gilded surrey rolled past, and both of them tipped their hats. Two ladies in velvet and lace rode there, with two gentlemen of spotless attire. Both ladies blushed, and one flicked open a fan to cover her face. One of the gentlemen turned to look back, scowling. Champon pursed his lips thoughtfully, then went on.

"What happened to him?" Thomas asked.

"To Luke Sinclair?" Champon shrugged. "A Dutch hide-trader named Kruger happened to him. A coarse man who flaunted the scalps of Indian women. The women had kin, and those kin followed Kruger to Fort Sinclair. The kin were *papayete*. Pawnee warriors."

"And Martha was there? She saw that?"

"She saw it all, Thomas. It was a hard thing to see. But she is a strong woman. With luck, she will find a friend." Wise old eyes glanced up at Thomas, seeing the set of his jaw, the troubled questions in his eyes. "It might just be that such a friend already is found, eh, *mon ami?*"

"I don't even know the woman . . ." Thomas started to protest.

Champon raised a hand. "Do not play coy with a Frenchman, *mon ami,*" he chuckled. "Haven't you heard? All Frenchmen are romantics. And old romantics like me have no time for the stumblings and blunderings of such play. Tell me truly, Thomas, you love her, no?"

Thomas blinked in surprise. He opened his mouth to argue, then closed it again. The man had asked an honest question.

"I think I have loved her all my life," he admitted.

"I think so, too," Champon nodded. "And so, with a bit of encouragement, matters can take their course. Tell me of this mill you want to build."

Thomas wondered, idly, whether he had ever had a stranger conversation. Behind them, Jack Christy had come from somewhere and fallen into step beside Andy Blain. "What are they fussin' about?" he asked quietly.

"They ain't fussin'," Blain said. "Least, I don't think they are. They're talkin' about bein' in love."

Thomas touched his hatbrim as a pair of matrons hurried by, followed by servants carrying bundles. "West of here," he said to Champon, "in the region called *Aux*

Arcs, there is a place where valleys come together. In all, there are several thousand acres of good bottom land there, and more people moving in each season to settle on it. A small piece of it is mine. A legacy. I have been there, and I've seen it. Good water, deep soil, and mountains to break the winds. Many crops will grow in those valleys, but the best of them will be grains. I want to settle there, and build a mill. A flour mill."

"You are a miller, then?"

"No, not a miller, but I've worked as a millwright. I can learn milling." He gazed off across the lower town and the river beyond. Far to the south, just coming into view, was another steamboat— a big one, by the look of its stacks, coming up from New Orleans.

"Some of that land out there can make ten bushels to the acre," he mused. "Maybe even more. Did you know, a man named McCormick is building a reaping machine that will harvest as much in a day as twenty men with scythes and rakes? All the *Aux Arc* growers need is a market."

"Markets mean buyers," Champon suggested. "St. Louis is full of buyers, but I see no one buying grain."

"They buy flour!" Thomas snapped. "Of course, flour means a mill . . . and everything that goes with it. If it was easy, it would already be done. But it can be done!"

"A vision," Champon nodded. "What makes you think you could make such a vision come true, Thomas Woodson?"

"I won't settle for less," Thomas said firmly.

Ahead, a gilded surrey rounded a corner and swung into a sheltered dive. It was the same surrey they had passed before, but the ladies were not in it now. Only the two men. Champon glanced back thoughtfully at Christy and Blain, following a few steps behind, then turned his attention again to the conversation at hand.

"Such a venture takes capital," he pointed out. "Do you have such funds?"

"I have enough to build the mill," Thomas shrugged. "At least, when I collect what's owed me, I will have."

"But a mill alone will fail. There must be silos and hoists, and wagon docks and a cooperage . . ."

"I have shares in the First Galena mine. I can sell those."

". . . and freight wagons and teams and teamsters and loaders. In short, Thomas, you need willing creditors . . . or a wise partner."

"I've thought of that, but . . ."

Champon stopped, looked around sadly at the busy street, and removed his hat. Beneath it, his hair was thin and as white as spun snow. The Frenchman held the hat up before him, as one might display a trophy. It was of the latest Eastern fashion, a tall "stovepipe" of lustrous black silk with a flat, narrow brim. Its weight was only a quarter of that of Thomas's gray beaver hat.

"Observe," the Frenchman said, "the epitaph of the fur trade. The beaver, the otter, the muskrat . . . the free trapper and all the industry he produces— all replaced by the secretions of a little worm. Silk is the thing, these days, Thomas. Felt is outdated, and the fine furs soon to follow. I'm thinking of finding a new trade."

A block away ahead of them, a gang of men had appeared . . . four rough-looking men who didn't match their surroundings. From fifty yards, Thomas could see the clubs in their hands. Without breaking his stride, he glanced at the old Frenchman. "Are those friends of yours?"

"No," Champon said. "Yours?"

"No."

Behind them, Jack Christy and Andy Blain had disappeared. One moment the two had been there, the next they weren't.

As they approached the toughs, two more men stepped out of the shadows of a hedge. They were the ones from the carriage. One raised a hand, pointing. "Louis Champon!" he shouted. "You have me to answer to!"

"Cartwright," Champon muttered. "This must be about Mitzi."

"Who?"

"Cartwright. He's a gambler. I had almost forgotten him."

"Who's Mitzi?"

"A vision of loveliness. At least, she was a few years ago, the last time I saw her. She was working as a shill for Cartwright." The old man smiled. his eyes twinkling above his glasses. "Ah, yes. I had nearly forgotten a very pleasant evening."

Like a storm descending, the four toughs crouched and charged, straight at Champon. The Frenchman's walking stick whisked upward and poised, elegantly like a fencer's épée, then struck like a viper. Thomas side-stepped a bull-like rush, saw a club aimed at the Frenchman and blocked it with his arm. In the same motion, he hit the tough as hard as he could, in the mouth. Another spun toward him, swatted him a glancing blow across the cheek, and turned to attack again. Thomas closed with the man, burying his knee in a hard midriff. The man doubled and Thomas took his cudgel away from him and hit him with it.

Thomas blinked his eyes to clear his vision, and turned, raising the club. But there was no one to hit. Both of the other toughs were down, one of them moaning and gasping, his hands clutching at his crotch. Louis Champon was sitting on the other one.

Thomas swung around, expecting an attack from up-street, but none came. The two dandies stood where they had been, looking pale and sheepish. They were staring into the muzzles of rifles held by Jack Christy and Andy Blain.

Panting, Champon got to his feet, tapped a fallen felon with his walking stick, and pulled out a kerchief to clean his glasses. Though there wasn't so much as a speck of dust on him, he carefully straightened his coat and dusted his lapels. Then with a sigh he marched up to the sweating gambler and demanded, "Is your honor satisfied, M'sieur Cartwright, or must I now give you great pain?"

A rifle nudged Cartwright in the ribs. "It . . . it's done," he gulped, edging away. "I accept your . . . your apology."

"Very well," Champon nodded. "Now go away. Go far away. I suggest Philadelphia, at least."

With Christy and Blain hovering over them, Cartwright and his partner gathered up their bruised employees and hurried off. The gilded carriage was waiting for them down the street, its Negro driver struggling to keep a straight face. When they were aboard, the carriage rolled away, toward the private docks upriver.

"Is that all?" Jack Christy growled. "Aren't there any more?"

Ignoring him, Thomas went and found his hat. He had a bleeding bruise on his face, and his coat was ripped at the shoulder. Champon looked him up and down, then resumed his stroll up the street as though nothing had happened.

"Aren't you a little old for that kind of problem?" Thomas suggested, catching up.

"I'm old," Champon said. "But I'm not dead. Besides, I am French." Cocking a silvery brow, he gazed into the distance. "I wonder how Mitzi is these days," he muttered. "I really should pay my respects. But as I was saying, I believe the hide and fur business has seen better days."

Trying to keep up with the old man's leaps of topic, Thomas decided, was like trying to catch fleas. "I've seen your company's registers," he protested. "It seems to me you do very well on buffalo hides."

"That too will end," Champon shrugged. "The great herds are harder to find than they were just a few years ago. And even now, buffalo tongues bring twice the revenue of the hides."

"Tongues?"

"Tongues are all the rage back east these days."

Behind them, Christy muttered sourly, "They always were." He felt distinctly uncomfortable in this fine section of the city. The encounter a few minutes before had looked interesting, but as far as he was concerned nothing interesting had come of it. He felt cranky and unfulfilled. Eyes attuned to the infinite variations of the wild woods were acutely aware of anything out of place, and it seemed to him that he and the plainsman, Blain, were as out of place here on these fine streets as a wolf and a badger at show-dog trials. "Let's go down by the water," he suggested to Blain. "Maybe there's more talk about Texas."

At a graded corner where steep, graveled roadway led upward from Bluff to the higher streets above, Champon pointed. "My house is up there," he said. "The one with the whitewashed gables. We can refresh ourselves there. It's been closed for two years, but I'm opening it again now. I've had enough travel for a while."

Far away, drifting in lazy echoes up the wide valley, a steam whistle trilled. The two men stepped to a high curb and paused there, gazing outward at the morning. From here the lower city spread before them like a bustling panorama, a crazy-quilt unsewn but pinned in place by a thousand rising smokes. Beyond, the big river spread outward to hazed distances, constrained only by the busy waterfront crowding in upon it and by the dark, forested silhouette of the Illinois shore on the other side. Small boats crawled like ants in a line, plying between the hide docks on this side and the tanneries across the river.

Off to the right, creeping upstream, the big riverboat was nearer now— a smoke-belching sternwheeler making its way northward. "That should be the Green River," Champon noted. "They say she'll try for the Gulf on her next trip."

"You mean for Texas," Thomas corrected.

"Well, they don't say that, of course. It wouldn't do for people to think Andrew Jackson has ambitions for Texas." He grinned, dipping his head to peer over his eyeglasses. "Such games they always play. Jackson has no interest in Texas, the way Madison was not interested in the Northwest Territories . . . or Jefferson in Louisiana." He peered up at Thomas curiously, his eyes pausing at the beaded talisman below the younger man's cravat. "Little Axe says he knows you. He says Tecumseh walks with you."

"Tecumseh is dead," Thomas said, startled at the flood of harsh memories suddenly released in his mind. For a moment it seemed that all his old memories— the best and the worst of them— had returned to torment him.

"To some of the Shawnee, nobody ever really dies," Champon said. "People come and go, but spirits live on. That's what *Chalacoma* . . . or *Ja'Lacoma* . . . means in the *Sawana'ki* tongue." He indicated the talisman. "That is a Shawnee device, isn't it?"

"I don't know," Thomas admitted. "I've always had it."

"And your sponsor, when you were a child . . . his name was Cadmont?"

"Salem Cadmont, yes. A fine gentleman."

Champon turned and started up the graded street. "It

will take time to air everything out, of course," he chatted. "Dust and mustiness accumulate behind locked shutters."

He was talking about his house again, Thomas realized. As though those moments of strange comment—about Shawnee and spirits, about Salem Cadmont and Tecumseh—had never occurred. "Who is Little Axe?" he demanded.

"Oh, that's Dekagathe. The name means little axe. He is the one you interfered for, at the steamer docks. You did him a favor, you know. He might have killed those hooligans, and then there would have been no end of trouble."

Jack was right about that then, Thomas noted. That Indian *was* Shawnee. He shook his head, deciding it wasn't worth sorting out.

"A house should be lived in," Champon chatted. "Otherwise it becomes lonely. Maybe I'll live in it for awhile now. I have been gone too much, I think. And when I am away, no one is there. I have never been fortunate enough to have family."

Where rose hedges bordered a wrought-iron gateway, Champon lifted a latch and bowed in invitation. "Welcome to my house, Thomas," he said. "Come in, come in. We'll have a bit of tea, and discuss flour milling."

A high, wide porch fronted the house. As they climbed the steps, the front door opened and Martha Sinclair stepped out, carrying a mop. A dusty apron covered her skirt, a scarf bound her auburn hair, and she was flushed with exertion. The two Sinclair girls came around the porch corner, carrying a pail between them. At sight of the men they stopped, wide-eyed.

"This house wants a thorough scrub, Mr. Champon," Martha started, then stopped as her eyes lit on Thomas, standing with hat in hand, gaping at her.

Never in his life, he decided, had he seen anything so pretty.

"Mistress Sinclair," Champon beamed, "may I present Mr. Thomas Woodson. You may recall him from the dock. Thomas, this is Martha Sinclair. And the two rosebuds yonder are Rachel and Emily."

"You're bleeding," Martha said, stepping close to Thomas to peer at his scratched cheek.

"It's nothing," he assured her. "I . . ."

"A slight misunderstanding on the street," Champon shrugged. "Well, don't just stand there. Come inside."

"Your coat is torn," Martha noticed.

"It's really nothing," he insisted.

"Of course I remember Mr. Woodson," she assured Champon. "From the waterfront."

"That was nothing," Thomas objected. "Just some rowdies on the dock. They . . ."

"Do come inside and give me your coat." She took him by the arm and Thomas marveled at the touch of her hand. Such a small hand, to be so firm and strong.

Clucking like an impatient old hen, Champon herded them into his parlor. The two girls twittered off into the nether regions and reappeared eventually with cups and a pot. Martha served tea, all the time gently chiding Champon on the neglected condition of his house. The fact that he had been away for more than two years, Thomas gathered, was a poor excuse for accumulated dust.

Eventually the Frenchman shooed the girls away, in the care of a Negro woman "borrowed" from some neighbor. Shortly after that he himself disappeared, and Thomas found himself alone with the substance of his dreams. For a time they sat and talked, then they walked through the overgrown gardens outside and talked. They sat together on the porch, looking out across the Mississippi River, and they talked. The sun was behind the bluffs and evening was in the air when Thomas took matters into his own hands.

"I'd like to have known your husband," he said. "But I didn't. I can only accept that he was a good man, and assume that he would approve of my feelings for you. They are honest feelings, Martha, and they go far deeper than you can know. You'll think this insane, but your face— the wonderful face I see before me at this moment— has been a lamp in my darkness for so long . . . so very long. All my life, it seems, I have followed a single light. And now I've found that light, and I will not let it go."

There was no pretended surprise in the long, searching look she gave him then. There was no pretense of any kind. Her blue eyes— as deep as the evening sky— seemed to search him out in every dark corner and to examine carefully what they found there.

"I can't know your mind, Martha," he pursued. "But I pledge to know your heart. And should the day come when you care to offer it, in any form, I want to be there to plead my case."

"Are you stating your intentions, Thomas?" A slight smile played on her cheeks— cheeks so exquisite that they took his breath from him.

"Intentions?" On impulse he took her hand in his. "Of course I am stating my intentions. I intend to court you unmercifully, Martha Sinclair. As much as it takes, for as long as it takes. And I intend to love you and care for you forever, just as I do now. Just as I always have. Those are my intentions."

"I can be headstrong and stubborn at times," she said.

"So can I."

"I have no tolerance for deception."

"Nor do I. It is a stupid waste of time."

"I've never cared for strawberries."

"And I don't eat peaches, unless there's nothing else."

The secret smile returned, and she giggled. Her hand in his was warm, and she made no effort to withdraw it. "Mr. Champon says you and he will be partners," she said. "I suppose he referred to your milling venture."

Thomas blinked in surprise. "He said that? When?"

"Yesterday, on the way here from the docks."

"How could he have said that yesterday? I didn't know it yesterday. I didn't even know *him* until yesterday!"

"Mr. Champon is a surprising man," she said. The breeze was chilly and she moved closer beside him. "Your place of valleys, is it far from here?"

"Not far," he said. "I'd like to show it to you."

"That would be nice," she murmured.

"You hardly know me," he reminded her.

"I know you better than you think, Thomas Woodson. I know that you grieve for my grief, and care for my happiness. I know Rachel and Emily like you, and I know Mr. Champon believes in you."

He didn't know what to say, so he said nothing. It was enough for now, just to be here with her, to feel her hand in his.

"I know something else, too," she whispered. "You see, I remember a boy who told me about the Raisan."

Not far away, in a vine-shrouded little arbor with a rocking chair, Louis Champon smiled contentedly.

I am an old meddler, he told himself. Maybe it's because I have never had family. But then, I have tended a good share of foundlings in my time. That's what I am— a collector of strays.

His eyes twinkled in the twilight, filled with a secret humor. It is interesting, he thought, to see what becomes of my strays in a world such as this one is . . . a world far smaller than it seems.

XI

To Follow a Dream

The steamship Green River called only briefly at St. Louis. Cargo and passengers were discharged and wood taken on, then the big sternwheeler continued her voyage up the Mississippi to Cairo, where the Ohio River came in from the east.

The landing at St. Louis had been like most such landings— a festive event for many, a crucial event for some. But among the passengers this time were a contingent of grim-faced men whose presence added a somber note. They gathered on the parade ground above the waterfront and pitched tents there. Each hour of the day, and by lantern light when day was done, they assembled to the fanfare of drums and fifes, and read aloud from rolled foolscap to all who would listen.

The words were the final message of Colonel William Barrett Travis, issued *"in extremis"* from a besieged old church called the Alamo, at San Antonio de Bexar in Texas.

For days, he— with one hundred and eighty-one other "Texans"— had held out against an army of thousands, the expeditionary forces of the man who called himself the "Napoleon of the West," General Antonio Lopez de Santa Anna.

The words of Colonel William Barrett "Buck" Travis had been penned in desperation, a message to a Council of Independence that he was not even sure existed. But now by torchlight on the St. Louis waterfront— and under the smoky skies of a hundred other rallying points— the words whipped like banners and echoed like cannonfire as men read them aloud:

". . . I shall have to fight the enemy on his own terms . . . I will do the best I can . . . the victory will cost the enemy so dear that it will be worse for him than defeat . . .

"Our supply of ammunition is limited . . .

"God and Texas . . . Victory or Death."

The men who brought the news were recruiters. It was too late now for the men at the Alamo, they said. Travis's letter had been dated March 3, the tenth day of the siege. Three days later, the Alamo had fallen. Not a single defender survived.

But with their blood, those hundred and eighty-two fierce Anglos had bought a bit of time. Whole battalions of Mexico's mighty army lay decimated. More than 1,600 of Santa Annas's elite troops were casualties, and twelve precious days had been handed to the infant republic, Texas.

Everywhere that riders could go, everywhere steamboats landed, the message was spread. Texas had declared its independence from Mexico. Texans had shed their blood to rid themselves of tyranny. Men were needed in Texas, fighting men who knew the taste of freedom.

At New Orleans and Vicksburg, at Memphis and Cape Girardeau, at Grove Bend and St. Louis, the word was spread and adventurous men saw to their packs and their rifles.

The Green River completed its northward run to Cairo, then headed south again. By the time it reached St. Louis, four hundred volunteers were aboard, bound for Texas. And more were waiting at the St. Louis docks. The wide, open deck of the big boat was so jammed with men and provisions, all bound for the new republic, that it had been dubbed the "Texas Deck."

Word from the south was discouraging. "Santa Anna's on the march," they said. "The whole damn Mescan army's on the move, burnin' everything in sight, drivin' the folks out ahead of 'em."

But where was Sam Houston? Where was the Texas army?

"In full retreat," they said. "Runnin' like rabbits, with Santa Anna right behind 'em."

Still, there was a fierce glint in the eyes of Jack Christy as he and Andy Blain shouldered their packs and headed for the loading ramp. "That Houston, he fought with Jackson down on the Horse Shoe, didn't he?"

"He was there, way I hear it," Blain agreed.

"So while we was fightin' Shawnee up north . . ."

"Not me," Blain said. "I wasn't quite weaned yet."

"Well, some of us were! And while we were up there, showin' the British an' the Shawnee a good time, Jackson and his bunch were down south, doin' likewise for British an' Creeks."

"That was two different times," Blain frowned. "They fought Creeks earlier . . . I think. And Jackson was over at New Orleans, anyway."

Christy glared at him. "Doesn't matter!" he snapped. "The thing is, there's ways of gettin' folks to chase you right where you want to go. Jackson's been known to do that, time to time, so maybe Houston does it too. Englishmen never did quite get the hang of that sort of maneuver, an' maybe Mescans are the same way."

"You reckon Houston's just lettin' that Santa Anna run 'til he gets him where he wants him?"

"That's what I said, isn't it?"

"I hope we get there before it's all over," Andy grinned. He had found an old coonskin cap somewhere and the disreputable thing resting just above his nose made him look more than ever like a happy badger.

Thomas hadn't gone down to see his old friend off. The talking was done, the decision made, and farewells would have embarrassed both of them. But tucked into Jack Christy's pack was a pouch of gold coin— his share of their lead trading venture— and in the tail of his coat was a certificate for shares in a milling company. Thomas had tried also to give him the little beaded amulet that he still wore on a thong around his neck. Thomas had never known what the thing meant— if it meant anything at all— but as far back as he could remember, it had always been with him. He had tried to give it to the old woodsman when they parted at Mistress Oakes's. For good luck, he said. But it was a Shawnee thing, and Christy wanted no part of it.

Sometimes he had nightmares, and Thomas suspected that those scalps he had collected— so many years ago now— were part of them.

"You watch yourself out there in Texas," Thomas had urged him. "A man could die in a scrap like that."

"We all die, boy," Christy had said, solemnly. "No way around that. But if a man's lucky, he can have a say in how it comes."

Now Jack and Andy made their way to the top of the Green River's gangway, then stepped aside as a gaggle of sooty-faced children scurried past them, shouting and pushing. There might have been a dozen of them, in sizes ranging from half-grown down to two or three that were barely more than toddlers. Most of the ragamuffins seemed to be boys, but there were girls among them, too. It was hard to tell which was which, covered as they were in ragged, cast-off clothing and an accumulation of grime.

Directly behind them, less boisterous but no less ragged, came a small crowd of people of various descriptions. Several women huddled in the midst of the group, some of them carrying babies, all hurrying to get off the boat. Flanking and following the women were as tough and hard-bitten a group of men as Jack ever recalled laying eyes upon, even in the grand old days of the "Kaintucks."

These all looked to be cast from the same mold— men so lean and lanky that they seemed taller than they were, men with lantern jaws and long noses, narrow, suspicious eyes and jutting ears that stood like jug handles beneath their dark hatbrims. Ragged, unshaven, and unkempt, they herded their flock like fierce, mangy dogs working sheep. Their eyes flicked this way and that, distrusting everyone, and each of them carried a long rifle as though he had been born with it in his hand.

As they hurried down the gangway, the men in the rear sidling to keep a sharp eye behind them, a half-dozen crewmen followed them part way, shouting and shaking fists at them.

"I ever see y'all near this ship again, I'll set dogs on the lot of you!" a burly ship's officer yelled.

A florid, square man with braid on his cap stood atop the gangway, big fists on his hips. "I want an inventory of stores," he ordered, angry eyes flashing at those around him. "And I want that rear hold searched and sealed. They've prob'ly stole us blind, damn them. Squatters and drifters! Movers! Worse'n Gypsies. They'll take anything that isn't nailed down."

"Said their name was Dekins," a purser offered. "Some of them, anyway."

"Hill trash!" the captain growled. He glared down at the crowded docks. The Dekins family had already disappeared, every last one of them, blending into crowds and shadows like rats in a warren. "I'd have the law on that bunch . . . if I thought they could catch them."

Growling his frustration, the captain turned and stalked aft, followed by his flock of crewmen.

"Dekins," Andy Blain muttered. "I wonder if that bunch is any of ol' man Matthew Dekins's kin."

"You know them?" Jack asked.

"Not this bunch, but ol' man Matthew Dekins had him a powerful lot of kin. Meaner'n snakes, mostly. I only knew one of 'em, once. Willy, they called him. He run with that buffalo crowd for a year or so, then disappeared. Guess Injuns got him. He was a mean one, sure enough. Steal yer poke right off yer belt, an' gut you if you noticed. Mighty good hand with a rifle, though. Awful sudden with a knife, too. An' he was skinny an' jug-eared, like this bunch. Folks used to say—back on th' Santee— 'you seen one Dekins you've seen 'em all.' "

Christy shrugged. The world was full of useless people, as far as he had noticed. And the real shiftless ones tended to get mean on occasion. For some reason though, the words called to mind Hall Stanton's two boys, back in Kentucky. More than twenty years had passed since those days in Michigan, but he could still see them as clearly as yesterday. Just plain ornery mean, they had been. It was just a shame a thirteen-year-old kid had to be the one to put that Jubal down. Plenty of grown men around, that should have.

Their daddy, Hall Stanton, had become a power in some circles in later years— a man of note in the Whig party, and a champion of federalism. His name came up now and then, when some of those northeasterners in the Washington government got to making noises. Jack had no idea what had become of Jason.

The Green River's long forward deck was crammed with bales and crates— goods that would be off-loaded at Memphis and New Orleans to make room for the powder, ball, stock, and provisions being assembled at Grand Isle. A few of the cabin passengers also would get off downstream. But most of those aboard on this voyage were bound for a more distant port. After negotiating the maze of channels south of New Orleans, Green River would put to sea. The stern-wheeler was bound for Texas. She was one of many riverboats that would risk such a journey in the next few months.

As the big boat swung into the southward current, a bristle-chinned Tennesseean at the starboard rail raised a jug in salute. "Remember the Alamo," he said.

It had a ring to it. It spoke to the dark souls of fighting men. It sang of hot blood and cold steel, of cannonfire and the acrid stench of powder smoke. Jack Christy repeated it: "Remember the Alamo."

Nearby, someone else took it up and it grew into a chant and a war-cry.

"Remember the Alamo!"

It wasn't so much Anse and the mule that set it off. That had just been kind of a last straw, for folks around Macklinville. It was just like everyplace else Coy Dekins and his brood had been. They were looked down on, for being poor. That was what set it off, every time.

Before Macklinville there had been the Long Hollow place, and before that the backwoods around Puckett. Everywhere Coy Dekins went, there was trouble, and it was always the same. Seemed like Luke and Shelby were in trouble all the time, and all the rest of them were in trouble most of the time.

They'd find a place and settle in, and take what they needed, then the trouble would start. Sometimes it was sheriffs with court orders, and sometimes highbinders sending their hired men around to push the Dekinses out.

But Dekinses didn't push easy. Generally they fought back, first. When they had to, they moved on. But they left their mark behind them. It had been old Daddy Matthew's way, back on the Santee, to root easy and set stubborn, and the boys had picked that up from him. Coy couldn't recollect a move that hadn't come to shooting first.

And when the shooting started, likely as not it was Luke or Shelby, one or the other or both together, who started it. "Wild blood," the kin said of Coy's oldest boys. They both took after their uncle Willy, that lit out on his own after he cut that high sheriff's throat at Logan Cross that time.

At Macklinville, it was Anse who got caught out. He'd been working an old mule, pulling stumps for hire for Mister Callinder, who had the big place on the hill. Mister Callinder told his friends that he calculated it was cheaper to hire white trash at fifty cents a day for work like that, than it was to wear out a good thousand-dollar darky. Mister Callinder and his friends laughed about that, up there on the veranda of that big house. But two of the Dekins girls were around there, doing scrub for Mrs. Callinder, and they brought the story home.

Anse didn't take to being compared to a nigger field slave, so he whipped that old mule 'til it fell down in its traces. Then he slipped over the ridge to the Walker place. He laid up in the woods for a day, then he went down and took Mr. Horace Walker's best mule. On his way back, he beat and robbed a man at Claybank. Anse Dekins was a man to hold a grudge, and he didn't care who he took it out on.

Anse got home all right, and showed everybody his new mule. But they came after him with dogs, and before it was done the Lord had taken George Dekins and two of his half-grown children, along with a schoolteacher named Mabry and three of Mr. Horace Walker's hired hands.

Then Luke put a bullet in the brisket of a Slack County deputy sheriff, and Coy decided it was time to move along.

They set out kith and kin, all but Shelby who had taken himself a fresh wife and went to stay with her folks over in Falls County, and one of the girls who'd taken to staying with old man Jutey Monroe because he bought her fancy things.

They didn't leave much behind them, just a couple of old cabins that somebody else had built before them and a corn patch that they'd never got around to tending anyway. Most of the game right around there was hunted out by then, and the best woodlots were all cut down, so there wasn't much for them to mind leaving. The Dekinses weren't long on farming, fencing, or fixing. It wasn't their way. They just mostly took what the Lord provided, and made do.

From Macklinville they made their way west along the ridges until they came to the big river. Then when a steamboat stopped at Grove Bend for wood, they slipped aboard and rode it to St. Louis.

Once they were west of the Mississippi, they never looked back. They just spread out through the town, to see what the Lord might provide here, and met up on the other side two or three days later.

But it was time for Coy Dekins to look ahead, then. One of the babies had already died of fevers, and two more were croupy. And Mama Rose was ailing so that the Lord might take her most any time. They all needed to find a place and set a spell, and Coy was tired of traveling, anyway.

To the west was high-up hills, that looked a lot like back home. "Yonder," Coy told them, pointing west. "Y'all keep a lookout now, for a passable place." Cradling his long rifle across his arm, he pulled off his hat and bowed his head. They all prayed with him, then they picked up and set out. Ahead were peopled places, but more and more spread out as they got farther from the city. In the distance, rolling hills rose one past another, and beyond them the shapes of mountains sat against the sky.

Yonder they would find a new place. The Lord would provide.

The gunsmith's shop was a shambles. Tools and spilled shelves littered the floor. Bins of small hardware— nuts and bolts, threaded rods, springs, tempered sears, and pins were strewn around, and a handful of wood splinters lay scattered across the doorway, where the frame had been chipped away to reach the bolt.

"Vandals!" Albert Voigt muttered, staring about him with stricken eyes. With a sigh that was almost a sob, he knelt to sweep aside a drift of litter, then stood, holding a twisted bit of brass, gazing at it as a man might gaze at a defiled Bible. It was his brass rule, a cherished tool now bent beyond repair. It had been spoiled and cast aside. "Vandals," he whispered, "misbegotten vandals."

His eyeglasses magnified the stricken pain in his eyes.

Thomas had met him on the street, had been with him when he came to his shop and found the broken door. Now Thomas stood in the doorway, his hat in his hand. "I'm sorry," he said. "Did they take anything?"

Albert Voigt walked around his shop, peering here and there, trying to see what was missing among the rubble of what was ruined. "Some coins that I had in a cup," he said. "A miter saw . . . some chisels . . . my good clock. A drill, a set of bits . . . maybe some fulminate caps." Again he stared around the little room, disbelieving. "All this, for a few tools and some coins!"

Shaking his head, he stepped to a closed cabinet and opened its door. Inside were a half-dozen rifles, an old musket, and a shotgun with a broken stock.

"Mr. Andel's Greener," he said. "Double barrel, presentation grade, with silver scrolling. They took that." From the back of the cabinet he withdrew a long, slim form wrapped in oilcloth. Sweeping litter from his counter, he laid it there and pulled back the wraps. Inside was gleaming brass, dark iron and rich maple. Lady Justice was different now. Gone was the tall firing assembly with its vise-jaws, leather-wrapped flint, and its proud, serrated cocking knob. Gone was the wide flash pan with its sleek, spring-action frizzen. In their place were a small, businesslike percussion hammer and a stubby drum with a shiny cap nipple set at a jaunty angle. She was changed now in silhouette and form. But she was still Lady Justice.

Thomas carried the rifle outside and studied it in the sunlight. The conversion was exquisite work. The only trace of pan and frizzen on the sideplate were three barely visible little circles where bolts had been removed and the holes filled with threaded steel plugs, dressed down until they blended with the facing metal. The new drum and hammer had been browned with chemicals to almost match the tone of the age-browned plate they adorned.

Thomas cocked the hammer, set the set-trigger, and touched the firing trigger . . . just the slightest touch. With only a whisper of sound, the hammer released against his thumb, and he let it down gently. Albert Voigt's work was that of a true artisan.

Back inside, he set the rifle down and counted out coin. "I am very pleased," he said, wishing there were something he could do to ease the gunsmith's pain at the ruin of his shop. But there was nothing.

As he turned away, Voigt stopped him. The man

handed him a little suede bag with a drawstring. "These go with it," he said.

In the bag were a matched pair of small contrivances— little crosses of polished brass, with a tempered-steel tool capping each arm of each cross. There was a driver for slotted screws, a nipple pick for cleaning a gun's flash-path, a little wire brush, and a bolt wrench.

Each little cross had Albert Voigt's insignia engraved at its center.

"I make these," the gunsmith said. "For each gun, I make tools to fit the gun. Two of them in case one becomes lost. They go with the gun."

"Thank you," Thomas said.

"She is a fine rifle," Voigt said, his voice soft, his thoughts distant. "I found her maker's mark, beneath the barrel. He was Otto Krupp of Pennsylvania. A fine man, who could never return to his own country. If she is his best, she will make a perfect shot." He gazed around him, sadly. "I wish that shot could find whoever did this."

Thomas placed one of the little tools in the ornate patchbox on Lady Justice's stock. The other he dropped into his pouch. Carrying his rifle and a tin of percussion caps, Thomas left the vandalized shop. He could feel the sadness and outrage of the craftsman whose tidy little world had been so brutally violated. But somehow he could not visualize men having done that. Somehow it seemed more like the work of children— vicious, mindless children looking for treasure and not knowing it when they saw it.

But for Thomas Woodson, there was no time right now to dwell on such things. By midday there would be wagons waiting at the Chenault crossroads, wagons laden with crates and parcels, and impatient teamsters ready to head west. In the wagons were a vast variety of things— coils of rope and cable, spools of pitch-impregnated belting, bolts of juteweave and bales of sacking, kegs of hardware, a brace of tempered steel axles, and crates of milled machine parts for drive wheels and reducing gears. At Charon Springs, bricks were being shaped and fired. In the hills above Rolla, stone was being cut and shaped for a pair of grinding faces.

He would need masons and coopers, fitters and carpenters. It was Wednesday, the sun was shining, and the produce markets on the south ground were in full array. There was no better place to find men looking for honest work.

It was spring, the morning was clear, the sun was shining, and the world seemed to sing as Thomas Woodson headed for the markets. He had a mill to build and a place to build it. He had a life to live and a woman— the only woman he would ever love— to live it with him.

The sky of morning sported tints as clear and pure as deep blue eyes, and the new sun touching the hills in the distance was soft and warm, like fresh-brushed auburn hair. He whistled a little tune as he walked, and the whole world seemed to echo the pure sweetness of it.

A cabin with a loft, he told himself. A cozy place, for us and ours. Too long have I wandered in this world alone. Come with me, Martha. Come lead me home.

XII

A Place of New Beginnings

Dekagathe, Little Axe whose clan-fathers had been of the free Shawnee, wasted no time in the white man's city. There was nothing there that he wanted. With the supplies Louis Champon had given them after their journey down the rivers, he and the Arapaho girl headed westward. For two days they drifted like ghosts through the lands of white farmers and woodcutters, staying off the roads and out of sight, stopping only briefly when they needed to rest, or when it was time for Kititsi to nurse her baby.

They understood little of each other's language, but they needed few words. They shared a common situation. Neither of them had any home to return to, or anyone of their own kind to shelter them. Dekagathe the rebel had turned his back on clan, tribe, and kinship. Once he had had a clan name. Now there was no such name among the people of the sunning turtle, and even if the people should see him they would not know him. He was no longer *Sawana'ki*. In the same way, he knew that the girl could never again be Arapaho, even had she wanted to. The blood father of her child was Shoshone.

One day the child might be Arapaho or Shoshone, if it chose to be. But its mother could not.

Their aloneness was a bond between them, and it was enough. Dekagathe was without people. Now he accepted that Kititsi and the infant, whom she called K'kyo, were his people.

Only when they were past the scattered farms and the network of little trails and wagon tracks that marked the lands tamed by the whites did Little Axe feel his spirit awaken within him. Names could be erased, but the *ja'la-coma* of a person—the spirit within him—could not. When they reached the first wild hills, where the silent grief of defeated wilderness no longer pressed him, his spirit opened its eyes and saw again the living forests. It sang to him and he responded. From a ridge top he saw the rising lands ahead, forested hills with higher places beyond. Where sunlight flooded a glade among hardwood stands, he knelt and built a little fire. As its first tiny flames flickered, his eyes followed the smoke of it upward.

When it had told him its secrets, he extinguished it and brushed out all traces of it. In the Shawnee way, it was gone as though it had never been there.

Two paces away, Kititsi stood, watching him solemnly. He was aware of the chant she had murmured while he read the smoke. Barely audible, and full of the sibilant whispers that were part of her language, her chant was a counterpoint offered so that his prayer would not have to fly alone. In her way, she had joined her spirit with his, so that the fire would hear him better—would know what he wanted and give it willingly.

Now an image rested in his mind, a suggestion of a white cow wandering astray among stone walls. It was the secret thing the smoke had told him. The white cow would show him the way.

The infant K'kyo cooed and gurgled as Kititsi lifted

him from the soft nest of leaves and bark where he had been resting. As she folded a blanket around him, Little Axe came close. He pulled back a corner of the cloth, and infant eyes as dark as the clear night sky looked up at him. The chubby face was the color of fresh roses and new copper, and his hair glistened like ravens' wings. A little hand fluttered, and tiny fingers closed around Little Axe's calloused thumb.

"K'kyo," he muttered, in the white man's tongue. "Not 'Rapaho. Not 'Shoneh. Not *Sawana'ki* . . . not Shawnee." He glanced at Kititsi. "K'kyo is like me. He is only himself."

One day, the boy would need a name. K'kyo was not a name. The word meant only "this baby." One day he would need a name, and the name would be his very own. Like Dekagathe— Little Axe— his name would be a personal name and no man, no clan or council, would ever take it from him.

"I will give him a name," he told the girl. "When he is ready to be a man."

Kititsi struggled with the words, but she understood the meaning, and her eyes shone with happiness. Her child was now Dekagathe's child.

With the morning sun rising behind them, they headed deeper into the forest. Here the *ladegui* grew tall and chuckling waters danced over tumbled stones in the valleys. It was a fresh, rugged land, a land as old as time and as new as morning. Once this land had been Osage range. Before that it had been the realm of the *Misuri*, whose blood soaked the hills when the Sauk and Fox came. Dekagathe knew none of this, but he felt the spirits of those who had been here before.

This land would have seemed unfriendly to some eyes. But to Little Axe it had the taste of home.

Evening shadows were on the climbing slopes when they found the white cow.

In truth, it was a draft ox, grazing on cattails at the edges of a seep. The seep was at the bottom of a narrow, brush-blocked canyon only a few yards wide. At a glance from the limestone wall of the cut, Little Axe could see the broken brush where the beast had blundered into the trap, and the crushed grasses told of its aimless wanderings in the small space over many hours of time.

At first he didn't see the man almost directly below him. Vines and shrubbery almost hid him from sight where he lay. But Little Axe saw the fresh-broken stone at the lip of the cut, and the path of the rubble as it fell. And the man was there in the rubble.

For moments Little Axe squatted above him, every sense searching. Then he let himself down the canyon wall, as nimble as a cat, and took a closer look.

It was a white man with blood-soaked hair and a broken leg. He had searched for the ox and found it. But he had fallen from above, and he was unconscious.

From willow withes and the limber, clinging vines of wild grape, Little Axe fashioned a collar and a lead. With these he captured the disinterested ox and led it out of its trap. Then he went back to the man, straightened and set his broken leg, and hoisted him over a sturdy shoulder. He found a battered old shotgun where the man had dropped it, and took that, too.

With the man secured face-down across the withers of the ox, Little Axe set out to backtrack the animal. Kititsi followed at a short distance, keeping to what cover she could but within sight. Where there was one white man, there would be others. Should anything happen, Dekagathe could signal to her by voice or by gesture, and she would know what to do.

The white people were not far away. Two heavy wagons and a bulky, high-sided cart sat askew on a stoney flat, ringed by dark forest. One of the wagons had a broken wheel. Oxen prowled restlessly within a rope corral, and a fresh fire was just beginning to flicker on the ashes of an earlier one.

From the forest's edge, Little Axe could see a scrawny young white man, two women, and several children. The little camp was tidy enough, but poorly arranged. The fire was off to one side, and some latrines at the other— bright blankets hung there as screening— both within steps of deep thickets. Clothing and bedding hung on a rope between branches at the east edge of the clearing, and little piles of gathered brush suggested three separate sleep-sites. The nearest water— a little spring fed stream among the rocks— was a hundred yards away.

If enemies discover them here, Little Axe thought, then they will die soon. Such a camp could not be guarded or defended. Their activities were scattered, and the things they had spread out were foolishly placed. "They think there are walls around them," Little Axe told himself. "But here the walls are only shadows where enemies can hide."

The man on the ox had begun to squirm a bit, and low moans escaped him now and then. He would awaken soon. Little Axe left the ox secured to a tree and worked his way slowly to the right, agate eyes keen in the deepening dusk. He found the place where the man— the one on the mule— had pushed through brush to enter the forest. He squatted there, peering around, and saw what he expected. Another man had come this way, too. Someone had gone to look for the missing one.

With another quick look around, Little Axe raised his hand, spread it and swept it down, palm downward. He didn't see Kititsi, but he knew she was nearby. The signal told her to hide and wait.

Slinging his rifle across his shoulder then, Little Axe retrieved the ox and stepped into the open. "Hello the camp!" he called in English, and went to meet the wagon people.

* * *

June Wakefield was the first of them to see the ox being led out of the forest. Rising from the stone circle where she had been trying to build a fire, she waved and shouted, "Polly! It's Bliss! He's found the beast!"

Nearby, Scat Ellis peered out from behind the downed wagon and peered in the gloom. "High time," he declared. "I can't raise this jack by myself." He started to wave, then paused, squinting at the approaching figures. It was their lost ox, all right, but the man leading it was not Bliss. Scat knew how his brother moved, and how he dressed, and that wasn't him out there.

The sinews in Scat's neck seemed to twitch as he made out broad shoulders, bare legs beneath a buckskin shirt, and long, flowing black hair. "Indian," he whispered. Then he shouted it, "Indians! Take cover!" and dived behind the broken wagon, searching for his gun.

He found his rifle where he had left it, leaning against the tailgate. He couldn't remember whether it was loaded, but this was no time to worry about that. Crouching, he hugged the tailgate and laid the rifle across it, trying to find the sights in the failing light. He heard scuffles and muffled shrieks as Polly and June gathered children into the shelter of the other vehicles.

The ox had stopped, just at the edge of the campsite. It stood there, slowly swinging its head this way and that, and there was a bundle on its back. But the man was gone. Like magic, he had disappeared like a ghost, almost in the blink of an eye.

Scat shifted his position, looking this way and that. He stood upright, and a deep voice behind him . . . almost at his shoulder . . . said, "Put gun down. Step away."

Scat froze in place, and felt the unmistakable sting of a knife tickling his ribs. A dark, muscular arm reached around him and took the rifle out of his hands, and the knife point left his back, though the sting of it remained. Slowly he turned, and gaped at the Indian standing before him. Eyes like dark agate gazed back at him, and the Indian touched himself on the chest with a thumb. "Little Axe," he said, then pointed, past the wagon. "You go, get white cow."

As Scat hurried away he heard the deep voice behind him, giving orders to the women. "Man hurt," the Indian said. "Make up fire. Bring blanket."

Scat reached the ox, grabbed its lead, and stared at the man on its back. At first he wasn't sure it was Bliss, his head was so matted with blood. Then he wasn't sure he was alive, until Bliss groaned and squirmed, struggling at the tied thongs which kept him from sliding off the animal.

Groggily, he tugged this way and that, then raised his bloody head. "Unhand me, damn you!" he demanded. "Don't you know a bargain when you see one?"

He wasn't making any sense, but Scat had no further doubt that this bloody mess was his brother. Only Bliss Ellis would say such a thing, lashed down on the back of a draft ox.

Little Axe got the people corralled and counted, and cached their weapons out of sight as a precaution. Then he helped the scrawny youngster unload the injured man and laid him gently on a blanket near the fire. The children gathered around, gawking, and the two young women fluttered here and there, trying to do things for the injured man, trying at the same time to stay between the Indian and their children.

One of them tried and tried again to build up the fire, and produced nothing but acrid smoke. Finally Little Axe chased her away from the fire, and called in Kititsi to attend to it.

The white women just stared at the girl at first, cringing from her. But as the fire came to life and they saw the baby in its wrap at her breast, they crept closer. Within moments they were all huddled together there, oohing and aahing, comparing children and chattering in at least two languages.

Little Axe stood back, alert and watchful. After a time he beckoned to the scrawny young man and repeated the introduction. "I am Little Axe," he said slowly, as though speaking to a child . . . or a simpleton. "Who are you?"

"Ah . . . S-Scat," the youth stuttered. "Scat Ellis."

"Bring water, Scat Ellis," Little Axe commanded him. "That one is waking up now."

Scat glanced toward the fire. Beyond the clustered women and children, Bliss was groaning and holding his head, trying to sit up. Polly had just turned to assist him.

"Yes, sir," Scat said. "I'll . . ."

But he was talking to himself. The Indian wasn't there anymore. As though he had never been there, Little Axe had disappeared in the dusk.

Where the forest began, on the backtrail of the ox, Dekagathe found a comfortable spot and sat down to wait. There was still another white man out there, looking for the first one. It was getting dark and he would return soon. Little Axe had no intention of letting the white man see him first, and react. From what he had observed, these people were lost and inept. They seemed as helpless as wolf pups in these surroundings, and would be easily frightened. It made them dangerous. There was no telling what one of them might do if he were surprised.

"We got lost, it seems," Ben Wakefield said sheepishly, panting as he inserted a large stone under the axle of the downed wagon. He stepped back and looked at it critically, then said, "Let it down easy."

At the far end of a long pole, braced across a fallen log, Scat Ellis and the two white women eased their weight off the pole and the wagon creaked as it settled onto the stone, the hub of its broken wheel jutting out at an angle.

Crouched a few feet away, Little Axe nodded. "Fix wheel now," he said.

They had been trying to use a clumsy wagon jack, without knowing how. The result was a broken jack lying beside their broken wheel. Little Axe had spent time on the hide-wagons. He showed them how to rig a lever and fulcrum, even helped them select and cut their lever. But that was all he intended to do. The problem was theirs, not his.

Ben Wakefield wiped sweat from his face. "We wandered around these hills for two days, but we couldn't find the road again. Then the wheel broke, and that ox got loose and disappeared . . . things been going to hell in a hurry for us." He chuckled, sadly. "I guess we should have stayed in Baltimore."

"Why didn't you?" Little Axe asked.

"We got land in Missouri," Scat Ellis said. "From our daddys."

Ben knelt to look at his hub. "My pa and Mr. Ellis— that's Bliss and Scat's pa— they served together in the war. Quartermaster Corps, at Washington City. After the war they took their grant as pay, and went back to Baltimore. They were in business together."

"Hardware and greengrocers," Scat added. "What business was your daddy in?"

"He was an Indian," Little Axe said.

Ben glanced at Scat and shook his head. The kid could ask the damnedest questions. "They gave their grants to us, so we thought we'd go to Missouri and set up a store.

We've brought goods enough to make a start. That's what's in these wagons. Everything we own is in these wagons."

Polly Ellis and June Wakefield— both of them hardly more than girls, although between them they had five children— laid the lever pole aside and went to see about dinner. Kititsi went along with them, chattering happily in Arapaho with a bit of fractured English, a smattering of Shoshone, and even a touch of Shawnee here and there. She seemed to have found new friends, and their conversation was as easy as if they were all speaking the same tongue.

"Where?" Little Axe asked.

"Our land?" Ben Wakefield climbed into the trail cart and came out with an oilskin parcel. There were maps in it, and he selected one and spread it on the ground. "Here," he pointed. "Where these valleys come together. I don't think the place has a name, but that's it."

Little Axe studied the map, tracing lines with his finger. Waterways were drawn on it as clusters of wavy lines. Rows of little arrowheads marked the main ridges. The Mississippi was there, and the Missouri River there, and St. Louis right there. He stood, got his bearings, and pointed. "There," he said, "past those hills and the next ones."

"Fine," Ben sighed. "It sounds so easy, when you say it like that." He turned his attention to the broken wheel. It needed new spokes in two places, and the hub needed to be reset. Then the iron tire would have to be sweated on, but Little Axe had the feeling the man knew how to do those things. It was just going from one place to another that defeated him. He tilted his head, listening to the breeze. Then he poked around, picking up fist-sized rocks, studying them carefully and dropping them to pick up others. When he had several that suited him, he drew his knife to cut fringe from his buckskin shirt.

"What are you doing?" Ben asked.

"Need some string," the Indian said.

"I have twine in the wagon. Will that do?"

Little Axe put his knife away. Twine would do nicely. From a fresh spool of it he cut two lengths, measuring them from his chest to his fingertips. Then he carefully bound a stone to each end of each string, picked up his rifle and turned toward the forest. In a few steps he was among the trees, and he seemed to simply disappear there.

Ben shook his head. The Indian was like a ghost. He came and went, unseen and unheard, as though he were a part of the forest itself.

When Little Axe returned, two hours later, he carried a pair of turkeys slung over his shoulder. "Supper," he said. Ben was shaving spokes for the wheel, but he paused. "Fat turkeys," he noted.

"I didn't hear any shootin'," Scat said. "How'd you get 'em?"

Little Axe held out his rock-weighted strings. There was blood on the twine. Shrugging, he untied the string and tossed the stones aside. The strings went into his belt pouch.

"Be done with this wheel tomorrow," Ben Wakefield said. "And Bliss will be up to traveling by then. His eyes focus all right, and he's fussing like a fishmonger. Says his leg aches like all hell. But it's straight." He set down his spokeshave and planted a boot on the repaired hub. "Where are you going, Little Axe?"

"West," the Shawnee spread his hands, a little puzzled at the question. Since childhood he had been on the move . . . always going, but never going anywhere in particular. The idea of a destination was strange to him. As a child he had heard the old stories. Once the Shawnee had gone where they wanted, free and proud. Now all the tribes were treaty tribes, and there were no free

Shawnee. But then, Dekagathe was no longer Shawnee . . . not in the way the old ones had been. He had broken the circle. He was a renegade, a rebel, and his name had been erased.

Once there had been ways for a man to go, but now there was only where he had not been before. "Just . . . west," he repeated.

Ben pointed, the same direction Little Axe had pointed earlier. "That's west," he said. "You could come with us, if you want to."

Little Axe arched a brow at him. "Why?"

"Why not?" Ben shrugged. "We all talked about it some. You know your way around wild country. We don't. You've helped us, and you might help us again. Then maybe, there might be a time when we could help you. We'd be grateful to have the chance."

Little Axe looked around. They had all stopped what they were doing, and were all looking at him, waiting. Even Kititsi was waiting, and her dark eyes said she hoped he would agree.

"We go west tomorrow," the last of the free Shawnee said.

Life had taught Dekagathe a truth that many of his predecessors— maybe even the great Tecumseh himself— had not understood. No one could see past tomorrow.

XIII

The Tempering Hills

The Ozarks, Mid-summer, 1836

Sim Holly and some of his boys were down from Candlestick.

For most of a day they had prowled around from place to place, dour and silent as they poked here and there. But they hadn't said what they were looking for. Now they had a little fire going down by the creek and since mid-afternoon they had kept to themselves down there, ignoring the people who came and went about the little settlement . . . just watching.

The place was nothing more than a crossroads— a stony little flat on the morning side of a ridge, where meandering trails came together among lonely lodgepole pines. But there were fresh artesian springs that flowed year round, and old mounds said it had always been a campsite for travelers, even before the white men came.

A scattering of log-and-stone cabins and several pole barns were sprawled about, along a pair of whispering little streams. The buildings were placed as though each had been the only structure in the region when it was built, but all together they formed a settlement. More or less in its center were a cluster of buildings— a smithy with shed wings to accommodate a farrier's stall and tackle shed, a carpenter's woodshop that held also a wheelwright's stall, a little stone-and-log "road station" with a cookery and washhouse, a church with a copper steeple, and a long, dog-run building connected by pole corrals to a produce shed.

Though no sign or marker proclaimed it, the settlement had come to be called Hays Junction.

Up on the ridge was a saw pit, and near it a stone quarry. Their early produce was evident in the stone foundations and fireplaces, in the board-and-batten walls of the little church building, the milled-lumber doors and shutters on some of the cabins and in stacks of cut limestone and hewn granite, and in racks of hardwood planking curing in a shed behind the carpentry. Both enterprises were busy again now, because of the new mill being built nearby on High Creek. Just visible around the slope was the mill site, Thomas Woodson's new flour mill, a ten-acre clearing alive with activity. Whole strings of wagons had come through in recent months, unloaded bales and crates out there, then gone back east for more.

Meandering little garden patches among the settlement's buildings were green with summer corn and bean crops, onions and squash. In the converging valleys that joined to curl around the ridge, little smokes rose from farmsteads where furrowed grainfields were patchwork patterns among the rolling woodlands. And on the shelf-lands under the hills, fields of wheat were ripening. There would be a mill now, and the planters were preparing their crop.

Hannibal Dean had his forge going on this gray afternoon, and his anvil rang cheerfully as he shaped and cut rods which would become the links of a new trace-chain. A gaggle of children played around his open swing doors, tarrying on their way home from school.

They ranged in size from a few shirt-tail tads and a pair of little girls in sack dresses up to some— hulking lads in outgrown canvas britches and burgeoning girls beginning to fill the garments they wore— who would soon be of age.

There might have been more around, but lately some of the older boys had taken to tagging after the Sinclair girls, who had come with the mill people. Several of the lads now worked at the mill evenings and weekends. Dean had jokingly accused Thomas Woodson, the millwright, of fishing for hired hands and using live bait.

About half of the rowdy little crowd around the smith now would be in for harsh words and maybe a lick or two when they got home, for tarrying while their chores waited. But that was the normal course of things, and Hannibal Dean made no attempt to shoo them away.

Distant thunder rumbled in the hills and he set down his hammer, wiped his grimy hands on a bit of sacking and stepped outside. The clouds that had stood atop the peaks earlier were now overhead, and there was a smell of rain in the air. Filling a pipe, the smith strolled up the road a short way, nodding here and there to people hurrying past— men with tools in their hands, women carrying baskets and bundles. The low clouds and the fresh breeze said summer storm was coming.

"Fixin' to pour, Cozy!" Dean called, waving to a man leading a brace of mules down the road.

Distant thunder growled and the mules' ears turned toward the sound. One of them tossed its head and threatened to balk. Cozy Kincaid hauled on its lead, bracing his feet and cursing under his breath. His stiff, clipped beard bobbed like a bird's beak. The mule subsided, and he led them toward his barn. Passing Dean he rasped, "Generally does, an' a man waits long enough."

Where a weed-choked gully opened toward the lower

creek, Dean glanced to his right. Sim Holly and his boys
were still there, and he wondered why. The Hollys were
reclusive folk, mostly. They came in now and again to
trade a brood sow or dicker for tobacco, but generally
they didn't stay. He had never seen their place up on
Candlestick, and didn't know anyone who had. The Hollys weren't long on hospitality.

Beyond the churchyard, the Creeds— Jim and his
brood— were scurrying around the downside of their
cookery, unrolling a large, stained tent. Hannibal Dean
turned and peered eastward. Sure enough, a blue and
white flag danced in the wind atop Lester Henry's flag
pole.

People were coming, the flag said. Dean squinted, trying to see the distant rise where the Rolla trace topped
out on east ridge. The road was a winding cut in the
distant forest, cleared by people passing through. It came
from the east, meandering like a snake track toward Hays
Junction. He couldn't see anybody out there, but when
the flag flew at Henry's it meant *somebody* had seen somebody. And they'd be coming from the east. Lester
wouldn't raise his best flag for anybody who'd come from
any other direction.

The Creeds had seen it, and they were setting up their
guest tent, getting the "hotel" ready for visitors.

Hannibal Dean finished his pipe and walked back to
his smithy. It was quiet now. The hint of storm had sent
the younguns scattering for home. He banked the coals
in his forge, gathered up his cut links and dumped them
in a larded sack, then went out and checked the poles
and uprights of his corral fence. From a hand pump he
drew water and filled the troughs. He had an ample
supply of grain, and plenty of baled hay, and he set out
a few small coils of rope for handling critters.

Folks on the move generally needed a place to rest
their weary bones for a day or two, and the Creeds would

see to that. But what they needed first was tending for their stock.

Hannibal Dean— like everybody else in these hills— rarely saw cash money. Hays Junction was isolated and remote from any place of size. Some coin was circulated— wages from the mill and now and then money from the sale of woodcrafts and such, down in the flatlands. Hannibal's own "cash crop" was knives— fine, tempered steel blades that he crafted now and then when business was slow. Most of these were bound for Santa Fe, judging by the currency he received for them— Mexican silver coins which he usually cut into quarters and bits.

Day to day though, folks made do on what they could swap with one another. But the outland trade grew a bit each season, and in recent times— as more and more land-grant pilgrims pushed through— Hays Junction had found travelers to be a good source of revenue.

There were a good many in these hills who didn't hold with travelers, newcomers, or any kind of strangers. But then, the smith reminded himself, glancing again toward the lower creek, there were some who didn't hold with *anybody*, stranger or not.

Distant thunders muttered, and he wondered again why the Hollys were hanging around like they were. The last time that bunch had camped here, a man had wound up dead— a ridgerunner up from Peabody. Dean had never heard what grievance the Hollys had with the man, but they had waited here, where trails crossed, and when he showed up, they killed him. Then they went away, back to Candlestick.

The Hollys were hard people. Tight-lipped and aloof, they kept to themselves mostly. Up on Candlestick— as much a part of the land there as the land itself. They rarely bothered anyone, but neither did they tolerate being bothered, and for any who harmed them and theirs, retribution was swift and final.

Hard men, fit for a hard land. Yet at the heart of their family was the matriarch, Tilda Holly, and she somehow balanced all the hardness of her kin. Hannibal Dean thought he had never met a finer woman . . . or a wiser person . . . than Tilda. And in her own way, she was the strongest of them all.

He recalled hearing Parson Swain say one time, that these hills were like a crossroads for the soul. It could go one way or the other, but every man had to choose. Devil hills, he called them, that must be somehow overcome if a man valued his eternal soul.

John Swain was a stern and unbending man, not one to dwell on the middles of things. To him, there were angels and devils, and not much in between. There was black and there was white. There was hot and there was cold, and light and dark and day and night. There was good and there was evil. Anything short of absolute, to the Reverend Mr. Swain, was only temporary, and in a grown man it was a sign of laziness.

Parson Swain could be an aggravating man, and mostly he was. But he had a point where these hills were concerned. Like the Hollys and a few others, Hannibal Dean was old family hereabouts. His daddy had claimed land on the Marais des Cygnes early on, and the Deans had been one of the first families to take root in these valleys. He had seen a lot of folks settle here, and a lot more pass through, and the hills *did* change folks. Often as not, the good got better and the bad got worse.

The Missouri hills were harsh land in some ways. They could be gentle and full of wondrous beauty. But they were whimsical. They would reward one man, and destroy another, with no more reason or common sense than Pastor Swain's Lord God seemed to have in such matters. Like that fierce old Hebrew deity, about whose mercy Pastor Swain and Hannibal Dean rarely saw eye to eye, this land could be bountiful sometimes. But then it could be suddenly cruel, and it didn't need a reason either way.

"It makes us better or it kills us," the poet Grant Axton had said of the Aux Arcs' region.

Dean had his doubts about that "better" business. What these hills did to people, it seemed to him, was make the strong stronger and the weak dead. Good or bad had nothing to do with it.

Satisfied that he was ready for customers, the smith stepped out on the road again, peering eastward. This time he saw them—two ox-drawn heavy wagons and a high-side cart, coming toward the little town. Maybe coming to stay, he decided. The true westerants—overland travelers with big dreams and big wagons, bound for the great trails to the west—didn't frequent the hill traces. That sort of traffic mostly followed the rivers as far as they could go, which usually meant to St. Joseph, or little Westport on the Missouri, before setting out by foot and wheel.

Across the way, Gustave Nilsson was out by his elm tree, leaning on an axe handle and looking at the weather. "Might have us some new neighbors, Gus!" the smith called, pointing eastward. Nilsson straightened, peered down the road, and nodded. "Ya, maybe," he said. "Yust maybe so."

Down the road a hundred yards, brush rustled and a men stepped partway into view. He was facing away, and the shrubbery hid most of him, but Dean could see a scraggly beard outthrust beneath a hook nose, and the dipping brim of an old slouch hat. He saw, too, that the man held a long, dark-stained rifle as lightly as though it were a toothpick.

"Jody Holly," he muttered. "So that's what they're doing. They're watching the roads."

The oldest of Sim Holly's boys stood there for a moment, then drew back out of sight. But Dean knew he hadn't gone away. Something was going on.

Lightning flared nearby, among the westward rises, and thunder cracked like cannon fire. As though it were a signal, a gust of wind danced along the street, kicking up whirls of dust and bits of debris. Here and there dogs barked and loose shutters banged against their frames. In only a moment, storm-dusk settled over the land, darkening the sky and hazing the distances. Scattered fat raindrops, carried on the wind, splattered and painted little designs as they hit.

Two women hurried past, both holding their bonnets in place with one hand, wrestling heavy baskets with the other. Dean put away his pipe and sprinted for the open front of his smithy. He clanged a grate over the banked forge, then hauled on his doors, swinging them closed one at a time. In the abrupt darkness inside he got down a lamp, lifted the glass and flared a match to light the wick. Trimmed and closed, the lamp cast a warm glow. He hung it on a swivel and turned.

An Indian stood a few feet away, dark-agate eyes studying him in the light. There were generally Indians around Hays Junction, but Dean knew instantly that this wasn't one of them. The man was young, but no child. He was sturdy of build, with sinewy bare arms that rippled with corded muscle at each slight movement. He wore buckskin, with a breechclout and high moccasins, and his long hair was coiled and held in place by a tufted ornament. There was a broad knife at his belt, and the rifle in his hand was a short-stocked Hawken— a plainsman's gun. The rifle of a long hunter.

Hannibal Dean gaped at him, startled, then regained his composure. With a casual gesture he indicated the blackened pot on the forge's lip. "Coffee?"

The Indian looked him up and down, then shook his

head. "Men are out there, in hiding," he said. "Who are they?"

"Who . . . ? Oh." Dean felt his shoulders ease a bit. The Indian spoke English. The smith had a good ear for languages, but he couldn't identify the accent. Not Cherokee, certainly. And not Osage or Peoria, like most of those who lived around here. But at least the Indian was willing to talk, and his English was good enough that they could. "I guess you mean the Hollys. That's their name. Holly."

"Why do they hide?"

"I don't know," Dean shrugged. "Likely they're look-ing for somebody. I wouldn't want to be him, whoever he is." Right now, he thought, Sim and his boys aren't fixing to do much but get wet.

"There is a flag on a pole," the Indian turned a thumb, eastward. "What does it mean?"

"That's Lester Henry's place," Dean said. "The flag means there are people coming in." He stepped to the lip of the forge. "If you don't want coffee, I do. Do you have a name I could pronounce?"

"Little Axe," the Indian said. Dean noted that he hadn't flinched when he stepped closer. He might have flinched. Hannibal Dean was a big man, and even un-armed he might seem a threat to a nervous visitor. But the Indian did not seem concerned, and Hannibal was suddenly glad that he had no hostile intentions. Little Axe was a man who could take care of himself.

He found his tin cup and sloshed steaming black cof-fee into it. Then he set it down and extended a grimy hand. "My name is Hannibal Dean," he said.

Little Axe ignored the gesture, but he set his rifle aside and found another cup. Dean sipped his own coffee and perched his backside comfortably on his anvil-stump. It seemed to be time for a friendly visit.

Outside, the wind was picking up and rain rattled like

birdshot on the copper shingling of the roof. Sloshing footsteps hurried past, and he recognized some of the voices. Workmen from the mill, coming in for a meal at Creed's table. They had shut down early, because of the weather.

"Those folks coming in will need tending for their animals," Dean said.

"Need a wheel, too," Little Axe told him. "But no hurry. They come to stay, if they are welcome." He glanced at the closed doors. "Those Hollys make trouble?"

"Doubt they would," Dean shrugged. "Not for strangers. I don't hold much with Sim Holly, but I've not known his brood to rob or ambush anybody. Sounds like you know the newcomers. Who are they?"

"Wakefield," Little Axe said. "And Ellis. They come to make a store."

"Then they'll be mighty welcome here," Dean nodded. "Place needs merchants, right enough. Good folks, are they?"

Dark-agate eyes held his for a long moment, and there was no expression there that he could see. "They're white," Little Axe said.

It was near dark and raining steadily when the wagons reached Hays Junction. Hannibal Dean had spread the word, and men with slickers and lanterns came out to help. They got the stock corralled at Dean's, and the people sheltered at Creed's place. Serenity Creed laid on smoked ham and sweet corn at her tables.

It flustered Serenity a little to have Indians in her house, but she took a shine to Kititsi the minute the girl unwrapped K'kyo. Serenity Creed had babies of her own. She liked babies, and it didn't much matter what persuasion they were.

Then when the Woodsons came in from the mill, and it turned out that Martha and Kititsi were old friends, that resolved any remaining concerns. If Martha Woodson accepted a body, Serenity Creed would accept her too.

As to Little Axe, he frightened her at first because he looked so fierce. But he accepted his plate courteously enough, and used a fork when he ate, and didn't make any fuss at all, and pretty soon Serenity got used to him being there . . . except when she looked around and he was gone. That made her uneasy, that the Indian could just come and go that way. It was as though he had never been there.

"We'll see if we can't find your husband some good boots," she told Kititsi. "Man ought to stomp some when he walks."

Kititsi understood hardly a word of it, but her smile was radiant. The friendly woman was talking about Dekagathe.

The big, low room seemed packed with people. The arrival of newcomers was an occasion, and folks had come in from all around, dripping with rain, to meet the new neighbors and share the smoked ham. A dozen conversations were going simultaneously at and around the plank tables.

"He ought to have some britches, too," June Wakefield chimed, shuffling children around to make sure each received a share. "Bare legs on a man just don't look Christian."

At the next table, Hannibal Dean glanced around, grinning, then turned back to the men. "I doubt he is," he muttered to Ben Wakefield.

Unfazed, Serenity Creed hauled fresh cornbread from the oven and set it out. "Man has good boots," she pronounced, "folks knows where he stands."

Polly Ellis poured coffee, pausing to check the fresh

wraps on her husband's broken leg. They were holding just fine, and the splints beneath them were the same willow staves the Indian had put there.

Bliss hardly even winced when his wife thumped his splints to test their set. He was absorbed in business. Just in the space of a good meal, some fine plans had been hatched. Lester Henry had title to the lot next to Gus Nilsson's, and was willing to put up a building for lease. By first frost, the new Wakefield and Ellis Company store would be in business there. In the meantime, they could start out in the school cabin. Classes would be dismissed for harvest soon, and they could finish up at the church. In return for this service, Pastor Swain wanted a bell. Thomas Woodson had offered to donate the bell, provided Ben Wakefield's uncle in Baltimore would market *Woodson's Superb* flour and meal through his brokerage in the east. Woodson had a partner in St. Louis who could arrange the details with the Baltimore uncle.

Through it all, Scat Ellis held aside from the dickering. His belly was full, he had a roof over his head, and he just naturally got out his fiddle and began playing little tunes over in the corner by the fire. He kept the strings muted and played mostly for himself . . . mostly, except that his eyes kept wandering toward Rachel Sinclair each time he hit a note that sounded especially nice. As a sort of adjunct to his brother's family the past few years, Scat hadn't given much thought to his own personal life. But suddenly, he was thinking a lot about such things.

Never in his sixteen years had he seen anything so pretty as Rachel Sinclair.

Outside, the rain had settled down to a steady rate. By threes and fives, people said their good evenings and headed for their homes. The newcomer children were bedded in the guest tent, and beds made ready for the rest. In the big room, women were tidying up from the meal, and the lamplit shadows were sweet with the warmth of the hearth, the aroma of good tobacco and the muted strains of Scat Ellis's fiddle.

The thunders had passed over, so it was abrupt and startling when a rattle of nearby gunfire broke the quiet. All around the room, men came alert and reached for their guns. Near the door Little Axe came to his feet, lithe as a shadow. He paused at the door, then opened it and was gone into the darkness. Others followed him, crowding through into the darkness outside, ready for anything.

There had been several shots. Four or five at least, in the space of a heartbeat. They fanned out from the doorway, their eyes searching the gloom, but there was nothing to be seen.

"Bring lanterns," Thomas Woodson said. Several of the men dodged back inside, to bring light.

As the lantern-glow spilled onto the wet roadway beyond, a tall, slickered figure stood there. Rainwater dripped from a slouch hat above deep-set eyes that were only dark shadows behind a prominent hook nose. Shadows, nose and beard, he seemed, atop six feet of lanky vengeance shrouded in rain gear. The rifle in his hand seemed a part of him.

Hannibal Dean pushed past the lanterns, peering at the figure in the roadway. "Sim Holly?" he asked.

"As ever was," the specter said. His voice was deep, but as thin and cold as skim ice on a pond. "We done our business here. Now we'll leave."

"And what business did you do?" Dean demanded.

"A thief," Sim Holly rasped. "Him an' his, they come by Candlestick. They stole from us."

"Who did?"

"Name of Dekins," Holly said. "He went into the crick."

With that he turned and walked away, fading into the darkness.

"What was that all about?" Thomas Woodson asked.

"Dekins?" Lester Henry rubbed his chin whiskers thoughtfully. "There's some Dekinses out at the old McDowell place. Gypsy bunch, seems like, but they've dug in like they mean to stay."

"Well, I'd say one of them outlived his welcome," Jim Creed allowed. "Them Hollys don't shoot for sport."

"I guess we'd better go find him," Thomas suggested, but Hannibal Dean spread his hands and shook his head. "If Sim Holly says he fell in the creek, then he fell in the creek. We'll look for him in the morning."

Back inside, the smith appeared dour and thoughtful as he collected his hat and coat.

"That Sim Holly!" Jim Creed grumbled. "Acts like Hays Junction is his own private killin' ground."

"I thought the McDowell place was abandoned," someone else said. "Wasn't anybody yonder last time I was over that way."

"Well, there is now," Cozy Kincaid rasped. "I was out there two-three days nigh, to look at a mule. Man wanted three dollars for it, but I didn't buy it 'cause it looked like one of Lester's string."

"You never told me that," Lester Henry snapped.

"None of my never-mind," Kincaid muttered. "You can't keep your mules in, that's your lookout."

"I encountered some stray children on the ridge," Pastor Swain announced. "Ragamuffin band, though they did speak well enough in the Lord's name. One of them could recite from the Book of Romans. As I recollect, they gave their name as Dekins."

Thomas was beside Dean, waiting while Martha and the girls found their wraps. "Trouble, Hannibal?" he asked quietly.

"There's the makin's," Dean said. "But I hope I'm wrong about that. The last thing we need around here is a feud."

XIV

The Outlaws

They found Anse Dekins the next morning, when the storm-rise had gone down. There were three bullet holes in him, and any one of them would have sent him to his maker. He lay like a soggy straw doll, wedged among stones in the new spillway just below the mill. When they lifted him out they found a strange thing. His spent rifle was still in his hand, clenched in dead fingers.

Cozy Kincaid brought a mule and a cart, and they hauled the corpse up to town for a proper burial. Lester Henry paid out two dollars for the man's old rifle, to cover the cost, and they voted to see who would go out to the old McDowell place to notify his kin. Pastor John Swain received that honor, by vote of nine to one.

But nobody had to tell the Dekinses what had happened. Three of the Dekins children, hiding in brush above the spillway, saw them bring Anse up from the creek. One of them was Anse's boy Harley. Harley wasn't much more than ten years old, but he was a Dekins. Maude and Wendell set out through the woods to spread the news, but Harley waited around to see what would happen next. While everybody was over by the church, Harley helped himself to coffee and corn bread at the blacksmith's shop, and picked up a patch knife and a good pouch belt in the bargain.

They laid Anse out in a shed behind the carpenter's barn, to be fitted for a coffin. When they were gone, Harley crept in and had himself a look. He knew no great fondness for the man who had sired him, and no particular regret that he was gone, but he was curious. He'd never seen his daddy dead before.

Within minutes after Lester Henry stuck the dead man's old long gun away in his shed, it was gone. Harley had it for his own, as a legacy from his father. He had always wanted it.

Satisfied with what he had acquired, Harley faded into the woods above Hays Junction and found twig signs where Wendell and Maude had gone. But he didn't follow their path. Instead he cut southeastward, toward Bald Knob. He didn't have anything to go home for, and no feelings about anyone there. But Bald Knob was where his Uncle Luke had gone after they crossed the river. Harley decided it was time to take up with Uncle Luke.

Behind him, at the forest's edge, a bramble thicket barely stirred as Dekagathe emerged. He had herbs in a sack, and a pair of fat rabbits.

The small person who passed within feet of him, even pausing there to glance back at the settlement below, was no more than a child. A little boy, begrimed and ragged but still hardly more than a baby. Yet there was something about him that was deeply disturbing to the Indian. This child, he felt, might as readily kill a man as suck on a sweet.

What Dekagathe's eyes had seen was a child. But what his spirit sensed was a small feral animal, snarling in shadows, a beast without conscience or remorse, awaiting only the appropriate moment to run amok.

Among the hide-hunters on the Platte had been a man named Kruger— a man who seemed not to have a spirit.

Dekagathe had sensed the void about him each time they met. At the edge of a farm field outside St. Louis, Negro people were herded together and made to watch as one of their kind was tied to a tree and beaten with a whip. Spirits had hovered there, like rainclouds. But the man using the whip could not feel them. He had no spirit of his own. And now Little Axe had sensed that void again, in a child.

Despite all he had seen in his life, Dekagathe still was amazed sometimes at how completely feral it was possible for people to be. But then, he was only an Indian. Nothing in his blood or his heritage had ever prepared him for the sheer savagery that could be found in this world. It took day-to-day association with white people, it seemed, to show him that.

Not all of them, he had learned, were human.

Cozy Kincaid and the Baker boys found Jody Holly, hanging from the limb of a white-oak tree. He was thoroughly dead— so badly beaten that he was probably dead before they hanged him. His boots were gone, along with everything of value that he might have carried. They weren't even sure who he was until Sim Holly and some of his other boys came down from Candlestick to identify him.

The boys— Grange and Bower Holly and a cousin, Mase Crenwell— waited at the shed door while Sim went inside with the preacher. With their wide hat brims shading their craggy faces, and their rifles across their arms, Martha Woodson thought they looked like the sentries must look at the gates of hell.

Thomas had his stones and troughs in place, and a drive-belt run to a spindle that Cozy Kincaid could turn with his mules. They were using sacked wheat from over by Jefferson City to test the reducing gears and "sweeten" the stone. The roughs would be reground, and the prized wheat germ was shared out to the mill crew. Martha collected the new flour and brought some of it up from the mill to swap for eggs and a bolt of yard goods. When a crowd gathered around the carpentry, she and Serenity Creed went to see.

Most of the men had gone in for a look at the hanged man, but few of the women cared to. They had heard how badly he was beaten.

Sim Holly was inside for only a few minutes. When he came out, his bearded face had no expression at all but his eyes were as bleak and cold as all winter. "How much for the box?" he rasped, speaking to no one in particular.

"A half-dollar, I reckon," the preacher said. "I expect he could rest yonder in God's acre. There's a corner there for strangers, and those not of the church."

"He's our'n," Sim said. "We'll mind him from here."

"But the Lord God said . . ."

"The Lord God's got all of Jody Lane Holly that he's entitled to," Sim growled, cutting him short. "The rest of him is ours, and we aim to take him home." Not looking around, he gestured with a thumb and his boys went into the shed, nailed the pine coffin shut and brought it out.

Gently and quietly, they strapped it onto a travois behind a docile mule. Sim Holly handed the preacher half a silver dollar, and they strode away, three fierce, unyielding men and a mule, headed for Candlestick.

"I wonder where the rest of them are," Lester Henry muttered, scanning the hills around.

"Who?" Martha asked.

"The rest of the Hollys. And the Crenwells and Lanes. There's a whole passel of them folks, ma'am, an' I'd wager they're around here someplace."

* * *

Three days later another Dekins was found dead, just a half mile out of town on the south trace. Children following a bee, looking for its hive, found him and brought men from town. They never learned the name of this one, but he was a Dekins, right enough. A man grown he was, but no more— maybe twenty at the oldest. Skinny and jug-eared, with big hands and big feet, a long nose and little, close-set eyes, he couldn't be anybody else but a Dekins. He had been shot one time, right through his chin. The big ball had crushed his jaw, smashed through the spine in his neck, and come out the back.

He hadn't lived long enough to blink his eyes. Nobody came to claim him, but dark shadows came in the night to call on the preacher, and he declared he would bury the man in God's Acre, out behind the church.

Not everybody was happy about that. "Them Dekinses is all white trash," some whispered. "Live from hand to mouth yonder in the hills, just like niggers or Injuns. Ought to be planted with their own, 'stead of here among God-fearin' folk."

But Pastor John Swain was adamant about it. "He was a white man!" he roared. "And a good Christian! The Dekinses might be poor people, but I've accepted them into my flock. I know for a fact they stand by the Good Book."

"Exodus, Deuteronomy, and Revelations," Hannibal Dean snorted. "An eye for an eye, a tooth for a tooth, and hellfire for any man that doesn't spout gospel like he was takin' a pee. I wish you'd read the rest of that dang book sometime, Preacher!"

"Blasphemy!" Swain hissed, but he turned his eyes away. Still, that dead Dekins was buried behind the church, among the flock like he wanted.

That same evening, an hour after full dark, there was

a glow on Candlestick that they could see from the town. A Holly barn was burning. The Dekinses had been busy.

In the days that followed, Hays Junction seemed to be full of Dekinses. Dour men with guns and stringy-haired women called at house after house, shop after shop, quoting scripture and implying retribution as they collected "donations" to sustain them in their struggle against evil. And while the grown-ups were holding folks' attention, the children were sneaking around behind, stealing everything they could carry.

Ben Wakefield and Bliss Ellis had been in business in their new store for less than a week when there was a ruckus there— some Dekins women squabbling over yard goods— and when it was over a year's worth of profit had disappeared from the shelves.

They went to Pastor Swain, who instructed them on the qualities of mercy and forgiveness. So Hannibal Dean and Gustave Nilsson took it on themselves to call a meeting. They met at the church.

Thomas Woodson came, because he'd had his own run-in with the Dekinses. Coy Dekins and some of his boys had come out to the mill, demanding money and food. The encounter might have turned nasty, but when Thomas came out with Lady Justice and pointed her at Coy Dekins's gizzard, the rest of his gang found themselves surrounded by angry mill crewmen with hammers, axes, and pitchforks. Every man there had a stake in Woodson's mill, one way or another, and about half of the young ones were secretly in love with Rachel Sinclair, who was just now beginning to look a lot like a woman.

Thomas chased the intruders away and told them not to come back. Then Scat Ellis and the Hagan boys followed them all the way to the south trace, to see that they behaved themselves. And Thomas puzzled over the beautiful shotgun Coy Dekins had been carrying— a presentation grade Greener double with silver scrolling at its breech and along stock and forestock. Abruptly, he remembered the gun that had been missing from Albert Voigt's gunshop in St. Louis.

"I don't want trouble," Thomas told the blacksmith when they met at the church. "But I don't like to be pushed, and those people are pushing."

"Them yaspers come to my door, I t'ink I shoot 'em, by God," Nilsson swore. "An' 'em chil'ren! You see my elm tree? Gonna lose 'at tree. Some yoker been drive copper nails in it. What kin' hoodlums kill a nice tree?"

A dozen concerned men gathered that morning in the little church, to share stories of the plague of Dekinses and to set a course of action. They were men with visions of a peaceful little town and a bright future, who suddenly found themselves caught up in a war, and they didn't know what to do about it.

"We should arm ourselves better," Ben Wakefield suggested. "From now on, there'll be a shotgun under my counter. I've lost all I can afford to lose."

"I agree," Bliss Ellis nodded, swaying on his crutch. "But that's only a gesture. I can't see us opening fire on women and children. Or even men either, for that matter."

"Or hitting anybody, even if we did," Ben admitted sheepishly.

"Wait'll they start shootin', right here in town," Lester Henry frowned. "Here where your wives and your kids are. You'll think differently when the lead starts flyin'."

"This is all Sim Holly's fault," John Swain declared. "Murderers and blasphemers, every one! Oh Israel, cast not thy lot with the ungodly." He bowed his head, intoning, "Repent . . . lest thou lift up thine eyes unto Heaven! Deuteronomy four-nineteen."

"Oh, Lord," Hannibal Dean growled. "Open the eyes of Balaam!"

"What is that?" the preacher stared at him, startled.

"Book of Numbers, twenty-two-thirty-one," the black-smith said. "Now let's stop quoting scripture and get down to fact. This thing is going to get worse before it gets better. I've seen a feud, once before. It goes like wildfire in dry timber. We need to stop it now."

"It's the Dekinses causing this grief," Jim Creed said. "We might all go out there to the McDowell place and drive them away."

From the doorway, Serenity Creed snapped, "You'll do no such a thing! You've got a family to look after!"

"We're not going to accomplish anything here," Thomas Woodson whispered to Hannibal Dean.

"I reckon not," the blacksmith sighed.

The meeting was interrupted by shouts from outside, and a moment later women scattered from the doorway as Sim Holly appeared there. Like a big, dark cloud he seemed to fill the portal, and his shadow cast a silence upon the little room.

"I've brought a soul for buryin'," he said. "Then I'll want Luke Dekins."

They had come with a mule cart, and in the cart was a body, laid out on green willow boughs and covered over with a fine old peach-pattern quilt, fresh-scrubbed and spotless. Peach-buds, wild roses, and clusters of deep green yaupon with vermilion berries were arranged in the cart to form a sort of bower.

It was Hannibal Dean who stepped forward to raise a corner of the quilt, and he pulled off his hat when he saw the face beneath. "It's Tilda," he murmured. "They've brought Tilda."

At his shoulder, Cozy Kincaid removed his hat and lowered his eyes. She had been a beautiful woman. She was still beautiful now, even with the marks of years and harsh seasons upon her . . . even in death. Her silver hair had been washed and brushed until it lay like a halo around her frail shoulders. It softened and highlighted the pattern of little wrinkles on her cheeks. A bright copper coin lay gently upon each eyelid, but their gleam did nothing to hide the beauty there— the strength, the wisdom and the bittersweet sadness that the little traceries beneath revealed.

"Tilda's gone," Dean murmured, as though he couldn't bring himself to accept the fact of it.

"Who was she?" Thomas asked, quietly.

"The heart of a family," Dean whispered. "She was the soul of the Candlestick clan. She *was* Candlestick . . . a light in the darkness."

"Tilda was Sim's mother," Jim Creed explained. "A truly fine old woman."

Sim Holly stood apart, awkwardly, neither at home nor at ease among these people, but intent on a purpose. There was iron in his greying hair and beard, and tempered steel in the eyes between. "She always said she wanted to rest down here, in the churchyard . . ." he said, "where she could keep an eye on us up yonder . . . an' all those who passed before."

"And not among the strangers," Dean nodded. "She should be at the crest."

"But she never set foot in our church!" John Swain objected. "The Good Lord told us to gather together as— "

Hannibal Dean whirled around, grabbed Swain by his lapels, and lifted him almost off the ground with one big hand. "Shut up, Preacher!" he hissed. "This is no time for sanctimonious fools! We have a saint to bury!"

So Tilda Holly was buried behind the Hays Junction church, in a place of honor among the flock. Nearly a hundred people gathered around, to pay their respects. Afterward, Hannibal spoke for a time with Sim Holly. Then he took Thomas and some of the other men aside. "She was killed by a gunshot," he said. "Sitting on her porch up there, just watching the sun come up, and a man on a gray horse rode in and shot her dead. Like he was just bound to kill somebody and she was the one he saw. Some of the other women saw him though. When Sim and the boys came in, they tracked that horse all the way to Bald Knob before they lost the trail. But they got the man's name. It was Dekins. Luke Dekins."

"I wouldn't want to be him when the Hollys find him," Jim Creed allowed.

"I hope they find him soon," Dean sighed. "A man like that, who'd do a thing like that . . . man like that ain't normal. Little Axe believes some people aren't human, and maybe he's right. A man like Luke Dekins might do most anything, and not care one way or another."

"Maybe it'll just blow over," Serenity Creed said, wistfully. "Can't imagine any of them showin' their faces around here now. Not after this."

They said Luke Dekins had been seen in Jefferson City. They said he had been seen at Westport. They said somebody with a big gray horse had waylaid a coach in the treaty lands and stole a gold shipment. They said he had violated a good woman over at Credence. They said Luke Dekins had a bunch running with him, out around Bald Knob. They said he had left the country and gone to California.

As time passed, the memories made way for other subjects and they didn't say much about Luke Dekins at all.

Dekinses and Hollys showed up around Hays Junction sometimes, the Hollys aloof and remote, the Dekinses furtive and silent. But they were never around at the same time, and the days passed peaceably enough.

It seemed the shocking death of Tilda Holly had washed away all that came before. The valleys bustled with industry now, and the highlands withdrew into themselves, inscrutable and aloof.

It was an odd thing to Thomas Woodson, the way this land sorted itself out. Here valleys converged among ridges and high hills, and in a way each valley seemed to be a fence— or an invisible wall— separating the various clusters of highlands.

And each highland was a little kingdom unto itself. Each was home and hearth to a family, or a cluster of related families— isolated clans shunning one another, as in Medieval times. In the valleys now there were little farms everywhere, roads and trails for produce wagons and a lively commerce with Hays Junction at its hub. But the highlanders took no more part in it than they had to. Candlestick remained Candlestick. Crosstimbers remained Crosstimbers and Spanish Ridge was still Spanish Ridge. The sawtooth breaks south of Hays Junction were more and more Dekins land as earlier drifters moved on and various Dekinses moved into their digs. And this, too, had become a highlands sanctuary.

The Dekinses were newcomers to the region, as were the Hanks and Farley families to the north. But some of the highland clans seemed to have been around forever. Thomas had heard that there were Hollys and Shelbys here when the first land-grant settlers came, and though generations passed, nothing changed. They remained as reclusive as ever, self-sufficient and imbedded in the land like monuments. The hills were their natural element, and they flourished there like the trees of the forest— separate forests on separate slopes, all the same in many ways but always apart.

Good fences make good neighbors, the old land seemed to say. And the fences were the fertile valleys among the hills.

Thomas asked Hannibal Dean about it one time, about how each ridge or mountain came to be like a fortress,

almost as though there were castles there. But the blacksmith had no explanation. He simply shook his head
and said, "Hill people."

Summer in the Ozarks went on in its easy, lazy way,
promising— as summers do— to never end. Then, just
when all the world seemed soothed by its lullaby, it
picked up its skirts, kicked up its heels and crescendoed
its performance with a blaze of color on the hills and a
sweet, sad song on the winds.

Overnight, there was a restless freshness in the air,
crisp edges on the breeze and a hint of chill that warned
of changing seasons.

In recent weeks, Thomas had seen a lot of this country.
Grains were ripening in the fields, and his mill was ready
for their harvest. Day after day he traveled, sometimes
by surrey but usually by saddle, going from farm to farm,
estimating yield, plucking a stalk's grain here and there
to rub off its whiskers, blow away its chaff, see its color
and taste its seed.

Some of the fields were barley and some durum wheat,
but many were of finer wheats, which would make ex-
cellent flour. His valise bulged with delivery schedules,
moisture estimates and penciled notes each time he returned to the rambling little house that was home to him
and Martha and her girls . . . and, it seemed sometimes,
to about half the rutting young bucks in the county. Rachel was nearing her full flower of womanhood, with
Emily not far behind.

Long past moonrise of a crystal evening, as he pulled
off his boots and poured a tot of brandy to ease the kinks
of three days in the saddle, he paused, listening to the
music drifting through the open front window. Out past
the dooryard, Rachel Sinclair sat on the top rail of the
fence while Scat Ellis paraded back and forth before her,
coaxing notes as sweet as new molasses from his old fiddle.

Martha leaned on the window sill, just listening, and Thomas stood beside her, resting his hand on her shoulder.

"He makes that violin sing like an angel," she said.

"I ought to go run him off, for his own good," Thomas mused. "I don't know when that boy sleeps. He works from dawn to wester at his brother's store, then he walks Rachel home from school. Then he works 'til dark on the mill roof, and now here he is, fiddling outside our window."

"He's in love, Thomas," Martha glanced around at him.

"He's too young to be in love! They both are."

Her eyes danced in the moonlight. "There's no such thing as too young. Shame on you, Thomas Paine Woodson! I'd think you of all people would understand that."

"But doesn't he ever get tired? Heaven knows I get tired sometimes."

Her shoulder quivered and he eased her close, wrapping her in his arm against the chill. Then he realized it wasn't a chill, but silent laughter. She raised to tiptoes to brush her cheek against his, almost purring.

Behind them the parlor door opened and candlelight brightened the room. Emily peeked in, said, "Mama, I turned the mattresses and . . . Mama! Hey, Thomas! How was the tour? You should both be ashamed of yourselves, you know."

Martha sighed and turned. "Go to bed, Emily," she said.

The girl giggled. "Old people!" she crooned, closing the door.

"Imp!" Martha huffed, then snuggled against Thomas again. "Where were we?"

"Old," he said.

"Nonsense."

Outside, the music had stopped abruptly. Now Scat

Ellis's face grinned at them across the window sill. "Evening, Mr. Woodson," he said. "Evening, ma'am. I, ah . . . I was just leaving."

"It's about time," Thomas agreed.

Outside somewhere, Rachel's indignant voice said, "Thomas! For shame!"

Martha shook her head and closed the window. "I know secrets about you, Mr. Thomas Woodson," she said.

"And I about you, Mrs. Woodson." He set aside his brandy and took her hand. The moon was high, the night was sweet, and they would sit on the porch for a while.

"You can be quite headstrong and stubborn sometimes," she said.

"So can you."

"You have very little tolerance for deception."

"Nor do you, and it *is* a waste of time."

"I know you don't care for peaches."

"And I know you don't favor strawberries."

Her hand in his was warm as they sat themselves in their rocking chairs, side by side. "I know another secret, too."

"Oh? And what might that be?"

"We'll need to add a bit of space to this house soon," she said. "You have been a good father to my girls, Thomas . . . to *our* girls. But it seems we aren't so old as they believe, you and I, because in the spring they will have a little brother or sister to deal with."

In a snug little cabin on the slope above the Wakefield-Ellis store, Kititsi and K'kyo slept. But Dekagathe could not sleep. Wrapped in warm wolf hides he crouched outside the low doorway, a shadow among shadows.

He had thought it was a sound that awakened him,

but now there was no unusual sound in the quiet valley. There had been distant music— the haunting strains of Scat's fiddle in over by the mill, but that was silent now and only the ordinary sounds of night came on the cool breeze. In the hills a red wolf cried for its mate. Lonesome pines whispered on the slopes, and somewhere a flight of geese squabbled among themselves as they winged southward, a ghostly vee of travelers between the bright moon and the dark hills.

Nearby, grazing mules sniffed and pawed, and hoofs shuffled on stony ground in the compounds. A dog barked at shadows and another, somewhere else, responded. Up the road, light footsteps on gravel said Scat Ellis was walking home.

Normal sounds, comforting sounds— it was not these that had awakened Little Axe. It wasn't a sound at all, he realized, but some other sense that disturbed him. Rising to his feet he stepped into the moonlight and turned slowly, full around, head up and nostrils twitching. He found nothing to catch his attention, but still the feeling lingered, an uneasiness that would not go away.

Something was out of place, he felt. Something was wrong. As subtly as premonition, the hills spoke to him, and Little Axe listened. Out there somewhere was a darkness within the darkness, shadows that were more than shadows.

Something in those hills was not normal. Something distorted prowled there— something that should have been human but was not. It prowled the hills, and it watched the valleys below.

XV

A Blending of Spirits

At more than forty feet from foundation to roof peak, with a pair of twelve-foot bins atop that, Woodson's millhouse was not the biggest structure in these parts but it was easily the tallest. Like a skinny tower of stone and timber, it stood above the bank of High Creek like a sentinel with two hats.

The building itself, though sound as a good barn, was nothing more than braced walls, rafters, and a roof, enclosing a series of ladders and platforms. It was a housing, a container for the mill itself, which occupied every level from the roof down to the big, wooden mill-wheel turning lazily to the flow of High Creek. Within the walls were an entire series of mechanisms powered by the turning wheel.

Pulleys and drive wheels were set on stone-braced butts at each of four platform levels, and a relay of belts—heavy, forty-gage canvas strips nearly a quarter-inch thick, edge-seamed and impregnated with tar— ran from the waterwheel's inset hub upward, connecting each level to the next. The running belts turned the drive shafts for the "breakers" beneath the roof— the main grinding stones of the operation— and those of the bran sifters, purifiers, and middling and tailing breakers below.

At the main floor— ground level at the slope's high side— were big chutes and hoppers to collect the ground flour.

"We grind eight times to the batch," Thomas Woodson recited to a group of local men as he led them on a precarious journey upward, along spidery rough-timber platforms, catwalks, and ladders. "The graded grain is cleaned in the wind-shed out back," he paused to point through a narrow window at the wide roof of the shed below. "That's to remove stones, chaff, and dust. Then the clean grain is carried up to the drop-bins on those conveyors. We use mule-power for that."

He scooted up a ladder, with men scrambling after him. "The bins are up there, above those big chutes. The chutes drop the grain onto those troughs over there," he pointed vaguely upward and men squinted to see what he was pointing at. To most of them, the whole thing was no more than a fantastic maze of timber uprights, ominous-looking enclosures and tilted panels. The air in the place was heavy with the sweet scent of fresh-ground grain.

"That belt there," Thomas pointed at a mystifying snakework of moving fabrics, "turns sweepers in the troughs, and they drop the grain through slots into the mill. Those levers control the size of the slots. And that," he indicated a large thing that resembled a little, round house suspended within the building, "is the heart of the mill, the main breakers. In there are two corrugated stones— fourteen groves to the inch— one above the other. The top one turns and breaks the grain against the bottom one. The clearance can be adjusted down to four one-thousandths of an inch at this stage."

"Good enough for cornmeal," Jim Creed noted.

"But not for wheat flour." Thomas pointed past the platform rail. "The first meal goes into that first sifter just below. About half the bran is removed at that point.

Then what's left goes back up to the mill and we grind it again, into that second sifter. That removes most of the remaining bran— about ninety percent in all. Then we do it all again. The third grinding and sifting gives us meal that's ready for the purifiers . . . we passed them coming up. The purifiers are like big sieves. They separate the flour into sizings, middlings— that's where the wheat germ is, at that stage— and what's called 'chunks.' All but the chunks go into little box-mills down below, for finer grinding and more sifting. The chunks go back through with the next fresh grind."

"When does it get to be flour?" Lester Henry prodded, impatient with the laborious details. "When will it bake bread?"

"It's flour as soon as it gets to the hoppers," Thomas said. "But it won't bake very good bread at that point. It still needs to mature for a while." Noting Lester Henry's scowl, he grinned. "It's good for other things though."

With a grandiose gesture, like a magician in a circus, Thomas stepped to the rail and tugged at a little rope. Somewhere below, a little bell jingled. He waited a moment, then selected another vertical rope and began pulling it downward, hand over hand. In the rafters overhead a pulley rattled, and the rope quivered as it ran. A moment passed, then a large wicker basket rose into view beside the rail. Thomas tied off his rope, loosed the basket from its hook, and turned, pulling back the cloth that covered it. Inside was a mound of freshly baked biscuits, still steaming from the oven.

Thank you, ladies, Thomas thought as the sunlight through high windows caught the golden-brown crusts of the little loaves. Martha was a hand at biscuits, and was teaching her art to the girls.

He set the hot basket on a bench, opened a wall cupboard beside the window and set out fresh butter and a pot of golden honey. "Help yourselves, gentlemen," he said. "The flour in those biscuits was wheat grain in Ned Butler's wagon two days ago."

"Hot dang," Lester Henry muttered, his whiskered cheeks round with biscuit, "Them is tasty!"

"A bit of saleratas from Soda Springs," Thomas grinned, "a touch of white salt from French Lick and some skim milk from Mabel Worley's jersey cow. The rest is *Woodson's Best Flour*." He helped himself to a biscuit and honey. "We thought you all might like to see how the mill works."

For a while they stood around on the high platform, a motley little crowd of rough men gawking at the contrivances around them, gazing from the high windows and stuffing themselves with biscuits.

Outside, the air was crisp, but here beneath the roof of the busy mill, with mid-morning sun on the split-cedar shingles and the glass panes, it was warm and cozy. From the east windows all of Hays Junction was visible: brisk traffic on the main road, people coming and going about their daily business, children pouring out of their classroom for a brief recess, Gus Nilsson out in his yard fussing around his elm tree. Somehow he had nursed it through its copper nail crisis, and it was doing fine. Half a dozen new buildings were going up along the street, one of which would be the Wakefield and Ellis store. Another would be a rooming house, the little four-square structure across from the church was the new school, and the square stone building just past Dean's smithy—though it was nothing now but some walls, a roof and a Bell & Sutherland steel safe—would soon be Lester Henry's new bank.

Moving along the road were mule teams, wagons and here and there a horse and rider. Traffic rolled also on the wagon roads winding away in all directions. On the near slopes were dozens of houses, some of them still greenbark-new. Their rooftops were bright patterns among the solemn pines and the brilliant reds and yellows of fall hardwoods.

Out on the east road a coach was approaching— the occasional mail run from Jefferson City. It occurred to Thomas that it was months now since he had seen a "visitor" flag on Lester's pole. With all the traffic nowadays, it was no longer a momentous occasion when somebody came up the road. The road now was busy most of the time.

The region was growing like weeds, and Hays Junction had almost overnight become a noticeable town.

And where there was commerce, there was money. Every man standing on this platform with him now had, in recent months, seen more cash and coin than in years before. Generally they shunned the paper scrip so often issued by big banks and investment cartels in the east. Such "wildcat currency," in the opinion of most people west of Philadelphia, was not money at all. It was nothing but premature promissory notes issued by someone they didn't know against money they didn't intend to lend and would probably never see again if they did. But there was plenty of real money around nowadays— good silver coin and now and then some gold.

The new mill, along with the latest explosion of westerers from the crowded places back east, had started a financial ripple in Hays Junction that had become a wave. It was like a snowball rolling down a hill. The further it went the bigger it got, and the bigger it was, the faster it grew.

"I believe you've got yourself some converts here, Thomas," Hannibal Dean said now, wiping honey from his whiskers. "This sure enough is a flour mill. If there were doubters among us, there are none now. But there's no such a thing as free breakfast, and we all know it. So tell us what you want."

"Wagons, teams, and drivers," Thomas stated. "And some big silos. The wheat's coming in, by the hundreds of bushels, and thousands more being harvested right this minute. We're buying it for cash on the bushel, but we can't grind it as fast as we get it. High Creek flows open ten months out of the year. With silos we can grade and clean, then store the grain and grind it as we're ready. But I need three times the rolling stock my partner can send out, to get the flour to Jefferson City. We'll use keels from there to the market at St. Louis."

"Wagons and teams don't come cheap," Lester Henry pointed out shrewdly. "Silos are expensive to build, and teamsters draw wages. It all costs money."

Thomas turned to him, fixed him with a knowing gaze and played his ace. "So what do you think we're making here, Lester? Biscuits? Mr. Champon and I are offering shares in this enterprise."

Beneath a limestone ledge under Copperhead Bluff, Luke Dekins sucked on a greasy bone and gazed thoughtfully out across the merging valleys. Behind him, faint scufflings said the kid was making for the fire again, but Luke ignored him. He'd had all he wanted to eat, and the kid could have the leavings.

In the hills beyond the bluff, a half-dozen little slap-up spreads now were Dekins places. Most of the kin had a way of finding a place and moving in on it, and pretty quick it was theirs. Like ticks on a hound dog, they just dug in and stuck, and took what the Good Lord sent their way. Many was the time Luke had heard old Coy say, "The meek shall inherit the earth."

They called Luke wild, because he had no time for such foolishness. "All things come to he who waits," Papa Coy said. But Luke had found that the Good Lord generally didn't shake a leg to get that done. God was quicker to provide for a man if he didn't mind taking matters into his own hands.

So far, the Good Lord had treated Luke Dekins just fine. He took what he wanted, and went where he pleased, and if anybody got in his way he put lead into them. Sometimes he even killed just for the fun of it, but that was mostly just niggers and Injuns and such, that a man could kill with no more thought than gut-shooting a stray dog. What a man had to be a little careful about was if he took a notion to kill livestock or white folks. That old woman he'd killed had set off such a ruckus that he'd had to stay scarce around these parts for quite a while. Even now he knew there were Hollys just itching to find him. Everyplace he turned, seemed like, some of that bunch wasn't far behind. And they kept poking around, asking about him. They even had likenesses of him tacked up on call boards around Jefferson City.

His little eyes glinted with mirth. That's how a man gets known, he told himself. Them Hollys are making old Luke Dekins a famous man.

The kid was at the fire now, scrabbling for bits of food Luke had missed or thrown aside. Luke glanced around just to see him jerk away, then went back to watching the valleys.

When the kid came along, Luke hadn't meant to bother with him. But now he allowed it was just as well he'd let him tag along. Harley had been useful a few times. Kid like that could go right into a settlement and poke around— sort of get the lay of the land— and people generally paid him no mind. He was just a kid. But then, with what he learned, Luke could ride right in and take what he wanted, light a shuck before hardly anybody knew what was happening.

All things considered, so far Harley was more use to him than he was a nuisance. And happen the kid had notions about catching his dear old uncle off guard some day and slitting his throat for him, for what he had, then the kid would have a hard lesson coming to him. Luke Dekins wasn't born yesterday.

Lot of busy folks down there, he noticed. Last time he'd seen it, Hays Junction wasn't but a slap-up little place where roads met. But now it just plain smelled like money. There was that tall, skinny building over on the creek, that hadn't been there before. Mill of some kind, he judged. And there were other new buildings, too.

Metal scraped against rock and Luke swung around. The kid had that old rifle again, and was scuttling back away from him, dragging it.

"What the blazes do you think you're doin'?" Luke snapped.

The kid stared at him, his eyes narrow and frightened. "Jus' . . . jus' thought I'd clean it," Harley said. "It's got rust on it."

Without rising, Luke shifted his weight for balance. His hand poised near the big knife at his hip. "Put it down," he purred.

"I can clean it if I want to," Harley glared at him. "It's mine!"

Luke chuckled, deep in his chest. "Yours? Did I say it was yours? Now put it down, before I decide to skin your hide off of you."

Harley turned the rifle and pointed it at his uncle's chest. In a panic he struggled to pull back the big hammer, and Luke's hand shot out, wrenched the gun from the boy's grip, and threw it against the rocks to one side. In the same motion he reversed his swing and cuffed Harley across the side of his head. The boy flipped over backward, lay sprawled against the rough ledge for a moment, then scooted out of reach. There was a bloody abrasion across his cheek and his nose was bleeding.

Luke drew his knife, fingered its razor edge, then put

it away again. "Clean your damn face," he ordered. "You're goin' down yonder to scout out that place. I want to know where they stash the money."

The mail coach from Jefferson City was an old slab-top army ambulance, refitted with six-inch oak axles and ten-slat hubs for rough country. The big, iron-shod wheels were nearly twice the diameter of the rims that had originally carried the rig. It looked for all the world like a stubby coffin on wheels. Four mules in trace, a driver, and a guard completed the United States Government's commitment to civilized communication in these hills.

Ben Wakefield had become postmaster at Hays Junction, by virtue of his keeping the post office in his end of the Wakefield and Ellis store. Thomas went there on this bright day to meet the mail.

There was the usual packet from Louis Champon—invoices, accountings, and information on sales and shipment agreements, along with a chatty letter in the Frenchman's usual florid style.

Champon's life, it appeared, had become quite humdrum of late. All of his investments and— as he put it— "divested interests" were pretty much running themselves these days. It left him very little to occupy his days, and he was certain he could sense senility creeping up on him. But he was undertaking to remedy all of that. He had agreed to stake a brigade of young adventurers who planned to follow Lewis and Clark's trail through the Nebraska Territory as far as the sand hills, then turn south and explore the Dismal River, in search of minerals. Part of his agreement with the explorers was that he would go along personally.

He bragged about his predictions regarding the fur trade, which was now in general decline. The blame for this, he assured Thomas, lay primarily with the ruling family of Austria and their slavish sycophants in Paris, and with John Jacob Astor, who should have seen the age of the silk hat coming.

He enclosed a clipping from the New Orleans *Picayune*, describing General Sam Houston's brilliant victory over General Santa Anna on the banks of the San Jacinto River in Texas. Texas had promptly declared itself a sovereign republic and Houston was in charge. In Champon's opinion, this meant that Andrew Jackson's party was in charge, though neither Texans nor Americans were ready to admit that openly.

There was no word from Jack Christy, but Thomas expected none. Christy could write as well as the next man of his time, but it had probably never occurred to him— ever in all his life— to write a letter to anyone.

Thomas was just putting his mail into his valise when Scat Ellis came around the corner of the store. "There's geese in Mr. Overmeyer's stubble," the youth said, excitedly. "Would you like to come along?"

Thomas hesitated for only a moment. He didn't have a scattergun, so he rarely hunted birds. But geese in a field were rifle game. And Martha and the girls might like a goose to bake in their new oven.

"I'll take this home and get down Lady Justice," he said. "Meet you on the ridge road in a little bit."

The ancient one lay beside a trickling spring on a hillside, sheltered by spreading arbor vines that he could not see. His eyes, which had seen far too much but not nearly enough in almost a hundred years of life, now saw nothing at all. They had failed him finally, just as everything else of this life was failing now.

Little Axe found him there, and at first he thought he was dead. But when he knelt beside him the old one stirred, and gazed up at him with sightless eyes. "Pasco-tateh," he said, his voice as faint and dry as wind in the pines. Long, thin hair like spider silk was a shimmering halo against the dark moss beneath his head, and his beardless old face was a maze of deep clefts and wrinkles, as brown as worn saddle leather. A century of suns had touched that face, and a century of living had left its tracks there.

"I am Dekagathe," Little Axe said. "Pascotateh died a long time ago."

As though he had not spoken, the blind eyes gazed at him and past him. "You always followed Tecumseh, Pas-cotateh," the ancient whispered. "You were always his strong arm. I am glad you follow him still."

Little Axe cupped water in his hand and let the old man sip it through his fingers. The old lips took the moisture eagerly, and when Little Axe moved his hand the old head turned to follow it. Again Little Axe cupped water, and again the old one drank. But only a little. Just that effort seemed to exhaust him. He relaxed, fight-ing for a few shallow breaths.

Dekagathe's eyes told him that the old one had come down the hillside, blind and lost, and had fallen here by this tiny spring. The emaciated old body said that he had wandered a long time through these hills, blind and helpless, starving.

He opened the old lips with gentle fingers and saw only a few teeth. He found a bit of pemmican in his pouch and put it in his own mouth, chewing it until it was a mush. Then he pressed his lips against the old one's and fed him the morsel.

The old jaws worked slowly, but finally the ancient swallowed the food. Little Axe gave him a few more sips of water, then sat back and waited. The old man was dying, and he had done all he could do.

Long minutes passed, then the blind eyes opened

again and the man's frail hand crept about until it rested on Little Axe's knee. "Who are you?" the ancient voice husked.

"Dekagathe," Little Axe said.

"Dekagathe," the old one repeated. "And Pascotateh. Both. Two spirits together, but not one. Dekagathe still lives."

"I found you here," Little Axe said. "Who are you?"

"Many Names," the whisper hesitated. "I am called Many Names. I am . . . medicine walker. I go to all the people. Everywhere."

"You are a pipe-bearer?" Awe flooded Little Axe. He had heard of the pipe-bearers— men of no tribe, yet all tribes, men who went from place to place and tribe to tribe, without fear because they were held in the highest respect by all. "You carry the great medicine."

"I carry . . ." the old hand moved this way and that, searching. Little Axe glanced about and found an ornamented pouch— a long, thin sheath of the finest doeskin. He lifted it, feeling deeply awed as he placed it into the old hand before him. The pipe within was holy.

Many Names clutched the pouch, and pressed it to his breast. "Very old," he whispered. "It was made in the moon when I was born. I have carried it since I became a man." He paused for a long time, barely breathing, then said, "Nicolet smoked this pipe. And Junaluska and Madricot and Vovoke, and Diwali of the Cherokee . . . Mandansai of the Mandan . . . Tamenot of the Delaware . . . Quicoy of the Pawnee . . . Coto'tsi of the Muskogi . . . Tecumseh of the Shawnee . . . Saskatwa of the Dakota . . . I knew them all. To each of them I handed the pipe in peace, and from each I received peace. I knew them when they lived. Now I know their spirits. Soon I will be with them, like the water joins the water . . ."

The blind eyes fluttered, closed, and the old voice

faded, and Little Axe bowed his head. Yet when he placed his ear against the skeletal old chest, a heart still beat there.

Nearly an hour passed, as Little Axe knelt by the medicine-carrier. When Many Names stirred again, he offered water, but the old man ignored it. "See the water, how it flows," he said.

Little Axe looked at the tiny stream, barely a trickle of clear water coming from the rocks to etch a little rivulet down the hill, toward the creek below.

"Each person is the water," Many Names said. "Each is born, and leaves his track as he goes. Each follows his own course in life. Then the stream joins other streams to make deeper tracks. The water below, is it the same water as this?"

"It is the same," Little Axe said. "But more, because it is many streams together."

"The water is the spirit," Many Names breathed. "It goes with each man while he lives, then goes on after he dies. The stream's water is part of all the water in the creek. The creek's water is part of the river. The waters mix and blend and become one water . . . when the spirit allows it to happen. But some that are in the river still are separate water. That's because they aren't through yet."

"Through with what?" Little Axe asked, enthralled.

"They know," the old man whispered. "They know. Why does Pascotateh stay with you, Dekagathe? Maybe Tecumseh still needs Pascotateh. Then why does Tecumseh not become one with the river?"

"Tecumseh died," Little Axe said. "Is his spirit here?"

"Near," Many Names began to cough, each spasm shaking him as a wind shakes a bough. "He still has something to do." With an effort he stifled the coughing. Now there was blood at his lips. "The medicine," he whispered. "The medicine should live."

"Where were you going?" Little Axe asked, trying to ease the ancient's head on the mossy stones.

"To the Osage," Many Names struggled with the sound. "The Osage need the medicine now. . . ."

As quickly as that he was gone, like a candle flame snuffed by a passing breeze. The heart that had beat for a hundred years beat no longer.

Little Axe covered the body with his own blanket, and swept leaves and twigs over it to hide it. Many Names would have wanted no more. He was part of the land now, and his spirit had joined the river, flowing away.

For a long time Little Axe stood there, deep in thought. When he left, he took the medicine pipe with him.

XVI

Judgment Day

Shadows lay long on the slopes when Thomas and Scat topped the "Tween-crik" ridge and headed down the road toward town, two men with long guns, and an old dog. Between them the men carried five good geese from the stubble fields to the west. Three of them would be for June and Polly and their families, and two for Martha and the girls. Though he hadn't said so, Thomas knew which table Scat intended to grace with his appetite when the time came. As always these days, wherever Rachel was, that was where Scat Ellis wanted to be.

"Ben has sent off for a piano," Scat chatted as the mill rose beside the road ahead, and the little town beyond. "He's gonna put a price on it, but 'til it sells he says I can practice on it."

"Like to see you play a piano and a fiddle at the same time," Thomas said drily.

"Oh, I got some plans," the youth assured him. "If I can learn some tunes on the piano, and make it sound good, I expect Newt Avery'll be after his pa to buy it for him. He likes tunes, too."

"So you're finagling yourself a band?" Thomas asked.

"Not 'specially," Scat admitted. "It's just that if Newt gets all caught up tryin' to learn how pianos work, that'll keep him busy for a while. He's a bother to have around, when I'm tryin' to talk with Miss Rachel.''

Thomas suppressed the chuckle that tugged at his gut. He doubted that it was a good idea for him to have any opinions regarding Rachel's suitors, but he did admire the devilish cunning that Scat displayed in his quest for the fair miss. If the kid didn't wind up with the grand prize, it wouldn't be for lack of trying.

They were almost at the Woodson house when the object of Scat's adoration stepped out onto the porch and waved at them. A moment later Rachel was coming to meet them, with Emily close behind.

Scat grinned, hoisted a pair of dangling geese over his head, and the girls both paused in mock amazement. Then Rachel clapped her hands in approval, and they came on, aiming to meet the hunters at the gate.

Abruptly, all of them slowed their pace. All eyes turned toward the town, as a gunshot rang out there, echoing from the hillsides. From the road above the mill, all looked ordinary enough below. But atop the mill a man working the bins yelled and pointed, toward town. He waved his arms frantically, and pointed again.

"What's he saying?'' Scat demanded. Thomas cupped his hands to shout at the approaching girls, "Get back! Go back inside!'' But more shots echoed up from the lower road, drowning his words. In the distance, people were shouting.

Then they heard running hooves, and a rider appeared below, coming up the road, gravel flying as he came. He wore a flat-crowned tan hat and a whipping long-coat, and his horse was a big, deep-chested gray racer. Almost as they spotted him, he was at Woodson's rail fence, rounding the corner of it. At sight of the girls just inside the gate he hauled back on his reins so hard that his horse screamed and pawed air, skidding on its rear hooves.

Running now, with the old dog yapping after them, Thomas and Scat were near enough to hear the man's words. "Well, now!" he drawled, a grin spreading across his stubbled cheeks. "Now that's a real pretty sight! You, honey!" he pointed an imperious finger at Rachel, "Get your sweet self on over here so ol' Luke can see you better."

Rachel's hands went to her mouth and she backed up a step. Emily said, "Rachel! Let's go in the house!"

Shocked at the man's rough manner and tone, Scat Ellis dropped his geese and waved his scattergun, still hurrying toward him. "Hey, you!" he shouted. "You just cut out that kind of talk! Those young ladies are . . ."

Lazily the rider glanced around, raised the barrel of his rifle and fired. Scat Ellis grunted, flailed backward for balance and sat down on the road. For an instant Thomas felt frozen. A sound long forgotten came back to him now, with sickening clarity as he heard it again . . . the sound of a lead ball striking human flesh.

Scat . . . suddenly frenzied, Thomas dropped his geese and swung Lady Justice around. For an instant her muzzle was pointed at the rider, then it was knocked aside as the man drove cruel spurs into his horse's flanks. The horse bowled Thomas aside and swept past, swinging to the left at the crest of the ridge. An instant later it was gone, hidden by the terrain. But even as Thomas got to his feet, raising Lady Justice for a quick shot, a ball sang past his ear. Up on the rise, some distance away, a little cloud of smoke billowed for a moment, and the crack of a rifle resounded through the hills.

The shooter was higher up, and back to the east, of the little crest where the rider had gone. There was another one up there then!

Voices came from down the road. A dozen or more townsmen were coming up the rise at a run. Thomas scurried to where Scat Ellis still sat spread-legged on the road, and bent over him. Scat looked up at him with stunned, empty eyes, and drew his hand from inside his coat. It was covered with blood.

With a glance up the hill, where the rifle fire had come from, Thomas dropped Lady Justice, grabbed Scat under his arms and dragged him backward off the road and through the gate. Then there were others all around— Rachel and Emily, gasping at sight of the bright blood, and the townsmen, pouring in through the gate. Strong hands lifted the boy and carried him at a run to the house. Martha met them outside, took one look, and pointed. "Inside," she said. "Put him on the table. Rachel, you and . . . Rachel! Emily! See to the lamps and bring water! Quickly!"

The men seemed to be all talking at once. "Luke Dekins," someone said. "Couldn't be anybody else." "Rode right into town brash as you please," another was saying. "Went straight for the bank." "I saw him shoot Lester," another voice cut in. "Did anybody look at Lester? Is he . . . ?" "Didn't get anything, though," someone noted. "Seemed like he didn't know about that safe. But it was all so quick . . ."

Thomas sagged against a wall, trying to sort it out while he gasped for breath. Somebody had shot Scat! And Lester . . . Lester Henry was shot too, they said.

Luke Dekins, they said. The man on the gray horse could have been a Dekins, all right. He had the look about him.

Ben Wakefield rapped his knuckles at the open door, then came in, panting. "He won't go very far," he announced. "His horse is over there on the ridge. It's dead." He spotted Thomas Woodson and handed Lady Justice to him. "Guess you hit it with that snap-shot."

They were doing things to Scat Ellis, over on the table. Men were crowded around there, holding up lamps, and Thomas saw Bliss Ellis hovering around, pasty-faced.

Martha's voice rose in the crowd, "If you don't have something to do here, stand back! Give us some air."

The crowd eased back, except those holding lamps. Martha was beside Scat, her busy hands covered with blood, and Rachel was just across from her, leaning over the boy, cupping his head in small, gentle hands. Each time Scat twitched or moaned, Rachel was right there to comfort him.

Hannibal Dean brought a bright little blade from the hearth . . . a knife of his own craft. "Use this, Martha," he said. "It's hot."

Then there were other women there, crowding the men back from the table. They wouldn't be bringing Lester Henry up for tending, they announced. He was dead. And so was Pastor Swain. They'd found him over at the graveyard. It looked as though the outlaw had been there, and Swain found him. The preacher had died without a sound, his throat laid open.

Cozy Kincaid stamped back and forth a few times, fuming, then picked up his old, converted musket. "Let's go find that son of a bitch," he rasped. A moment later most of the men were gone, headed for Thomas's gate and the slope beyond.

Thomas sat on a bench, turning Lady Justice over in his hands as though she might speak to him. His fidgeting fingers released the catch on the patch box and he glanced inside. There was the little brass-and-steel tool Albert Voigt had made, the twin of the one Thomas carried in his pouch. Beneath it, beadwork gleamed darkly, and he lifted the old Indian talisman from its hiding place, gazed at it, and slipped its thong around his neck.

I've had this thing as long as I can remember, he chided himself, and I don't even know what it is. Nevertheless, it felt comfortable dangling at his breast. As though it had always been there.

With a grunt he stood, opened his belt pouch and found a cleaning jag, a tin of soap water, and swabs. Working deliberately, his eyes gazing out through the open door at the rugged slopes beyond the road, he cleaned and greased Lady Justice . . . just as he had so many years before, for Salem Cadmont.

When the rifle was ready, he set a cap on its nipple, stepped outside, held its muzzle an inch from a rose leaf, and popped the cap. The leaf fluttered. The rifle's firing-path was clear. He removed the spent cap and set the rifle upright on its curved brass butt. Then he measured out sixty grains-weight of black powder and poured it down the barrel.

He spread spit-damp patch cloth over the muzzle, set a cast ball on top of it and set it in the barrel with his starter. With a razor-sharp patch knife he trimmed away the excess fabric, then set his ramrod and rammed the load down to the breech. He returned the ramrod to its ferrules beneath the long barrel, raised the gun and put a fresh cap under its hammer.

From inside, he heard Martha's voice: "There! It was lodged under his shoulder. He might have a broken rib, but it didn't get to his lungs."

And Rachel's voice was a constant, reassuring murmur, like a lullaby. She kept talking to Scat, easing him through his pain, reassuring him. But she didn't call him Scat, now. She called him Sidney.

Thomas secured his pouch, hefted Lady Justice, and gazed up the darkening slopes. Up there was Tween-crik Ridge. Beyond and above it rose the rugged mass of the mountain that folks called Old Sky. Evening shadows crept up the slopes, herded by the push of nightfall in the valleys. Off to the east, a full moon was rising over Candlestick.

As though no time had passed, the wilderness years came alive in Thomas Woodson's mind—all those seasons so long ago, when Jack had been with him, guiding a boy in becoming a man, teaching him what he knew about the kind of country he understood.

"More Injun than ary Injun," some long-ago Kentuckian had said of Jack Christy. "Man don't just get by in the wild woods, he *wears* 'em like they was his second skin." As easily now as though they were his own, Thomas saw these Ozark lands as Jack Christy would see them . . . and the land told him what he wanted to know. Luke Dekins was up there. The man who shot Scat had gone to ground in the high-up hills, and Thomas knew where he was.

There was no hurry, just yet. Thomas took off his heavy boots and pulled on thick-soled hightop moccasins. He turned, and Emily was there, watching him. "You're going after that man, aren't you, Thomas?" she whispered.

"I have to," he said.

"Mama said you would. But she doesn't want to see you go, and anyway she's busy with Scat. She says he'll mend, though it may take a while."

Thomas took a deep breath and let it out slowly. Scat would live. Rachel would have the young man she had chosen . . . that gangly kid who made such plans and such music, and who didn't even know yet that his angel had picked him out.

"Mama says be careful, Thomas," Emily said. "She wants you to come back. We all do."

When the moon was high—a traveler's moon, the Kaintucks had called it—Thomas slipped away from the house and out the gate.

The other Hays Junction men would be back soon. The trail they were on led nowhere. Afoot, Luke Dekins would know they'd be after him. He would send them off on a blind chase, while he dug in to rest. They wouldn't find Luke Dekins and that was just as well. If they had, some of them would be dead.

Still, the man must be found. He was a rogue, a thing run amok. He was an outlaw and a merciless killer, a lurking menace as real as a rabid dog running loose among innocents. There was the ring of truth in the stories they told about Luke Dekins. Thomas had seen the frail old Holly woman, Miss Tilda, when they brought her body down from Candlestick. He had heard the grief in Hannibal Dean's voice— in the voices of all those who knew her alive. And now Scat Ellis lay bleeding . . . young Scat whose greatest sin was an occasional sour chord on his fiddle.

Voices drifted from the house, and Thomas's throat went tight. Beyond that fragile door was everything that mattered in his world— Martha and the baby growing in her womb . . . all his hopes and dreams, the people he cared about, and the life he had won.

A mad dog can't be tolerated, he told himself. While it runs free, nobody is safe. Luke Dekins must be found and Thomas knew how to find him. The lay of the land— as Jack Christy had taught him to see it— told him where the outlaw must be. And something else— an instinct too strong to ignore, an instinct that was like a voice whispering to him— told him he was right.

A half mile from town, in the rising forest, he abruptly was no longer alone. Thomas hadn't seen him come, but now Little Axe was there, moving with him up the rugged slope.

It was as though he had always been there. On impulse, Thomas raised a hand to touch the old Indian talisman dangling beneath his shirt. Then he went on, and Little Axe was a savage shadow at his side, gliding soundlessly among brush and deadfall, nearly invisible in the forest's patterned moonlight except as he moved.

Thomas set an easy, climbing pace. Though Luke

Dekins was nearby in straight distance, there were no straight distances in these hills. It would take hours to get where they were going.

At first dawn on the mountain, Luke Dekins saw his pursuer. For a moment he had a clear view of him below— a tall, angular man carrying a delicately ornamented rifle. But before he could act, the man was out of sight behind an outcrop. With a curse, Luke found a new vantage point and cocked his rifle. The man had to reappear, and Luke could see where he would come out, less than a hundred yards away. From here he would have a clear, easy shot.

Harley was in back of him, somewhere, higher up the mountain. The kid had that old rifle of his, and was staying out of sight. You better hide good, Luke thought, because when I catch you we're going to talk about that bank building and why you didn't know they had a damned safe.

Maybe I'll cut a notch in one of his ears, Luke told himself. That ought to teach him to pay attention.

But the kid could wait. Luke had his dander up now. He didn't like coming out of a place empty-handed. It made him mad. It made him want to kill folks. The one coming toward him now, just past those rocks, he was one of them from down there. He was the one who'd killed Luke's horse— that flour miller, Woodson. Luke needed that horse, and losing it made him furious. He needed to see some folks die and Woodson would do for starters.

Like a duck in a rain-barrel, he thought, sighting along his rifle. The miller had gone behind the rocks just yonder. He had to come out . . . right . . . *there*. Luke eased back his set trigger and laid his finger on the firing trigger, light as a breath. It was a hair trigger. It needed only a touch.

A minute passed, and Luke growled and shifted his shoulders. They were beginning to ache. What was the bastard doing back of those rocks, taking a piss? Luke squared himself again, elbows on the stony ledge, and realigned his sights . . . and froze in place as a deep voice directly behind him said, "Bad guess, Dekins. Lay the rifle down."

Luke hesitated only an instant, then he rolled, swung his rifle down, and fired. Even before the echoes came he was over the edge, among rockfall, scurrying for cover. Then behind him he heard the sound of a man falling. "Got him!" he breathed. The echoes of his shot faded, and there was silence on the mountain. Luke waited a dozen heartbeats, just listening, not moving a hair. Then he picked up his rifle, trudged upslope to the little ledge and climbed over it, peering ahead.

There was no one there. Luke stood for a moment, astonished, then turned full circle, crouching, peering into the brushy shadows. Nothing. "God damn it!" he muttered. "I killed him. Where is he?"

Slowly it dawned on him that he had been out-slicked. The damned miller had foxed him. Here he stood, in plain sight, with a spent rifle, and somewhere the man was looking at him right this minute . . . somewhere near, and Woodson's rifle was still loaded.

With a curse, Luke ducked down, his eyes darting around from shadow to shadow. He raised his rifle, reaching for its ramrod, and it seemed to explode in his hands. A ball smashed into its side plate, driving the iron against its delicate housing, and the rifle broke apart, showering Luke with stinging splinters. He jumped back, fell over a broken stump, scrambled to his feet and ran. Blind with fear, he crashed through a thorn thicket, bounced off a cedar, fell and rolled downhill until a standing boulder stopped him.

Woodson was right behind him. Luke heard stones rattle as pacing moccasins dislodged them. "Let me alone!" he screamed, and ran again, angling down the slope. He fought through a thicket, scrambled over a flint outcrop and plunged into a stand of scrub oak. Deep gashes on his knees and his back soaked his clothing and left a trail of crimson drops. He was bleeding from a hundred scrapes and stone cuts, but none of that mattered. He had to get away! The miller was right behind, and it seemed that nothing Luke did could shake him. In desperation, he turned and drew his knife, but there was no one there. Yet somewhere close— so near that he would swear he could hear the hardwood brushing against the steel— there was the sound of a fresh load being thumped home in a long rifle.

Gibbering with panic, Luke whirled this way and that, then ran again, bounding down a long slope to burst into a little clearing . . . and then there was nowhere else to go. There were men there— tall, bearded men with long, dark rifles that seemed as natural to them as the fingers on their hands.

With his boys keeping good sight on the bleeding, whimpering scarecrow before him, Sim Holly stepped forward and nodded. "Luke Dekins," he said, "we have business with you. Time's come to settle up."

Thomas had never expected the man to move so fast. Luke Dekins had been down on his belly on a little ledge, with his rifle aimed at a cleft in the rocks across the draw. Thomas was behind him, and the situation was well in hand. In the next instant though, the outlaw had flipped around and his rifle was spitting fire.

Instinct had thrown Thomas aside as the ball sang

past, but his foot had slipped. Next thing he knew he
had been flat on his back in a cedar break, with Dekins
coming to find him. Calling on everything Jack Sinclair
ever taught him, Thomas snaked himself into cover, then
changed his direction and climbed.

When Dekins crouched on the outcrop, turning this
way and that in his search, Thomas had been only thirty
feet away, shielded by nothing more than a droop of
grapeweed fronds. Hide where nobody thinks about
hidin', Jack had told him once. That way nobody'll think
of lookin' there.

When Dekins reached for his ramrod, everything of
Jack Christy in him said shoot the man. But some other
part of him didn't want to kill a man if he didn't have
to, and at the last instant— as he touched Lady Justice's
feather-light trigger, he had shifted his sight and shot
the man's rifle instead.

But then the outlaw seemed to go crazy. He turned
and ran, hollering like a scared pup. Thomas saw him
crash into a briar thicket, then lost sight of him. He
never saw him again, though for long minutes after that
he could hear him, scrambling and crashing down the
hill, sometimes screaming curses as he went.

When all was quiet, Thomas cleaned his scrapes at a
little stream and reloaded Lady Justice. Then he headed
for home. There was nothing more he could do. Once,
some distance away, he thought he heard a gunshot. But
he wasn't sure where the sound had come from.

Dekagathe watched the hill men take Luke Dekins
away. They went eastward, toward Candlestick. Agate
eyes narrowed, he squatted on a rock and waited, every
sense alive. For a time, nothing happened. Then, a quarter mile away, horsemen emerged from a copse, moving

slowly along a tiny trail that wound away across a mountainside.

It was the hill men. Somewhere they'd had horses, and now they rode . . . all except Luke Dekins, who stumbled along in their midst. They had tied his hands behind them and put a rope around his neck, and they were taking him home, leading him by the neck the way they would lead a stray cow.

Dekagathe concentrated on them, and on the hills above them, and when a rifle cracked in the distance, he saw where it was fired from.

On the little trail, the trudging prisoner fell on his face and the horsemen milled about for a moment, their eyes searching, but then they got their prize on his feet again and went on their way. No one had been hit.

Little Axe noticed that, but it didn't matter to him. What mattered was where the shooter was, and even before the echoes died away he was on his way there, darting through the wild lands like a running deer.

He found the shooter within an hour, and was not surprised. It was just a little boy, carrying a long rifle, or so it seemed. Dekagathe knew otherwise. This was a child, but not a human child. This child had no spirit to temper and shape him, no constraints of any kind upon him. He was small, but he was a feral animal, as cruel as anything that walked these hills and far more dangerous for having no qualms about what he did.

He had tried to kill his own uncle, even when he had nothing to gain by it. He would try again to kill others, and would not fail. He needed no more reason to kill than the plain joy of the killing.

Dekagathe wasted no time stalking the boy. He simply stepped into the clear before him, and when Harley raised his gun Dekagathe struck it aside, crushing the small fingers that held it in the process.

The boy screamed, stared at his ruined hand and

screamed again, and Dekagathe grabbed the hair on his head and raised his broad knife. But then he hesitated. Somewhere within him a hollow old voice whispered, "Even this one is part of the river, son of Pascotateh. The river must flow its course."

Little Axe held the boy suspended for a moment, then flung him aside. When Harley looked up, pure hatred blazing in his young eyes, the Indian was gone.

It was as though he had never been there.

Harley got to his knees, cradling his injured hand at his breast. He looked at it once, then didn't look again. The sight made him sick. Smashed between the flat of a belt-axe and the curve of a rifle-stock, the fingers weren't fingers any more. They were broken, bleeding things, twisted and beginning to bloat, and the pain of them was excruciating.

". . . kill that redskin," he breathed, his hatred a blaze to keep the pain at bay. "Crippled me, sure. I'll kill him!" The pain and the hatred blended and were like a fever, carrying him along on great, rolling waves. The Indian . . . he had seen that Indian somewhere. Down there, at the town! He had been with that flour miller, over by the mill. The miller . . . Woodson.

"I'll kill him," Harley swore. He didn't know whether he meant the Indian or the miller, but it didn't make any difference. "Kill him!" his fever screamed. "Find him and kill him!"

He slept for a time, then found a cold spring and let his ruined hand soak in the water while he slept again. Faces blended together in his feral dreams, and were just one face. Woodson. The miller, Woodson.

The Hollys spread the word around, so everybody would know: Luke Dekins wouldn't be bothering folks anymore. But when somebody asked who had killed the outlaw, Sim Holly swore solemnly that nobody killed him.

Eventually it sorted itself out, the way mysteries do in the hills, and folks understood. Nobody *did* kill Luke Dekins. He was still alive when the Hollys buried him under six feet of clean earth in Tilda Holly's wildflower patch.

On a spring evening, Little Axe came to the house to see Thomas Woodson. They sat on the porch watching the stars come out, and when Martha brought tea for them Little Axe gazed solemnly at the rounded belly of her and told Thomas that he would have a son.

They drank their tea, then Little Axe said, "I will go away now. I will find a new place for my Kititsi, and for K'kyo to become a man. This is not the right place for us, Thomas."

Thomas stared at him. "Why?"

"White man's place," Little Axe spread his hands in a shrug. "Pretty soon, people will begin thinking about Harley Dekins. Then they'll remember what happened to his crippled hand. An' what they'll remember is that an Indian laid hands on a white boy."

Thomas thought about it, and understood. "Where will you go?" he asked.

"I met a pipe-walker. His path has no feet on it now, but it's still there to walk. We will go west, Thomas. I want to share a smoke with the Osage."

Thomas wanted to object, but he knew the decision was made. "We'll miss you, Little Axe," he said.

"We'll probably meet again," the Indian told him. "I think you'll come along some day."

"Me? Why?"

"Because the Osage need a mill for their wheat maybe," Dekagathe chuckled. "Who knows?" Then, as sudden as a shift in the spring breeze, he was serious again. "Let me see the *la'sawana'i* again, Thomas."

"The what?"

"The thing in your rifle."

Obediently, Thomas went in and got down Lady Justice. Sweet music drifted through the open garden windows of the west parlor and he paused for a moment, enjoying the sound of it. Somewhere out there, among Martha's prized rose bushes, Scat Ellis was playing his fiddle. Thomas didn't have to look to know where Rachel was. She would be sitting beside Scat, as usual nowadays, and the music he made was for her, like always.

Carrying a lamp, Thomas took Lady Justice out to the porch and handed her to Little Axe. By lamplight the Indian opened her patch box and lifted out the little beaded talisman that rested there. He studied it in the light, tracing the patterns of its tiny beads, and muttered, "Tecumseh."

When Thomas made no answer, Little Axe held out the talisman to him. "Tecumseh gave you this," he said. "These are his own marks."

"I don't know," Thomas admitted. "I've just always had it."

But Little Axe shrugged it off. "Tecumseh put his sign on you, Thomas Woodson. Now he rests in this rifle."

"Tecumseh died at the Thames," Thomas said. "I was there. I saw him fall."

"This rifle killed him, didn't it?"

"How did you know that?" Thomas squinted at him, mystified. Little Axe had not been at the Thames. He couldn't have been more than a baby then.

"It had his permission," Little Axe nodded. "The rifle, the *la'sawana'i*, he touched them both, and his spirit spoke to them. Tecumseh was *Ja'lacoma'i savata*, Thomas. A world person. His spirit is still his spirit. It is very strong."

Thomas shook his head, perplexed. He hadn't any idea what Little Axe was talking about. Yet— somehow— it seemed to make sense.

Little Axe put the ornament away in the patch box, stood for a moment gazing at the rifle, then returned it to Thomas. "Take good care of this, white man," he smiled. "I think some day you will be glad you did. Some day that rifle will make a perfect shot." He stepped off the porch, glanced around, and said something in Shawnee.

"What?" Thomas prompted.

"I said, keep your powder dry, Thomas Woodson. I'll see you down the road." With that, the Indian turned and was gone in the darkness.

Gone . . . as though he had never been there.

Epilogue I

Time of the Scavengers

Western Missouri, 1866

John Henry Dean seemed, to Thomas Woodson, almost a reincarnation of his uncle Hannibal. A quiet, thoughtful young man, he packed two hundred pounds of muscle and cautious optimism onto a frame that was deceptively square and plodding. Strong as a horse and happy as a puppy, Thomas had often mused, but woe to the man who ever offends his Emily or threatens his children.

His hands on the reins as his buggy made its way northward along skinny roads clinging to hillsides were as gentle as a kitten's touch, but as strong as the iron they shaped. Just like Hannibal, Thomas thought, riding beside him while Tip perched on the rolled calash behind them, gawking at the vertical scenery. Hannibal rested now in the old Hays Junction churchyard, very near the grave of Tilda Holly.

Orphaned by cholera at seventeen, John Henry had been taken under Hannibal's wing, learning the ways of forge and anvil, of cherry-red iron and alloy steel. By

1847 John Henry Dean was a master smith in his own right, and had the prospects to ask Emily to be his bride. He was probably the only one in these hills to be surprised when she agreed, Thomas had thought at the time. Emily had been waiting for him for years. Thomas and Martha attended their wedding the following spring.

Those had been good years for Thomas Paine Woodson— the best he had ever known. With his Martha at his side, and little Caleb growing like a mischievous weed, with Sidney Ellis— he would always be Scat to Thomas— working with him in the mill, with Rachel and Emily bringing their young husbands around as many evenings as not to share a pie or trade yarns, Thomas had learned what "home" truly meant. He had adored every minute of it.

But then new opportunity came, and the Woodsons had picked up and moved to Kansas. The Osage settlements along the Kaw and Neosho were producing wheat, and white settlers overflowing from Westport and Independence to stake new claims in the Territory were a ready market for bread flour. Osage leaders offered Thomas land and patronage for a mill.

From that start, he had added mills at Lawrence, Osawatomie and Fort Scott, and then one at Leavenworth using the new roller-mill processes perfected in Austria.

Those were good years, too, despite the chaos that sometimes seemed to be enveloping the world around them. Raiders and night-riders from the Missouri border were increasingly a threat. Quantril and Anderson, the Haver brothers and numerous others, all leading gangs of ruffians who came to be known as bushwhackers, repeatedly stormed across the border to harass Kansas Free-state settlers, and the Kansans' own breed of troublemakers— they called themselves jayhawkers— retaliated in kind. In the midst of it, an Ohio-bred fanatic named John Brown was collecting a private army at the

little town of Osawatomie. The border between Kansas
and Missouri became virtually a war zone, and there was
little that a scattering of federal marshals could do to
stop it.

Thomas had seen the town of Lawrence a few days
after Quantril's raid there. The invasion had been brief,
but cruel. The issue was not a local one, he knew. It
stemmed from distant disputes in the east, between people who favored a strong central government— and, in-
cidentally, one on the side of those whose interests were
vested in the northeastern states— and those who relied
on a plantation economy and so favored the sovereignty
of states as a shield against stifling federalism.

But agitators in both camps had camouflaged the issues. They had fallen back on the old question of slavery,
and made that the cause of the day. The fact that human
bondage was already becoming barely more than a tradition was lost in the outcry. This was politics, played
on a national level. Politics, Thomas himself had proclaimed one time, is a game played by the few at the
expense of the many, with gibbering zealots as the pieces
on the board.

The conflict had been inevitable, Thomas realized
later, wise with hindsight. Slavish emancipationism ran
headlong into lunatic pride, and the clash demanded a
contest. The politicians in Washington City designated
distant Kansas as the bleeding ground, to test their prin-
ciples. Thus this two hundred mile stretch of arbitrary
border became a battle ground long before the cartels
of Massachusetts and New York and the hotheads of
South Carolina ignited a formal war.

Now that war was over, Thomas mused. But not
where it began. Its seeds still produced bitter fruit on
the Missouri-Kansas border. The law was whatever each
locality could make of it, and hordes of rootless, ruth-
less men ran free, coming and going as they pleased.

There were the remnants of Quantril's Raiders and Bloody Bill's guerrillas, the escapees of John Brown's army and untold numbers of freelance robbers and killers.

One of the worst, according to the newspapers, was a cold-blooded murderer known only as Devil Luke. He had committed dozens of atrocities around Independence, then disappeared, only to reappear in the Springfield region. They said he always worked alone, and had committed a dozen capital crimes in as many months. They said he killed purely for the fun of it. They said he was like a ghost, who came and went and could not be caught.

The past several years had been bloody times. And before them had been worse.

Still, the world had been bright for Thomas Woodson in those pre-war times, despite the turmoil. Those things that most mattered to him were in good order. He was busy, he was in love with his wife, he adored their offspring, and he was the luckiest man he knew.

But abruptly— in the spring of 1858— the warm heart of Thomas Paine Woodson's comfortable world stopped beating. Martha Speer Sinclair Woodson rested now in a little cemetery on a hill near Lawrence. Cerebral hemorrhage, the doctor had called it. Martha— his beloved Martha— had died in her sleep at the age of fifty-six.

Thomas wiped his eyes now, fighting back the cold grief that was always there, always ready to overwhelm him. I've been lucky, he reminded himself again. So lucky . . . why did it have to be so brief? John Henry said, "About five miles now, just past that rim of hills ahead. The Langenkamps are caring folk, Thomas, but don't expect too much. Lot of things they just don't talk about. It's their way."

"I see people," Tip said.

At first the men saw nothing where he pointed. Then,

small in the distance, they saw riders coming from the west. "Crossroad ahead," John Henry said. "They're on the other road."

The riders disappeared behind a rise, but a mile further on, they saw them again, much closer. There were five men on horses, and they were making time.

The crossroad was exactly that— a flat spot between hills, where trails crossed. The mounted men reached it first, not slowing down. But when they saw the buggy approaching from the south, one of them raised a hand and reined in, the others following his lead. They milled about for a moment, then three of them spread out, blocking the crossing. They all wore sidearms and they didn't look friendly. A fourth one stayed back, holding the reins of the fifth horse. The man atop it wore no hat, and his beard and shirt were caked with dried blood. His wrists were shackled.

Thomas unbuttoned his coat and noticed from the corner of his eye that John Henry had done the same.

"Hold up, there!" one of the nearer men ordered, raising am imperative hand.

John Henry eased his reins back, and his horse slowed, coming to a halt twenty feet short of the blockade. "Regulators," he muttered. "Hoodlums, mostly."

The man who seemed to be in charge, a dark-bearded individual with bull shoulders and a jagged scar on his cheek, walked his horse forward a few steps and stopped, looking them over. "Who're y'all?" he demanded.

John Henry sat quietly, letting the man study them. Then he said, "John Dean, from Springfield. Who are you?"

"You mind your tongue," the man snapped. "We'll ask the questions. Where you bound for and what's your business?"

"Where I'm bound is north," John Henry said levelly.

"And my business is my own. Now state your purpose or stand aside."

Another rider closed in, looking them over. "That kid's totin' somethin', Foley," he pointed, edging closer. "You, kid! What you got there in that sheath?"

The man sidled his horse up to the buggy and reached for the rifle cradled in Tip's arms. Then he froze as a hammer clicked back and a gunbarrel prodded his ribs. Right under his outstretched arm, out of sight of the rest of them, the gray-haired man beside the buggy driver held a slim, businesslike Dragoon Colt, and it was ready to fire. "Leave my grandson alone," the old man purred. "Don't you have any manners at all?"

The rider hesitated, then withdrew his hand. "I reckon there's nothin' I want," he admitted.

"Good decision," the gray-hair said. With a quick motion, he lifted the bushwhacker's revolver from its holster and dropped it on the buggy's floorboard. "Now you and your friends just go away, and you can reflect on how lucky you are," he smiled. "Old codger like me, there's just no telling what I might do if I get excited."

"You aim to keep my pistol?" the man asked, very politely.

"It will be around here somewhere," Thomas said. "You can come back and get it later. Just don't be in a hurry about it."

His coat hiding his empty holster, the rider reined around carefully and waved. "They're all right, Foley. Just home folks passin' through."

The others continued to stare at the buggy for a moment, then Foley snapped, "Well, let's get on then! We're wastin' time." They rode away eastward, leading their prisoner, and the disarmed one followed sheepishly when Thomas told him he could.

"I'll be damned," John Henry breathed. Thomas noticed for the first time that the smith had a revolver in his hand, just under the dash. A big, blued-steel .44 Army, it looked like a trinket in John Henry's fist.

"Does this happen a lot?" Thomas asked.

"Not usually, up here. Down around Hays those hooraws are thick as thieves . . . which most of them are. But they usually don't bother up this way. Must have been after a runaway." His glance at Woodson was full of admiration and puzzlement. "I never saw the like, Thomas. Sometimes you amaze me."

"You never knew Jack Christy," Thomas shrugged. "He taught me some things, a long time ago. Who were those men?"

"Home guard," John Henry sneered. "Regulators, they call themselves. That Foley is one of Tolliver's crowd, I think."

He snapped the reins, and they headed up the road. At the crossing, Thomas gave the "Regulator's" gun a heave. It disappeared in the brush. "Who is Tolliver?"

"Purdy Tolliver. White trash from over by Rolla. Wiggled his way into politics during the war, now he runs things around Hays. He calls himself 'Judge Tolliver,' and he's collected a dozen good farms that he runs with convict labor. It's just like slavery, except he gets his slaves for free."

"How did he come to settle at Hays?" Thomas asked.

John Henry shrugged. "Natural place for him, I guess. It's pretty isolated. And he married one of the Dekins girls."

"Will this mean trouble for you?" Thomas put away his Dragoon. "They know your name."

"No matter," John Henry shrugged. "Springfield is a federal town. Troop headquarters. The 'Judge' doesn't want trouble with federals. He's supposed to be on their side." They rolled another mile, the light buggy traveling easily even on a long grade, and he pointed ahead and to the right. "Jacob Langenkamp's place is just over there, past that rise and to the east. Good spot, for times like these. 'Way off the road, and you'd have to know it's there to find it.''

In a secluded little valley among the hills, they rolled into a tidy, well-kept farmyard. A bright-eyed young girl and an old dog watched them come in— the child peeking from the shelter of a fence corner, the dog stiff-legged and alert. At the house, a young woman stepped out onto the porch, drying her hands on her apron. She was pretty, but plainly dressed in severe clothing which seemed designed to hide her prettiness. Thomas noticed that, though the farmstead had a solid, comfortable look, nowhere was there any ornamentation or anything even slightly ostentatious.

"Are they Mennonites?" Thomas asked John Henry as the buggy rolled to a stop.

"I don't know," Dean shrugged. "They don't talk about it. But there are quite a few around these parts just like them. I've heard it said they might be Mormons, though if Jacob Langenkamp has any plural wives I haven't met them."

A fringe-bearded young man came from the barn, waving. "Mister Dean!" he said. "Get down and come in. Let us meet thy friends!"

They stepped down from the buggy. John Henry snapped a keep onto his horse's headstall, and introduced Thomas and Tip to Jacob and Placid Langenkamp. "This is the gentleman I told you about," he said. "His son served in the war, then disappeared. He's looking for him."

"Mr. Dean called thy . . . called *your* son's name Caleb," Jacob said, shrewd blue eyes studying the older man.

"Caleb Woodson," Thomas nodded. "He served as a

quartermaster sergeant with the Kansas Brigade, attached to the Fourth Infantry."

"I see the family resemblance," Jacob said. "There was a Caleb here, some months ago. He had been beaten and robbed. We tended him for a time, then sent him on."

"Was he badly hurt?"

"A broken arm, which was mending nicely," Jacob said. "And some painful bruises. But he'd had a blow to the head, that cost him his memory."

"You sent him on . . . where?"

"Come into the house," Jacob invited. "Placid has tea and cool buttermilk." He turned to Tip, who was still clutching Lady Justice in her sheath. "Thee'll not need thy weapon here, youngster," he smiled. "There are no wolves or catamounts hereabouts."

"Some men on the road tried to take the rifle from him," Thomas explained. "Tip is fond of that old rifle."

"And of his grandfather as well, I warrant," Jacob said, noting the boy's defiant stance. "But come in, come in. We'll speak of thy son, and thee can . . . you can tell me of those men on the road."

They walked to Langenkamps's open door, removed their hats, wiped their boots, and started through, then Thomas looked back. Tip wasn't with them. Greta Langenkamp had come from the shelter of the fence corner, and Tip stood just where he had been, as though he were frozen in place. His eyes were as big as dollars and he stared at the girl as though she were the first of her kind he had ever seen.

Thomas chuckled to himself, remembering the stunning sight of auburn ringlets and evening-sky eyes. Remembering as though it were yesterday. "It's all great circles, Martha," he muttered. "Around and around, on and on."

* * *

"What ails thee?" the girl inquired curiously, staring at Tip Woodson, who hadn't moved a muscle in the past minute. The grown people had gone into the house, and he just stood there, clutching that long suede case in his arms and staring at her. "Are thee dumb?"

He seemed to find his tongue then, and lowered his eyes. Hot color crept upward from his collar. "I . . . I'm Tip," he stuttered. "Thomas Speer Woodson. That's . . . that's my name."

"Well," she nodded. "At least thee remembers thy name. Some are not able. I'm Greta. Was that thy father?"

Tip glanced toward the house, a little confused. "Mr. Woodson is my grandfather. We're . . ."

"I mean the man who was hurt. He abided here for a time. Was he thy father?"

"My father's name is Caleb Woodson," Tip clarified. "We're looking for him."

"I hope thee finds him," she said. "Biscuit found him after he was hurt. We tended him. Is that a spear in thy case?"

"Of course not," Tip snapped, then blushed again as his voice betrayed him, shifting from tenor to baritone and back. "Why would you think that?"

"Thee said 'spear,' " she reminded.

"It's my middle name. It was my grandmother's maiden name. Speer."

"Thee seems confused," Greta said, lifting a pretty eyebrow.

"And you talk funny," Tip snapped.

"It is our manner," she shrugged. "Would thee care for some buttermilk?"

With Biscuit presiding, they sat on the wide porch and drank buttermilk. "Thee looks like thy father," Greta decided. "He told me he had a little boy . . ."

"I'm not so little. But I guess I was when he left."

"Why did he go to war?"

"I don't know. Some said it was to free the slaves, but my grandfather says that would have happened anyway. Folks just have to have wars sometimes, I guess."

"Then those who want to fight should go off and fight and leave those who don't alone," Greta declared, as though the words were carved in stone. "I don't believe thy father wanted to fight a war."

"I don't either," Tip agreed. "What he wanted to do was finish our house."

For a time they just sat there, side by side, and Tip was enthralled with her presence. He had talked to girls before . . . there were girls everywhere. But never had he encountered anyone who seemed to tie his soul in tidy bow knots as this person did. Greta Langenkamp was by far the prettiest thing he had ever seen. On impulse he rolled back Lady Justice's sheath, revealing the sleek, brass-fitted maple of her stock.

"Oh," Greta said. "It's pretty."

Tip opened the patch-box. Inside were two things—a little beaded amulet on a rolled thong and a cross-shaped brass tool. He took out the tool and handed it to her. "You can have this, if you want it," he said.

Greta looked at the tool, then up at him, her blue eyes confused. "I already had this," she said. "Thy father left it with me. For luck, he said."

"That wasn't this one," Tip explained. "This is the other one. We have two of them. My grandfather has the other one."

"Thee said *this* is the other one."

"I mean the other . . . the *other* other one! My grandfather has that one. It's the one Pa had for luck. This is *this* one! It's from me! Do you want it or not?"

"Thank thee," she smiled, and Tip saw sunrises. "I shall keep it then."

"Good!" he snapped, feeling suddenly cross and wondering why. It was just that she confused him so, he decided.

An hour passed, and the men came out, putting on their hats. "I wish thee well," Jacob Langenkamp was saying. "I would say more if I could, but possibly one of those I suggested can guide thee."

"We'll find him," Thomas Woodson nodded. "You've given me reassurance. Now I *know* my son still lives."

John Henry removed the keep from his horse's head-stall and set it in the buggy's tiny boot. "God keep you and yours, Jacob," he waved.

The men climbed in and Tip followed, carrying Lady Justice. Atop the rolled calash he turned and called to Greta, "It isn't a spear! It's a fifty-caliber rifle! Her name is Lady Justice and she's real old!"

Thomas turned, squinting at his grandson, but the boy offered no explanation. John Henry lifted his reins and they headed back the way they had come.

"Where will I find this Brother Lawrence?" Thomas asked John Henry as they turned southward on the public road. "I don't even know his full name."

"Lawrence Mason, probably," John Henry said. "I've heard these people mention someone they call the 'Angel of Gedde.' My guess is he and Lawrence Mason are one and the same. He's of their faith. Mason's a good man, but not one you'd trifle with. He has a place not far from here."

"And he can send us to someone else," Thomas sighed. "And they can send us to someone else. These are secretive people."

"They've had to be," John Henry said.

"Well, *somebody* knows where they took Caleb. I guess we just keep at it until we find that somebody."

"Culver's Hole," Tip said, behind them.

Thomas turned. "What?"

"That's where they took Pa," the boy said. "Culver's Hole. Greta told me."

"I'll be damned," John Henry said.

"Where is Culver's Hole?" Thomas asked him.

"Almost nowhere," the smith shrugged. "It's a hole in the mountains. Only one way in, and not much of a way at that. Nobody goes to Culver's Hole. Most folks don't even know it's there. But it isn't far from Hays Junction. Do you remember those saddle peaks southwest, that we could see from your mill? That's where it is. It's under them."

John Henry wanted to go with them to Culver's Hole, but Thomas wouldn't let him. That was Regulator country now, by his own account, and some of those bushwhackers had reason to remember him.

"They saw you, too!" John Henry objected. "You're the one who disarmed that fella."

"I'm an old man," Thomas said. "People don't notice old men much. I'll be fine, but I wouldn't want anything to happen to you. Emily and the children need you."

They had slept and breakfasted in Springfield, and Thomas had packed away his broadcloth suit and good hat. Now he wore an old slouch hat, buckskin jacket, and denim pants, with sturdy muleskin boots on his feet. He would be traveling cross-country from here.

Emily handed him his shoulder pack and gave him a hug. "Well, at least Tip can stay with us 'til you get back," she said.

"I appreciate that," he agreed. But when he went to find Tip, the boy was nowhere around. And when Thomas had a good horse saddled and a pack mount loaded, ready to set out, Tip still could not be found. Lady Justice was missing, too. They searched the house, the grounds, and the neighborhood, then Thomas understood. "I'll need a second horse and saddle, John Henry," he said.

"Fine," the smith nodded. "I swear, though, I don't know where that boy has got to." He stopped and lifted a brow. "Another horse . . . for Tip? Do you know where he is?"

"No, but I reckon I know where he will be. I was just like him, once upon a time."

On the street, a newsboy was peddling week-old copies of the *Post-Tribune* and he bought one, scanning it briefly. It was the first newspaper he had seen in a month.

President Johnson was under fire from both the north and the south, because of his actions in the Reconstruction program. His positions were far too lenient to please some, far too harsh for others. England was still mourning the death of King George V, and the Boers were fighting again with the Basutos in Africa. A new amendment to the United States Constitution would regulate voting and prohibit certain former rebels from holding office. By the same instrument, the war debts of the Confederacy were repudiated.

At the same time, certain Confederate units were still waging war in Texas, even though the war had been over for a year everywhere else.

A man named Alfred Nobel had invented solid-form explosives, and an English engineer was perfecting an underwater torpedo. The London Stock Exchange was in shambles, and thirty-six new commercial buildings were under construction in New York City, all funded by war profits. Critics were hailing something called *Crime and Punishment* by the Russian, Dostoevsky.

Prussian troops had invaded Saxony, Hanover, and Hesse, and Italy was at war with Austria. Sailors reported sighting a giant sea monster off Barataria, and an Arkansas woman had given birth to a child with two heads.

More locally, two men and a crippled woman had been shot down by the outlaw Devil Luke, near Pilot's Knob.

Thomas folded the newspaper and put it away in his saddle-wallet. I'm growing old, Martha, he thought. The more things change nowadays, the more they remain the same.

He was past the outskirts of Springfield, leading an extra saddle mount and a pack horse, when Tip appeared on the trail ahead of him. The boy was sitting on a light pack, and holding Lady Justice across his lap. "I thought I'd just wait for you here," he said innocently.

"I know," Thomas nodded. "Have you written to your mother?"

"I wrote a letter last night," Tip said. "I told her we are both well, and have been visiting with relatives. I told her we plan to meet Pa and come home with him." Every word of it was true, as far as it went. Thomas sighed and nodded. "Well, come on then, climb aboard. We don't have all day. We need to go find your Pa."

Epilogue II

Hill Justice

As though forty years of his life had never happened, Thomas Woodson found himself once again traveling wilderness lands, relying mile by mile, minute by minute on his senses, his instincts and the skills that an untamable adventurer named Jack Christy had taught him a long time ago. Like the donning of a comfortable old cloak, the long-forgotten ways of the wild land came back to him now, and he saw again the land as it once was, before men bent it to their own shifting patterns.

The knowledge once learned was there, as it had always been— knowing which trace was passable and which not, how to thread a deadfall or negotiate a slope, where the winds were and what the flutter of a leaf might mean, and how to follow a direction with neither sun-shadow nor line-of-sight.

They followed no road, but struck out cross-country through the Ozark wilderness, and it seemed that at each turn there was a new thing to show the boy, a new skill to teach him. In an odd way, Thomas felt as though he were twenty again and seeing each hour's raw, new world through the eyes of Jack Christy . . . seeing it and showing Tip how to see it that way, too.

Still, there were reminders that those days were very

long ago. A few hours of riding made the muscles in his neck and shoulders ache, and after a day on the move his very bones whimpered with fatigue. To make matters worse, every seam in his britches seemed to have etched its likeness into his time-softened rump, and the boots on his feet fairly begged to be swapped for moccasins.

I'm not twenty anymore, he admonished himself. I'm sixty-six years old, and I ought to be dozing in a wide-bottom rocking chair on my own front porch, howdying the men who pass by, and harboring unpardonable thoughts about the ladies. Why in blazes, he asked himself, am I here?

But he knew why he was here. His boy— his and Martha's— was out here somewhere, waiting for Thomas to find him and take him home. And his boy's own son rode at his side, ready to take on the world with his Grandad any time he said the word . . . or on his own if he didn't.

I've got it to do, Martha, he thought. All these years, and I'm still here, and no other reason that I can see. So I guess what I'm doing now is why I'm here. I'll find him, Martha. I'll find Caleb, and Tip and I will take him home to his Mary.

They made tight camp by a little stream— a "crick" in this country— and Thomas dozed by a tiny fire. He dreamed of past times, and he dreamed of good times, and as always, he dreamed of his Martha. A twig shifted somewhere and he turned to see a shadow among the starlight shadows. It didn't move, only stood there, but he knew who it was. *Tacom'the,* he thought . . . Tecumseh, why are you here? Is your spirit so great that it flows this far without losing itself in the river? Behind the shadow was another shadow— a young warrior who might have been the one he saw just before Tecumseh died— and he was Little Axe, who understood about the spirits.

They were no more than shadows, but it was as though they had always been there.

He awoke with a start then, and the shadow he saw now was real. Tip was crouched a few feet away, Lady Justice unsheathed and ready in his hands.

"I heard something," the boy whispered.

They listened in silence, then heard it again— the slight shifting of a twig. "Beetles," Thomas said. "Beetles in the grass. If it was a larger thing, you'd hear the twig's other end move too."

When Tip was asleep again, Thomas sat by the coals, listening to the night. On impulse he slid Lady Justice away from the boy's hand and opened her patch-box. He took out the little, beaded amulet and hung its thong around his neck. He had worn it thus for such a long time in wild country, that he felt naked without it.

The rising hills here were a patchwork quilt of settled places and wilderness. In the bottoms were tilled lands and clusters of buildings, sometimes only a few miles apart. But above them rose forested slopes and rugged crests where few found cause to pass and even fewer to linger.

Thomas and Tip avoided the peopled places and shunned the roadways. In remote lands, chance encounters could lead to trouble. More than once they faded into thickets or found shelter among rocks while people passed within sight. Tip learned quickly the skills of the trail. By the end of their second day the boy was as alert as a ferret to the ways of the wild, and as elusive as an Indian when he chose to be.

From the beginning, he had taken it upon himself to tend and carry his grandfather's long rifle, and now it began to seem a part of him. He handled it easily, despite its weight and its five-foot length, and he kept it clean and its load fresh.

She's more his gun than mine these days, Thomas mused sometimes. And it seemed a proper thing, when he thought about it. Early on the third day, they stopped to rest their horses where a spring trickled from a limestone cleft. On impulse, Thomas took the Shawnee talisman from his neck and dropped it around Tip's. "I've had this by me as long as I can remember," he told the boy. "I don't know what it means, but I was told that a Shawnee Indian gave it to me when I was still a coddling tad. I've even been told that the Indian was Tecumseh himself."

"Why are you giving it to me?" the boy asked, shrewd eyes studying his grandfather's face.

"It seems right to," Thomas shrugged. "It's always been with me, and as long as you keep it, it will be still." He grinned and added, "It belongs to Thomas Woodson, and that's who you are."

The boy turned away, then swung back, looking startled. But it was only for an instant, then he shook his head. "You said the forest can play tricks on the eyes," he said.

"It can, if you let it. Why?"

"Oh, I just thought . . . well, just for a second there, I thought there was an Indian standing here, right here with us."

A little later, as they topped a ridge, Tip turned and asked, "This came from Tecumseh . . . and it was Lady Justice that killed him?"

"It was her ball," Thomas assured him. "I was there. I even loaded the rifle, for Salem Cadmont. But it wasn't me that fired the shot. It was a man named King."

They had been on the trail almost four days when Thomas spurred to the top of a ridge and waved Tip up beside him. The land was even more rugged here than in those places they had seen coming down from the plateau. In every direction, it seemed, there were vertiginous slopes and hidden creases. It was as though a great hand had swept aside a broad land to make room for more land, and the old part now was a crowded terrain of wrinkles.

Thomas stepped down from his saddle, stretched his aching old bones, and peered eastward. The mountains fell away in that direction, and snake-track valleys came together among the hills. In the bottoms were smooth fields of ripening grain, and beyond them in the distance a little town.

"Yonder is where your Pa was born, boy," he pointed. "That's Hays Junction, and the little tall building there by the creek is Woodson's Mill. It was the first one I ever built."

"Does it still work?" Tip asked.

"Last I heard, it did," Thomas said. "Your Uncle Scat runs it now. That house just up from it was our house. Now it's Rachel's."

"Uncle Scat . . . that's Uncle Sidney?"

"That's him," Thomas grinned. "Though when I first knew him he was just Scat."

The boy viewed the distant place for a moment, then turned, his eyes searching. "Where's Culver's Hole?"

Thomas pointed ahead, the way they were going. "See where that saddle-back ridge is, yonder? That's where we're going. Culver's Hole is in there."

Devil's Den, the thought occurred to him. Jim Creed used to speak of a place called Devil's Den, off yonder somewhere. Maybe that was Culver's Hole. Names change in this country. They float around. A place might be called one thing today and another tomorrow. And what a place used to be called might be the name of some other place now.

That reminded him of a place they had seen somewhere along the line, where a trail had forked. One of the forks was a fine, graded road leading off into the woods, and there was a sign on a post. "Galena City," it said. But the road only went a few hundred yards, and there was nothing at the end of it but a tiny graveyard and the skeleton of a burned cabin. There were no markings on the graves and nothing to say who had lived there. The only things that remained of whatever grand dream had ended there were a graded road and a carved sign that proclaimed, "Galena City."

And us, he thought. Tip and me were there for a little while. I'm probably an old fool on a fool's errand, Martha, he thought. But then, the world is full of fools.

Tip fidgeted. He wanted to cater to his grandfather's moods and whims, but they were so close now. He was impatient with the delay. Finally he urged, "Time's wastin', Grandad. Let's go get Pa."

It was coming on evening when they reached the rim of the deep, hidden valley called Culver's Hole. There was a trail here, but it was weedy and there was no fresh sign. It was a while since anybody had passed this way.

A few minutes later they stood at the top of a nearly vertical cliff, where the little road curled away to the left and began a torturous, snaking descent into the shadowed depths below. It was a hole, right enough . . . a deep, vertiginous hole in the mountains— a hole full of nothing but daunting slopes, empty twilight, and rising mists. Vague, rectangular shapes in a jumbled pattern far below suggested buildings, but there was no smoke, no movement, no sign of habitation.

Tip stared into the depths, then gave Thomas a stricken look. "There isn't anybody down there," he said. "It's empty."

Thomas shook his head slowly. They had come so far,

searching. . . . "Let's take a look," he said. "Maybe we'll find sign."

Leading their horses, with the pack animal between them on a slip-knot lead, they started down the trail. They were halfway down and running out of daylight when the boy hissed and pointed. Below them, among the vacant-looking structures, was a tiny flicker of light. Somebody had made a fire.

There had been three of them in Culver's Hole, ragged scavengers picking through the ruins of an abandoned little settlement. Now there was only one, and a pair of little stone mounds covering fresh graves.

"Devil Luke," the sole survivor told them, the words slurred by toothless jaws and bad whiskey. The man might have been any age, fifty or eighty or thirty, but he was old— the kind of old that comes of a lifetime without direction or purpose. He had stopped caring about much of anything a long time ago. Still, there was a trace of outrage in him as he looked at the graves he had labored over. "That Devil Luke. It was him, all right. I seen him, bad hand an' all. He come down here, pokin' around. When he seen Jake an' Ben, he just shot 'em dead. No reason, no warnin', nothin'! Just hauled out a big pistol an' let fly."

"Where did he go?" Thomas asked. "We came down the trail. There weren't any tracks."

"Dunno," the scavenger shrugged. "Mebbe they's some other way out. Y'all got any vittles you don't need?"

At Thomas's nod, Tip dug a chunk of bacon out of a pack, and found some flatbread. The man gazed at the food, his pinched lips working, but he didn't move from the fire.

"There were folks here," Thomas prodded. "This place hasn't been empty long."

"Them?" the old man looked around at the dilapidated hovels and slap-up sheds that had been a town.

"Regulators run 'em out, three-four months back. Foley an' a passel of 'em, they come down here after 'scapers. Rounded up a mess of 'em, for Judge Tolliver. The rest just run off. Me an' them . . ." he glanced at the graves, ". . . we're th' onliest ones as come back."

He had said all he was going to say. From somewhere among his tumbled clothes and bedding, he produced a small clay jug and pulled its cork. He drank and a few minutes later he was asleep.

"We'll get us a wink or two over by that spring," Thomas told the boy. "Smell here's enough to make a man sick."

"What about him?" Tip wondered.

"Leave the food," Thomas said. "When he wakes up . . . if he wakes up . . . he'll want it."

They slept fitfully, both of them alert to every sound in the night. With first light, they packed and headed back up the twisting trail. Regulators had rounded up men in the hole for Judge Tolliver. "We'll take a look at Hays Junction," Thomas said.

Twice during the day, Thomas reined in and eased into cover, studying their backtrail. He saw nothing, but the feeling persisted that someone was back there, behind them. A very long time ago, Jack Christy had told him, "Your bones have eyes, boy. If somebody is lookin' at you, don't look straight back at him. You can't see an ambusher by lookin' at him. Look away, and let your bones tell you where he is."

His bones were telling him something now. They said somebody was following. But for the life of him he couldn't catch a glimpse of who it was. And that worried him. It meant whoever was back there didn't choose to be seen.

The old woodsman had taught him that a man can be

invisible if he knows how. "The trick," he said, "is to be part of what's around you. Hiding isn't not being seen. Hiding is not being noticed."

It was woodsman's lore. And whoever was back there knew how to be a woodsman.

After a time, though, the bone-sense— the feeling of being watched— faded. And in late afternoon they crossed a skyline ridge and saw Hays Junction below.

Thomas took his time scanning the little town. Much of what was there was as it had been, but there were changes. A few more commercial buildings now fronted on the main road, two large barns with pole corrals had been added, and there were maybe twice as many houses as he remembered. And at the east end of town, built squarely on the road so that the road now curved around it on both sides, was a solid, two-story stone building with brick trim. A federal flag hung there on a white-washed standard, and above it was a red and yellow banner. Apart and to one side were a double row of little, shed-roof buildings, with a high, tight-rail fence around them.

At the other end of the road, the flour mill was much as he remembered it— tall and skinny, forty feet of vertical shell with its water-wheel turning lazily in the creek and grain bins on its high roof. And behind it was his old house, now Rachel and Scat's house. There were children in the yard and a plume of smoke drifted from the kitchen chimney.

"Look!" Tip's hand closed on his elbow, and the boy's voice broke with excitement. He was pointing toward the nearest grain field, just above the mill. Tall wheat was ripening there, and gangs of men worked in the narrow rows, their heads and shoulders rising and falling among the gauzy mist of bearded grain as they swung hoes, preparing the field for harvest.

There were dozens of them, working in long, erratic

lines, while armed, mounted men patrolled the perimeters. Convict labor, Thomas thought. That, or slaves. At this stage, they're the same thing.

But Tip was tugging at his elbow, pointing impatiently, almost jumping from excitement. "There's Pa!" he crowed. "I see Pa!"

Rachel Ellis stood like a woman dazed, gawking at the newcomers while Scat drummed slow, hard fingers on the table top.

"Caleb?" Rachel whispered. *"Our* Caleb . . . he's here? But those are convicts, Thomas! Felons and outlaws, Rebels off parole . . ."

"He's here," Thomas repeated. "We saw him, right out there in Kincaid's field."

"Not Kincaid's any more," Scat Ellis growled. "It's Purdy Tolliver's. Half the bottom land around here is his, now. The Kincaids, the Crenwells, the Applebys . . . all burned out or driven out by night riders. And now the Judge has their land."

"Night riders!" Rachel sneered. "Dekinses and Dekins kin. That's who they are."

"What about the Hollys?" Thomas pondered. "Any of them still around?"

"Sure," Scat said. "Up on Candlestick. Old Sim died a couple of years ago. Some 'busher shot him in the back, about the time General Fielding's troops came through. Or right after that, I guess. But Grange Holly is still up there. They don't get involved here, though. They lost a good many boys in the war, an' now the Dekinses are practically the law around here. I guess the Hollys don't want any more grief."

"Who's still here, then?"

"Some you'd know, I guess. My brother Bliss still has the store. And Ben Wakefield's still here. Bliss bought him out, and Ben started up a produce business . . . milk, butter, an' eggs mostly. The Creeds have held on, though their rooming house business is only what the Judge allows now. Folks don't come here much, 'less he says so."

"How about the Swede, Gustave Nilsson?"

"Gone," Scat sighed. "There's an old stump down the road, that used to be his elm tree. A Confederate troop came through here just ahead of Fielding's regiment. They took what they had to have, but they were polite about it, and didn't burn anything. But they set a hitch-brace on that tree, and wore off the bark all the way around. The tree died, and ol' Nils didn't live a month after that." ·

"Why is Caleb here?" Rachel demanded. "What did he do?"

"He was on his way home," Thomas said. "Somebody beat him up and robbed him. He's been holed up with a bunch of fugitives, and I guess the Regulators took him for one of them."

"But *how*? They can't do that. Even Tolliver can't just . . . just *conscript* people to work his fields! Caleb's a discharged soldier. Honorably discharged! He's no de-serter, or unreconstructed rebel. They can't keep him!"

"Pa doesn't know who he is," Tip said.

"Caleb's lost his memory, lass," Thomas explained. "He doesn't remember his name, or where he's been, or where he lives. He has no papers, no identification, and he can't tell them anything."

"Well, *we* can!"

"Easy, darlin'," Scat took her hand and put a finger to her lips. "Think. What's Purdy Tolliver going to do if he finds out he's been enslaving a free citizen? Word of that gets out, the federals will be on him like ticks on a hound. The last thing the Judge wants is federals pokin' around in his business. Remember Jody Cain?"

Thomas raised his head, his eyes suddenly hard. "What about Jody?"

"They hanged him," Scat said. "They said he'd knifed one of the Judge's men, but we don't think so. Jody wasn't like that. We think he was buildin' a case against Tolliver to present to the court at Jefferson City."

"He used to work for me," Thomas muttered. "A good kid. That crooked leg of his, he got that pulling Bol Shanks out of the way when the drive belt failed."

"Yeah," Scat nodded. "I was there, too. Anyhow, I sure wouldn't go demandin' anything from the Judge . . . not if we want Caleb to stay alive."

"Then we'll just have to get him out ourselves," Thomas breathed. "Who'll help, Scat?"

"We'll find out," Scat said. "Meantime, you and Tip best not be seen around here."

The campaign against Judge Purdy Tolliver would have done William Henry Harrison proud. Even Salem Cadmont would have approved, Thomas thought. And Jack Christy would have been delighted. The plan was straightforward, almost entirely legal and still devious enough to have a distinct Shawnee flavor to it.

On the morning of the seventeenth, Ben Wakefield and his oldest boy left town on a freight wagon loaded with empty kegs and baskets. The fact that the wagon sat heavy on its wide iron tires, and the fact that it was pulled by a four-mule team, went unnoticed.

A little later, Jim Creed and his two grown sons drove out the other way, toward their little truck patch on the slopes past the near fields. About the same time, Bliss Creed also left town, heading east with a canvas-covered load of various goods obviously bound for the hill farms around Candlestick, and Billy McCoy headed out with a small herd of horses, toward the high meadows.

In all, more than twenty Hays Junction men were no longer in town by noon. Then the Judge's Regulators began to quietly disappear. At a cove just north of town, a patrol guard stepped down from his saddle to get a closer look at a bright thing lying beside a thicket. It looked like a gold watch.

He stooped, stared, and squatted to pick the thing up. When he rose to his feet, four guns were trained on him. A storekeeper took his guns and a blacksmith's swamper tied the rope that secured his wrists. He was led away still astonished and confused.

On the east road, four Regulators waiting for the outbound mailcoach were quietly and efficiently surrounded, disarmed and herded away. The coach was stopped, but only briefly. When it resumed its journey it carried several parcels of paper addressed to the civil and occupational authorities in Jefferson City and Springfield. The parcels were postage-paid and duly stamped by the postmaster of Hays Junction.

At three separate wheat fields above Hays, the widespread labor guards disappeared one by one, and mostly in silence, as a little squad of young Missourians moved around the perimeters and along the rows. Army-trained and war-hardened, with a little camouflage assistance from a tall, old man who could do wonders with a bit of shredded linen, a daub of clay mud, a few dashes of barn wash, and green buggy paint, they were practically invisible as they went about collecting their prisoners.

"That's sort of how the Shawnee used to do it," Thomas had explained to an enthralled Tip as he put the finishing touches on Emanuel Creed's warpaint, on the wooded slope south of town. "A man can just disappear, if he becomes part of what's around him. The Shawnee were better at it, of course, but I learned it from some Kaintucks who were better at it than even the Shawnee."

When the field squad was on its way, Thomas cleaned his hands, put on his coat and picked up his hat. "This time you stay here," he told Tip.

"I can help!" The boy objected. "I can . . ."

"You can tend the horses and have them ready to ride if I need them," Thomas said sternly. "I mean it, Tip! I don't want you down there until I send for you! Do you understand?"

The boy dropped his gaze, abashed. "Yes, sir," he muttered.

"I want your word on it, Tip."

"I'll stay here, Grandad," the boy sighed. "My word."

With a quick smile, Thomas Woodson turned and walked away, down the hill toward the town. Tip watched him go, then he walked back over the little rise to where the horses were grazing. He looked them over, inspected the saddles, packs and gear stacked nearby, then picked up Lady Justice and her possible pouch and returned to his vantage point on the crest. With nothing better to do, he pulled the load, cleaned the rifle carefully, oiled its plates and mechanisms, tested its firing-path, and began reloading.

It was a good eight hundred yards from here to the center of the little town below, he estimated.

In the Citadel, Purdy Tolliver's pet name for his combination house, office, and headquarters straddling the main road, the Judge had barely finished his breakfast when T.J. Foley was banging at the door of his private quarters.

"You better come out here, Judge," Foley said. "We got a problem."

Tolliver fixed his captain with a stare of disbelief. "What is it, that you and your men can't handle it?" he demanded.

"You better come see for yourself," Foley grunted.

Irritated, Tolliver straightened his cuffs, buttoned on

his starched collar, pulled on his coat, and followed Foley through the empty guard quarters to the massive front door. Foley slipped the bar and pushed the door open.

Tolliver found himself confronted by angry women. There seemed to be dozens of them, waving skillets and rolling pins and all screeching at him at the same time. The instant the door was open, they flooded through it like an angry tide, crowding him back.

". . . ever' last penny's gone!" one of them was shouting. "I want some answers, an' I want 'em right this minute!"

". . . hooligans scattered my wash all over kingdom come!" another shrilled. "Y'all supposed to keep law an' order around these parts, or not?"

". . . hens won't lay . . ." a high voice griped.

". . . paid three dollars for them windows," another chirped, pushing forward and waving a heavy skillet almost under his nose.

His arms raised in startled defense, Judge Purdy Tolliver stared this way and that, trying to sort it out. "What in hell . . . ?" He backed another step, then shouted at Foley, ."Get these damn women out of here!"

Foley blinked in bewilderment, then reached for his gun. A rolling pin cracked across his knuckles. "You mind your manners!" a woman snapped.

"Don't shoot 'em, damn it!" Tolliver roared. "Just get 'em out!"

Foley hesitated, then began grabbing wrists, shoulders, and whatever else he could reach, herding women before him as he headed for outside.

"Keep your filthy hands to yourself!" a sturdy matron barked, and glanced a skillet off his skull. His hat went flying. By the time he had them all crowded outside and pulled the iron-bound door shut, Foley had a dozen assorted bruises and a blossoming hatred toward all members of the female persuasion.

"What was that all about?" Tolliver demanded, brushing down his coat. It was covered with flour.

"I'm damned if I know," Foley shrugged, wincing as he discovered a new bruise. T.J. Foley had been a bully all his life. He had beaten and maimed men, even killed a few, and was used to being walked wide around. But suddenly he found himself completely out of his depth. Tolliver was right, he realized. You can't just shoot women or knock them around. But what *can* you do? Taken one at a time, in privacy, he knew exactly what to do with women. But this was something else entirely.

"Well, go put a stop to it," Tolliver ordered. He turned and pointed an imperious finger at two payroll Regulators who had just come from the back. One was rubbing sleep out of his eyes, the other hopping on one foot while he pulled on a boot. "You men go with him! I wants to know what's going on out there."

Followed by two of his toughs, T.J. Foley stepped outside and closed the door. Then he looked around and his eyes widened. There were no women out there. Not a one anywhere in sight, Instead, four men stood waiting for him. Three of them he knew— the miller Sidney Ellis, big Sam Barrett from the smithery and old Landen Henry. The latter pair were holding shotguns.

The fourth man was a tall, aging individual who looked vaguely familiar. This one spoke first. "My name is Woodson," he said. "That's as in Woodson's Mill."

"Cap'n," the Regulator on Foley's right hissed. "That's him! That's the jasper that took my gun away from me."

"I'll have all your guns," Woodson said. "You men are charged with kidnapping, false imprisonment, impersonating officers of the court, and maybe murder and treason."

"Who says?" Foley snorted. "By God, I'll . . ."

"We say," Woodson said, his voice precisely level, "this is a citizen's arrest."

"The hell you say!" Foley roared. In one swift motion he half-turned and side-stepped to knock Landen Henry's shotgun aside, and drew his revolver. He thrust it toward Woodson, cocking the hammer as he did, then gasped as the older man imprisoned his gun-hand in iron-hard fingers, hauled him sideways and whirled to plant a boot in the pit of his stomach.

In the instant of falling, Foley squeezed his trigger, but nothing happened. The old man's hand was wedging the hammer. Then T.J. Foley was flat on his back, a knee was dug into his belly and his own gun, no longer in his hand, collided with his left temple.

Thomas glanced around. One of the Regulators was a foot off the ground and going blue-faced as Sam Barrett's huge arms crushed the breath from his lungs. The other had both hands in the air, and was staring cross-eyed into the twin bores of Landen Henry's scattergun.

An upstairs shutter slammed open, and Judge Purdy Tolliver stared aghast at the scene below him. He spun away from the window, reappeared with a pistol in his hand, then ducked and closed the shutter as a business-like Colt Dragoon was aligned on his collar button. The gun was held by a distinctive-looking, gray-haired gentleman sitting on the belly of T.J. Foley.

Sam Barrett dropped his unconscious Regulator and turned to Thomas Woodson. "That was real pretty," he said.

"Thank you," Thomas nodded. "You know, I wondered if I could still do that. It's been a long time."

He stood, put away his revolver, and dusted himself off. Landen Henry herded his Regulator toward the stockade compound, and Sam Barrett followed, dragging the two unconscious ones. They would keep them there while other citizens brought in as many of the others as they could catch.

I guess that's that, Martha, Thomas mused, starting toward the old mill. I'll go get our boy, and we'll take him home. In time, he'll mend. He has to. He's a Woodson.

The road was deserted now, and felt eerily lonely as he approached the mill he had built so long ago. Memories are strange, he thought. They all change flavor each time a new one is added.

A shadow moved, and he looked up, startled. Directly in front of him was a man with a gun, and abruptly he knew who it was. The jug-handle ears, the close-set little eyes, the clawlike left hand . . . it had been a long time, since the day the kid tried to kill him, and he was grown up now. But he was still Harley Dekins. Only he didn't call himself that anymore. Now he was Devil Luke.

Epilogue III

The Way Home

"I know you," Devil Luke purred. "You're the flour miller that got me hurt an' got my uncle killed. I been lookin' for you for years an' years." The gun he pointed at Thomas was a sleek .36 Navy revolver, a weapon quick and deadly, and his grip said he knew how to use it.

Thomas didn't move, but his mind was racing. There wasn't a chance he could get his Dragoon out before Harley fired, nor any doubt that the outlaw would shoot to kill. Devil Luke killed for the pure fun of it. "I didn't kill your uncle, Harley," he said. "Or bust up your hand, either. You know that."

"Your fault, though," the outlaw said. "Don't matter about my uncle. I aimed to kill him anyway, for his name. Now I got that. *Devil Luke*, they say. Sounds right nice, don't it?"

They were alone on the road. For the moment at least, there wasn't another soul in sight. Looks like I'm through here now, Martha, Thomas thought. Everybody dies. Maybe this is as good a way as any. Wish I could have brought Caleb home first, though.

"I can shoot you right through the heart," Harley grinned. "I heard that hurts like hell, but not for very long. High in the gut takes longer." The .36 shifted downward slightly. "Right in the brisket ought to be a sight to see. I seen that kid ridin' with you, you know. Maybe I'll just shoot him, too. Why not?"

Thomas held the outlaw's eyes, staring him down out of plain, stubborn pride. But he knew it was over. Be there for me, Martha, part of him thought. Let us be together again . . .

The .36 steadied on its target— the middle button of his coat. Get away, Tip, his mind cried out in silence. Hide, like Jack Christy taught me . . . like I taught you! He braced himself for death and Devil Luke's throat seemed to explode before his eyes. Blood sprayed from beneath the outlaw's chin, his head rocked back and there was no throat there, only a gaping void that gushed dark gore. And in Thomas Woodson's ears was a sound he had heard long ago, a sound like no other sound— the sound of a lead ball striking human flesh.

Harley Dekins swayed, tottered and fell, crumpling like a broken wood doll. Stunned beyond comprehension, Thomas stared down at him for long seconds, then raised his head as the sound of a distant gunshot drifted down the slopes— the whiplike crack of a fine rifle, far away.

Up on the slope, impossibly far, a little cloud of white smoke drifted for a moment on the errant breeze, then dispersed, and Tip stood there, just lowering Lady Justice. Somewhere in Thomas Woodson's stunned mind a small, argumentative voice was raised in protest. No rifle could shoot that far, it reasoned— not shoot and hit anything smaller than a barn. The range from the slope was at least eight hundred yards. Nearly half a mile! And it was downhill.

A few people had appeared along the road now, nervous and curious about the gunshot they had heard. At first, most of them didn't notice Thomas standing over the dead outlaw. They were scanning the hills, looking into the distance.

Up on the slope, Tip stood frozen for a moment, shading his eyes as he looked down the hill. Then he waved, and kept waving, literally jumping up and down.

Thomas took a deep breath and let it out. You won't believe this, Martha, he thought. I hope you're where you could see it. Otherwise you'll never believe it.

The perfect shot. Lady Justice had fulfilled the promise of a long-dead Hessian gunsmith in Pennsylvania. The perfect rifle was the rifle that could make a perfect shot.

They brought the "convicts" in from the fields, guarded now by Missourians wearing the warpaint of the long ago Shawnee. Some among the Judge's laborers probably were criminals or parole-breaker rebs. They didn't know which ones, but they would keep them in the Judge's labor compound until some law arrived to sort it all out.

When all the prisoners were accounted for, they brought in eighteen more captive Regulators and put them there, too. They wouldn't be going anyplace. Bliss Ellis had sent a rider out to Candlestick to say that the killer of Sim Holly was probably in custody at the junction. Nobody was sure which prisoner was guilty of that, but it seemed likely that one of them might be.

Thus when Purdy Tolliver finally came out of his Citadel—after Sam Barrett removed the hinges and took out the front door—it was Grange Holly and a dozen of his boys who were there to meet him.

Putting Tolliver in the prison compound to wait for the law was a mercy, in a way. Several of the Hollys would gladly have taken the Judge off the town's hands if they had let them.

In evening light, Thomas Woodson made his way back to the house of Scat and Rachel Ellis. He paused at the gate, letting his heart bask in the quiet wonder that his eyes beheld. Caleb Woodson sat on the porch, his hand clasped in the hands of his son. Tip was talking to him. The words didn't carry, but the tone did, and Thomas felt a kind of awe he had felt only twice before— the day Martha first showed him his infant son, and later when that son was a young man and Thomas first held the infant who was his grandchild.

He stood by the gate for long minutes, just looking at the two of them. Then they looked up and saw him, and Caleb's face split in a huge grin. "Pa!" he called. They stood, and Thomas hurried up the path to them.

Caleb's embrace nearly crushed his ribs. Then the young man backed up a step and his grin widened. "My name is Caleb Woodson," he said proudly. "I seem to have been away for a while."

Thomas reached up to remove his hat, and realized he had lost it somewhere. It didn't matter. He looked at his son and his grandson through eyes that refused to be dry, and their grins were just like his.

"Let's take your Pa home, Tip," he said. "Your Ma will sure be glad to see him."

A LITTLE INCONVENIENCE

Judy Christenberry

A KISMET™ Romance

 METEOR PUBLISHING CORPORATION

Bensalem, Pennsylvania

To my sister, Peggy
for her enthusiasm and support

JUDY CHRISTENBERRY

Judy Christenberry lives with her two daughters in Plano, Texas, where she teaches high school French. She writes both contemporary and regency romances. Reading is one of her favorite pastimes but she is also a sports enthusiast. She hopes to travel more now that her children are older.

ONE

Drat! Elizabeth Broadhurst looked down the back of her slim leg and wearily noted the wide run zipping its way up her nylons. She hadn't expected to wear her hot pink silk suit and spike heels on the flight to Denver, but the fashion show she was covering had been delayed. There was no time to change into more casual garb if she was going to catch her plane.

So here she was in Denver's Stapleton International Airport, dressed for the cocktail party that followed the show, but on her way to a camping trip. And probably no one would meet her. It had been that kind of a day. She tried to see over the passengers ahead of her as they wended their way slowly through the exit, but her five-foot-six-inch height wasn't enough. With a sigh, she trudged along, ready for the day to end.

This ridiculous assignment was enough to depress anyone. She couldn't let her editor Joe Pierson down, after all he had done for her. But to chase all the way out to Colorado to interview a recluse who wanted it about like he wanted the measles was not smart. She still didn't understand why this man she'd never met had picked her personally from the entire staff of *Star* magazine to write the article. At least Joe told her he had.

The people in front of her melted into the waiting crowd with kisses, hugs, and laughter. Liz looked at them with envy.

Shaking her head impatiently, she scanned the faces. There were no signs held up with her name on it, so she moved with her huge duffel bag to a central position and waited. She hoped *someone* would meet her.

Jason Harmon. All she knew was that he was incredibly wealthy and even more camera shy. There had been a fuzzy newspaper photo, a ten-year-old picture taken at his wife's funeral. Everything else in the file dealt with his business operations. How could she do a personal profile from that?

She leaned against the wall and eased her right foot from the black silk three-inch heel. Normally, she wouldn't be caught dead in these torture chambers, but she couldn't wear her customary loafers to a fashion show.

She put her right shoe back on and slipped out of her other one. Ah. If someone didn't come soon, she'd find a chair and ease both feet at once.

"Liz!" someone exclaimed as strong arms wrapped her in a bear hug. She struggled to get her nose out of a dark-blue suit coat to identify the voice's owner.

Without warning, her face was lifted and warm lips covered hers. With her hazel eyes wide open,

Liz stared at a smooth, slightly tanned cheek before her eyes traveled up to the crisp dark hair. She barely registered the fact that she had never seen this man before in her life when she was distracted by the movement of his mouth on hers.

What was he doing to her? she protested to herself indignantly. But the frantic warning her mind screamed was filtered out by confusion.

After what seemed like hours, or only a second, the man pulled back and grinned. "Nice to meet you," he said in a throaty baritone. It took a minute before she understood what he had said.

"Who are you?" she demanded, hoping her voice was less shaky than her knees.

"Jason Harmon. You didn't know?"

Liz stared at him in shock. This was the wealthy, reclusive industrialist? A man who grabs a stranger and kisses her as if they had been lovers for years? "You can't be!" she replied heatedly, even as her eyes took in his elegant suit and silk tie, well suited to his large but lean frame.

"Why not? How else would I know you were due to arrive today to write an article about me?" The grin never left his face, a handsome one, Liz had to admit, though his features were rugged rather than classic. She shook her head.

"You still don't believe me? Here," he said as he reached into his pocket and pulled out a billfold. Flipping it open, he showed her a Colorado driver's license.

"This doesn't make sense," she muttered, wishing she sounded more like her normally decisive self.

"Never mind. It's the altitude." Another kiss, thankfully brief, left her unprepared for his next move.

Swinging her in the opposite direction, his arm wrapped around her shoulders, he started off across the waiting room. Liz almost fell over when her foot parted company with her shoe.

"Wait!" she yelped, hopping along, her free hand clutching his lapel.

"What's the matter? You changed your mind?"

She frowned at the eagerness of his question. "I stopped you because my shoe is about three yards behind us."

He swung the two of them around as if they were joined at the hip and stared first at the shoe and then at her bare foot. "I see what you mean."

"Would you let me go so I can put it back on?" she asked in exasperation.

"Allow me, Cinderella," he said with a laugh as he retrieved her shoe and knelt at her foot.

Liz considered herself immune to embarrassment at the age of twenty-seven, but this man had a knack for it. "No, I can . . . Oh, all right," she agreed in disgust since he knelt patiently for her to insert her foot into the shoe.

"How do you walk in those things, much less travel halfway across the country?" the man asked scornfully.

Liz felt the urge to hit something . . . or someone. Wearily, she said, "It's a long story."

She hoped the sharp glance he gave her didn't go past mussed blond hair and pale cheeks. This man made her feel vulnerable, and it wasn't a feeling she liked. She had spent the last few years shoring up her defenses.

That strong arm came around her shoulders again, and she couldn't find the energy to shrug it off.

Without a word, he had them moving in the same direction as before.

"Are we late for something?" she gasped as he strode through the airport, pulling her along with him.

"I can't wait to be alone with you," he growled in her ear without slackening his pace.

Liz stared up at him, her mouth open, until she almost fell on her face because she forgot to move her feet.

"You really shouldn't try to walk in those shoes," he advised as he set her back on her feet.

"I—you—this . . ." she spluttered, her anger and shock rendering her speechless.

"And I always thought reporters were particularly coherent," he murmured, a wicked grin on his face.

When he clutched her to his side again, preparing to continue his sprint, she rebelled. Wrenching herself out of his hold, she dropped her duffel bag and stood with her hands on her hips. "Just *one* minute!"

"Oh. The ladies's room is over there."

"You *know* that's not what I meant."

"I just met you. I'll know you a lot better *real* soon, but I don't—"

"*That's* what I mean!" she exclaimed. "I'm a reporter here to interview you for a personal profile, not an applicant for the position of mistress."

"Why, Liz, what do you mean?" The sight of the tall, virile man trying to pose as a misunderstood little boy, his blue eyes rounded in innocence, almost broke through Liz's irritation. But not quite. She was too tired, angry, and bewildered to be amused by his playacting.

"Stop it," she hissed, sparing a glance to the people around them, pausing to watch the spectacle.

"Stop what?"

She closed her eyes. Her prescient thoughts about how ridiculous this assignment was were coming back to haunt her.

"Are you feeling faint?" His solicitous tones did nothing to soothe her.

Drawing a deep breath, she opened her eyes and stared up at him. "No, I'm not feeling faint, Mr. Harmon. Frustrated, confused, and angry, but not faint."

"If you'd rather take the next plane back to L.A., I'll understand," he offered.

Liz frowned. Why did his offer sound like a big piece of cheese in a mouse trap? "I'm a professional, Mr. Harmon, and my editor is counting on me."

The grim look on his face vanished almost before Liz saw it. "Great! I don't have any objections to working *closely* with you." When he used his body to emphasize his words, pulling her against him again, Liz pushed against his solid chest. For a businessman, he was certainly in good shape, her reporter's mind noted even as she spoke.

"We won't be working that closely, Mr. Harmon."

"We will if you want a *personal* interview, Liz darlin'," he explained with a leer.

What had her editor gotten her into, Liz wondered. She'd heard horror stories from other reporters about sexual harassment, but she'd never experienced it herself.

"Mr. Harmon—"

"If you're determined to do the interview, we'd

better be on our way. We've a long drive ahead of us."

"Aren't we staying in Denver tonight?" That would give her time to call Joe and ask for help.

"No. I don't like crowds. I want to have you all to myself." He moved closer again, his breath hot on her face as he bent toward her.

Had she gone mad? Or perhaps *he* was the sick one. Her eyes narrowing, Liz scanned the area for assistance. Even for Joe, she wasn't willing to leave herself in this man's clutches.

"Let me take your bag for you, honey. I should have done so before now. I guess I was just so happy to see you I forgot my manners."

"No, I . . ."

He left her no choice, yanking the large bag from behind her without compunction. Okay, so he had her bag. That just meant she could run faster. She had her round-trip ticket and a credit card in her purse.

On the verge of flight, she almost jumped out of her skin when Harmon spoke to someone over her shoulder. "Here, Archie, take Liz's bag, and we'll be on our way."

Off balance, Liz found herself led willy-nilly from the airport against her better judgment. *I'll call Joe the minute I get to a phone*, she promised herself.

A short time later, the airport faded from view as Archie, an elderly man, dignified in a dark-blue suit, drove the polished gray limousine through the crowded traffic west toward the Rockies. Liz was momentarily distracted by the beauty of the towering mountains, with the sparkling lights of Denver spread out beneath them.

She pushed her blond hair behind one ear, a habit that was easily accommodated by her casual style. It was time to sort out this mess. "Mr. Harmon—"

Since he was seated next to her in the backseat, he didn't have to lean over far to plant a kiss on her lips. "Now, honey, there's no need to call me that. I told you my name's Jason."

"*Will* you stop that!" she demanded, even angrier as she heard the shrill tones in her voice.

The man winked at her. "Don't tell me you're shy. I thought reporters were experienced." He imbued that word with all kinds of lurid ideas.

"You've got the wrong—" she began, but was cut off again by his lips. She intended to fight her way out of his embrace, but the warmth of his touch held her until he withdrew. Wide-eyed, she put as much distance between them as she could.

"Have you ever been to the Rockies before, Liz?" he asked casually, as if they hadn't just exchanged a passionate embrace.

"What?" She felt herself in a fog, totally confused by recent events.

"Been to the Rockies before?"

"No. No, I haven't."

"You'll love 'em. The mountains are great. Of course, they're kind of wild, lots of bears, mountain lions and all. You're not frightened by wild animals, are you, Liz?" When she didn't immediately respond, he added with a smile, "Or the cold? Or being alone with a stranger up in the mountains?"

By now, however, Liz was finding her feet, helped by a certain distance from him across the limo, and she noted that the smile did not extend to his blue eyes.

Her reporter's instincts told her there was something going on beneath the surface. Watching him carefully, she asked, "Are we going up into the mountains tonight?"

He gave her a speculative look, but Liz kept her face void of any emotion. "No, we'll spend the night at the ranch."

"I didn't realize you had a ranch. Is it far from Denver?"

"Not too far."

Which told her exactly nothing, a technique of which she was sure Mr. Harmon was an expert. She hadn't managed to stay afloat in the tough world of journalism for five years because of meekness, however. "Good. I'm looking forward to changing clothes. I had to go to a fashion show this afternoon and didn't have time to change before my plane left. You must think I'm crazy to dress like this for a camping trip."

"And here I thought you were just trying to impress me," he said, leaning forward. "And, I must say, I'm impressed."

His compliment left her cold. She raised her chin and stared straight ahead. Was he serious with his sexy talk, or was he trying to distract her from something else? Her instincts said the latter, but what was he hiding?

Without warning, the dark-haired man slid across the seat and nuzzled her neck. "No!" Liz protested. "Don't do that."

"Well, that cuts it," he finally exclaimed. He said nothing more until she reluctantly looked at him. "I thought you'd be friendly." When she continued to stare silently at him, her hazel eyes wide, he said,

"Look, if you aren't interested in having a good time, you might as well leave. I'll have Andy take you back to the airport."

"Are you refusing to do the interview, Mr. Harmon?" Liz asked with a frown, trying to gather her thoughts.

"Hell, no, I'm not refusing!" he growled, shooting her a glare that would have conquered almost any adversary. His next words were softened. "But I'll understand if you want to give it up."

"I told you my editor was depending on me. I've never backed out on an assignment yet."

His arm snaked around her again. "Then I expect we'll become real close friends."

This time Liz steeled herself to resist the shakiness that invaded her every time he drew near. Something was rotten in Denmark. Keeping her voice unemotional, she asked, "Just how close do you want to get . . . Jason?"

The surprise in his eyes gave her a boost of confidence. "I just like to know where I stand," she murmured in explanation when he didn't answer.

"I reckon as close as you'll allow, sweetheart," he whispered, putting her resolution to the test as he nibbled on her ear.

Trying to quell the shivers that coursed through her, she said sweetly, "Oh, I can't wait to tell my sisters."

Only a grunt was heard from the man exploring her neck in a way that melted her insides.

"They've always said I'd find the right man one day, if I just waited," she cooed. Her stillness paid off. There was a slow withdrawal as Jason Harmon sat back and stared at her cautiously.

"I look wonderful in white," she assured him with a girlish giggle while fluttering her lashes.

"Wait just a minute! I never said anything about a wedding." He ran his finger around the collar of his crisp white shirt.

"Well, of course not. Not yet." She giggled again. "And to think, I thought this would just be a dull, boring interview. Oh, Jason," she enthused, sighing, as she cast a lingering glance at him.

He didn't respond to her invitation, drawing farther from her. She'd been right. Whatever game he was playing, it wasn't seduction . . . at least, not with the price tag she'd just revealed. His body was taut with tension, not desire. She almost felt sorry for him as panic flared in his eyes. But he deserved it. She didn't like playing any game blind, and it was time she let him know she wasn't a puppet whose strings were in his pocket.

With an abrupt movement, he picked up the phone and buzzed the chauffeur. "Archie, turn around and go back to the airport."

"You're refusing to do the interview?" she asked, assuming her professional air.

"No! But I . . . that was all a show, wasn't it?" he asked slowly.

"My desire for a wedding ring?" she asked, smiling coolly. "Not entirely, Mr. Harmon. I intend to marry someday. But it won't be to someone like you."

"I find your behavior to be very unprofessional," he said stiffly.

He was right. But she couldn't believe he had the gall to say so after his behavior. "I could say I was led astray by your incredible performance."

He had the grace to drop his gaze, and she noted his flushed cheeks in the dim light. "I had my reasons." His harsh voice didn't invite friendliness.

"As did I."

"Look, lady, you'd better just forget doing this interview. I don't think things will work out between us."

"*Things* don't have to work out between us, Mr. Harmon. As I stated earlier, I'm a professional. I don't have to like my subject to do a good interview." Looking out the window of the limo, she added, "And I don't intend to go back to L.A."

"You're in way over your head. This trip up into the mountains is going to be difficult. And I wasn't joking about the wild animals earlier." His growl was as bad as any bear's, Liz decided.

"I'll hide behind you, Mr. Harmon. I'm sure there isn't a bear in the Rockies that would dare attack you."

As if her cool jab had snapped his patience, Harmon grabbed the phone again. 'Archie, pull over!"

Liz felt sure she had gone one step too far. She braced herself for what would follow.

Jason Harmon yanked open the door of the limo and got out, his tall frame impressive in silhouette. Liz didn't move until he reached back in and, grabbing her arm, snapped, "Out!"

I'm going to look pretty silly standing by the road dressed in spike heels and a silk suit, she thought grimly. Sliding out of the car, she turned and faced her enemy.

He wrenched open the front door of the car and motioned to her. She stared at him dumbfounded.

"Get in!" he ordered, and she could tell he was

hanging on by the threads to what little civility he had.

"I don't understand."

"I gave my word to do this interview, so if you insist on going on with this farce, I have no choice. But I don't have to like it. And I don't have to spend any more time with you than necessary. You ride with Archie." He leaned into the car. "And, Archie, keep the dividing glass up. I don't want to hear this woman until I have to!" When Liz didn't move, he circled her, getting into the backseat and slamming the door. She stared after him.

"Miss? Would you get in, please?" The chauffeur's kind words prodded her, and Liz slid into the comfortable seat. At least it was better than being abandoned in the Rocky Mountains. But interviewing someone who didn't want to talk to her was going to be a little inconvenient.

TWO

Liz spent the rest of the ride in silence. Though there were several sideways looks from the chauffeur, she made no attempt to strike up a conversation. She had a lot on her mind. Over and over she traced the evening's events, from her arrival at the airport until her exile from the man in the backseat. Had she misjudged him? Was he simply a lecher, thinking every woman would submit to his passes because he was wealthy?

She didn't think so. There had been no desire in his eyes, no enthusiasm for his victim. In fact, in spite of his actions, Liz got the feeling he didn't like her very much even before she turned the tables on him. And if she was right, why the act?

The problem could be connected to the interview, not herself personally. Joe told her the new owner of the magazine had arranged it, that he was a personal friend of Jason Harmon, who had refused all interview requests for ten years. Why had he suddenly decided to break that rule?

Liz frowned. And why had he chosen her? She wrote about the soft issues. Fashion, charity balls, society, that was her milieu.

Archie slowed down before turning into a gravel road. There was no building in sight. "Are we almost there?" she asked.

"Yes, ma'am," Archie responded politely.

She didn't ask any more questions, even though the elderly man reminded her of those patrician southern planters who would never forget their manners.

A few minutes later, Archie halted the limo and Liz realized with a jolt they had reached their destination. The fleeting headlights had given her a glimpse of a sprawling two-story house with a wide veranda running across the front of it.

A woman came out of the house as Jason Harmon got out of the car and swung open her door. Liz found herself face-to-face with the plump woman, somewhere in Archie's age group.

"My, don't you look elegant," the lady said with a smile, the first real warmth Liz had received since her arrival in Colorado.

"Thank you. I'm afraid I didn't have time to change after covering a fashion show this afternoon."

"A fashion show? Oh, I can't wait to hear all about it. What designer?"

Liz told her the designer's name and was surprised to discover the lady knew of him. "Oh, yes, I do like his clothes. I saw him on *Donohue*."

"Mamie, if we could go inside, maybe Miss Broadhurst could tell you about it in comfort." There was no lazy charm in the man's voice, but at least her host was not going to make her sleep in the barn, Liz thought in relief.

There must have been something in his tone to alert the housekeeper that all was not right. "Of course, right this way, Miss Broadhurst. I'll show you to your room at once," she offered, but her eyes were on her employer.

Liz caught his curt nod of approval but said nothing, meekly following the woman.

She discreetly looked around her as she entered the house. It was tastefully decorated, the hallway's wooden floor gleaming with wax and covered with several Navajo rugs. There was a mahogany side table with a floral arrangement that picked up the reds and blues in the rugs. She wanted to pause at the charcoal drawings of Indians that hung on the walls, but the lady moved steadily toward the stairs and Liz followed.

Tasteful but simple. She liked the honesty of the decor. Nothing shouted incredible wealth, but it also didn't pretend to be average America.

The room at the end of the upstairs hall was decorated in cornflower blue and cream. The queen-size bed was piled with pillows on top of the sprigged-blossom bedspread. On the other side of the room stood a small couch and chairs in front of a stone fireplace. And best of all, in Liz's opinion, were the ceiling-to-floor double windows that lined two of the walls.

"What an incredibly beautiful room," she said in appreciation.

"I'm glad you like it. Jason likes his guests to be comfortable. By the way, I'm Mamie, the housekeeper, Archie's wife. If there's anything you need, you just let me know."

Liz hoped the woman's friendliness didn't disappear after she had a few words with her employer. She was like an oasis in the desert of displeasure she had just survived.

"Thank you, Mamie. Please call me Liz, and I'm sure I'll be very happy in this room. I've never stayed anywhere lovelier."

The woman beamed even more at her praise. "It's a real shame that you have to leave it so soon. But maybe when you get back, Jason'll ask you to stay a while longer."

Liz didn't know how to respond to her words. She was sure if Mr. Harmon had a choice, she'd be out the door now, much less increasing the length of her stay. Finally, she murmured, "That's a nice thought."

They were interrupted by Archie's sliding the big duffel bag inside the door. Liz thanked him as he nodded and slipped from the room.

"Well, I'll get downstairs and put dinner on the table. It should be ready in about half an hour. And we're casual folks. No need to dress up." With a motherly smile, Mamie went downstairs.

Liz checked out the two doors that led from the room and found first a huge walk-in closet that she would have died for in her cramped apartment in Los Angeles. The other led to a sparkling bathroom done in the same color scheme as the bedroom, with a tub that invited a luxurious bubble bath. No time for that now, but if she hurried, she could take a shower and still not be late to dinner.

When Liz came down the stairs half an hour later, she was dressed in gray slacks topped with a pale-pink cotton sweater. Her makeup was lightly done and her blond hair shining clean. She looked like America's ideal of the girl next door. Pausing in the hallway, she tried to decide where she should go.

"There you are," Mamie said, opening a door behind her. "I was just coming up to get you. My, don't you look nice." Her smile was just as warm as before and Liz wondered if Mr. Harmon had not had an opportunity to tell her how unwanted Liz was.

"Thank you. Something smells delicious."

"Good. I like people to have big appetites. Just come this way." She turned back to the open door and Liz followed her. She entered a huge kitchen with an incredible array of gleaming appliances and stared around her in wonder. Voices drew her to the center of the room where a large table was located.

"Liz is here, Jason," Mamie prompted, looking at him in surprise.

Her host had remained seated, greeting her with only a hard look. At Mamie's words, he rose from his chair and said with no warmth at all, "Please be seated, Miss Broadhurst."

Unfortunately for Liz, the chair he waved her to was beside him. In a move that surprised her, he pulled her chair out.

After she was seated, he introduced her to the three men at the table besides Archie. "This is Al, Matt, and Jesse. Miss Broadhurst from Los Angeles," he added, making his displeasure clear in his voice. With even greater reluctance, he added, "And these are my children, Robert and Roseann."

The three nodded, looking from their boss to her with interest. Either the man was always a bear with outsiders or they knew the reason for his antagonism,

Liz thought. Probably a combination of the two. The two children, twins and carbon copies of their father with dark hair and blue eyes, neither smiled nor looked at her. She said, "Please, call me Liz."

Jesse, who appeared to be the youngest of the men and was of Mexican-American descent, asked, "You lookin' forward to the camping trip, Liz?"

"Yes, I am. I love being outdoors."

"You do?" Jason asked sharply, causing Liz to look at him with a frown.

"Why, yes, I do. Is that a problem?"

He dropped his eyes to his plate. "Just unexpected in a city girl."

"I've only been a city girl for five years, and even then I've gotten out of the city when I could."

"Where you from?" asked Al, the most mature of the three men, his grizzled hair and leathery skin attesting to his age.

With a grin, Liz said, "Texas."

"Aw, no, you done brought home another of those pesky Texans, Jason. What's the matter with you?" Al said plaintively with a big grin on his face.

Every year, Colorado was inundated with Texans who arrived either for the winter sports of skiing and hunting or for the summer coolness of the mountains. Colorado natives protested the invasion, but Texans continued to come in large numbers.

Even Jason smiled at Al's remark, but he made no comment.

"You won't like this camping trip," Roseann suddenly piped up from her seat across from Liz. "It's going to be terrible!" She scowled in accompaniment to her words.

Understanding the child was much easier than understanding the father. The child's flushed face made her unhappiness with Liz's presence quite clear. Liz smiled and said, "Oh, really? Why?"

Not expecting a challenge to her words, the little girl had no answer. Her father assisted her, however. "Because the terrain is quite rough and we'll be gone for a number of days. It won't exactly be an easy time for you, Miss Broadhurst." His continued use of her last name only emphasized his antagonism.

"I certainly don't want to be a burden to you, Mr. Harmon. Suppose we just do the interview here? We could probably cover everything tomorrow and only delay your trip by one day. It might be a better alternative than my accompanying you on the camping expedition." Instinct already warned her what his answer would be, but she waited to see if she was right.

"No!" he snapped. "Either you follow the conditions, or no interview."

"Then I guess I'll be going with you on that trip, because I must do the interview."

She met his eyes with a challenging look.

"That may be a decision you live to regret, Miss Broadhurst," he warned.

"It wouldn't be the first time, Mr. Harmon."

"That was a wonderful meal, Mamie," Liz said warmly. "It reminds me of my mother's cooking."

"Well, I'll take that as a high compliment, young lady. I do enjoy feeding people."

Liz liked Mamie more and more. She had an unpretentious warmth that even overcame Mr. Harmon's lack of welcome. She turned to the dark-haired little boy seated beside her and noticed he had scarcely touched his meal. "Don't you like steak, Robert?"

His face flushed, he only nodded his head no. His sister, however, had no hesitation in answering for him. "Robbie can't eat when he's upset." Her words left no one in doubt as to the cause of Robert's disturbance.

Liz wasn't sure why her presence was so bothersome, but she would never want to hurt children. "I'm sorry, Robert, if my being here upsets you."

He turned even redder, if possible, and refused to meet her eyes.

"Never you mind, Liz. He'll be sneaking back down here later for some of my homemade ice cream," Mamie assured her, easing Liz's concern somewhat.

"May I help you with the dishes, Mamie?" Liz offered.

"That's real friendly of you, Liz, but I always make Archie help me."

"I'll be glad to give Archie a break. After all, he had to pick me up at the airport."

The housekeeper looked at Jason Harmon before answering. "Well, all right, if you don't mind, I'd enjoy the company."

That was the signal for the men and children to leave the table and they did so without hesitation. Before Jason Harmon could leave the room, however, Liz stopped him.

"I wonder if I might have a word with you after I finish in here, Mr. Harmon? Say, in half an hour?"

"If you insist," he clipped, staring at her grimly.

"Thank you. Where shall I find you?"

"I'll be in the den with the kids. Mamie will show you."

She stared at the door through which he had disappeared until Mamie asked her if she was all right.

"Oh, yes, of course." She moved over to the table and began stacking dishes. She longed to ask Mamie about her boss, but she was sure the lady would not gossip about him. And she had no intention of giving the man reason to accuse her of pumping his employees.

Jason Harmon, his children, and Archie were all playing a card game when the two women entered the spacious den, filled with comfortable easy chairs and sofas that encouraged one to stretch out in contentment. The family scene struck Liz in the heart, reminding her of her intention to leave Los Angeles as soon as she did this one last interview. She wanted to be part of her family again, to surround herself with loved ones.

"Who's winning?" Mamie asked cheerfully, announcing their arrival.

There was a definite lowering of the temperature as the players greeted the other two. *And it's not because of Mamie*, Liz ruefully assured herself.

Mr. Harmon got to his feet and beckoned for Mamie. "You come take my place, and I'll have that talk with Miss Broadhurst."

Mamie agreed and seated herself in his chair, but she called out over her shoulder, "You let me know if you need anything before you go up to bed, Liz."

"I will, Mamie, thanks." She turned and silently followed her host from the room. He led her to what must be his office, though its furniture was luxurious and comfortable. A large desk with several computer terminals behind it dominated the room.

He moved behind the desk, and she sat down in a

leather chair across from him. After several minutes, when it was obvious he was not going to initiate a conversation, she stood up.

"Please sit down, Miss Broadhurst, or good manners will force me to stand again."

His growl did nothing to soothe her nerves and she snapped, "You'll forgive me for not realizing you operated under the constraints of good manners, I'm sure."

"If I didn't, Miss Broadhurst, you would have been left beside the road." The iciness of his blue eyes should have turned her into a popsicle, she thought, shivering.

"Look, Mr. Harmon . . ." Liz began earnestly, reseating herself, "I asked to speak to you privately because there seems to be something going on here of which I am unaware. Have you changed your mind about the interview? Because, if so, I'll be out of your way first thing tomorrow morning."

"I agreed to the interview, Miss Broadhurst."

She had never heard words spoken with more loathing. Frowning, she asked, "Since it is clearly not what you want, why did you do so?"

"I had no choice. The new owner of your magazine is an old friend who has done me several favors in the past."

Liz stared at the man until he dropped his eyes. She still couldn't make heads or tails of what was going on. But she had a job to do, and she needed some information. "Since I'm here, Mr. Harmon, I would like you to tell me any limitations you wish to set. After all, you have final approval of the article, so it would be foolish of me to include something you don't want."

It was Harmon's turn to frown. He seemed surprised by her words. "You mean you'll abide by my rules?"

"Of course. I don't do hatchet jobs, Mr. Harmon. I assumed that's why you chose me."

His blue eyes flashed at her before looking away.

"I was told you specifically asked for me," she persisted.

"Yes, I did. But I haven't actually read any of your writing." He was bending an acrylic letter opener back and forth and Liz watched his hands in fascination.

"Then why—"

"It doesn't matter," he said, dismissing her question. "I appreciate your attitude, Miss Broadhurst, but I think it would be best if you gave up the idea."

"If you're recanting your consent to the interview, I have no choice, do I, Mr. Harmon?" Liz said carefully.

"I'm doing no such thing!" he roared. His reply was accompanied by the snapping of the letter opener. He stared at it in disgust and threw the pieces in a trash can beside his desk. More calmly, he said again, "I am not refusing the interview, Miss Broadhurst. I can't do that. I gave my word. I realize women don't always understand how important that is, but my reputation as a straight-shooter is at stake."

Liz bristled at his words. "Honor is not unknown among females." When he didn't respond, she added, "And if you are going to permit the interview, why did you suggest I return to Los Angeles?" There was no response. "Have you decided you want another reporter?"

"No."

He seemed unwilling to add anything to his bald

reply. Liz glared at him in frustration. "Mr. Harmon, I am simply trying to do my job. But you seem intent on blocking me at every turn. What is going on?"

As if he were explaining a complicated problem to his twins, he said carefully, "I cannot take back my agreement to the interview, but you could refuse to write it."

"What?"

He started to repeat his words, but Liz stopped him. She was finally beginning to understand her confusing evening. "That's what you've been doing, isn't it? Trying to convince me I should quit, give up, go back to L.A."

Shrugging his shoulders, he added, "The camping trip is not going to be easy. You really should consider it."

"Like you, Mr. Harmon, I gave my word," she said stiffly. "Unless you refuse to give the interview, I, too, have no choice."

"You'll regret your decision, Miss Broadhurst," he said, rising. "I can promise you that." When she stood also and returned his stare, he said, "Very well. We leave at dawn. Please be ready. I don't appreciate layabouts."

"My editor said you would provide any camping equipment I might need." She hadn't wanted to ask, but she didn't want to find herself stranded in the mountains with no sleeping bag.

"Of course, Miss Broadhurst," he assured her in a tone of voice that made Liz promise herself to check the bedroll for snakes before she got in it. Then he added, "But I'm afraid we don't have any spare hiking boots or proper clothing for you to wear. I just assumed you would know enough about camping to bring your own."

"Your worries are over," she assured him sweetly. "I did."

She was almost to the door when she turned around to face the man still standing behind the desk. "Will you tell me one thing, Mr. Harmon?" He made no response, but she continued anyway. "You're a sophisticated, intelligent man. Why are you so irrational about interviews?"

The anger in his face and the shaking of his strong hands should have prepared her for his bombshell. "It's reporters I'm irrational about, Miss Broadhurst. After all, two of them killed my wife."

THREE

Mamie found Liz in the hallway with the door to Harmon's office closed behind her, though she couldn't actually remember leaving the room.

"Why, child, what's wrong? You're white as a sheet."

Liz blinked, trying to focus on the lady. Finally, she replied, "Nothing, Mamie. I'm just tired."

"Well, you just scoot on off to bed. Would you like me to bring you up a cup of cocoa?"

Her motherly concern warmed Liz. "No, thanks. Will you wake me an hour before we're to leave in the morning?"

"Of course."

Liz moved toward the stairs but then stopped to call to Mamie who had continued on her way to the kitchen. "Mamie? I need to call my editor. I'll put it on my credit card, of course."

"Lands, Liz, don't worry about that. There's a phone in your room. Feel free to use it."

Hurrying up the stairs, Liz could think of nothing but Jason Harmon's last words. The assignment had only been given to her yesterday when she was still working on the article about the fashion show. She had grabbed what the business reporter had in his files and read through most of it on the plane, but she had seen nothing about his wife's death.

The woman died ten years ago, when the twins were a year old. Liz herself was a senior in high school in a small town in Texas. She wouldn't have heard of it. As soon as she reached her room, she dialed her editor's number at home.

"Joe?" she greeted the grumpy voice that answered.

"Liz? Is that you? Is everything okay?"

He asked that question as if he didn't expect it to be, Liz mused. Yet he had sent her out here without any warning. "Joe, everything isn't okay. What can you tell me about Mrs. Harmon's death."

"Oh."

"Why didn't you warn me?" Liz demanded, exasperated. "I haven't a clue to what the man meant, but he said his wife was killed by two reporters."

"That's not true, Liz. Well, yes, but there were extenuating circumstances. It was before your time."

"The facts, Joe!"

"It was a couple of years after Harmon burst on the scene as a boy genius. The press hounded him for interviews. He gave a few, but he drew the line at exposing his family. One evening, two reporters spotted his wife out alone. They tried to talk to her, but once they identified themselves as reporters, she ran. Jumped into her car and sped off. Well, you know reporters. They don't give up that easily. They followed her. It was raining and . . . well, she lost control of the car and hit a bridge embankment. The reporters got help, but it was too late. She was killed instantly. Harmon blamed the reporters. He's never given an interview since.''

"You let me come out here without telling me that?" Liz demanded, outraged.

"Come on, Liz, what difference did it make? You have to do the interview anyway.'' His cajoling tones fell on deaf ears.

"No, I don't, Joe. Send someone else. I've had it with you and Mr. Harmon!''

"Liz, I can't do that. If you don't interview him, the deal's off. And if we don't get this interview, Parks is going to fire me.'' His voice wavered on the last sentence. Liz didn't know if it was acting or genuine fear that caused it.

"Why does it have to be me?''

"Because Harmon agreed to the interview under his conditions. He requested you, and he insisted the interview had to be conducted in the mountains.''

"Joe, he hasn't read any of my stuff. Why would he pick me? I'm not a business expert.''

After clearing his throat, Joe muttered, "I'm not sure.''

"Now, why don't I believe you?" Liz asked in cool tones.

"He said something about you looking like the one the least able to stay the course. He warned Parks that if you backed out, the whole deal was off.''

Liz blew out a heavy breath in frustration. "And you didn't think it was necessary to mention that, either?''

"Maybe I handled it all wrong, Liz, but . . . but I'm worried. Please get the interview. I'm too old to be pounding the sidewalks." Joe had given her a job when she first came to L.A. She could remember how scared she had been.

"I'll get the interview, Joe," Liz assured him in grim tones, "but that's the last you or Los Angeles will see of me."

"Thanks, Liz. I knew you wouldn't let me down."

"Bye, Joe." She put down the receiver and leaned back against the pillows. Thanks a lot, Joe. He'd let her stumble into a hornet's nest with no warning whatsoever. Oh, she had known that her subject was reluctant, but she knew how to handle that kind. Jason Harmon was different.

Now she thought she fully understood his act at the airport. He'd hoped she'd turn tail and run if he made her think he was going to waylay her at every turn. She'd been confused by his behavior, as unexpected as it was. Now that she knew she was the enemy, she'd be on her guard.

It was still dark when Mamie entered the room and woke her the next morning. With a groan, Liz rolled over and opened one eye. She had had difficulty getting to sleep the night before and it was a very comfortable bed. "So soon?"

" 'Fraid so. And Jason's not the most patient of men on the subject of tardiness."

"I haven't found him patient on any subject," Liz muttered, bleary-eyed.

"Well, when it comes to the kids, he is. He's a wonderful father."

Sitting up, Liz asked, "Has he raised them by

himself? I mean, I know you're here, but . . . he's never remarried?''

"No, he hasn't. I've suggested it, but he says he won't have them live in Los Angeles, and most women don't want to live in the country.''

"I don't think Mr. Harmon has a very high opinion of women, Mamie. Except for you, of course.''

"Well, now, that could be true. Maybe you're the one to change his mind.''

Liz caught the twinkle in the woman's eye. "Don't get any matchmaking ideas. Mr. Harmon would as soon run over me as look at me. And besides, I'm not interested, either,'' she remembered to add.

"Whatever you say, honey. You'd best get a move on. I'll have breakfast ready in half an hour.''

"I don't eat much breakfast, Mamie. Just a piece of toast and some juice.''

"Reckon you'd better change your habits this morning. It'll be a long time till lunch,'' the housekeeper warned as she left the room.

She had a point. And if Mr. Harmon was going to make this trip as difficult as possible, she'd better be prepared for anything. She rolled out of bed and hurried to take her last shower for the next few days. Outdoor plumbing left a lot to be desired.

Liz was the last to arrive at the breakfast table. Again, the only empty seat was beside Jason Harmon. She offered a general greeting and avoided looking at her host. When Mamie set a plate full of eggs, bacon, and toast down in front of her, Liz swallowed her protest and gave the hearty breakfast her best efforts. The hot cup of coffee did more for her appreciation of the morning than the food, but she might feel differently later in the morning.

"Are you packed?"

The clipped tones of her host roused Liz from her thoughts. She looked up to find him staring at her. "Why, yes, I am."

Her self-congratulation was forgotten when he said, "Then you'll have to repack. All your gear must go in the backpack over on that chair."

Eyeing the nylon bag, Liz knew Mr. Jason Harmon expected her to protest its size, but she only looked at him and nodded. His eyes narrowed, but he said nothing else.

"If you need some more room, Liz, I reckon I've got a little space going empty," Matt drawled. His generosity earned him a black look from his employer.

With a warm smile, she said, "Thanks, Matt, I may need to take you up on your offer. I'll see how compactly I can fold my clothes."

"We're not doing a fashion show up in the mountains," Jason growled. "You just need a change or two." When she didn't respond, he added begrudgingly, "I hope the rest of your gear is as appropriate as what you're wearing."

Liz was dressed in worn jeans, a denim shirt covered with a blue pullover, and lightweight leather hiking boots, and she'd pulled her blond hair back in a practical pony tail.

"They are," she replied crisply, her chin up. This man could take niceness lessons from the Ayatollah Khomeini, she thought in disgust. She drained her coffee mug and rose. "If you'll excuse me, I'll go repack. I don't want to keep anyone waiting."

A few minutes later, Liz came down the stairs with

the bag Harmon had given her stuffed like a Thanksgiving turkey. It would've been helpful if he'd told her earlier. But then being helpful wasn't his goal, she reminded herself.

"Miss Broadhurst."

Jason Harmon's irritable tones jerked her from her thoughts. He was standing in front of the office where their previous night's interview had taken place.

"I'm ready, Mr. Harmon." Her response didn't seem to please him, she noted as his frown deepened.

"I want to talk to you," he snapped, and turned on his heel to enter his office without waiting to see if she would follow.

Liz considered ignoring his order. In no way could it be construed as a request. But that kind of behavior would only increase the tension between them. She reluctantly entered the lion's den.

The man was seated behind his desk, his hands clenched in front of him. Liz didn't sit down. She hoped their conference would be brief.

"I thought you might have changed your mind."

Liz played the innocent. "Oh, no, I managed to get everything in the bag you gave me, Mr. Harmon."

"You know what I mean!" he ground out.

She gave up the game for frankness. "I explained last night that I had to go through with the interview unless you stop me. If you want another reporter, then I'll return to Los Angeles as soon as you call my boss and tell him that." She wanted to force the man to be honest with her, to confirm what her editor had told her.

One fist smashed into the rich mahogany of the desk. Liz jumped in surprise.

"I can't do that!"

"Why? It happens all the time. If the person being interviewed isn't happy with the reporter, then—"

"I understand the concept, Ms. Broadhurst." His heavy sarcasm didn't faze her.

"Then why don't you call him?"

"Because I insisted you were the only reporter I would accept, and if you didn't write the story, then the deal was completely off."

Liz sat down. "Why would you do that? Insist that it only be me? You said last night you've never read anything that I wrote."

He avoided her eyes and his face darkened. "You looked soft," he muttered.

"I beg your pardon?" Liz demanded, outraged.

"I planned on scaring you off!"

Liz jumped to her feet, followed by Jason Harmon, and they glared at each other.

"Scare me off? You and who else?" she retaliated, resorting to childish taunts.

"I don't need any help! You're a city woman! And you'd better think twice before you go camping with *me*!"

"What are you going to do? Push me off a mountain?" She wanted to stick her tongue out at him, but she retained at least enough control to submerge that desire.

Her outrageous suggestion must have shaken the man because he shook his head, as if clearing it, and took a deep breath. "Look, Miss Broadhurst, let's not get carried away."

"I'm not the one who was issuing threats," she muttered.

"I didn't mean . . . I was just trying to persuade you to give up the interview."

Liz sank back down into the chair, her knees wobbly. "I've told you I can't," she protested.

"But why? What difference does it make?"

"A lot. The new owner will fire the editor if I don't get this interview. And Joe gave me my start. I can't let that happen just because you go a little crazy around reporters."

"I have a right to my privacy," he said stiffly.

"*You* are the one who agreed to the interview, Mr. Harmon, not me."

A knock on the door interrupted the tension. "Boss, you ready?" Matt's voice called.

Frustration was evident on the man's face as he called back, "We'll be there in just a minute, Matt." He turned back to stare at Liz. "I'll help your editor find another job. Hell! I'll buy the magazine and let him keep his old job."

It was tempting to accept his offer. She could then get on with her life. But Liz didn't think the magazine could be bought. The new owner was too enthralled with his new "toy." And besides, as she had told him earlier, she had given her word. She regretfully shook her head. "I'm sorry, Mr. Harmon. I can't go back on my word. But I can assure you that I'll write a fair article."

"I don't want fairness! I want to be left alone!"

"Mr. Harmon, you're too young to be a hermit." Liz hesitated but couldn't resist adding, "And you really should get over your fear of publicity. It must make your work more difficult."

"Oh, of course, Miss Broadhurst," he agreed nastily, "I'm in great danger of going bankrupt because I don't kowtow to every reporter I meet."

Perhaps her remark had been unjustified, but he

needn't have been so rude about it. Liz stood again
and challenged the man with her eyes. "Shall we go,
Mr. Harmon? We don't want to keep the others
waiting."

He strode around his desk to tower over her. "Listen to me, woman. I don't want you talking to my
children. Do you hear me?"

"Very clearly, Mr. Harmon. But I don't pump
innocent children. Nor do I chase people and cause
their deaths." She wished she hadn't added that last
bit, as his eyes darkened with pain. "I . . . I'm
sorry," she added with little effect.

"People always are afterward, Miss Broadhurst."

He didn't wait for a response. Almost before Liz
realized it, he was out the door, leaving it open for
her to follow. With a sigh, she picked up the bag in
which she had repacked her belongings and trod after
him. She hoped this camping trip was going to be the
shortest one on record. Because she was quite sure it
was going to be the most difficult.

Liz undid another button on her denim shirt. She
had already removed her sweater and laid it across
the saddle in front of her. It might be October in the
Rockies, but the sun was beating down on her back,
and she was hot. And tired. And extremely sore. She
was in good shape, but her legs were not used to
hugging the big horse beneath her.

When they had stopped for lunch, a cold snack
that only took fifteen minutes, she thought she couldn't
walk to the shade of a nearby tree. But she was just
as determined as Jason Harmon, she reminded herself.

Getting back upon that horse was the hardest thing
she'd ever done. She wanted to tell the devilish Mr.

Harmon that she would follow on foot. But when he'd cocked an eyebrow in her direction, she remained mum and pulled herself back up onto that torturous saddle.

Now she was boiling in the sun. The one thing she hadn't remembered was a hat. She envied the others with their broad-brimmed cowboy hats. In the city, she always scorned the men who pretentiously paraded around in boots and hats, but out here, they were a necessary part of the uniform. She would have given a lot to have one of her own.

When Jason Harmon dropped back beside her on his mount, Liz straightened her back and assumed a nonchalant expression. She would give him no weapons to use against her.

"How are you doing, Miss Broadhurst?" he asked, the blue eyes that matched his plaid flannel shirt glinting.

That's probably how the sharks look at their victims before they rip off a leg, Liz thought wearily. "Just fine, Mr. Harmon."

"You'd better call me Jason," he said abruptly, surprising Liz. At her questioning look, he added, "The men wouldn't understand our formality. Coloradians are friendly by nature."

Though she searched his suggestion for hidden dangers, she found none. "All right. As long as we're on the camping trip, I'll call you Jason."

"Right."

"Daddy, how much farther?" Roseann called out.

"Not far, little one," Jason said as he rode ahead to speak with his daughter.

Liz watched him. That was one thing she had

already discovered about Jason Harmon. He loved his children.

Liz grimaced as she thought about her editor's reaction to such a discovery. She knew that wasn't what he hoped her article would contain. To Liz, however, it was an important part of the man she was here to study.

Jason Harmon's "not far" turned out to be two more hours, with the terrain growing steeper each step her horse took. When they finally pulled up at a small flat area, she wanted to fall to the ground and never rise again.

Come on now, Liz, she encouraged herself. *You can do it. Just remember that Jason Harmon is trying to force you to quit.* Her words were more appropriate than she knew as her enemy strolled over to hold her horse while she slid from the saddle.

"Are you all right?" Jason asked with what she considered to be mock concern on his face.

"Fine," she mumbled, clutching the saddle horn to allow her rubber legs time to solidify.

"Because if this is too much for you, I could arrange for you to return to the ranch with Al," he added as he crossed his arms over the saddle, his cowboy hat tipped back on his head.

As if he had jabbed her with a miracle cure, Liz straightened and gave her tormentor a bright smile. "Don't be ridiculous. I'm enjoying myself immensely." Besides, she added to herself, she'd die in these mountains before she'd mount another horse!

"Good," Jason said tersely. "Then I guess you won't mind helping with the camp chores. It's tradition that everyone pitches in."

"Of course. I insist on it." She was sure her task

would be that of camp cook. That would be typical of macho men.

"Why don't you help Robbie distribute the sleeping bags and unroll them after Matt and I set up the tents."

Liz stared at him in surprise. When he looked at her questioningly, she nodded.

"Fine. Go find Robbie and he'll tell you what to do."

Liz nodded again and watched over her saddle as the infuriating man strolled away, his form-fitting jeans emphasizing his muscular legs. If only she could be assured of walking so casually, she moaned. She was afraid to let go of the saddle horn in case she crumpled up without support, but Al was approaching. She took a small step away from her faithful steed and breathed a sigh of relief when she stayed upright.

"You all right, Miss Broadhurst?" the older man asked kindly.

"Yes, thank you. And please, let's make it Liz. Formalities seem silly up here."

"Yes, ma'am," Al said with a grin. "I'll unsaddle your horse. Why don't you just wander on over there and sit down."

"Oh, no. I'm to help Robbie with the sleeping bags. Really, I'm just fine," she replied in response to the skeptical look on the leathery face of the man beside her.

With great caution, she stepped around her horse, moving slowly, and headed toward the boy who was untying a large bundle.

"Robert? Or should I call you Robbie?" Liz asked.

"Robbie," the child mumbled, never looking up.

"Your dad said I should help you lay out the sleeping bags. You'll need to tell me what to do since I'm new at this."

Though Liz smiled in a friendly manner, there was no response from the boy, who never looked up. Liz stood there patiently waiting. Finally, she caught a sideways look from her companion.

"These are yours and Rosie's. You're gonna share a tent."

Liz glanced doubtfully over at the girl, who continued to give her baleful stares. "Does Rosie know that?" she asked conspiratorially, surprising her young friend into a hastily concealed laugh.

"Yes, ma'am, she knows."

Robbie's tone of voice told Liz Rosie's opinion of their sharing even if she couldn't have guessed. With a sigh, she said, "I see."

"It won't be so bad," Robbie suddenly said with a half smile. "She just pretends to be mean."

"Ah. I'll try to remember that." Taking the two sleeping bags indicated, she asked, "Which tent will we use?"

"The one Daddy and Matt are finishing now. Girls always get the first tent 'cause Daddy says they have more gear to stow away."

"I bet Rosie loves that," Liz muttered, surprising her companion into another grin.

"Yeah," he agreed before catching a stare from his sister. He wiped the smile from his face and turned back to his chores. Liz looked at that young lady regretfully.

Clearly Rosie's problem was jealousy over her father, Liz thought as she walked slowly toward the first tent to be erected. She was there only to write an article, but she couldn't blame Roseann for thinking otherwise. Apparently her father didn't invite women to share their life very often. It was perfectly normal for the child to assume more than was true.

"Rosie, does it matter to you which side you're on?" she called out, determined to bridge the gap between the only two females.

"My name is Roseann," the young lady said icily, more formal than the snootiest of society ladies.

"Sorry," Liz said with a cheerful grin, determined not to take offense. One fight with his daughter, and Liz was sure Jason Harmon would call off the interview, promise or no promise. In fact, she wasn't sure she would be allowed to do anything more than breathe. And do camp chores.

Liz crawled into the small tent as soon as the two men had moved on to the next one, untied the sleeping bags, and rolled them out, first checking for any sharp objects that would affect their comfort. The bending over necessary to maneuver in the tent caused her stiff muscles to scream out in pain, but Liz ground her teeth and continued.

The tent set up only a few feet from the ladies' tent was for Jason Harmon and his son. Liz dutifully unrolled the two sleeping bags pointed out to her by Robbie.

The third tent was slightly larger and Al, Matt, and Jesse would share it. When she emerged from that tent after arranging the sleeping bags, she looked around camp.

Al had unsaddled and tethered all the horses, after

leading them to a nearby stream that Liz just now noticed. Matt and his boss had set up all the tents. Robbie was in charge of unpacking the necessities, and Jesse and Roseann had built a campfire and were preparing a delicious supper if the aroma was accurate.

"Can I help?" Liz asked Jesse.

"Sure. I need a couple more potatos peeled," the man said easily.

"I'll show you where to wash your hands," Roseann offered suddenly, jumping up, her black pigtails flying at her sudden movement.

Liz eyed her suspiciously, but the child turned a cheerful face up to her, and Liz couldn't hold back a smile in return. She wasn't going to refuse an olive branch from anyone. Following the child toward the stream, Liz hoped she was taking the first step to breaking through Roseann's animosity.

FOUR

"Here's a good place," Roseann said, gesturing to the foot of the path where the stream ran cold and swift. There were several large rocks surrounded by smaller ones where Liz could kneel down to wash.

"Thanks, Roseann," Liz said, turning to the little girl with a smile. The child was searching the area with her eyes, an intent look on her face. Liz was reminded of that suspicious feeling she got when Roseann offered to show her the way. She looked back at the stream, but she couldn't see any problems. Shrugging her shoulders, she squatted down and reached for the water. Just as she leaned forward, a long black ropelike creature whipped between her feet and into the stream.

The scream that rent the air came from Liz without conscious volition. She fell back on her bottom, ignoring the rocks on which she landed. A shaking hand covered her lips to hold back any more screams that might try to escape.

"Are you okay?" Roseann asked in monumental unconcern. "There isn't anything to be upset about. It was only an old water snake. They aren't dangerous."

Eyeing the calm young lady with irritation, Liz said between gritted teeth, "It surprised me, that's all."

There was a scattering of stones and the rush of several feet as the male members of their camp joined them. "What's wrong?" Jason demanded in urgent tones, his concern lessening as he saw both females safe beside the stream.

Though still white of face, Liz rose to her feet and faced the others. "I'm sorry. I shouldn't have screamed, but . . . but a snake went between my legs as I stooped down to wash."

"What kind of snake?" Jason demanded.

"Only a water snake, Daddy. I told her it wasn't poisonous," Roseann said.

"They're really harmless, Liz, but I reckon they could put a fright into you. They move awful fast," Matt said, showing some sympathy.

Liz shot him a grateful smile. "I didn't mean to upset the camp. But I couldn't hold back the scream."

"Well, I don't think it hurt anything," Al assured her.

"Unless our steaks are burning!" Jesse exclaimed, turning on his heel and racing back to camp. The others, after exchanging rueful shrugs, moved in that general direction.

"I'll wait for you to wash, Liz," Jason offered gruffly, since she didn't follow.

"I can do that, Daddy," Roseann protested, sending Liz a malevolent glance.

"You were supposed to help her the first time, Rosie. You know to check out an area before you do anything else." Jason watched his daughter's reaction.

"Yeah. I guess I forgot."

While they were arguing over who was going to wait for her, Liz quickly washed her hands and face and stood. "It doesn't matter. I'm ready now."

"Go on ahead, Rosie," Jason commanded. After a backward look, Roseann obeyed her father. When she was almost to camp, he turned back to Liz. "I apologize for my daughter."

Liz didn't argue with his conclusion. She nodded an acknowledgment and waited.

"But perhaps you'd better reconsider your decision to continue. We're likely to run into some bigger wildlife than snakes, you know. There's bear up here and mountain lions."

"And if I really want to, you can arrange for me to return to the ranch, right, Mr. Harmon?"

"You catch on quick, Miss Broadhurst," the man replied stiffly.

"Yes, don't I just? Shall we go back now? I promised Jesse I'd peel potatoes."

As the light faded, the mountain air grew sharper, and the warmth from the campfire felt good. Liz put down her tin plate with a sigh. "Jesse, that was the most wonderful dinner I've ever eaten. You're a marvelous cook."

"Thanks, Liz," the cowhand said with a grin. "But I suspect your appetite influenced your taste buds."

"You could be right," she agreed. "That long ride today took a lot out of me." Realizing what an opening she had given her host to recommend she quit, Liz threw a challenging look his way.

"Did you want me to offer?"

Robbie, leaning against his father's knee, looked up and asked, "Offer what?"

"To send Miss Broadhurst back to the ranch if the trip is too difficult for her."

"No, I didn't *want* you to offer. It's just that you've become rather predictable," Liz responded, her voice as cold as the night air.

"That's me, dull and predictable," Jason said dryly. There was laughter among the men, but the children's faces wore puzzled looks. Liz felt sure they were the only ones unaware of their father's reputation for steely negotiations and unusual compromises.

"How do you find time to come camping when you are responsible for so many companies?" Liz asked.

"I have an incredible staff and I keep in constant touch. It's impor— Wait a minute. We're not doing the interview now." Jason leaned forward to lay another piece of wood on the dying campfire, a scowl on his face.

"Sorry, I was just curious. After all, the image you're presenting now is quite different from how most people see you." Liz studied his muscular figure, clad in tight-fitting jeans and a blue plaid shirt, the shadows from the flames dancing across his strong face.

Jason stood up abruptly. "You'd better turn in, since you're determined to stick this out. We'll be leaving at dawn in the morning."

Liz saw the others' surprise and realized her host was uping the ante in their little game. "And just when will the interview take place?" she asked softly, her hazel eyes trained on him.

"Not now!" he snapped, and turned to walk off into the woods.

"Uhuh," Matt muttered.

"Did you say something, Matt?" Liz asked.

"No, ma'am, I didn't. Since we're going to get such an early start, I reckon I'll turn in, too. Kids?"

The two youngsters got up, but Roseann turned to Liz. "I wish you'd just leave Daddy alone. We're here to have fun, and you're spoiling it!" Then she ran after her father.

Robbie scuffed his toe against a rock, saying nothing, his dark hair shading his troubled eyes. Al walked over and put his arm around the boy and smiled at Liz. "Don't pay any attention to Rosie. She's used to being the only lady in her dad's life."

"If any of you could reassure her that I'm only here for an interview at Mr. Harmon's request, it might help. In fact, if he'd give me the interview this evening, I'd leave in the morning with you, Al."

Matt, Jesse, and Al ignored her appeal, confirming Liz's idea that Jason Harmon had explained the situation to his cowhands. But Robbie looked at her curiously. "Is that the only reason you're here? You and Daddy aren't . . . I mean . . . we thought—"

"Time for bed, young Robbie," Matt interrupted. "You'd best find your dad and Rosie."

Liz watched the boy walk out of the circle of light provided by the fire. "I can accept that the kids are off limits for the interview, Matt, but I don't understand why they can't know the situation."

Matt smiled down at Liz as she remained seated on her rock. He was about the same age as Jason Harmon and had a rugged attraction. His lazy smile would have drawn a lot of women in Los Angeles, Liz thought. "I'll tell you, Liz, Jason doesn't pay me to make his decisions for him, especially about his kids. I do my job. You got any questions about all this, you talk to the boss."

The same closed expression was on Al and Jesse's faces, and Liz shrugged her shoulders. "Okay. Sorry about the early start in the morning," she added with a sweet smile that drew a grin from the other two. Matt stared at her but made no reply.

Liz made a quick trip to the stream, taking a long stick to disperse any friends of her earlier acquaintance and then returned to bed down in the small tent allotted to her and Roseann. The child had not yet put in an appearance.

She could hear the others moving around the campfire, putting away provisions, banking the fire. Jason and his children came back just as the others were going to bed. Liz sat up as she heard her name mentioned. Matt was speaking in a low voice, and she could just barely distinguish what was being said.

". . . a sharp one. She figured out we don't normally leave so early. You'd better watch your step."

Liz strained forward, but all she could hear was a low murmur. Matt laughed before adding, "Yeah, she is."

Frustrated, she crawled a little closer to the flap that hid her wakefulness. The murmur continued. ". . . early . . . wait . . ." a low chuckle ". . . beautiful."

"What was beautiful?" she whispered to herself.

Or it could be *who*. Maybe Jason meant her? She dismissed such an idea. It didn't matter what Jason Harmon thought, she assured herself.

"Kids, time to turn in," Jason called across the small area.

"Just a minute, Daddy," Robbie called. Then, in a whisper, he said, "How did you get that snake to do that?"

Liz's back stiffened. The kids must be just outside her tent.

"I saw him earlier and just hoped he'd be around. It never occurred to me he'd act like that," Rose explained with a giggle. "Wasn't it great?"

Liz rolled her eyes in the darkness. That depended entirely upon your point of view, she thought.

"Rosie, I think we're wrong. I don't think Liz is wanting to . . . well, marry Dad, like your friend told you. She said she only wanted her interview and would leave tonight if she could."

"And you believed her?" Rosie responded with scorn. "Don't you know anything about women?" Her world-wise tones almost caused Liz to burst out laughing.

"Probably as much as you," Robbie protested.

"Well, if they're interested in a man, they never let on. They pretend they're not interested. That's all she's doing. I've seen it on *Dynasty* a hundred times."

"Yeah, and Daddy said you weren't supposed to watch that show."

"But it takes place in Colorado, Robbie."

"Kids!" their father's voice intruded. "I want you in your tents in ten seconds. One . . . two . . ."

Liz flopped back down in her sleeping bag and pretended to be asleep only seconds before the flap was pulled back and Roseann entered, calling back over her shoulder, "Good night."

" 'Night, sweetheart. We'll see you in the morning."

By the time the even breathing from the little girl signified sleep, Liz had done a lot of thinking. If she understood anything in this world, it was children. The five brothers and sisters who had come after her had run the gamut from meek and mild to fierce and independent.

Liz knew she was in for a difficult trip because the child next to her was protecting her territory. And until Liz could convince her that she wanted no part of her father, there would be rocky times ahead on several fronts.

Roseann was the first out of her sleeping bag the next morning, a fact for which Liz was grateful. The little girl slipped into her jeans and sweater with total unselfconsciousness, gave her companion a scornful warning to hurry and left the tent.

It wasn't that Liz was asleep. On the contrary, she was very much awake and aware of every bone in her body. After dismounting yesterday evening, her muscles had stretched out a little and she had managed to move around with minimum discomfort. But this morning, even breathing brought a painful sensation that made her never want to move again.

The sounds Jesse was making as he prepared breakfast and the movement of the others told her time was running out. She really had no choice. She could not let Joe down. And she could not let Jason Harmon win! No matter how much she suffered, she would not concede a victory to the difficult man waiting for her to raise the white flag.

With a groan, Liz sat up and unzipped her sleeping bag, sliding her legs out of its soft warmth. It seemed to take her forever to get to her knees. She stayed in that position for several minutes, grateful there was no one to witness her agony. Her long underwear kept the chill of the morning air from her body, but she could feel the bite in it.

She inched herself up to a stride position, her legs spread out, but she remained bent over from the waist because the roof of the tent didn't allow her to stand upright. Stretching began to ease the pain, giving her hope she might walk again.

Just as she was considering pulling on her clothes, the flap of her tent was thrown back. "No sleeping in, this . . ." Jason Harmon began but stopped when he discovered himself face-to-face with Liz's rear end.

Shocked by the intrusion, Liz's legs crumpled up under her and her already sore bottom, from the hours in the saddle and her meeting with the snake, crashed into the hard earth. *I may never sit down again*, Liz thought as she looked over her shoulder at the man responsible for her misery.

"Sorry to interrupt." After a brief pause, as if he couldn't help himself, Jason asked, "What the hell were you doing?"

Thank goodness for long underwear to preserve her modesty, Liz thought. "Stretching," she replied abruptly.

"Are you okay? If you aren't, you can always . . ."

"Go back to the ranch with Al. Thanks, but no thanks."

Jason didn't seem surprised at her response, but his face hardened as he warned, "You'd better think twice. Sore or not, you're expected to pull your own weight.''

Liz's face became the stiffest part of her anatomy as she said expressionlessly, ''I have every intention of doing my part. If you'll excuse me now. I'll dress and be right out.''

The man silently withdrew, and Liz tugged on her jeans and a red sweater, tears in her eyes as she gritted her teeth and tried to ignore the aches. She pulled a hairbrush through her hair and did a short braid at the back to keep it from catching in the trees as she walked. She rolled up her sleeping bag and then turned to do the same to Roseann's.

By the time she emerged from the tent, she could almost walk normally as long as she didn't make any sudden moves. The others were just sitting down around the campfire to eat fluffy scrambled eggs. Jesse handed her a plate with a smile. She gave a general greeting and seated herself carefully on a rock and ate her breakfast.

The other men responded to her greeting, but the Harmons didn't speak at all, and there was no conversation during the meal. The sun wasn't visible over the mountain on which they had climbed the day before, but its effect was gradually seen as the sky lightened and the stars disappeared. Liz checked her watch and discovered it was only six-thirty. She kept her groan to herself. Jason Harmon was a sadist.

By the time the sky was light, their camp had been disassembled, and Al had the horses tied to a lead string, ready to head back toward the ranch. No words were needed when Jason Harmon stared at her, a question in his eyes. Liz shook her head no and turned her back on her tormentor.

"Bye, Al," she called gaily. "I'll see you in a few days."

"Right you are, Liz. Have a good climb," the older man called, a grin on his face.

Liz watched as Jason, clad in his form-fitting jeans and another plaid shirt, moved over to have a few words with his cowhand. When he caught her eye on him, she swung around and moved over to pick up the lightweight aluminum frame she was to carry. Each of the men would carry one of the three tents and the cooking supplies were divided among the adults, in addition to their own belongings.

Turning around to watch Al move down the trail, Liz discovered Jason Harmon approaching, a black hat in his hand. She recognized it at once as Al's, a glance at his bare head confirming her thought.

"Al thought you might want this," Jason said gruffly.

"But won't he need it traveling back to the ranch?" she asked, touched.

"No, he'll be there before the sun gets very high," Jason answered absentmindedly as he set the hat on top of her blond head and adjusted it.

Liz almost missed the significance of his remark, distracted as she was by his closeness. No question about it, the man exuded sexual attraction. She dropped her eyes and his words repeated themselves in her head.

"What did you say?"

"Hmm? That looks pretty good."

"How can Al be home before the sun gets hot? It took us almost ten hours to get here yesterday." Liz stared at the man as his cheeks flushed.

"Uh, there's a shortcut, but . . . ."

"Do you mean to say you brought us up that tortuous path for ten hours when we could have gotten here in half that time?" Liz's voice rose in outrage as she finished her question.

Matt walked by and murmured to his boss, "I told you you'd better watch your step." He ambled off to check the campfire one more time.

"The way we came was more—more scenic," Jason said, moving away from the seething Liz.

She stood there, immobilized by her anger. Liz knew he was trying to discourage her from interviewing him, but she hadn't realized he would play such a trick. Even now, after being up for an hour, her pain was agonizing. Right there, she promised herself that if it was the last thing she ever did, she would get that interview with Mr. Jason Harmon . . . and then they'd see who had the upper hand!

Without another word, she reached down and slipped her arms through the straps of her backpack. The hat slipped sideways, reminding her that the man had at least shown a little consideration. Her anger ridiculed that thought. He probably got the hat for her because he was afraid she'd have a heat stroke and sue him.

And that wasn't such a bad idea. She'd start a journal of all his dirty tricks, and that might scare him more than an article would. With relish, Liz waited for the others while she planned the torment she would work upon Mr. Harmon to pay for every moment her muscles were screaming.

By ten o'clock, four hours later, Liz could think of nothing good enough to repay James Harmon for her discomfort. The sun was unusually warm and the trail steep. When he finally called a break, she sank down onto the nearest boulder, ignoring the bruises on the part of her body that met the rock. Surprised when Jason stopped alongside her, she jerked her head back and stared at him.

"Wishing you'd gone with Al?" he asked.

"No, but I suspect the rest of the party wished I had," Liz challenged as she stared at the weariness on the children's faces.

"What do you mean?"

"Look at your children, Mr. Harmon. You've overtaxed them in an effort to make me pay for being here."

He frowned as he looked over his shoulder. "They're all right," he protested.

Liz said nothing else, sure she had already said enough to disturb this difficult man.

He turned abruptly and walked over to Roseann. "Rosie, are you doing okay?"

"Sure, Daddy," the little girl said with a gallant smile. He reached behind her and took her canteen, offering it to her. "Have a drink, sweetheart. I'll see what Jesse has for a snack."

"Great, I'm starved," Robbie chimed in, plopping down beside his sister, his cheeks flushed.

Jason walked on ahead and conferred with Jesse, and Liz smiled at the children. "You're great hikers. Do you do this much?"

Roseann ignored her, but Robbie said, "Not too often. Usually Daddy can't get away for long trips."

"I know he travels a lot. You must miss him."

"Yeah. He—"

"Miss Broadhurst!" the topic of their conversation roared. "You will *not* interview my children! That was not part of the agreement."

"But I wasn't," Liz protested. "I was just chatting with them."

After giving her a malevolent stare, he ignored her. "Kids, Jesse suggests we eat lunch now since we made such an early start. Why don't you go help him?"

"I'll help Jesse. The kids are already exhausted," Liz interrupted.

"No. Kids," he repeated, watching them as they dragged themselves ahead to where Jesse was opening his pack. "He knows not to work them too hard, so you can save your concern, Miss Broadhurst." His heavy sarcasm tightened Liz's features. "I wanted you alone to make it clear to you that you are to keep away from my children. I don't want them in the article and I don't want you talking to them."

"Why did you bring them along?" Liz demanded angrily.

"Because I don't get enough time with them as it is." His black brows snapped together as he added, "I didn't expect things to—"

"You thought I'd back out before we ever got this far?" she asked coolly.

He acknowledged her statement with a brief nod.

"You wanted to intimidate me with your kisses at the airport or scare me with tales of wild animals so you could get out of the interview."

"You're a perceptive woman, Miss Broadhurst," he said before adding, "I'll do whatever is necessary to protect my children, and you would do well to keep that in mind."

"I have no intention of harming your children . . . or you for that matter! And I don't appreciate being threatened."

"That was a warning, not a threat. You're not worth going to prison for, Miss Broadhurst," he snarled.

"You do say the sweetest things, Mr. Harmon," Liz cooed in return. "Now, If you'll excuse me, I'll go offer my assistance to Matt and Jesse. After all, I believe in pulling my own weight," she said pointedly, giving him the once-over.

"Just remember what I said," he called after her.

With a cool smile thrown over her shoulder, she said, "Oh, I will. I certainly will."

FIVE

Because of their early start, the hikers reached their destination long before sunset. Diamond Lake, surrounded by aspens and pines, was limpid blue and icy cold. Liz knelt by its edge and splashed the refreshing liquid on her hot cheeks.

"This is heavenly," she said with a sigh, her eyes tracing the shoreline.

"Yep," Matt agreed, going down on one knee beside her. "It's our favorite campout."

"Do you come here often?"

"Well, we try to get away two or three times a year. The fishing's great and you get a different perspective on all those little problems up here."

"Even Jason?" Liz asked doubtfully. Her eyes found the handsome man unbuckling Roseann's backpack.

Matt chuckled. "Yeah, even Jason. He's human, you know. I think that's one of the things he hated most about the publicity he received when he first started out. They made him out to be some kind of superman.''

''You knew him then?''

''We were in college together,'' Matt said before he abruptly rose.

Frowning, Liz stood also and caught a scowl on Jason Harmon's face that must have halted Matt's conversation.

Liz hesitated before moving over to join the others. She was too tired to fence with Jason right now. But she also didn't want him to accuse her of shirking any chores. Finally she took the few steps necessary and asked, ''Where do we set up camp?''

Jason looked at her as if she were intruding, she thought indignantly. He had ignored her ever since their argument at lunch, and she was growing tired of his attitude.

''Under those trees,'' he said, pointing to a particularly lovely stand of aspens only a few yards from the edge of the lake.

''Shall I help Robbie with the sleeping bags again?''

Did he think she was usurping his authority by daring to suggest her chore, she wondered as he gave her a cold stare. A nod was his only response, but Liz kept her chin up. With a smile at Robbie, she said, ''I'm ready when you are, boss.''

The youngster grinned, his blue eyes dancing. ''That's the first time I've ever been called boss. That's what everyone calls Daddy.''

His show of friendliness warmed Liz's heart. She was quite willing to leave the presence of the real boss and follow Robbie's directions for setting up their camp at Diamond Lake. ''Well, you're the best boss I've ever worked for, Robbie. If you ever want a recommmendation, let me know.''

With a delighted laugh, the boy led the way over to the pile of backpacks. Liz knelt beside him and together they unbuckled the tents and sleeping bags. When a long arm reached over her shoulder to lift one of the tents, Liz rocked back on her heels in surprise.

"Didn't mean to disturb you," Jason said before turning his back on her. He moved off a few feet where Matt was waiting and the two men began setting up the first tent.

"Is your father always this cranky?" Liz asked, her eyes focused on his broad shoulders, but she regretted her question at once as a cloud settled on Robbie's brow. "Forget it, honey. That was a silly thing to say."

The uncertain look the child gave her made Liz feel doubly guilty. She sought for another topic. "Are you and Roseann missing school this week?"

With a grimace, Robbie nodded. "Yeah. Daddy said if we got our assignments and brought them with us, it would be all right."

"If you need any help with your homework, I'll be happy to volunteer."

"Thanks." Robbie paused before asking, "Do you really write things?"

Liz looked at him in surprise. "Why, yes. I write articles for a magazine."

"Do you ever write, you know, stories?"

Liz hesitated. "Yes," she finally said, "I've been doing that lately." Something in the child's silence prodded her to ask, "Do *you* write stories?"

Robbie's eyes darted first to his father and then to

his twin, assisting Jesse by gathering wood for the campfire. Then he turned back to Liz and barely nodded.

"You haven't told anyone?"

There was a quick shake of his head. Liz understood his secrecy. She had written a short story over a year ago. After polishing it for a number of months, she had finally gotten the nerve to send it out three months ago. But she hadn't told anyone because she didn't want to admit it if she received a rejection.

"What do you write?" she asked in a low voice.

"Just stories about kids living on a ranch," Robbie muttered, his eyes not meeting hers.

"That sounds interesting."

Robbie said nothing else and Liz didn't mention his secret again. She understood his not wanting to talk about it. She entered the tent the two men had completed and unrolled the sleeping bags. As she finished, she noted that there was more space between the two beds than before. She stuck her head out of the tent. By comparing the tent the men were now erecting with her own, Liz realized they had first put up the larger one.

She ducked back inside and rolled up the two bags. As she came out of the tent with one under each arm, Jason turned around.

"What are you doing?" he demanded.

"These are Roseann's and my sleeping bags. I didn't realize this was the larger tent. I'm going to exchange them for the guys' sleeping bags."

"That's the right tent."

Liz gave him a confused look.

"You and Roseann get the larger tent now that Al has returned to the ranch." His furrowed brow didn't invite any excess of appreciation, but Liz offered a thank-you anyway. He only nodded and turned his back again.

She backed into the tent and replaced the sleeping bags. Roseann would probably move hers as far away from Liz as she could, but in the meantime, Liz centered them each in its half of the tent.

After the sleeping bag detail, Liz joined everyone in gathering a large stock of wood to be burned. Because they had camped here many times before, the fire was built in a small pit surrounded by large, smooth stones. Jesse had set up a grill over part of the fire, and the smell of steaks sizzling made the wood-gatherers work a little faster.

"Man, that Jesse can cook," Matt commented as he came over to help Liz with a heavy log. "Here, I've got it."

"Thanks, my eyes were bigger than my muscles," she said with a laugh. "And I agree with you. The smell of dinner is driving me crazy."

"Well, it won't be long now. And we won't have to get up before sunrise in the morning, either."

"Are you sure Jason won't decide to march us around the lake just to be sure I'm uncomfortable?" Liz teased.

Matt grinned. "If he does, sweetheart, you won't have to keep up with me, 'cause I'll be tucked into my sleeping bag."

Grinning ruefully in return, Liz said, "I hope that's where I'll be, too."

"Well, I'm willing, but it might be a little snug with the two of us."

"Matt!" Liz protested, her cheeks a bright red. "You know that's not what I meant."

"Can't blame a guy for hoping, can you?" he teased.

The pair came to an abrupt halt when Jason stepped in front of them. "Is anything wrong?" he asked stiltedly.

Liz flashed a pleading look at her companion and remained silent.

"Naw, Liz and I were just gettin' to know each other, friendly-like, you know."

Jason shot her an angry look. "Careful. She may decide to write about you, too."

Jason's words stayed with Liz the rest of the day. After a delicious meal had been eaten and things stowed away, everyone sat around the campfire in the growing darkness. Liz was between Robbie and Matt, and she took the opportunity to quietly ask Matt a question.

"Would you object if I interviewed you, also, Matt? I'd like to do a story about modern-day cowboys. I could talk to Jesse, too, if he doesn't mind, and maybe Al when we get back to the ranch."

"If you think anyone would be interested, I don't mind," Matt agreed. "Sure you'll have the time?"

"Jason's not exactly rushing to fill pages in my notebook, or haven't you noticed?"

"He's a mite shy, it's true." Matt's grin was wide.

Liz ignored his comment. "I can't promise you the article will get published, you understand, but if it does, I'll be sure to send you a copy of it."

"What article?" Jason barked from across the campfire.

Liz shrank back into the shadows. She had hoped

to keep her question quiet enough to avoid Jason's hearing it. She should've known better.

Matt had no problem with informing his boss. "Liz here is gonna interview me and Jesse, if it's okay with him, and write an article about modern-day cowboys."

"I don't think that's a good idea."

Liz said nothing.

Jesse sat up straight and looked across at her. "I kind of like that. I'm sick and tired of how most people write about us."

Liz couldn't resist that opening. "What do you mean, Jesse?"

"Most people picture cowboys as ignorant country people who can't do anything else. And that's not true. Most of us do this kind of work because it's what we prefer."

Liz nodded, her eyes urging him to go on.

"Take Matt, for instance . . ." Jesse began, only to be interrupted by him.

"Here, now, I can talk for myself."

"Sure you can, but you might not tell her how you've built your herd. Why, Liz, he can practically name his own price for the calves he produces. Matt's almost famous in the breeding world for his herd."

"Really? I had no idea, Matt. Will you tell me about it?"

"Sure. I brag about my cows all the time. But I couldn't have done that if it weren't for Jason."

"That's not true," Jason protested, but his blue eyes avoided Liz's.

"You know it is, boss. You see, Jason's too busy with his business ventures to spend much time running the ranch, so he hired me to do that. And we struck a deal. I wanted to raise cattle but I had no land. So he lets me run my cows on his ranch, and I give him every fourth calf.''

Liz eyed the ''boss'' across the campfire, but his face gave nothing away. He stared into the fire as if he were all alone. ''That sounds fair,'' she murmured.

Matt snorted. ''Fair? Hell . . . uh . . . heck, it's more than fair. I offered half the calves. The first year he took them and gave me back half of them at the end of the year. He said he couldn't look after that many cows.'' Liz noted the affectionate look the cowboy sent his employer.

''That's enough, Matt. You're the one who's done all the work. And it's your expertise that's made my herd worth ten times more than my neighbors'.''

''He's modest as well as shy,'' Matt said in a stage whisper that had the children giggling.

''And what about you, Jesse? Are you happy with your work?'' Liz asked, turning to the other cowboy.

''Sure. I love being outdoors, riding horses. I don't even mind the cows.'' Liz laughed at that, and Jesse grinned.

''I think you should write a cookbook for campers,'' Liz said. ''I've camped out before, but I've never eaten so well.''

''That's not a bad idea. Maybe I will someday. In the meantime, I'll be glad to tell you all about the life of a cowboy cook for your article. Do you want to start tomorrow?''

Liz looked across the campfire again. ''Are we going to work on your interview tomorrow, Jason?''

''I'm taking my kids fishing,'' he snapped.

Liz allowed no irritation to show in her face.

"Then if you're not going fishing, Jesse, I'd like to interview you and Matt tomorrow."

"Matt's going with us."

Liz just smiled. "Are you leaving early?" she then asked. "Because if not, I could—"

"We're leaving very early."

After shooting a revengeful grin at Liz, Matt leaned toward Jason and said, "If I were you, boss, I'd take her with me. That way you can keep an eye on her. Besides, if anyone deserves to get up early, it's Liz."

Liz watched her host with a sinking feeling as he considered Matt's words. "I guess you're right, Matt. Prepare to rise early in the morning, Liz. We're going to teach you how to fish."

Rosie's angry look seemed a fitting end to a long day.

Jason's voice brought Liz's eyes open before dawn the next morning, but she didn't stir. She wasn't ready to face the man yet. She had just spent her entire night dreaming of him. Or maybe she should call it a nightmare. She'd been in a dark forest, with the elusive Mr. Harmon somewhere just ahead of her. No matter how fast she ran, he was always out of sight, taunting her, but never allowing her to catch up.

Roseann struggled out of her sleeping bag and began dressing.

"You'd better hurry," the child warned, standing over Liz's sleeping bag. "Daddy'll be angry if you make us late."

With a sigh, Liz shoved back the top layer of warmth as Rosie left the tent. The air was just brisk enough to remind her they were on the edge of winter in the Rockies. She pulled a sweater and jeans over her long underwear and laced up her boots before looking for a brush.

"I don't see why the stupid fish have to be caught at sunrise," she muttered as she smoothed her blond hair into place. A little face cream was all the makeup she used. High gloss and the Rockies just didn't go together.

When she approached the campfire, Jesse became her friend for life by silently extending a steaming cup.

"Thanks. I was afraid there wouldn't be time for coffee and I couldn't face Jason, much less a lake full of fish, without it."

Jesse grinned. "That's something you and the boss have in common. We're never without a pot of coffee."

Liz thought that was probably the *only* thing she had in common with the man she had come to interview, but she didn't voice her thoughts.

"Here's a breakfast sandwich. You won't have time to sit and eat. The boss is loading the boat already."

With a guilty look over her shoulder, she took the napkin-wrapped breakfast he had given her. "Sandwich?"

"Yeah, toast and scrambled eggs. It'll last a while. We had to develop something for the guy to eat in the saddle. Sometimes you just don't have time for a leisurely breakfast."

"Thanks, Jesse. Let me know what I can do for you in return."

"Bring me plenty of trout to cook tonight," he suggested.

Matt loomed over her shoulder before she heard him arrive. "You'd better get a move on, young lady, or he may make you swim along behind."

No need to ask who the impatient "he" was. With a sigh, Liz shot Matt a dark look and turned downhill toward the lake. "It's your fault I'm going on this trip."

"Turn about, fair play. After all, you brought on the early departure."

She could tell she'd get no sympathy from Matt. "What are you two going to do all day?"

The men exchanged happy smiles before Matt said, "I'll curl up in my sleeping bag and catch forty winks. If there's any time left over, I've got a good murder mystery in my pack."

"I've got some letters to write," Jesse added, "and I brought a book, too."

Liz groaned. "You're killing me, you rats. What a perfect day!"

"Fishing won't be too bad, Liz, if you just remember to be quiet and not rock the boat," Matt assured her with a wink.

Several hours later, after the rising sun had tinted the blue water a shining gold and taken the frost off the morning, Liz could agree with the two cowboys. Jason Harmon didn't shout his wealth, but he didn't go without comfort, either. The boat had seats with cushions and backs that made sitting still relatively easy. In fact, a nap crossed her mind several times.

They had rowed slowly across the lake earlier, each of the children taking an oar and rowing until they tired out. Liz had offered to take a turn, but Jason had simply shaken his head no and taken both oars. Since that time, they had alternately drifted away from the lake's source, a rambunctious mountain stream that submerged its ripples into the deep lake, and rowed back to it.

"Why do we keep returning here?" Liz asked quietly.

"Because the stream carries in vegetation and insect eggs that attract the trout. They can catch it here before it settles into the deeper water."

Another few minutes passed in silence before Jason murmured, "I didn't think you knew how to fish."

Liz rejected the snippy remark she might have made another time. "I've fished before, but never for trout."

"Daddy says the hardest part is keeping quiet," Rosie said, unable to pass up a conversation.

"Just for you," Robbie teased, sharing a smile with Liz.

"I get bored!" Rosie protested a little too loudly, drawing a frown from her father. "Sorry."

"I used to make up stories for myself when I'd go fishing as a child. The time always flew by." Liz's thoughts drifted to the fishing trips to a small lake near her house. Her grandmother had taken her there often as a child to fish for brim.

"Me, too," Robbie chimed in, again smiling at Liz.

"What kind of stories? I can't think of any." Rosie watched the woman sitting alongside her father, in Rosie's favorite place.

"Stories about things I liked. What do you enjoy, Rosie?"

Rosie listed many things that occupied her mind, and in a quiet voice, Liz began spinning a tale that incorporated Rosie's preferences.

By the time she'd finished, Rosie's eyes were drooping and a contented smile was spread across her face. Her father, with the ease of practice, slipped a pillow behind the child's head and encouraged her to sleep a while.

Robbie, enthralled by the story, too, had a different reaction. He was more interested in the making of the story than the telling. After a while, however, he, too, succumbed to the lure of dreamland and drifted off to sleep.

"Nicely done. Can you put a spell on me, also?"

Liz turned toward the low voice and studied Jason Harmon's face. The admiration for her Scheherazade act was there, but there was also resentment.

"Was I too loud?"

"No. I said you did a nice job." He looked away, his tanned features strong but relaxed.

"Yes, but I heard a 'but.' "

He shrugged his shoulders and turned his attention back to his fishing. They sat in silence, the children's deep breathing the only sound as they drifted out into the lake.

"Where did you learn to fish?"

"At home, in Texas. My grandmother was an avid fisherman."

"I just misjudged you all the way around, didn't I?"

"Does that mean you'll cooperate for the interview?'' She regretted that question as soon as it was out of her mouth, but it was too late to take it back.

His lips pressed together in a tight line and he looked away. "I never said I wouldn't cooperate," he finally ground out.

Liz said nothing. What he said and what he did were two different things. But she wasn't going to point that out to him in the middle of a lake when his was the only available boat.

A trout eased the tension by gobbling the lure on Jason's line, and Liz watched with admiration as he neatly played the fish toward the boat. There had been several other trout offering themselves for Jesse's frypan, but Jason had carefully removed the hook and returned them to the lake to grow another year.

Liz didn't think this one would be so lucky.

"Get the net," he muttered, and Liz picked up the large black net lying near his feet. She eased her way toward the edge of the boat, careful not to rock it, and scooped up the silvery, twisting fish.

"Jason! That was terrific, and he's a real beauty," she exclaimed softly, looking at his catch.

"Thanks. That was good teamwork, Liz," he said, surprising her.

"My part was easy. Where did you learn to fish like that?"

He deftly removed the hook and put the fish in the mesh bag that hung over the side of the boat. "My dad took me fishing a lot as a boy."

"And you're doing the same for your children."

He shrugged his denim-clad shoulders, almost as if he were embarrassed. "I don't get to spend as much time with them as I'd like. I try to make up for it by taking them camping."

Liz bit her bottom lip. A caring parent was tops in her book of important things in life. "I'm sorry I'm intruding."

Jason stared at her for a long moment before shifting away from her and reaching for the oars. Over his shoulder, Liz could just hear him say, "You have nothing to apologize for. I forced you up here."

As she sat behind him, watching his muscles strain as he rowed the boat against the current back to the mouth of the lake, she pondered the man she was slowly coming to know. His earlier treatment of her was abominable, but a sneaky liking was insinuating itself in her feelings. A man who made time for his kids, who cared about them, was so much the opposite of her stepfather, the only father she'd ever known, that she found it impossible to condemn him. And now, to admit that their situation was his fault showed an honesty she'd not expected.

From that moment on, the day was a delight. When the children awakened from their nap, Jason deemed it time for lunch. He found no objectors in his boat.

He pulled the boat into a grassy bank, and they moved ashore and settled down against the aspens to munch Jesse's sandwiches.

"How much longer are we gonna fish, Dad?" Robbie asked, after wolfing down his food.

"You tired, son?"

"No! I just want to have time to catch up with Rosie. She's caught a couple of fish and I haven't even had a nibble. And I've been as quiet as can be!"

"There'll be time, Robbie," Jason assured his son.

"It's probably just because Rosie's a girl," Liz said, a smile on her face.

"You think girls are better than boys?" Robbie asked, hurt in his blue eyes.

"Of course not, silly, but I bet these fish were all gentlemen and wanted to let the lady go first."

Even Robbie chuckled at Liz's joke.

"If that were true, you'd have made all the catches, Miss Broadhurst," Jason said in low tones as he stood and took Liz's hand to pull her up. "I can't imagine a gentleman passing you by."

Her mouth wide open in surprise, Liz snapped it closed only after Jason had walked away. Unfortunately, Rosie had also heard her father's remark and glared at the other female. "Daddy was just joking," she assured Liz sturdily.

"Of course he was, honey. We were trying to cheer Robbie up because he hasn't caught any fish."

Though Rosie's look still held suspicion, she said nothing more and the fishing resumed.

Late afternoon found them rowing back to camp, a satisfied quartet. Robbie had caught only one fish, but it was the biggest of the lot. Even Liz had snagged one, but Jason had thrown it back in, assuring her it was only a baby.

When they reached the shore, Jason sent the kids on up to camp. They were eager to brag about their prowess to the two cowboys. Turning, he then extended a hand to help Liz from the boat.

"You know, Liz Broadhurst, if you weren't a reporter, I think we'd be friends."

She looked up at his serious face and felt a real regret somewhere in the region of her stomach. With a wry smile, she said, "You know, Jason Harmon, if you weren't prejudiced, we could be friends anyway."

The warmth left his face, and he dropped her hand, turning away without a word to retrieve their gear from the boat.

Liz sighed. For a few hours, she and Jason Harmon had shared sunshine and laughter, peace and warmth. But now they were back on dry land and the war had resumed.

SIX

A pot of stew was simmering on the fire when Liz reached camp. Its delectable smell coupled with an appetite sharpened by the fresh air made her ready for dinner at once.

Jesse, however, had a different idea. "Everyone needs to go pick up firewood before they get any dinner."

Rosie groaned. "But I'm tired!"

Matt walked by and tugged at her black braid. "How could you be tired? All you did was sit around all day. Come on. You can tag along with me."

With a huge sigh, Rosie agreed, following in Matt's footsteps.

Robbie fell in beside Liz as she moved away from the campsight looking for firewood.

"I really enjoyed today," the boy said, watching Liz out of the corner of his eye.

"Me, too, Robbie."

"The story you told was neat."

"Thank you, kind sir."

Liz bent over and picked up several sticks of wood. "I tell stories."

Standing up, Liz turned to the owner of that whispered confidence. With a smile, she draped her free arm around Robbie's shoulders. "Do you write them down?"

"Yeah."

They walked in silence for several minutes, ignoring numerous prime pieces of wood.

"Would you read it?"

"I'd be honored to, Robbie."

"I . . . I may not be very good," the boy admitted, stopping to look up at Liz with anxious eyes.

She fought off the urge to wrap him in comforting arms. "Very few people are good at something when they first begin."

"Were you?"

"No, sweetheart, I wasn't, and I hope I'm still learning," Liz assured him with a rueful laugh.

"Will you help me?"

No one could resist those innocent blue eyes, the little nose with just a hint of freckles. Robbie looked so much like his father, she thought with a sigh. "Of course, Robbie."

The child responded by throwing his arms around her.

She returned his hug but released him at once when he pulled away.

"I'll go put it under your bedroll," he whispered, and scampered away.

Liz stood watching the child's departure, bemused by the warmth she felt for Robbie.

"Just what do you think you're doing?"

Whirling around in surprise at the menacing words, Liz dropped the wood she was carrying.

"G-gathering wood. You scared me, sneaking up on me like that." Her hazel eyes were wide as she watched him.

"I'll do worse than scare you if I catch you pumping my kids for information." Jason's grim expression bore no resemblance to the man out on the lake.

"I was doing no such thing!"

"Then I'll ask my question again. Just what *were* you doing?"

Liz took a step back from his powerful body as she considered her answer. "I can't tell you what we were talking about, but I can assure you it had nothing to do with you."

"Not good enough," he growled. "I haven't seen Robbie voluntarily hug someone in a long time. And what concerns my kids concerns me."

Liz stooped down and scooped up the pieces of wood she'd dropped. "You'll have to ask Robbie, not me," she said as she stood.

She met his glare with defiance. His blue eyes, so much like Robbie's, refused to release her, holding her by their intensity.

"You should've stayed in L.A.," he finally muttered.

His words hurt, but she raised her chin and said, "You made that impossible with your bizarre stipulations."

He leaned closer, until Liz could feel his breath on her chilled cheeks. His eyes focused on her lips as he murmured, "I know."

Whether or not he would have actually touched

her, Liz didn't know. At that moment, Matt's voice rang through the trees—''Timber!''—accompanied by Rosie's giggle.

Jason spun away from Liz and walked toward the area from which the noise had come, leaving her trembling as she recovered from their encounter.

Without thought for any more firewood, she walked back to camp, laid down the few pieces of wood she'd found, and entered her tent, never seeing Jesse's puzzled stare or hearing the greeting he'd given her.

Sheltered inside the canvas, she sat down on her sleeping bag and wrapped her arms tightly around her. What had just happened? Their confrontation involved more than Robbie. For a moment she'd even thought he intended to kiss her.

Even more upsetting was the disappointment she'd felt when he didn't. She'd avoided involvements in L.A. after her first disastrous one. Now that she was leaving, she certainly wouldn't want an attachment to anyone living in that world.

What was she even thinking about? She shook her head in confusion. Jason Harmon hated reporters. Even if she were Marilyn Monroe, he wouldn't get involved with her. Besides, he was the subject of her interview. Never had she mixed business with pleasure.

Sounds of the others returning to the campfire roused Liz from her thoughts. She sat up and stared straight ahead. It was time she got started on the interview. After all, that was the only reason she was here. And when it was over, she could escape Jason Harmon's confusing company and never see him again. She assumed the emptiness she felt was hunger and answered the call to dinner.

*   *   *

Contrary to what Liz expected, dinner was a pleasant meal, in spite of the fact that Jason never spoke to her and avoided looking at her.

The children were happy and chattered away about the fishing they'd done that day. Robbie included Liz as well as his father in their conversation. Even Rosie wasn't as antagonistic as usual. Of course, she had no reason to be, since her father completely ignored Liz.

Their conversation led the men to tell of earlier fishing trips. Matt had them all laughing with his wild tales that always ended with him catching the most fish.

"That's not true, Matt," Robbie protested. "I know 'cause you're always the one who has to clean the fish."

Everyone laughed but Liz, who looked puzzled. "But why would that prove you didn't catch the most fish?" she asked.

In his best cowboy drawl, Matt explained. "Well, I reckon it's because we always have a bet. Whoever catches the fewest fish has to clean them."

"You mean you were being dishonest, Matt?" Liz teased, her hazel eyes rounded in mock innocence.

"We'll just call it stretching the truth a little. And I consider it real unsporting of you to spoil my act, young Robbie," the cowboy growled, but his grin took away the sting his words might've had.

"At least it means you're an expert at cleaning fish," Jason added.

"True. By the time you finish with those poor critters this evening, there won't be much left for Jesse to fry."

"You could volunteer to do it for me."

It said a lot for Jason's fairness as an employer that Matt didn't hesitate to reject his suggestion.

"Fat chance! You could make Liz help you," he added with a grin.

Liz was sure no one was surprised that he rejected such an offer, but she wondered if she was the only one to notice how pleased he was to do so.

"Maybe I'll help Jesse with the dishes instead," she offered, pushing up the sleeves of her pink sweater. "I'm better at that than I am at fishing."

"I thought you were a good fisherman," Robbie assured her, his little-boy face wreathed in a warm smile.

"Thanks, Robbie, it was fun." Liz hoped the child didn't notice the identical scowl on his sister and father's faces. She wouldn't want him to suffer for his friendliness.

"You must come from a big family," Matt said, looking at Liz.

"Why do you say that?"

" 'Cause you're comfortable around kids." He turned to his employer. "Remember that lady you brought to the ranch? Must've been six or seven years ago 'cause the kids were little. She screamed anytime one of them got close to her."

Interest flared as Liz noted Jason's red cheeks.

"That was a mistake," he growled.

"Sure was," Matt agreed with a grin.

"That was right after I started here," Jesse recalled. "Boy, she was some looker, a blond like you."

"What happened to her?" Liz asked casually.

"She returned to L.A.," Jason snapped.

"And do you still see her?"

"No."

She had angered him by her questions, Liz knew, but, after all, that was why she was here. And she'd better keep reminding herself of that. Jason Harmon had a strange effect on her.

With studied casualness, Jason stood and stretched, and Liz discovered her eyes had a will of their own, drawn to his masculine form in tight jeans.

"Well, it's time I clean our catch," he said, moving over to the table Jesse had constructed by laying long sticks across two low branches and securing them with rope. He picked up the extra kerosene lantern. "I'll be back with tomorrow's breakfast in a little while, Jesse. Kids, you'd better get ready for bed."

Without acknowledging her presence at all, Jason strode out of the circle of light cast by the fire and disappeared into the darkness, only the glow of the lantern marking his progress.

"Maybe I should go help Daddy," Roseann offered.

"I reckon you'd better do what he said," Matt said firmly but with a smile. "You got up awful early this morning." The teasing look he sent Liz reminded her of his enjoyment in turning the tables on her.

"But I'm not really . . ." Roseann's words were broken by a yawn she wasn't able to hold back. "Tired," she finished sheepishly.

Everyone laughed, and the little girl joined in before the two children got up to follow orders.

"Ready to turn in, Liz?"

"What?" Liz jerked her eyes to Matt, who was staring at her with a smile on his face.

"You seemed miles away. I wondered if you were ready to hit the sack."

"Oh, uh, no. I'm not tired."

"Like Rosie?" he asked with a grin. "I bet it won't take you long to fall asleep tonight."

Liz grinned. "You could be right, but I think I'll stay up a while longer. What's on the agenda for tomorrow? Jason didn't mention any early-morning hikes or chopping down trees, did he?"

"I didn't hear him if he did. 'Course, I try not to hear any plans about getting up early," Matt assured her.

"You managed to get up this morning when we did."

"We did get up, me and Jesse, but we went back to bed as soon as you were out of sight," he informed her with particular relish.

"Maybe I can mention to Jason how much you'd like a day of fishing, starting tomorrow at dawn," Liz suggested, a grin on her face.

"Uhuh, you wouldn't do that, would you?" Matt pleaded.

Liz ignored his joking, her eyes trying to pierce the darkness beside the lake where a faint lantern glow proclaimed Jason's presence.

"We'll ask Jason when he gets back to camp," Jesse assured her.

"I think I'll ask him now," Liz said slowly. After all, he'd promised her an interview. Never put off until tomorrow what you can do today.

"Hey, Liz, I was only teasing. Jason not gonna roust you out in the morning," Matt called as she stood and started toward the lake.

Waving a hand over her shoulder, she continued on her way. She was tired of being ignored, as she had been all evening. He had offered an interview, and it was about time he honor his agreement. She wasn't sure why she was so determined to do the interview this evening, but she was.

Liz slowed down once she was out of the firelight, giving her eyes a chance to adjust to the darkness.

Ahead of her, she could see the steady glow of the lantern Jason had taken from camp. She was still yards from reaching him when the lantern was raised and his husky voice called out, "Who is it?"

"It's Liz," she replied, stopping in the darkness.

"What do you want?"

She started walking again, treading carefully. When she drew up within the circle of light, she said, "You promised me an interview."

"I have to clean the fish," he said abruptly, setting the lamp back down on the ground and kneeling beside the water.

Liz chose a rock near him and settled herself there. "That's all right. You can talk while you're working."

There was enough light to see the angry glitter in his eyes, but he said nothing.

"I thought we'd get some of the background information out of the way tonight," she said chattily, as if they were seated in someone's living room having coffee.

"How did you get your start in business?" she asked. She held her breath when there was no response, but she knew better than to speak.

Finally, with a sigh, he replied briefly. "I earned my M.B.A. from Stanford and got a job as a management consultant with an accounting firm."

For the next half hour, Liz asked easy questions, confirming what little was already known about Jason Harmon. He talked freely about his business ventures. Only when she touched on anything personal did he cut short his responses. But she knew her magazine would not be satisfied with an article filled with numbers and dates. *Star* magazine had built its reputation on in-depth, personal interviews. She stared at his strong features in the lantern's glow as he kept his eyes on the trout he was fileting.

Jason Harmon was a dynamic, sexy man. That alone would draw the women. Add to it his immense wealth, and she wasn't naive enough to think women didn't clamor for his attention. Why was there no gossip about him in Los Angeles, where gossip was always a record crop?

When he finished his technical explanation of the latest takeover, she plunged in. "Jason, why do I never read anything about you in the L.A. gossip columns?"

His hands stilled, but he didn't look up. Finally, he continued with his work. "Because you're reading the wrong part of the paper. I'm in the business section."

"You know what I mean. You're an attractive, wealthy man, a rare breed, what half the female population in Los Angeles is looking for." He didn't respond. "Do you have a girlfriend?"

"Next you'll want to know if I'm going steady," he ground out. He rinsed off the last fish and tossed it in the dishpan he had brought with him. Then he knelt by the water again and washed his hands.

Liz refused to respond to his taunt. "And are you?"

"I'll tell you anything you want to know about my business dealings. My personal life is none of your business."

He had his back to her as he continued washing his hands, and Liz was sorely tempted to boot him into the lake. This man provoked her as no one had in a long time. "My instructions were to include both your career and your personal life in the interview. That is the hallmark of *Star* magazine. Did the owner promise you anything different?"

The look he sent her was pure anger, but he didn't deny her words. He rose to his feet and turned his back on her again, his large hands resting lightly on his hips as he stared out across the lake.

"I'm not interested in dirt, Jason," she added, "but it is strange that there's no lady in your . . . Oh, no! Surely you're not . . ." She broke off, unable to voice the horrible thought that had struck her.

He wheeled around, his face a dim glow from the lamp on the ground. "No, I'm not!"

"Not what?" Liz carefully said.

"Gay! That's what you thought, wasn't it?"

"It's really none of my business," she muttered, keeping her head down.

"Damn it, I will not have you even thinking such a thing, much less printing it!"

"I would never . . ." she began when she found herself lifted from her rock by strong hands on her shoulders. Only inches from his stern features, Liz gasped, "I believe you!"

He stared into her eyes and Liz couldn't tear hers away. When his gaze dropped to her lips, she tried to back away, but her heels were up against the rock. "N-no," she protested, but it only came out in a whisper.

His hands dropped from her shoulders to slide inside her down jacket, almost spanning her narrow waist. "Yes," he murmured just before his lips took hers.

The memory of those airport kisses disintegrated in the fire of his caress. This time, his kiss was loaded with emotion, and it packed an incredible wallop as his lips moved across hers and he pulled her against his large frame.

Transported by a myriad of sensations, Liz didn't know how long that kiss lasted, only that she never wanted it to end. When his lips left hers, she involuntarily moaned, calling them back to her. Almost before the sound left her mouth, his lips returned.

Liz Broadhurst hadn't even dated in over a year. She'd given up on men. But this man's caresses set off a spark that turned into a raging fire before she knew it. Her arms encircled his neck, and she pressed against him.

Only when his lips left hers to bury themselves in her neck did rational thought return. Jason Harmon had tried to defeat her at every turn. Now he was returning to his original tactics. In a flash, all the pain she had suffered, the rejection she had felt, the anger she had stored up, erased the pleasure his touch gave her. With a mighty shove, she removed herself from his arms.

Unfortunately, she also removed Jason from solid earth. Liz stared in horror as the man fell, as if in slow motion, backward into the lake. The resulting splash almost drowned out her cry, but not quite.

Running steps, preceded by a dancing spotlight, came tumbling down the slope as the two cowboys joined them. Liz, kneeling on the bank, the lantern in her left hand and her right one outstretched, found herself lifted out of the way. The two men reached out hands to pull the sputtering Jason from the chilly waters.

"You all right, boss?" Matt asked as Jason sprawled out on the grass.

Though he glared at Liz, Jason muttered through chattering teeth, "Sure. Fine and dandy."

Jesse stripped the down vest off Jason and, shrugging out of his own jacket, draped it around his employer's shoulders. "Come on, you've got to get out of those wet clothes or you'll catch your death of cold."

Jason accepted Jesse's assistance without comment and strode off toward the camp, water squelching from his boots at every step. Liz nibbled on her bottom lip as she watched him leave.

"How about you?"

Liz drew her eyes reluctantly back to Matt. "What?"

"Are you okay?"

She swallowed a sudden lump in her throat and willed her eyes to remain dry. "Yes, of course." The cowboy said nothing else and after a minute Liz added, "It was an accident."

With a gentle smile, Matt assured her, "It's none of my business, lady. But going swimming at this time of the year can be dangerous."

"Truly, Matt, I didn't intend to . . . It just happened," she finished lamely. She couldn't confess what had led up to Jason's falling in the water. "Do you think he'll be all right?" She hated the way her voice trembled.

"I reckon. He's a tough bird. Come on. Little girls with big eyes need to be in bed."

She didn't realize he was talking about her until he took her elbow and tugged. "You mean me?"

He grinned and nodded, and Liz fell into step beside him. He reached over and took the lantern from her, holding it aloft to light their way.

There was no sign of Jason or Jesse when they reached camp. Liz assumed they were both in one of the tents, getting Jason out of his wet clothes. Roseann stuck her head out of the women's tent. "What's going on?"

"Nothing, honey," Matt assured her.

"Where's Daddy?"

Matt and Liz shared looks before she answered the child. "He's in his tent."

"Daddy?" Roseann called across the campfire.

Jason's head appeared out of the cowboys' tent. "What?" His rough growl wasn't encouraging.

"Why are you in Jesse's tent?"

"Go to bed, Roseann!"

Liz knew that his anger wasn't intended for his daughter, but Roseann didn't. With trembling lips, she disappeared inside.

"Damn!" Jason muttered, glaring at Liz, before he, too, withdrew from sight.

"If I were you, Liz, I'd be sure I was tucked up nice and tight inside my tent before that bear reappears," Matt warned.

"I think that's good advice, Matt. Thanks," Liz whispered before she hurried to heed his words.

It wasn't long before Liz was sliding into her sleeping bag. Like the other nights, there was no greeting from Roseann. She had consistently ignored the fact that she had a roommate, only speaking to Liz when it was absolutely necessary.

But tonight, as Liz made herself comfortable, she heard the unmistakable sound of a sniff. She lay still, unsure what she should do. The decision was made for her when several more sniffs followed the first.

"Roseann?"

There was no answer.

"Roseann, your dad was mad at me, not you."

More sniffs occurred before a small voice asked, "Why?"

Liz didn't want to answer that question, but she couldn't let the little girl think her father was angry with her. "He fell into the lake."

Roseann bolted upright, but Liz couldn't see her face in the darkness. "Is he all right?"

"Yes, I think so. But he had to change out of his wet clothes."

There was no response until Roseann asked, "Why would he be mad at you if he fell into the lake? Did you push him?"

There went any chance Liz had of making friends with the only other female within miles: "I didn't mean to."

"And you're sure he's not mad at me?"

Liz smiled grimly in the darkness. "Rosie, your daddy loves you very much."

"All daddies love their daughters," Rosie returned in a worried voice.

"No."

Again there was silence in the tent that seemed to thicken the longer it went on. Liz wished she could retract her answer.

"Why do you say that?"

"Nothing, honey. Just don't worry about it. Your dad was mad at me, not you," she repeated.

Liz sensed, if she couldn't see, Roseann lie back down in her sleeping bag. She sighed silently and closed her eyes. The evening's events were catching up with her.

"Didn't your daddy love you?"

Liz jerked to attention. She lay still, frantically trying to find an answer. "It . . . it doesn't matter, Roseann. You'd better go on to sleep. You got up early this morning."

There was a rustling movement, and Liz hoped the child was settling down for sleep. She almost screamed as a small, warm hand touched her cheek.

"I didn't mean to make you sad," Roseann whispered, and Liz marveled at her sensitivity.

She planted a kiss on Roseann's hand. "Thank you, honey, but it was all a long time ago."

"But I thought daddies had to love their children." Liz had forgotten how insistent a child could be, worrying away at a bone that had already been gnawed clean.

"My daddy died when I was a baby, Rosie. Just go to sleep now."

"Then why did you say he didn't love you?" Roseann asked. "You probably just forgot."

"Probably."

Liz lay still, hoping that would end the questions.

"Then why did you say that?"

"I wasn't talking about my real daddy. My mother remarried when I was three years old."

There was a childish eagerness in Roseann's voice as she asked, "Was he wicked, like a stepmother?"

Liz almost laughed, but the memories hurt a little too much. "Nothing as bad as Cinderella's," she said, understanding Rosie's thinking. "He wasn't mean . . . very often. He just didn't care, even about his own kids."

"I'm sorry," the child murmured, her hand reaching for Liz's cheek once more. Liz discovered it was a very comforting feeling.

"Thanks, honey."

"Do you have lots of brothers and sisters?"

"I have three sisters and two brothers." Liz was looking forward to seeing all of them again when she returned to Texas. Her stepfather had passed away last spring, and she hadn't returned for the funeral. But now she was planning on going home for good.

"Wow! That's a lot."

"Yes, it is. But I love them all. And I miss them."

"I'd miss Robbie if he went away. And I don't ever intend to leave Daddy." The earnestness in Roseann's voice was sweet.

"Your daddy wouldn't ever want you to leave him." Liz raised up and leaned over until she found the little girl's cheek. She gave her a kiss and lay back down. "Go to sleep now, Rosie."

"Okay." Sounds of the little girl sliding back down into her sleeping bag told Liz she was following directions. When everything was still again, Roseann whispered, "Liz?"

"Yes, Rosie?"

"Thank you for telling me Daddy wasn't mad at me."

"Sure."

"And . . . and I'll share Daddy with you, if you want?"

Liz was more shaken than she cared to admit by the child's abrupt about-face. "Rosie, you have a big heart. I'm a little old to share him, but thank you for offering."

"Okay. Good night." The satisfaction in Roseann's voice brought a smile to Liz's lips.

Whatever else she discovered about Jason Harmon, one thing Liz knew for sure. He had done a good job raising his children alone. They were both warm-hearted, intelligent, and loving. Children anyone should be proud of. She'd like to have the opportunity to tell Jason that, but she thought he'd send her packing first thing in the morning.

In spite of her worries, she almost chuckled aloud at the look Jason would've given her had he heard Rosie's offer to share him. Roseann had kept her distance until this evening. The turn-around in the little girl's attitude would just be one more thing to displease him.

Of course, it couldn't compare to pushing him in the lake. But she really hadn't intended to cool him off quite so effectively. It just happened. Somehow she didn't think she'd be able to convince him of that.

But then he shouldn't have resorted to kissing her again. He ought to know by now that wouldn't work on her. *Oh, yeah?* a derisive voice demanded somewhere within her. Well, okay, so it had almost worked. His kisses had stirred her as none ever had before. But she was no longer the naive young woman who had landed in Los Angeles five years ago.

That first year, she thought she had fallen in love. At last, she had found a man who loved her. Her thoughts weren't that clear at the time. It was only later that Liz realized she was seeking a replacement for the love her stepfather had never given her. And she found it. He had taken advantage of her, just as her stepfather had taken advantage of her mother.

Demanding the house be kept spick and span, dinner on the table at exactly six o'clock, even if he didn't bother to call, coming in at midnight stinking drunk. Ignoring her mother's needs.

Don wasn't that bad, at least not in the beginning. At first, he had made her feel wonderful, telling her she was the most important thing in the world to him. He insisted they live together, moving in with her. Since she was a virgin, Liz hesitated, but he convinced her they were making a commitment together.

Her happiness lasted about a month before Don began staying out late. To work, he said. Liz was working at the magazine and writing free-lance articles at night, saving her money to send back home. She wanted her brothers and sisters to go to college also and there wasn't much money.

She put up with his absences, his tantrums when the laundry wasn't folded a certain way or arranged in his drawers to his liking. She stopped making food she enjoyed and fixed only his favorites. She gave him money when he claimed he was short.

One Thursday, he came home late and told her he'd have to go to a convention in Las Vegas over the weekend. Offering to go with him, Liz saw the trip as a badly needed jolt to their relationship.

He refused her company. It would be a working weekend and would bore her. He asked for money, telling her he would give it back to her the next week when he turned in his expense vouchers. Any extra money Liz had that month had already gone to his pockets. All she had left was her savings.

Like a fool, she took a substantial portion out of the bank the next morning and gave it to him when he met her for lunch. Almost a thousand dollars down the drain.

Of course, he was taking another woman. She hadn't believed it when one of his co-workers called and told her. She'd gone to the airport and watched as Don and a young brunette got off the plane, arms locked. They stood by the luggage rack embracing, embarrassing most of the people around them.

Liz went back to the apartment and looked at herself in the mirror. There was the one person she had sworn she would never be: her mother.

Getting rid of Don had been easy. It cost her a thousand dollars, but it was well worth the price. Getting rid of the pain and fear was another story. Could she ever trust herself to see a man clearly? Her mother had been miserable for twenty years, trying to hold a marriage together that wasn't worth saving. She didn't want that to happen to her.

Liz flopped over in her sleeping bag. She didn't want to think about the past. It was too painful. And she didn't want to think about the future, either. She avoided men, particularly sexy men. They were the worst kind. Too much attraction clouded her judgment. She'd already learned her lesson the hard way.

She wasn't about to give Jason Harmon the opportunity to teach her another painful lesson. Even if she had to shove him off a mountain.

SEVEN

Breakfast the next morning was a strained affair. Jason's good humor had not returned. He sat by the campfire, his shoulders hunched over in a green corduroy shirt, and avoided looking or speaking to Liz. He even snapped at his children.

Liz chatted with the kids and the two cowboys and pretended not to notice her host's inhospitable manner. "Is there a climb we can make today?" she asked. "I feel rested after our hike up here."

"Oh, yes!" Roseann answered enthusiastically. "We could climb to Superstition Rock. We always go up there, don't we, Daddy?"

"That would be fun!" Robbie agreed. "Jesse, could you fix us a picnic lunch?"

"You can't go without an adult," Jason growled. It was clear to everyone he wasn't about to volunteer.

"Liz is an adult," Roseann stated, surprising her father, Liz guessed, by the look on his face.

"She's not an experienced hiker."

"Why don't you come with us, Daddy?" Robbie asked, a frown on his face. "You always do."

"No."

Silence fell over the group, and Liz concentrated on her scrambled eggs. When she next looked up, Jason was giving her a fulminating look.

"I'll take the kids to Superstition Rock, but you'd better not come. The climb would be too hard for you."

As if anyone would believe he was concerned about her health, Liz thought in derision. Well, she wasn't going to play the meek little women. "Oh, I think I can make it, but if you don't feel up to it, maybe Matt will come with us."

Liz smiled calmly at her adversary while the children's eyes darted from their father to her, waiting to see who won the duel.

Abruptly, Jason rose to his feet. "Fine! Be ready in five minutes." He stalked off into the woods without another word.

"Lady, you sure do like to live dangerously," Matt murmured, watching his boss disappear among the trees.

"What's he going to do? Push me off the mountain?" Liz asked, remembering her thoughts the night before.

"I doubt it. And he can't even make you get up early. But he sure can wear you out climbing all over these mountains."

Liz smiled at the anxious faces of the children. "I have Robbie and Rosie on my side, Matt. They'll take care of me."

The cowboy's eyebrows rose as he looked at the

little girl, a question in his eyes. What he saw there must have reassured him. "Then I reckon you'll be just fine. You two take care of our lady reporter, you hear?"

"Aren't you coming with us?" Robbie asked.

"Naw. I've climbed it before. I think Liz will do just fine with you two. You gonna tell her the story of Superstition Rock?"

"Sure!" Rosie promised. "She'll want to make her wish when she gets to the top."

"I get to make a wish when I get to the top?" Liz questioned, intrigued with the idea.

"*If* you get to the top," Jesse corrected. "It's not an easy climb."

"Nothing ever is with Jason Harmon," Liz muttered.

"It'll be all right, Liz," Roseann assured her. "You can make it. Me and Robbie will help you."

"Thanks, honey. I'm sure I'll need all the help I can get. And if your dad isn't going to leave us behind, we'd better get ready."

Liz leaned against the rock wall and unzipped her down jacket. "It feels like a hundred degrees," she complained to Roseann, who stood beside her.

"I'll ask Daddy if we can take a breather," Roseann said with a conspiratorial wink. Moving ahead a few steps, she called to her father. "Daddy, I'm tired. Can we rest a few minutes?"

Though Jason flicked a suspicious look in her direction, Liz was glad to see him give in to his daughter's request. His pace was punishing, just as Matt had predicted.

"Come on up here, then. There's a place where we can all sit down."

Roseann motioned for Liz to follow her and scrambled up the path to where her father and Robbie waited. Liz drew a shuddering breath and followed slowly. The cold stare that greeted her almost cooled off her hot cheeks.

"Tired, Miss Broadhurst?"

With a rueful grin, Liz said, "Yes, Jason, I'm tired . . . just as you planned."

His mouth tightened in anger, but the movement reminded Liz of his lips on hers last night. With a shake of her head, she settled her tired body on a flat rock.

Robbie sat down beside her, his jacket unzipped also. "Look, Liz, you can see our campfire from here."

Reluctantly, Liz looked down the mountain to discover a wisp of smoke near the sparkling blue water of the lake. "You're right, Robbie." She shuddered at the steep drop and turned around to stare up the mountain.

Roseann had joined her father on another rock across from her and Liz smiled at the child. "Tell me the story of Superstition Rock, Rosie."

Roseann unzipped her red jacket and would have taken it off except for her father's intervention. More comfortable, she settled herself to tell the story. "Well, you see, these two gold miners were very compe-compet— Anyways, they would always compete. You know, to see who could find the most gold and all.

"Finally, one of them challenged the other one to race him to the top of the big rock that hung over the valley. The winner would get all the gold." Roseann leaned against her father's strong arm. "Well, when the race ended, it was a tie, but on the way back down, they discovered a big gold strike. They shared it and both became rich. And since then, everyone's always said that if you climbed to the top of the rock, you got your wish.''

"And have you ever gotten your wish?" Liz asked curiously, wondering if the little girl really believed the story.

"Not yet. Robbie did once, though.''

"He did?" Jason asked in surprise.

"Don't you remember, Daddy? He wished for a puppy, and when we got back to the ranch, Binky was there waiting for him.''

"Binky?" Liz asked, choking back a laugh.

"He's my dog," Robbie explained. "He was a stray, but Daddy let me keep him.''

"He has a rather, um . . . large nose," Jason assured her, the corners of his mouth turning up as he fought to control a smile. It was the first time he had acted human to her in several days.

"I don't think I met Binky while we were at the ranch.''

"Daddy won't let him come in the house," Robbie explained. "But when we get back, I'll introduce you to him. He's a great dog.''

"I'm sure he is, Robbie." A thought occurred to Liz. "Is the dog in your . . ." She broke off as she realized she was about to give away the boy's secret about his writing.

The alarmed look on Robbie's face as well as Liz's behavior drew Jason's attention. He looked first at his son and then at Liz. "Is it what?"

"I . . . I just meant, uh . . . Robbie was showing

me a book he liked, and I wondered if the dog in the book was named Binky.''

''No, it's not,'' Robbie said swiftly.

''I didn't think it would be. Binky is such an unusual name,'' Liz added, knowing she was chattering but unable to remain silent. ''Well, I think I'm rested. How about you, Roseann? Ready to hurry on up to Superstition Rock? I've got some wishes to make.''

''What will you wish for?'' Roseann asked as she slid off the rock.

''Will they come true if you tell?''

Liz watched out of the corner of her eye to see Jason finally turned away from her as Roseann asked, ''Will they, Daddy?''

''What, honey?''

''Will your wish come true if you tell it?''

''Probably not. How about you, Robbie? Are you ready to go on?''

''Sure, Dad,'' the little boy said as he sent a grateful smile to Liz. He stood up and offered a hand to help her from the rock.

''Thank you, Robbie. You have terrific manners.''

''Daddy taught me,'' he assured Liz, who managed to hold back a stinging comment about do as I say, not as I do. Jason must have read her mind, since he sent her another angry look.

Liz smiled demurely. ''You go first, Jason, and I'll bring up the rear.'' She didn't add that she felt much safer when he was in front of her.

They trudged up the mountain with Jason leading the way followed by the children and then Liz. Occasionally she'd fall behind, but Robbie or Roseann would check on her and encourage her or call to their father to wait.

The sun was high overhead when they reached the top of the mountain. Liz was in no state to appreciate the beautiful view as she collapsed on the ground. "Aaah. I don't think I can climb another step. That was hard work."

"I warned you it wouldn't be easy," Jason commented in a superior manner.

"True, but you didn't add that we were going to climb double-time."

"That was our normal speed," he assured her loftily.

"Boy, Daddy, we really got up here fast today," Roseann said as she walked over to the two adults. Liz didn't bother to hide her triumphant grin.

"Yes, well, I wanted to have lunch up here, and I figured you two munchkins wouldn't wait much longer," Jason informed his daughter, avoiding Liz's knowing eyes.

"Good. I'm ready to eat," Robbie said.

A short time later, they were settled in a circle, munching on the delicious lunch Jesse had prepared for them.

"Mmm, food has never tasted so good," Liz said.

"That's one of the nice things about camping out. It helps you appreciate the good things in life, the important things."

Liz looked at Jason in surprise. "Matt said something about that, too. I guess everyone feels that way when they come to the Rockies."

"I think that's why they draw so many tourists. Problems don't look so big compared to a rock like this one," Jason said with a grin, gesturing to Superstition Rock.

The children, having finished their lunch, wandered off to explore while the adults talked.

"Is that what gives you balance in your business dealings?" Liz asked, unconsciously seeking the key to this fascinating man.

She was surprised to see anger on his face. "No more interviewing. You did enough of that last night."

"Are you blaming me for what happened last night?" Liz demanded.

"*I* was cleaning the fish. You're the one who insisted on horning in. It's a wonder I didn't catch pneumonia!"

"You promised me an interview! Do you think fifteen minutes on the way back to the ranch will be enough?" Liz asked angrily. "And besides, I'm not the one who . . . who grabbed anyone!"

"No, you just shoved me in the lake!"

"That was an accident!" Liz shouted.

"Sure! Tell that to the Marines!" Jason yelled in return.

"Daddy!" a voice shrieked. The two combatants stared at each other and then at the surrounding area for the children. "Daddy! Daddy! Hurry, come quick!" Roseann's frantic voice repeated, even though she wasn't in sight.

Jason leaped to his feet and rushed toward the sound of the child's voice, and Liz followed him as fast as she could. It was only a short distance to where a crying Roseann was hanging over the edge of the rock.

"Rosie! Don't move!" Jason shouted as he ran to his daughter. Liz prayed under her breath, fearing the little girl would slip before her father could reach her.

When Jason grabbed Roseann, Liz slowed her running and sighed deeply, but Roseann's next words took that breath away.

"It's not me," she sobbed. "It's Robbie."

A low moan rose from below and all three peered over the edge of the rock.

"Dear God," Jason muttered. "Robbie?" he called as he leaned over as far as he could. "Robbie, can you hear me?"

A faint yes floated back up as Liz took a trembling Roseann in her arms.

"Son, don't move, okay?"

"Can you reach him?" Liz asked in a whisper.

Robbie was wedged on a ledge about ten feet below the edge. The rock sloped down rather than dropping sharply until it reached the ledge. From there it was a straight drop to the valley below.

"No! We didn't bring any rope with us, either. I don't want to take the time to go back to camp. I don't know if anything's broken, or if he'll be able to stay there for long."

Liz admired his calm as he considered his options. She had come to understand that nothing in the world mattered as much as his children to Jason Harmon. And yet, faced with the possible death of his only son, he was using all his faculties to rescue him, rather than falling apart. Liz clutched Roseann closer to her.

Jason stood and stared at the trees nearby.

"Are you looking for something? Can we help?"

"A long stout stick," Jason muttered, and she and Rosie immediately helped him search. Five minutes later, they gave up. With no axe or hatchet, it was hopeless.

"So close," Jason muttered, looking down once more at the child on the ledge. "Robbie? How are you doing?"

"F-fine," the boy's weak voice floated back up to them.

"I don't suppose you two could . . . No, that would be foolish."

"What?" Liz demanded.

"I was going to suggest you hold on to my feet and let me slide down and pull him up, but you couldn't hold me."

Liz knew he was right. She and Roseann didn't have enough strength to hold his almost two hundred pounds. Liz leaned over to stare down at the boy. If Robbie could reach up, it was just possible . . . She drew a deep breath."

"Jason, I'll . . . I'll go down."

"What?" he demanded in surprise, staring at her.

"You're strong enough to hold me. I'm not as tall as you, but I think it will be enough. I'll slide down to Robbie."

"You realize it's dangerous?"

With a laugh that turned into a sob, Liz nodded. Roseann hugged her tight, and Liz returned her hug. After a long look, Jason nodded his head.

"Take off your boots and socks. It will be easier to grip your bare feet." While she sat down to do that, Roseann helping her untie the boots since she seemed all thumbs, Jason leaned back over the edge. "Robbie? Do you think you've broken any bones?"

"N-no, Daddy . . . but I'm scared."

Liz could almost feel the anguish in Jason's voice.

"I know, son. Listen to me carefully. We're going to lower Liz down to you. But she won't be able to reach you while you're lying down. When she tells you, I want you to sit up. If you can't reach her, you'll have to stand. Do you understand?"

"Yes, Daddy."

"Be very careful. And . . . Robbie? I love you very much."

"I love you, Daddy, and Rosie, too. And Liz, too."

Liz pressed her lips together to stop their trembling. She tiptoed over to Jason and tapped him on the shoulder. "I'm ready," she said in a low voice.

They exchanged a look that spoke volumes, but no words were exchanged. Liz got down on her knees and took one look at the valley below before resolutely fixing her eyes on Robbie. She felt Jason's strong hands grab her ankles.

"Okay, Liz. Inch your way forward. When you can reach him, be sure to double-lock your grip and hold on tight."

"I'm holding on, too, Liz," Roseann's trembling voice called out as Liz flattened out on the rock, the blood rushing to her head. Slowly she extended herself to her full length.

"Robbie?" she called softly. He looked up at her.

"I'm scared, Liz," he whispered.

"I know, honey. But your daddy is counting on us. Can you sit up?"

The ledge was about a foot and a half wide where Robbie was, and he pushed himself up with the outside arm. His fingers were only inches away from Liz's when the earth at the edge of the ledge crumbled and his support hand slipped. Liz screamed as the child fell back. When she opened her eyes again, she gave a thousand thanks to see him still on the ledge.

"What happened?" Jason's raw voice called down.

"Nothing. It's o-okay," she assured him. Then she turned her efforts back to the child, knowing Jason couldn't hold her like this forever. "Come on, Robbie. Be careful where you put your hand this time. In just a few minutes, we'll both be safely back to the top."

The little boy reached up to her again, fear plainly written on his features, and Liz felt sure hers said the same. Their fingers were only inches away. "Robbie, you'll have to reach farther. And hurry."

Slowly, the boy inched his way, his trembling legs pushing up. When his hand touched hers, Liz almost shouted for joy, but the battle had just begun. "Slide your hand past mine and grab my wrist," she told him. His confidence grew as he touched her and he pushed up straighter. "Good, Robbie. Now the other hand."

"I-I can't. I'd have to turn around and there's not room," he cried out.

"Robbie, your daddy can't hold me much longer. I've got you. Now swing quickly around and grab my other hand."

The sternness in her voice had him obeying. Fortunately he moved quickly, because just as their hands met, more of the ledge crumbled and his feet were suddenly dangling in midair.

"Jason!" Liz screamed, hanging on for dear life as Robbie swung beneath her. "Pull us up!"

The strain of being pulled on both ends of her body was intense, and the excruciating minute it took to reach the top seemed to go on for hours. The rock scraped her stomach as her clothing was pushed up her body, and her raspy breath filled her ears. Or perhaps that was Jason's breathing, or Robbie's. She didn't know or care. She just wanted the awful moment to end.

Finally she was on flat ground, and Jason's hands reached over hers to grab the boy and pull him to a rest next to her. Liz could feel Roseann's young arms hugging her and hear the sobs from someone. After a minute she realized they were hers, not Rosie's. Struggling to sit up, she looked at Jason and discovered him sitting still, hugging Robbie tightly to him, with tears running down his face.

Roseann sat with an arm around Liz and another around her father, a dazed look on her face. Pulling down her shirt and jacket, Liz hugged the little girl close to her and extended a hand to Robbie. It seemed important to touch him, as if to prove that he was safe.

"Is . . . is he okay?" Rosie asked in a whisper.

Her question snapped Jason awake. He loosened his tight hold on his son and extended a hand to Roseann. "Robbie? Are you all right?"

"I think so," he said with a sob. "Sorry, Daddy, I don't mean to c-cry, but I was s-so scared!"

Jason hugged the boy to him again. "Cry away, son. You're not the only one who was scared."

When the shock began to ease, Liz found Jason's eyes on her. "I can never thank you enough for saving Robbie."

Embarrassed, Liz replied, "It was a joint effort. I couldn't have done it at all without you and Rosie."

Jason stared at her intently but only said, "Let's

get away from the edge. I don't feel too comfortable here."

They moved back to their original picnic spot, and Jason sat down with his back against a large boulder. He extended his arms to his two children who gathered one on each side of him. Liz stood awkwardly, watching the little family.

"Come on, Liz," Rosie prompted, holding out a hand to her.

Jason's eyes seconded the invitation, and Liz found herself joining the collective hug, the warmth of Jason and Rosie's arms around her lessening the horror of the past few minutes.

"Let's all just rest here for a while until we get our second wind," Jason suggested soothingly. "We've still got that hike back to camp."

Liz shuddered at the thought. Her legs were so rubbery right now, she wasn't sure she could make the long trek back down to the lake.

A few minutes later, Liz realized it wasn't fear that was making her feet numb, but cold. She had left her socks and boots over by the edge of the rock. When she started to move both Jason and Rosie stopped her.

"I have to get my boots. My feet are cold," she explained.

"I'll get them," Rosie offered, but before she could move, both her father and Liz shouted, "No!"

"Thanks, honey," Jason explained, "but we've had enough scare today. I'll get them. You wait here with Robbie and Liz."

When Jason returned with her footgear, Liz reached out a hand to take them, but he refused to give them to her. "I'll put them on for you."

"No, I can—"

"*I'll* do it," he insisted, and Liz realized he needed to do something for her, even if it was as simple as putting on her shoes and socks. She relaxed against the rock and extended her feet.

When Jason took hold of one foot to put on the sock, he exclaimed, "Good Lord! Your feet are blocks of ice." He began to massage her foot with his big hands. "Rosie, come work on the other foot. We've got to get them warm before we put her boots back on or it will take forever for them to warm up."

The little girl left her place beside Liz and joined her father, her small hands rubbing Liz's flesh. Robbie scooted over to sit next to Liz, his hand holding hers. Surrounded by Harmons, Liz thought with a grin. It was a nice feeling.

A few minutes later, with her boots on nicely warmed feet, Liz realized the warm interlude was over. "I'm afraid it's time we start back down the mountain," Jason said.

Roseann scrambled to her feet. "I'll be glad to get there. Wait until Matt and Jesse hear about our adventure."

Jason and Liz exchanged a look that showed amazement over the resiliency of children. Robbie, however, didn't share his sister's excitement. He lay still against the rock, making no move to stand. Jason extended a hand, but the boy didn't take it.

"Robbie?" he questioned.

"Daddy, I don't think I can stand."

Jason was down on his knees at once in front of the boy. "Why not, son?"

"M-my ankle hurts. I didn't say anything because I thought it would go away, but it hasn't."

Liz knelt beside Jason and looked at the swollen ankle when Jason removed the boy's sock and boot. "Is it broken?" she whispered, hoping the child couldn't hear.

"I don't think so. I think you just sprained your ankle, Robbie. It'll mend in a couple of days." Jason's cheerful voice belied the frown on his forehead.

"But how will Robbie get to camp? Do we have to leave him here?" Roseann demanded, rising fear in her voice.

"Of course not, Rosie!" Jason growled. "You're being silly. We would never abandon Robbie. I'll just have to carry him down."

"It's a long way," Liz said, an unspoken question in her voice.

"I can make it, if we take rest stops and don't go down as fast as we came up," Jason assured her, a grin on his face.

Liz grinned back, warmed by his admission. "That suits me just fine."

"Will you be able to help Rosie?" he asked.

"I don't need any help," the child protested indignantly.

"She'll probably help me more than I'll help her. But we'll manage together, won't we, Rosie?"

"Yeah, we'll manage, Daddy," she said with a proud smile.

Jason sent Liz a grateful look before he turned back to Robbie. "Okay, son, I'm going to help you stand on your good foot. Then Liz and Rosie will boost you up on my back."

When that awkward maneuver was accomplished, they headed back down the mountain, Rosie and Liz leading the way.

EIGHT

The weary hikers were still a half hour from camp when they saw Matt and Jesse coming up the path. It had been an arduous trip down, particularly for Jason, as he carried his son to safety.

"Matt, Jesse!" Rosie called out, racing toward them in a burst of speed.

Liz turned back to make sure Jason realized help had arrived, and he greeted her with a weary smile. "I think the cavalry has arrived, Liz."

Moving behind him to help Robbie slide to the ground on his good foot, Liz murmured, "You must be worn out, both of you."

"All I had to do was ride," Robbie said, guilt coloring his voice. "I'm really sorry, Daddy."

Jason hugged the boy. "Don't even think about it, Robbie. You're worth the effort."

"What happened?" Matt called as he reached Rosie. Jason and Liz could hear the little girl chattering away as the trio approached.

"I think Rosie has a flair for the dramatic," Jason whispered before he called out to the others. "We're fine. Just a little accident."

"We got worried about you when you didn't get back. It's going to be dark in a few minutes," Matt explained, his eyes taking in their disheveled state.

"We're glad you did. I could use a spell as pack mule," Jason said. "Robbie sprained his ankle and can't walk."

Matt immediately turned his broad back and knelt in front of the boy. "Saddle up, cowboy."

Robbie, with his father's help, clambered on and held tight as Matt stood. "What's this about Robbie falling?" Matt asked as he shrugged his burden into a more comfortable position.

"Later," Jason muttered, stretching his sore muscles.

Jesse looked at Rosie. "I feel kind of left out without anyone to carry," he said. "How about you, Rosie? Could you use a lift back to camp?"

Liz could have kissed the man for his thoughtfulness. The little girl was drooping with weariness and reaction was beginning to set in.

"Sorry we can't offer you a lift as well, Liz, but I did warn you that hiking with the boss could be a dangerous proposition," Matt added as he turned to follow the trail.

"That's all right, Matt. It's not much farther, and I've enjoyed my day—at least most of it." She looked up at Jason, and time seemed to stand still as he smiled back at her, a lock of dark hair falling across his weary face.

"Come on, you two. Jesse left dinner on the fire. I sure don't want it to burn up," Matt called.

"We're right behind you, Matt," Jason replied as he took Liz's hand in his and started down the path.

They all lingered around the campfire that evening as if reluctant to lose sight of one another. Robbie's ankle had been bathed in cold water and wrapped up for support. His father had settled him by the fire on a sleeping bag with his foot elevated on one of Jesse's pots turned upside down.

Rosie leaned against Liz, her eyelids drooping as she fought against her weariness. "It was scary today," she whispered.

"I know, honey," Liz replied, giving her a hug. "But your daddy kept his head, and everything turned out all right."

"I should've warned Robbie not to get too close to the edge," the child continued.

"It was an accident, Rosie," Liz said sternly. "You're not responsible for Robbie, and you couldn't have prevented it."

"What is it?" Jason called from across the open fire, his ear picking up the tone of Liz's response.

"Rosie was thinking she should've done something to prevent the accident," Liz explained, hoping Jason would know how to relieve his daughter's worry.

Jason stood up and came around the circle. He stooped beside his daughter and kissed her forehead before tugging on her black braid. "Listen, my darling child, if anyone is responsible, it's me. I'm the parent here. But accidents happen, no matter how careful we are. Let's just be grateful Robbie's okay."

"Yes, Daddy," Rosie whispered, throwing her arms around his neck as she squeezed her eyes shut. Liz watched in compassion as tears slipped through the child's defenses. A glance over at Robbie showed him asleep. At least his sister's fears wouldn't upset him.

Jason sat down on the rock beside Liz and held a sobbing Roseann in his lap, murmuring soothing words over and over as he hugged her tight.

"I-I was so scared, Daddy!"

"We all were, honey," Jason assured her, kissing her again.

"W-we mustn't ever let Robbie out of our sight again!" The fierce protectiveness in the child's voice brought wry smiles to the four adults. Jason pushed Rosie back far enough to see her face.

"Rosie, do you know how often I've felt that way about you two? After your mother died, I . . ." he broke off abruptly, hugging the child to him again.

"But, Daddy, I've never done anything like that!" Rosie assured her father.

"Do you think Robbie did it on purpose? There are so many things that could go wrong, Rosie. It scares me to death!" Jason rocked his child back and forth, a fierce frown on his face.

Matt, sitting behind Robbie, his face partially in the shadows, said evenly, "But if we all stand around watching each other, just to be sure we're safe, we miss out on life, Rosie."

"I don't care! I don't want Robbie to be hurt!"

Matt's words seemed to have brought Jason back from whatever frightening world he had been in. He wiped Rosie's tears away with gentle fingers. "Of course you don't," he said. "And we'll take the best care of Robbie, and you, too, that we can. But we can't hide from life, sweetheart, just like Matt said.''

The child sniffed into her father's shirt front, burrowing inside his down jacket. Liz smiled sympathetically.

''How about letting me tuck you into your sleeping bag, Rosie?'' she finally suggested. ''Then your daddy can come in and kiss you good night.''

A few minutes later, Liz stepped out of the tent and motioned to Jason to enter.

She returned wearily to the fireside, leaving the man and his daughter alone. Noticing Robbie was no longer ensconced in front of the fire, she raised a questioning brow.

''Jesse put Robbie to bed,'' Matt explained. ''It wasn't too hard. The kid was dead to the world.''

Liz shuddered at his expression.

''Sorry, Liz, I didn't think. I guess today was kind of tough.''

''Yeah,'' Liz murmured, unable to say more.

Jesse, however, didn't notice her reluctance. ''Tell us what happened? Jason didn't want to talk in front of the kids and we still don't know.''

Liz shivered inside her coat. She didn't want to think about those terrible moments up in the mountain when she hung upside down, Jason on one end and Robbie on the other. ''It . . . it just happened. Robbie slid off the rock and onto a ledge.''

''But how did you get him back up? Could Jason reach him?''

It was Jason who answered Matt's question as he stepped out of the tent. ''No, I couldn't. And we had no ropes. We tried to find a long stick, but there was nothing.''

"What'd you do?" Jesse asked, leaning forward intently.

"Liz saved Robbie's life. She let me lower her down to him, holding on to her ankles. She got hold of him and we pulled them back up."

Liz could feel his blue eyes burning into her, willing her to look at him, but she stared at the fire.

There was silence after his words. Then Matt cleared his throat. "Good job, Liz," he said, and Jesse murmured like words.

"It was a team effort," she mumbled, shifting in embarrassment. Her movement reminded her of the raw skin on her stomach and she winced.

"What's wrong?" Jason demanded, at her side immediately.

"Nothing," Liz said in alarm.

"You must have hurt yourself today. Where? Your ankle? Did you hurt your ankle?" he asked.

"Jason, I'm fine," she insisted, drawing a deep breath and wishing he would move away.

"Then why did you grimace like that?"

All three men were staring intently at her and Liz felt as if she were a prime suspect in a police line-up. "Please, it's nothing."

"Tell me what hurts."

The steel in his voice told her he wouldn't stop until she explained. With a sigh, she admitted, "The skin on my midriff is scraped a little." She had had to change shirts after their arrival at camp because the dried blood caused the material to stick to her.

"Let me see," Jason said at once, reaching for the buttons on her flannel shirt.

Liz reared back in astonishment. "No! I . . . I can take care of it."

"You can't. You won't even be able to see it clearly. I have some salve in my tent."

"Jason, I'm not going to . . . to undress in front of all three of you."

Jason blinked, as if he had forgotten they had an audience. He looked at the other two, a frown on his forehead. "Aren't you two ready for bed?"

Liz watched as the two men stared first at Jason and then each other with grins on their faces. "Come on, Jason, give us a break. It's only eight o'clock," Matt finally said.

"Just give me the salve and I can put it on by myself," Liz assured her determined medic.

"No. I have to make sure it's clean before the salve goes on. Come on, we'll go down by the lake and wash it. I'll take the lantern so I can clean it, and then I'll put on the salve. The guys will stay here to listen for the kids in case they have nightmares."

Liz wondered why this man thought she would be any more comfortable undressing in front of him than the other two. But the hand on her arm left her little choice about accompanying him.

Stopping by his tent, Jason reached inside for a tube she supposed held the salve and a clean handkerchief. Sticking those two items in his coat pocket, he picked up the lantern, never turning loose of Liz's arm. *That's just one more bruise I'll have in the morning,* she thought wearily as she trod along behind him.

"Jason, must we run? I'm really tired," she finally protested.

"Sorry, Liz," he said with a half-smile, slowing his pace. "I just—I'm still a little overwrought from earlier today."

The rigidity to his lips in the lantern glow made Liz want to hug him close, just as he had comforted his children. But she didn't. Her middle was too sore for close quarters. And anyway, she knew better.

When they reached the lake's edge, the campfire a dim glow behind them, Jason set the lantern down on the ground. Without a word, he reached for the top buttons on Liz's shirt. Her hands shot up to stop him.

"That's not necessary, Jason!"

"Don't be skittish, Liz. We've got to be sure the scratches are clean." His irritation was obvious.

"It's not necessary to remove my shirt to look at my middle," she protested in exasperation. "I can lift it up. That's how I got the scratches after all."

"Well, then, do it!" he snapped.

Liz carefully pulled the shirt away from her skin, lifting the shirttail until her midsection was exposed. Jason's gasp as he lifted the lantern didn't improve her spirits.

"Dear God, Liz, why didn't you say something earlier?" he demanded roughly.

She kept silent. Whatever she said wouldn't matter anyway. Waiting numbly for his next move, she stared over his shoulder into the dark woods.

"You'll have to lie down so I can clean it without holding the lantern," he said briskly, as he set the lantern down on the ground. Liz sat down on the hard, cold ground and leaned back gingerly on the bed of pine needles.

The first touch of his handkerchief, saturated in the icy cold water of the lake made her gasp and sent shivers over her entire body.

"Did I hurt you? I'll try to be careful," Jason promised. Liz stared up at his face as he concentrated on his task. The lantern cast a yellow glow over his features, revealing their strength, and yet those very features created shadows. Like their owner, Liz thought hazily. He was an incredible man, and yet there were shadowy depths yet to be explored.

"Your skin is too soft," he said gruffly. "Even a tan would have toughened it up a little. Don't you ever go to the beach?"

"Occasionally," she said, "but I wear a one-piece."

"Why?"

His abrupt question brought a frown to Liz's face. What difference did it make? "I feel more comfortable in a one-piece."

"You've got a good figure. A bikini would look great."

Liz shook her head. "Am I crazy? Or are we up in the Rockies in late fall discussing whether I should be wearing a bikini? What difference does it make?"

"None. I was just curious." He peered down at her middle, but Liz saw his eyes stray higher, skimming over her covered breasts. She couldn't hold back a shiver.

"Cold? I'm hurrying," he assured her. "I'll put on the salve now. It may sting a little, but it will keep the wound from getting infected until we can get you to a doctor."

"I don't need a doc— Aaaah!" she protested as the cure bit into the wound. "A little? You did say a little, didn't you?"

"Isn't that what the doctor always says?"

"I just hope you don't send me a bill like the doctor," she grumbled.

His hands stilled. "I owe you more than I could possibly ever repay, Liz. You know that."

"You don't owe me anything."

"You don't think it important that you saved my son's life?"

"Of course it's important. But I didn't do it for you. I would have done the same for anyone."

"I see."

Liz peered up at his face as he resumed his ministrations, but she couldn't read his expression. With a sigh, she quit trying and looked out across the lake, biting her bottom lip as the salve continued to make itself felt.

"All finished," Jason said, but as she moved to pull down her shirt, he stopped her. "Not yet. Give it a chance to take hold. We don't want your shirt to rub it off before it does its job."

Liz remained where she was, extremely uncomfortable stretched out on the ground, her middle exposed. Jason rocked back off his feet and settled on the ground, staring down at her.

"What is it?" she finally asked, pushing back a strand of blonde hair, unnerved by his look.

With a half-smile, Jason said, "You know, when you got off that plane the other day, I was sure my plan would work. You had big city written all over you."

"Of course I did," she said crossly. "That's where I live."

He ignored her response. "You're also a beauty."

Liz stared at him in amazement. It was quite a change for Jason Harmon to be passing compliments in her direction.

"Beauty and practicality, that's an interesting mixture." He paused, but Liz had nothing to say. "So why aren't you married?"

That question jolted her. "What?"

"You're an extremely attractive woman, intelligent, sincere, all the things a man is looking for. So why aren't you married?"

"I'm a career woman!" she snapped.

"There's no such animal. Just smarter women out for bigger catches. Is that what you're doing? Looking for your very own millionaire?"

Somewhere the conversation had taken a different tone. Gone were the compliments. Instead, Jason seemed to be attacking her. Was he afraid she would expect more than he was willing to give in exchange for saving his son?

Liz started to rise, but a hand on her shoulder forced her to continue to lie down. "What's the matter, Jason? Afraid I've got my sights set on you?"

"You wouldn't be the first one," he growled. "And it won't do you any good."

"Is that why you've never remarried? Because you're too cynical?"

"Give it up, lady. My love life is none of your business."

"And mine is your business?"

"Forget it! I was just making conversation."

"Well, I can do without that kind of conversation."

There was no talk for the next two minutes. Liz wanted to go back to her tent and get away from this frustrating, fascinating man, but she felt sure he wouldn't let her rise just yet.

"Are you one of those frigid virgins?"

Outraged, Liz turned to stare at her questioner. The angry look on his face made her want to smack him. "I thought we had agreed to forget this topic," she ground out.

"That must mean you are. It's easy to recognize a virgin. She's afraid of life."

"For your information," Liz fired back, her temper gaining control, "I am neither afraid of life nor a virgin!" Her words rang out in the silence of the cold night air. The thought that the two men around the campfire might have heard her was mortifying.

"Go away and leave me alone!" Liz exclaimed.

She thought he was going to do just that as he reached for the lantern. Instead, he snuffed out the light, leaving them in darkness except for the silver of moonlight and the campfire in the distance. "What—" She never finished her question because his lips covered hers, taking her breath away.

Her thoughts were jumbled, confused by the passion that rose within her. She couldn't deny her attraction to this bewildering man, but she wanted to. Feeling his body stretch out alongside hers as his arms pulled her to him, Liz tried to move away, but his lips followed hers, caressing, molding, and the sweetness of his mouth seduced even as she withdrew.

Finally twisting her face away from his, she gasped, "Jason! Stop! We can't—" But his lips assured her they could.

Hands shoved her shirt up above her breasts and stroked her, leaving a mounting desire in their wake. Even in his ardor, she noted how careful Jason was of her wounds. His hands avoided touching her sores, but they trailed down her bare flesh on the side, and searching fingers slid beneath the waist of her jeans.

Shivers ran over her body as Jason's kiss deepened, sending her spiraling into the depths of desire. She hadn't ever wanted a man as she wanted Jason at that moment. Her hands sought the buttons of his shirt, searching for the warmth of his flesh.

All the reasons she had used to shun men for the past three years were useless against Jason's caresses. Caution was abandoned, and she sought his touch as she explored his body with her fingers. His scent mixed with the heady perfume of the pine needles and the fresh night air, an elixir more intoxicating than the costliest cologne.

A moan rose from one of them, but Liz didn't know if it was hers or Jason's. The exquisite pleasure was drugging, and when his lips left hers to seek the soft skin of her neck, she gladly offered herself to him. "Jason," she whispered, imploring his touch as she pressed against him. His hands slid down to free her breasts and his lips soon joined them, his tongue tasting each one.

While his mouth continued its devastation, his fingers sought the opening to her jeans, and Liz made no attempt to stop him. She felt as if she were on a runaway train heading downhill and had no power to prevent what was happening.

Even more frightening was the knowledge that she would not have put on the brakes if she could have. She shoved that thought away, and sought the pleasure offered.

"Jason? Is everything okay?"

Both of them went rigid as Matt's voice penetrated their euphoria. Jason withdrew his hands from her jeans and rolled away from her. "Yes, Matt. We'll be up in a minute."

Even in the dark, Liz felt exposed. It was her soul more than her body that she wanted to cover. She had shown her desire, her need for this man, and that

Tomorrow she would finish the interview, get away from Jason Harmon, and never see him again. She wasn't stupid enough to repeat such a disastrous mistake.

NINE

Sometime during the night, Liz surfaced from a restless sleep to hear Rosie whimper. Foggily, she reached out to the little girl, shaking her awake. About the time Rosie responded, Liz's hand told her the temperature had dropped considerably since she had gotten into her bed.

"Rosie?" she asked, trying to stop the shiver that was going all over her. "Are you all right?"

"What? What is it, Liz?" the child's sleepy voice asked before she added, "Brr, I'm cold."

"Me, too. But I heard you cry and I thought you might be having a bad dream."

"I don't remember." Liz could hear her stirring in her sleeping bag. "I'm so cold. Maybe we should wake up Daddy and see if he can find us some more covers."

"No! No, we don't want to disturb your father's sleep." Liz thought frantically. "I know. Why don't you get in my sleeping bag with me. We'll keep each other warm that way.''

''Hey, that's a neat idea,'' Rosie said with enthusiasm. Though they made the transfer quickly, the cold air rushed in the bag along with the little girl, and Liz wasn't sure their body heat would be enough. Momentary concern about the weather was dismissed as useless, however. There wasn't anything she could do about it. Besides, she didn't intend to be around here much longer, and she could stand the cold for a little while. Rosie snuggled up against her, taking Liz back to her childhood when her younger siblings had crawled in bed with her on a cold morning, begging her to tell them stories.

'' 'Night, Liz,'' Rosie said softly.

''Good night, honey.''

The child's even breathing soon told Liz she had returned to her dreams. With determination, Liz closed her eyes to do the same. She refused even to think about the previous evening. Mr. Jason Harmon wasn't worth losing a night's sleep over.

Liz came awake much later because of an insistent whisper in her ear.

''Liz? Liz? Are you awake?''

''What a silly question, my pet, when you can see my eyes are closed.'' She opened one eye and semiglared at the cherubic face smiling up at her. ''What time is it?''

''I don't know, but it must be really early 'cause there's no sunshine and I can't smell the fire burning.''

Liz sniffed the air just as Rosie had done, but she could detect nothing. ''That means Jesse hasn't started breakfast yet," she said with a grimace. She would have loved a cup of hot coffee.

Liz worked her left arm to the top of the sleeping bag and looked at the plain watch on her wrist. After staring at it, she shook it and held it to her ear.

"What is it?" Rosie asked.

"My watch says it's eight-thirty," Liz said in astonishment, still peering at it in the gloom of their tent.

"But Daddy and Jesse and Matt never sleep that late when we're camping!"

The bitter cold that had driven them into one sleeping bag was attacking Liz's exposed arm. She slid back down into the warmth. "Let me get warm again and then I'll dress and see what's going on."

"I'll come with you."

"I don't think so, Rosie. It's really cold. We must have had a norther blow through last night."

"One time it snowed on us up here," Rosie told her with a giggle.

"The way that wind's blowing, if it were snowing, we'd have a blizzard." Liz took a deep breath and located her clothes with her eyes. "Okay, here goes." She launched herself from the sleeping bag and into her clothes in the shortest possible time, but she felt chilled all the way through. "Stay put, Rosie. It's really cold. I'll be right back," she assured the little girl as she knelt to unsnap and unzip the tent door.

The white, whirling world she discovered before she had pulled the zipper even a foot apart astounded her. She quickly unzipped it the rest of the way. Their campsight was unrecognizable with swirling snow covering everything. Liz could just barely make out the other two tents even though they were less than ten yards away. Even as she stared, they seemed to fade from view and all she saw was blinding white. The stinging snow on her face awakened her and she quickly slid the zipper back in place, snapping the snaps with shaking fingers.

"Rosie," she gasped. "We're in the middle of a *big* snowstorm. I can scarcely even see the other tents." She picked up Rosie's sleeping bag and unzipped it. Sitting on one end of it, she wrapped it around her Indian-style.

"Really?" Rosie squealed. "I want to see!"

"No, young lady. You stay snug in that bag. You'll catch a terrible cold if you're not careful."

Before Rosie could argue, and it was clear she intended to, both were startled when the zipper on their tent slid up and a human snowman burst in upon them.

"Daddy!" Rosie cried. "You look like a snowball."

"So would you if you went outside," Jason muttered. Liz felt his eyes rake her face, but she kept her eyes lowered. "Are you two okay?"

"We're fine," Rosie said blithely. "We snuggled together to keep warm."

"Good. Well, Jesse and Matt are going to rig up a shelter to block off the wind and snow and build a fire so we can have hot food."

"Coffee?" Liz couldn't help asking.

With a wry grin that acknowledged a mutual need, Jason said, "Jesse promised it would be the first thing he fixed."

"I want hot chocolate!"

"I think Jesse knows you well enough to figure that out, little one." He cleared his throat. "Anyway, we're going to bring Robbie over here and use this tent as kind of our living area, since it's the largest. All of us in here will be a little snug, but the body heat should make it cozy."

Liz said nothing, but she vowed to stay on the opposite side of the tent from her host.

"I have to get dressed!" Rosie assured her father in alarm.

"There's time, sweetheart. I'll go back and help the others while you get ready for the invasion."

He turned to go but Rosie called him back. "Daddy, I have to, you know, go outside. What do I do?"

"Can't you . . . no, I don't suppose you can." He avoided Liz's eyes. Finally he said, "I'll get a rope. We'll tie it to your tent and if Liz will go with you, you go as far as the rope and—and take care of your business and then follow the rope back to the tent."

"Is the rope really necessary?" Liz asked in surprise.

"People have died in storms like this only a few feet from shelter. You lose your bearing very easily. Don't turn loose of the rope."

His stern warning convinced Liz, and she nodded her head.

"I'll be right back."

As soon as he was gone, Liz hustled the child into her clothes and then rolled up the sleeping bags. She placed them as backrests along the walls of the tent. All six of them would completely fill the tent, but Jason was right about body heat. And in this weather, any heat at all was welcome.

When the two ladies returned from their escapade at the end of the rope, they discovered Jesse sheltering behind the canvas wall that had been erected, working over a sputtering fire. His grin in spite of the intolerable circumstances cheered both of them.

Dashing into the tent they found Jason and Matt settling Robbie. They had apparently carried him in his sleeping bag.

"Hi, Robbie," Rosie greeted him happily. "Isn't this neat?"

Matt groaned. "Rosie, I swear, no one but you would think a storm like this was neat."

"But, Matt, the snow is beautiful, and when it stops, we can have snowball fights and everything!"

Liz watched the two men exchange looks and frowned. Surely they weren't in any danger? She started to ask, but Jason's glare in her direction made her change her mind.

"I'd better see if I can help Jesse," Matt muttered, and turned to go back out into the storm.

"Can I help?" Liz offered.

"No, you stay in here with the kids," Jason said abruptly. "I'll help with the food."

A short time later, everyone was crowded into the tent, all but Robbie sitting cross-legged to conserve space. Liz was feeling much better after a breakfast of oatmeal and hot coffee. In fact, she would've felt a lot better even if she'd only had coffee, but the oatmeal left her with a warm feeling in her tummy.

"Doggone," Matt complained, "God didn't mean for a man to sit like this. My legs feel like parts of an accordian."

The two children giggled, and even Jason cracked a smile, a rare occurrence so far.

"That's because you've had them wrapped around a horse for too long," Jesse assured him with a grin. "Since I spend most of my time squatting down by a fire, it's no problem."

"I'd be careful, Jesse. By the time this storm ends, you may be complaining, too," Jason warned.

"You think it will last a long time?" Liz asked in concern.

The three men looked at each other, but no one volunteered an answer.

"Well?" Liz prompted.

"It's hard to tell," Jason said calmly. "But as strong as this one seems to be, it could last several days."

Liz gasped, and even the children seemed subdued by such a possibility. After a moment, she asked, "Do we have enough supplies to last us?"

Jesse nodded. "Sure. We had planned to stay a couple of more days, and I always take some emergency rations along. The big problem may be finding wood for the fire. We moved the wood we had collected behind the canvas, but when that's gone, we'll have to find some more. It won't be easy in this storm."

"We'll manage," Jason said crisply, sending a warning glance to his cook.

" 'Course we will," Matt added. "Why, I remember back in '87 when we had that terrible storm . . ." he began, spinning a long tale that entertained the children for at least half an hour. After that, each of the adults took turns telling stories or finding some form of entertainment for their little group, keeping the children's minds away from the storm raging around them.

Lunch was a cold affair—and never had those words been truer, Liz thought with a chuckle. When their hunger had been satisfied, she dug through her bag and came up with a deck of cards.

"Why didn't you tell us you had cards, Liz?" Matt demanded. "We could've avoided some of Jesse's tales."

"Because I enjoyed every word of his stories, Matt, just as I did yours," Liz assured him with a grin. "But I thought everyone might be ready for a change of pace."

"*I* sure am," Jesse agreed. "What'll it be? Poker?"

"I don't know how to play poker," Rosie said anxiously.

Liz, sitting between the two children, gave her a hug. "Of course you don't, Rosie. And I thought we could play go fishing. Have you ever played that game?"

The two children shook their heads enthusiastically, and Liz glanced at the men with a grin. In no time at all, they were launched into a game of go fishing that had Rosie doubled up with giggles as the men teased and joked their way through the game. Robbie struggled to stay awake, and after the game ended, Liz suggested the two children take a nap.

"I'm not sleepy," Rosie protested.

Liz leaned down and whispered, "I know, honey, but Robbie isn't up to par, and it will make him feel better about sleeping if he thinks you're tired, too."

"Oh, well, maybe it wouldn't hurt to rest a little," Rosie said, and was rewarded by Liz's warm smile.

There was a rearrangement of the party as they made room for Rosie to stretch out on the opposite end of the tent from Robbie, and Liz discovered herself next to Jason, across from the other two.

"What shall we play now?" Jesse asked. "Strip poker?"

His leer didn't even faze Liz. "In this weather? You're crazy," she assured him.

"And what if it were summer?"

Liz frowned at the man beside her. He acted as if she had no morals. Stiffly, she said, "I don't play strip poker at any time."

"Darn!" Matt joked, even though his curious eyes were on both of them.

"Why don't we play hearts?" Liz suggested.

"That's what women always want to play."

The bitterness in Jason's words had nothing to do with cards, and Liz refused to say anything after that.

"Aw, come on, Jase, give the lady a break. She hasn't tried to steal my heart, even though I offered several times." Matt winked at Liz.

There was a tense silence as the others waited for Jason's response. Liz kept her eyes focused on the cards in her hands.

Abruptly, Jason's big hand reached over and took the deck from her. "How about spades? Does everyone know how to play spades?"

Everyone did, and the subject of hearts, any kind of hearts, was dropped for the moment.

By the time the kids awakened, it was time for Jesse to start dinner. The kerosene lantern that had given off a little additional warmth in the tent had to be carried outside to the shelter so he could see to work. Matt and Jason, each with a rope tied around his waist, wandered out in the storm to pick up any wood they could find. Liz sat with Rosie and Robbie in near darkness.

"How long do you think it will snow?" Robbie asked.

made her vulnerable. She pulled down her bra and shirt even as she turned away, sitting up with her back to the man beside her.

"I didn't intend for that to happen," he said harshly.

She didn't answer, continuing to adjust her clothes.

A hand on her shoulder pulled her back around in spite of her efforts to dislodge it. "It doesn't change anything. Do you understand? What happened doesn't mean anything except that you're an attractive woman and I wanted you!"

"Afraid I'll sue you for breach of promise or something?" she demanded, her voice shaking.

"That's been tried before, too."

Liz looked at him for the first time since he had turned her to face him. The bitterness she saw there in the pale light struck her, leaving her with no response.

"Hell! I should never have started this whole mess," Jason muttered, jumping to his feet. Before Liz could agree with him, he strode off into the darkness, away from her and the camp.

She sat still, her limbs shaking with the rapid emotional descent. Her thoughts were chaotic, disturbing her even more than her physical reaction. Since her disastrous engagement, she had held herself aloof from men, avoiding them whenever possible. She would not be bound to a life like her mother's. But tonight, just because Jason Harmon had wanted her, she had offered herself to him on a platter.

Nausea stirred her stomach. How stupid could she be? The man had already told her he wouldn't offer marriage. And even if he did, that wasn't what she wanted! Was this what had happened to her mother? Had she been betrayed by her body?

Liz reached out and squeezed his hand. He sounded a little forlorn. "Oh, probably by tomorrow it will have blown itself out, Robbie."

Rosie leaned against her other side. "You know, when Daddy first told us you were comin', we didn't think we'd like you."

You weren't supposed to, Liz reminded herself silently.

She said nothing, and Rosie continued. "But now, it's almost like you're our mother."

"Rosie, you shouldn't say that," Liz warned, just as a snow-covered Jason entered the tent.

"Ooh! Daddy, you're frozen," Rosie protested as a shower of snow fell from him.

"Rosie shouldn't say what?" Jason demanded in a hard voice, ignoring his daughter's words.

"She . . . she was just teasing," Liz said.

But at the same time, Rosie repeated her words. "I just said Liz almost seems like our mother."

Liz knew Jason was angry with her last night, though she wasn't quite sure why. After all, *he* had initiated their embrace, not *her*. But that anger paled in comparison to the burning stare he gave her now. *It's a wonder steam isn't rising from him,* Liz thought, annoyed herself.

"She's not at all like your mother!" he snapped.

"I didn't mean she looked like our mother, Daddy. I can't even remember what she looked like. But Liz *feels* like our mother 'cause she's always there to help us, and . . . and she loves us. Don't you, Liz?"

Not even to appease Jason's anger could Liz have lied to Rosie as she smiled up at her. "Yes, I do love you and Robbie, but that doesn't mean . . . I love you as friends, sweetheart."

"But isn't that the way mothers love you, like best friends?"

Liz avoided Jason's eyes. "I guess so."

"Liz is helping me with my story," Robbie announced abruptly.

Jason stared at his son. "What story?"

"I've been writing a story, Daddy. But I didn't want to tell you or Rosie 'cause I thought it wasn't good enough. But Liz read it and said she liked it. And she's going to help me make it better." Robbie beamed at Liz as she fought to hold back a groan.

Jason's words were as cold as the blizzard. "How kind of Miss Broadhurst."

Matt's entrance, bumping into Jason and throwing him forward almost into Liz's lap, ended their conversation.

"Whoops, sorry, big guy. I didn't know you were blocking the door."

Jason righted himself, settling down by Robbie. "Did you find much?"

"Naw, everything's covered. I brought back one or two sticks, but that's about it. You?"

"The same. But Jesse thinks it may be tapering off."

Liz looked up eagerly. "He thinks the storm may be ending?"

"Maybe."

Jason's laconic answer didn't hold much joy at the prospect.

"Isn't that good?"

Jason said nothing, but Matt explained. "You see, Liz, when the clouds go away, the bottom falls out of the temperature. So if it stops snowing, it'll probably get real cold, and we'll have to figure out a way to keep all of us warm.''

Liz sobered. They had managed with all of them packed into the one tent and the heat from the kerosene lantern during the day. But it wasn't warm by any means. And if the temperature dropped considerably during the night, it would be impossible. ''What will we do?''

''We'll manage,'' Jason muttered, his eyes flickering on his children's faces.

Reminded of little ears, Liz tried a heartiness she didn't feel. ''Yes, of course. I just wondered what measures we would take.''

''We'll probably all sleep in this tent,'' Matt put in, ''like one big slumber party.''

''Or like a big family,'' Rosie added, her face split in a big grin. ''This is the best camping trip ever, Daddy.''

From the look on his face, Jason didn't seem to agree with his daughter.

Once dinner was out of the way and the lantern brought back into the tent, everyone seemed at a loss for entertainment. The cardplaying had lost its novelty and the stories were all told.

''How about some songs?'' Liz finally suggested. ''I used to be in the Girl Scouts, and we always sang around the campfire.''

The children agreed enthusiastically, but the men looked a little doubtful. ''Unless you'd rather tell more stories or play cards?'' Liz offered.

With a look at the others, Matt capitulated. ''Nope. I believe we'll sing.''

They all took turns suggesting songs and singing

riotously along, frequently off-key. When the enthusiasm began to lag, Liz offered one of her favorite songs as a child. "How about the crocodile song?"

"We don't know that one," Robbie said, a frown on his brow.

"It's easy, and it has hand motions. Just follow me," Liz said, extending her two hands, the palm of one facedown on the back of the other hand. "Here's the way it goes:

" 'She sailed away on a happy, summer day

"On the back of a crocodile. (She made wave motions with her hand).

"You see, said she, he's as tame as he can be.

"I'll float him down the Nile. (Liz used the top hand to pet the second one as she continued the wave motions.)

"The croc winked his eye as she waved them all good-bye,

"Wearing a happy smile, (After waving good-bye, Liz pointed to her broad smile.)

"At the end of the ride, the lady was inside,

"And the smile on the crocodile.' " (She continued the wave motions, but turned her palms together, opening and closing them to simulate the crocodile's mouth.)

Rosie clapped with glee. "I love that! Sing it again. I want to learn how to do it."

After several rounds of the crocodile song, with Rosie insisting everyone join in, silence fell. It took several minutes for Liz to realize what was so strange about it.

"Listen!"

Jason frowned at her. "I don't hear anything."

"But that's it. The wind has stopped!"

Matt reached for the zipper of the tent and opened the canvas door. Overhead was a clear, velvet-blue sky with stars twinkling down. On the ground, deep snow lay in drifts, covering everything.

Liz shivered as the cold stole into their little home. She thought it was already more frigid.

"Well, it's time we all settled down for the night," Jason said. "Rosie, you'd better make a trip outside with Liz."

When the two of them returned, Liz brushed the snow off Rosie and then herself before they stepped back into the tent. Robbie had gone out with his father, and the two cowboys were building a large fire near the entrance of their tent. Liz sent Rosie into the tent and turned to Matt.

"Will we have enough wood?"

"Sure. We'll be leavin' in the morning, so we'll build a big fire tonight and keep us all toasty warm."

Liz could feel the heat building from the fire they had started, but it was very close to the tent. "Isn't it a little dangerous to have it so near the canvas?"

"We'll have to take shifts staying up and keeping the fire going anyway. We'll just keep an eye out for sparks at the same time," Jesse explained with a grin.

"I'll be glad to take a turn," Liz offered.

"Well, that's right neighborly of you, ma'am," Matt responded in a thick western drawl, "but here in the West, we men take care of our womenfolk, not the other way around."

Liz stared at him in exasperation. "I can't believe you said that!"

"Now what?" Jason questioned as he helped Robbie into the tent, having come up behind them without

Liz realizing it. He turned back around to them after making sure Robbie made it to his sleeping bag.

Matt grinned at her and said nothing, leaving it up to Liz to explain. ''I just offered to help share the watch tonight to keep the fire going, and Matt made some chauvinistic remark about the men taking care of the women.''

''Here, now. I was just being a gentleman, not a chauvinist,'' Matt protested.

''There's no reason I shouldn't do my part. After all, keeping a fire burning isn't that difficult. It only makes sense because the more sleep we all get, the easier the trip tomorrow will be.''

''And that's why you'll need a full night's sleep,'' Jason explained in steely tones. ''Now get inside and get to sleep.''

Liz stared at him in frustration. She always pulled her own weight and she didn't like being treated this way.

Jesse stepped forward and said kindly, ''It really is the best way, Liz. The kids will settle down a lot better with you in there with them. They've really taken to you.''

Liz nodded, since she had no choice, and slipped into the tent. But at least she had the satisfaction of seeing Jason's mouth tighten in anger at Jesse's words.

TEN

Liz had settled the two children in their sleeping bags when Jason entered the tent. She looked at him questioningly but refused to say anything.

"Hi, Daddy," a sleepy Rosie said. "Are you going to sleep in here with us, too?"

"I guess so," he replied grumpily. "Jesse and Matt have moved the lean-to over by the fire and are going to bed down there, taking turns staying awake."

"You mean they're going to take care of you, too?" Liz asked silkily, willing to endure his anger for the price of a little dig.

He glared at her but said nothing.

Robbie grinned. "It'll be just like a real family, Daddy."

His father shifted his glare from Liz to his son.

Robbie, thinking his father didn't understand his remark, added, "You know, a mommy, a daddy, and two kids."

"I've heard enough about Liz being a part of our family. She's not! And that's all I want to hear about it!"

A deathly silence followed his outburst. Finally, Liz asked, "How's the best way to arrange the sleeping bags? Shall we put the two kids in the middle?"

"Yeah."

"I guess we can all cuddle together," Rosie added, peeping at her father to see if he would be angry.

Jason Harmon's saving grace, as far as Liz was concerned, was his love for his children. She watched his face show guilt when he caught Rosie's look and he immediately melted. "Sorry, baby, I didn't mean to yell at you."

"That's all right, Daddy. Liz says lots of people get cabin heat." The child nodded her head wisely while her father stared at her, perplexed.

"Cabin *fever*, Rosie, not heat," Liz amended as she tried to hide her laughter. When Jason's eyes met hers, however, she gave up the effort and matched his grin with one of her own.

That moment relaxed the tension that had existed between them the past twenty-four hours. With little discussion and no animosity, they moved the children to the center of the tent and Liz bedded down beside Rosie and Jason beside Robbie.

Rosie giggled and whispered for a while before Liz settled her down. Robbie was already snoring softly when Rosie's even breathing told Liz she had finally succumbed.

"You must be a natural with children unless you have some of your own."

The disembodied voice startled Liz. She peered across the tent in the darkness but could see no movement. "I don't have any of my own, but I helped raise five brothers and sisters."

"That's a big family."

"Yes."

"Do they all live in Los Angeles?"

Liz found it disturbingly intimate to carry on a whispered conversation in the dark, even though they were separated by two sleeping children. But she could hardly object.

"No, they're all in Texas."

"Ah. That's where my plan failed."

That non sequitur left her confused. "What?"

"If I'd known you were from Texas, before I picked you, I wouldn't have expected a camping trip to scare you."

"I assume you believe the rumor that every Texan was born on a horse?"

Her sarcasm didn't seem to faze him. "No, I think you disproved that theory the first day. But most Texans are just about as stubborn as they come."

A small smile crept on Liz's face and she was glad they were in the dark.

"Do you intend to have children of your own, or are you fed up with kids?"

"I . . . I intend to have children of my own someday."

"How old are you?"

"Didn't your report tell you that?"

"As a matter of fact it did. I'd forgotten. You're twenty-seven."

Liz said nothing.

"You've still got time, I guess." When she still said nothing, he asked, "Have any prospects?"

"Children?" she asked, startled.

Even though she couldn't see his face, she felt the smile in his words. "No, honey, prospects for a husband. I've heard one is necessary if you want a family."

"Then you heard wrong. A lot of single women are parents these days." She regretted the stiffness in her words, but she was uncomfortable with their discussion.

After a moment, he said, "I don't recommend being a single parent. I've got a lot of help, but it's still difficult."

"It must not be too bad or you would've remarried."

Now it was Jason's turn to stiffen. "That's not a very good reason for marriage."

"Do you ever date?"

"Volunteering?"

Liz gritted her teeth, trying to hold back the hot words that wanted to pour forth. After a deep breath, she said, "No, but I'm curious. You are in Los Angeles frequently where beautiful women are readily available. Yet you never make the gossip columns. Either you're incredibly discreet or you have no social life at all."

"There's more to a woman than her beauty."

"I couldn't agree more. But that doesn't answer my question."

"It's all the answer you're going to get. Neither of us has a relationship and there's no reason we have to explain that to each other. Maybe we're both frigid," he said flippantly.

But while Liz might have once considered herself unresponsive, rather than frigid, she had discovered only last night that the right man could build a roaring fire inside her. And that man could never be considered frigid, even in a blizzard.

When Liz awoke the next morning, it was because someone was shaking her shoulder. She slowly opened her eyes to find Jason standing over her.

"Wake up, Liz."

"What time is it?"

"Seven o'clock. Jesse almost has breakfast ready. We want to eat and be underway in half an hour. It'll be light enough then."

"Will we be able to make it back to the ranch in one day?" she asked as she slid down the zipper on her bag.

"I think Al will meet us with the horses before we get too far. Then it will go faster." He moved over to wake up the kids, and Liz pulled on her cold boots.

Half an hour later, almost to the minute, just as Jason had said, Liz watched as the men kicked snow on the remaining embers of the fire. They had taken down the tents but were leaving them there along with a lot of their supplies.

"We'll return for these things later," Jason told her. "There's no sense burdening us down when we need to travel fast."

During the night, while tending the fire, Matt and Jesse had made a bed for Robbie out of two long tree limbs and some shorter ones tied crisscross fashion between them. The men would take turns carrying him.

"Everyone ready?" Jason asked.

There were nods all around. He looked at Liz. "Matt is going to lead for a while, and Jesse and I will carry Robbie. You and Rosie follow Matt. Be sure to step where he does so you're not surprised by a deep drift.''

Liz knew he was reminding her that he depended on her to help Rosie. She nodded and turned to the little girl, pulling her knitted hat farther down over her ears. Liz also wore a knitted hat, red to match her down jacket, but she added Al's black cowboy hat. She didn't want to leave it up here.

"Off we go, then," Matt said. He led the way back toward the lake and around its edge for about a hundred yards before striking off down the slope the way they had come.

Two hours later, Liz wasn't sure she could go another step. After yesterday's inactivity, her legs seemed to have forgotten any strength she thought she had. And plowing through snow was as difficult as running underwater. Just when she thought she would drop, Matt called a halt.

They had reached a flat, open space with several large rocks. Matt brushed the snow from one and gestured to it. "Ladies, your couch awaits you."

Rosie gave a tired chuckle and Liz helped her up before she sat down also. Jason and Jesse leaned Robbie's traveling bed up against another rock, leaving him aslant. "Gosh, it feels good to be still for a while," the little boy said.

"Rough ride, son?" Jason asked with a weary grin.

"Sorry, Daddy. I know you and Jesse must be tired."

"As light as you are?" Jesse teased. "I'm beginning to think you don't really like my cooking. If you did, you'd weigh a lot more."

"Aw, Jesse," Robbie protested with a grin. But the cowboy's teasing had taken the child away from worrying about being a burden.

"How much farther, Daddy?" Rosie asked, the same question that Liz had been holding back for fear of worrying the kids.

"Well, we're taking the shortcut," he explained, avoiding Liz's eyes, "but if Al doesn't meet us with the horses, I don't think we'll get there until late this evening."

"Can we keep going after the sun goes down?" Liz asked.

"Yeah, with the brightness of the snow, we should be able to see okay. But we'll keep our fingers crossed that Al will show."

"I didn't think I'd ever want to get on a horse again," Liz said fervently, "but now I'd throw my arms around its neck and give it a big hug."

"Careful now," Matt said with a grin, "or you'll have us fellows jealous of a horse."

"Would you be jealous, Daddy?" Roseann asked with the air of a bird spying a grain of corn.

With a shrug, Jason said, "Probably not, honey."

"But Liz is very pretty, don't you think?"

"Rosie!" Liz protested.

Jason, however, answered his daughter calmly. "Of course Liz is pretty." Before she could ask anything else, Jason said, "Your hands and feet are warm enough, aren't they, Rosie? You can still feel your toes?"

The little girl frowned. " 'Course I can, Daddy."

"You let me know if they start going numb. Robbie, how about you? Are you warm enough?"

The little boy assured his father he was comfortable, and that seemed to signal to Jason it was time to move on. Liz would have preferred another fifteen minutes, but her opinion wasn't sought.

This time Jesse broke the trail and Matt and Jason carried the litter, with Liz and Rosie slipping and sliding in between the two.

As the sun rose higher, its brightness reflecting off the glittering whiteness of the snow, Liz's spirits rose even as her energy fell. When Jesse spotted a solitary figure down below leading a string of horses, she and Rosie let out a cheer of relief.

Jesse's grin showed his agreement with them, but he added, "We've got at least half an hour before we meet up with him, so keep moving, you two."

"Aye, aye, sir," Liz said, but her spirits were lifted by the thought of the once-dreaded ride back to the ranch.

Their pace quickened with the end of the hike in sight. Jesse offered to switch off with Jason, since he had carried part of the litter the entire way, but he refused.

A short time later, they heard Al's call, letting them know he had spotted them up above him. Jesse waved back. "Not much farther now, ladies," he called over his shoulder.

Rosie and Liz exchanged grins and slid after him. When they met up with Al, Rosie prodded Liz. "Are you going to hug your horse?"

Liz grinned but whispered, "I'd rather not, if you don't mind. I'm afraid he might object and bite me."

Rosie giggled, drawing a sharp look from her father. When he walked past Liz, he asked in a low voice, "Collecting more secrets from my children?"

Liz stared after him in surprise. She finally realized he must be referring to Robbie's writing. His son's secrecy must have hurt him. Remembering Robbie, she moved over to where his bed was resting. "How are you doing, Robbie?"

"Just fine, Liz."

"Are you going to ride a horse back?"

"I don't know. Daddy and Al are talking about it now. I told him I could, but he said I needed to keep my foot up."

"I'm sure he's right, Robbie. Just think, tonight you can sleep in your own bed." The prospect of a hot shower thrilled Liz most of all, but she wasn't sure a boy would appreciate that.

Jason returned to his son's side. "We're going to tie the litter to the back of the horse, Indian-style, Robbie. I want to put some more padding beneath your ankle because it may be a rough ride."

"Can I help?"

Jason gave Liz a hard look, but she didn't flinch. Finally, he said, "Ask Al to give you the blankets he packed."

Liz hurried over to the cowboy. "We're glad to see you, Al."

"I'm glad to see all of you, too. When that storm came up all of a sudden, we were right worried about you."

Liz smiled her appreciation. "Jason wants me to bring over the blankets you packed so he can make Robbie comfortable."

Al moved over to one of the horses and untied a stack of several blankets from the saddle. "Sure you can handle 'em?"

"I'm sure. I'm stronger than I look," she assured him as she moved back to Jason. Matt had joined him and they were unstrapping Robbie. Once he was untied, Jason helped the boy upright, balancing on one foot.

"Spread a couple of the blankets across the litter," he instructed brusquely. Liz did so, and the two men lowered the boy back onto the bed, still encased in his sleeping bag.

"Now, fold the other two blankets and make a pad underneath his feet," Jason instructed. Liz carefully followed his orders and they restrapped the boy to the bed.

"Why do I have to be tied, Daddy?"

"Because with all the bouncing you're going to do, you might fall off." Jason's face softened. "We'll be home in a few hours, son, and we've already radioed the house for Mamie to call the doctor."

"You have a radio?" Liz asked in surprise.

"Al brought one with him. If the snow weren't so deep, we'd have one of the vehicles meet us, but it'd be more trouble than it's worth until some of the snow melts."

Liz thought longingly of a nice cushioned seat in a pickup. She never thought that would be her first choice, but compared to a saddle, she would take the pickup any day.

"Buck up, Liz," Matt said with a grin. "You can make it."

"You're probably right, Matt, but something with springs would've been nice."

Again she received a hard stare from Jason, but he didn't speak to her. As he turned away, she sighed. For a short while, they had achieved a rapport that she had enjoyed. But it never lasted long. And since they started down the mountain, it hadn't returned.

* * *

By the time the ranch came in sight, Liz was ready to get back down and walk the rest of the way. Her stiff and tired muscles only grew more so on the back of her horse. Besides that, when the horse slid in the snow, her heart bolted to the roof of her mouth. She felt insecure and increasingly fragile.

Even though dark had almost fallen, the lights of the house drew them like a beacon. Al stopped their procession in front of the house. "You all get off here, and I'll take the horses to the stables and get 'em rubbed down."

Jason helped Rosie down and then went to Robbie's side, along with Jesse, while Matt helped Liz dismount.

"I may have to crawl up the steps, Matt," she said.

"Naw, you'll make it just fine, Liz. You've been a real trouper."

"Thanks," Liz said, but she couldn't resist a look in Jason's direction. Either he didn't hear Matt's remark or he was ignoring it.

Mamie was at the front door waiting for them. "Lawsy me! I've never been so glad to see anyone. You really had us worried," she announced to everyone. "The doc's here, Jason." She stopped as someone appeared behind her. "Oh, here you are, Doc. They're bringing in Robbie now."

The tall, grayhaired man moved out on the front porch. "Evening, Jason. Is Robbie the only injury?"

"I think so, Caleb. Unless someone got frostbite on the way down today." He glared at Liz as if he was sure she had done so.

With her eyebrows raised, she protested, "Not me, Jason."

"Would you even know what it feels like?" he demanded.

"I've been snowskiing, and it was explained to me then."

"You can feel all your toes and fingers?" the doctor asked with a smile.

"Yes, I can."

"Then you'll do. Any other problems?"

Liz grinned. "Only aches and pains from the walk down and then this bone-jarring ride."

"Aha! A tenderfoot. I prescribe a long, hot bath." He turned back to Robbie, but Liz heard him comment to Jason, "I'm surprised, Jason. I didn't know you ever took inexperienced campers with you or I would've volunteered."

"I don't if I have a choice, Caleb. But you know you're welcome anytime."

So he could be gracious if he wanted, Liz thought to herself. Just not to reporters.

It only took about fifteen minutes for Liz to follow the doctor's orders. Running the bathtub as full as she could with steaming hot water, she added the bubblebath she had longed for before their trip and sank into the heavenly concoction.

She leaned her head against the inflatable pillow she had discovered in one of the drawers and decided she would never get out of the tub. For the first time in several days, her toes were getting warm and her aches were fading. Man had made a miraculous discovery when he built bathtubs and running hot water.

*　　*　　*

"Liz? Liz!"

Someone calling her woke Liz from the dream she was having of lying on the beach in a bikini, accompanied, of all people, by Jason Harmon. Her eyes jerked open and she looked around her, trying to gain her bearings.

She was stunned when the very man in her dreams came bursting through the bathroom door. Fortunately, the bubbles had not yet dissipated, but she didn't feel very secure clothed in such vaporous objects.

"What are you doing?" she demanded in horror, sinking even further into the water.

"What am I doing? Just trying to be sure you were still alive, that's all!" The ferocious frown on his face fit the irritation in his voice. "Why didn't you answer when I called?"

"I must've fallen asleep," she mumbled.

"Don't you know that's dangerous? You could've drowned in that bathtub."

"I didn't intend to. And could you please leave? This is embarrassing." She pushed a fallen blond lock back to the top of her head. When she saw Jason's blue eyes tracing her raised arm, she quickly submerged it.

An unreadable expression filled his eyes. "I thought you said you were experienced."

Liz's eyes flew to his face. She couldn't believe what he had just said. "What does that have to do with anything?"

He shrugged his shoulder. "If you're not a virgin, then you're used to men seeing you without your clothes."

"Just bcause I'm . . . because I'm experienced,

doesn't mean I'm a nymphomaniac! Now get out of here!''

"How many lovers have you had?"

"None of your business!" She felt like screaming. It wasn't fair. He was dressed in clean jeans and a dark blue corduroy shirt, handsome and at ease, while she was trapped beneath rapidly disappearing bubbles.

"Maybe not, but you keep harping on my not dating. Yet you don't want to talk about your social life, either."

"I'm not the one who agreed to an interview!" Liz reminded him angrily.

"You mean, was coerced."

His bitterness made Liz uncomfortable, if being more uncomfortable was possible in her position. "I had nothing to do with that."

"But you could make it right if you refused to do the interview."

She shoved upright in her anger but submerged at once when his eyes lit up, reminding her of her nakedness. "We've already had this discussion! I told you I don't have a choice. And besides, this is not . . . not an appropriate time to talk about it."

"Maybe not, but I'm finding it a lot more pleasant than any of our other discussions."

"Mr. Harmon! This is sexual harassment! Get out of my bathroom!"

"This is *my* bathroom, Miss Broadhurst," he pointed out lazily.

She closed her eyes in frustration, wishing she could wave a wand and make this difficult man disappear.

When she opened her eyes, she discovered her adversary had sat down on the wide rim of the sunken tub. "I want to ask you something," he said, a serious look on his face.

"I've already told you I have to do the interview," Liz whispered, disturbed by his closeness.

"No, that's not what I want to ask."

She waited, saying nothing.

He stared down into her hazel eyes as he said, "The other night, by the lake, would you have stopped me?"

Liz could feel the heat in her cheeks as she struggled to find an answer. She had asked herself that question a number of times, but she had never discovered the truth.

"Daddy! What are you doing in the bathroom while Liz is taking a bath?"

If the situation hadn't been so fraught with difficulties, Liz would have laughed as Jason almost fell into the tub with her at his daughter's sudden appearance.

With her hands on her hips, a miniature immitation of Mamie, Rosie prodded, "Well?" when neither adult answered her question.

Liz finally said, "I fell asleep in the tub, and your daddy had to wake me up. He was afraid I'd drown, Rosie."

"That's dangerous, Liz," Rosie said with a very serious face, but she turned back to her father. "I'm glad you saved Liz, Daddy, but I don't think you should be in here. After all, you said Liz wasn't part of our family."

"I just wanted to be sure she was all right, Rosie. I'm leaving right now," he assured his child, avoiding Liz's eyes. "Why don't you stay with Liz and make sure she gets out of the tub without falling back to sleep?''

"Okay.''

Liz said nothing, and Rosie turned and watched her father's departure without comment. Then she turned back to her charge. "I think you should get out now. Mamie has dinner ready. She sent me up to see what was taking so long.''

"Good. I'm starving. Would you hand me my towel?''

The little girl turned her back to preserve Liz's modesty when she exited the tub. At least Jason had taught his daughter good manners even if he didn't have any himself, she thought.

With her back turned, Rosie asked, "Liz? Do you think Daddy is handsome?''

Cautiously, Liz said, "Yes, of course, honey.''

"More handsome than Matt?''

"They're both attractive men, each in his own way.''

"But which one do *you* think is most handsome?''

"Rosie, why are you asking these questions?''

"I was just curious.''

Liz rubbed herself down and grabbed up the robe she had carried into the bathroom with her. Belting it around her, she walked into the bedroom to find the clean clothes she had laid out.

"Well?''

"Well, what, Rosie?''

"Which one is most handsome?''

"Rosie—your dad is most handsome,'' Liz finished honestly, giving up the attempt to avoid the question.

She slipped into her underwear, slacks, and sweater, the same outfit she had worn on her first night at the ranch. That seemed so long ago, though it was only a few days. "Let me comb my hair out of my face, and I'll be ready, Rosie. I bet you're as hungry as me, aren't you?"

"Mmhmm. Liz, how does a lady choose a husband?"

Warily, Liz said, "I wouldn't know, honey. After all, I don't have a husband."

With a satisfied smile that gave Liz pause, Rosie said, "I know."

ELEVEN

There was an air of celebration around the big kitchen table that night. Even more enjoyable to Liz was the sense of camaraderie. It was a stark contrast to her first meal at the same table.

"How did you like the lake, Liz?" Al asked before taking a bite of Mamie's golden fried chicken.

"Oh, it was lovely, Al, though the water was very cold."

"You didn't go swimming, did you?" Mamie asked, startled.

"No, of course not," Liz assured her with a grin. "But I washed my face in the water when—"

"Damn!" Jason interrupted, drawing all eyes. "I forgot to have the doctor look at your middle."

Liz's cheeks flushed as the attention shifted to her. "It doesn't matter," she mumbled. "I'm fine."

Jason ignored her. "I'll drive you to Doc's office first thing in the morning."

"What's wrong with her?" Mamie asked.

"She scraped her midriff pretty badly when she rescued Robbie," Jason explained.

"When *we* rescued Robbie," Liz corrected. "It was a joint effort with you, me, and Rosie."

"Maybe I'd better look at it before you go to bed, Liz. I've got some salve to keep it free from infection." Mamie looked first at Liz and then at Jason for agreement.

"That's a good idea, Mamie," he approved. "I put some on it last night, but I haven't checked it today."

"Why didn't you look when you were helping Liz take her bath, Daddy?" Roseann asked.

Liz plummeted to the depths of embarrassment as everyone stared at first her and then Jason, while he appeared to have been left speechless.

A niggling suspicion arose when she turned to Roseann, however. Frequent dealings with her siblings had always made her suspect that wide-eyed, innocent look Roseann wore at the moment.

Quietly, she said, "Rosie, you know your father came in the bathroom because I had fallen asleep. *And* that I was covered with all those lovely bubbles." She added a confident smile that had shaky foundations. She hoped no one could see them.

There was a sigh of relief from someone at the table, but Liz wasn't sure who gave it.

"Of course, Liz," Roseann readily agreed, building Liz's suspicions, "and it's almost like you're family, anyway. After all, the four of us slept together last night."

"Rosie, I think it's time for you and Robbie to go

to bed. After all, you've had a strenuous day," Jason said firmly.

"But, Daddy, *I'm* not doing anything," Robbie protested, piercing his father's pretense of concern.

A flustered Jason stared at his son but said nothing. Matt came to his rescue.

"Tell you what, Robbie, why don't you and Rosie come to the playroom with me and Al and we'll teach Al how to play go fishing. I'm a dab hand at that game, Al. But you got to watch Robbie. Just when you've saved up three of 'em, Robbie'll grab 'em away."

Jason gave his friend a grateful look as the two children eagerly agreed. Under his breath, he added, "I owe you one, pal."

An awkward silence fell after their departure. Then Jesse jumped to his feet. "Why don't I help Archie with the dishes while you doctor Liz?" he offered to Mamie.

"I'm fine, and I'll be glad to help with the dishes," Liz protested.

Jesse grinned back at her. "Liz, you're a great sport. But today was a tough day. Give yourself a break."

"Jesse's right. Come on upstairs and let me look at you. Then I'll tuck you in and you can get a good night's sleep," Mamie promised.

That program sounded too tempting to pass up. With a grateful smile at Jesse, Liz excused herself, carefully avoiding Jason's eyes, and she and Mamie headed upstairs.

"Seems like you and Jason are getting along a little better," Mamie said, looking sideways at Liz as they climbed the stairs.

Unsure how to answer, or even what the answer was, Liz finally said, "Maybe. He'll never be friendly toward reporters, but he tolerates me now."

As she opened the door to her room, Mamie murmured, "Be patient, Liz. He needs to chase away the bogey man."

Liz turned to stare at Mamie. "What?"

"Has he talked to you about his wife?"

Nodding, Liz waited for what Mamie would say.

"He always says it was the reporters' fault, but I think he blames himself. That's why he won't have any interviews and why he won't remarry."

"But he's an intelligent man," Liz protested.

Mamie moved over to sit down on the couch, patting the place beside her. Liz followed her lead. "One thing I've noticed," Mamie continued, "is that emotion doesn't have much to do with intelligence. Jason had a happy childhood. His parents did a good job raisin' him. But things came easy to him. Whatever he set his sights for, he achieved. I think Marty's death was the first thing to happen that he couldn't turn around."

"He must've been devastated," Liz murmured.

"Yep. They were very happy."

Liz ignored the sudden twist of pain. She would not regret Jason's happy marriage. She had no reason to.

"Anyway, he's shut every woman out since then. I've tried to encourage him to find a new mother for the twins, but he ignores me."

Liz's curiosity suddenly changed to discomfort. "Mamie . . ."

"Now, don't get me wrong, child. I'm not trying to push you into anything. But when he was so concerned about getting you to the doctor . . . well, I just hoped maybe he had had a change of heart.''

Liz stood up and walked over to the window to stare out at the snowy night. ''I think he's just grateful for my helping to save Robbie, that's all. Or afraid I'll sue him,'' she added with a mirthless laugh.

Mamie said nothing until Liz turned back to face her. Then she rose from the couch. ''Well, let's have a look at those sores. I want to be sure you're okay.''

Liz pulled up her sweater, and Mamie guided her over to the lamp. ''My eyes aren't what they used to be.'' Bending over, she studied the scabs that had formed. ''Hmm, looks pretty clean to me, but I'll go get that salve. You wait right here.''

When Mamie returned, she had Liz lie down on the bed. After lathering Liz's skin with the salve, she suggested Liz dress for bed while she put the salve in the connecting bathroom where she could use it the next morning.

Slipping quickly into her nightgown and lightweight robe, Liz bid Mamie good night after thanking her for her help.

Mamie paused by the door. ''Don't worry your head about what I said. Things have a way of working themselves out.''

''I know. Thank you, Mamie.''

''Good night, child. Sleep as late as you please in the morning.''

Liz leaned against the closed door and breathed deeply. She had wanted Mamie to talk about Jason when she first arrived, but she shied away from hearing about his past life now. And she didn't want to ask herself why.

She had enough information now to write an article about Jason Harmon. It might not have a lot of substance, or be as long as Joe would want, but Liz came to the decision that the wisest course for her would be to pack her bag and head back to Los Angeles in the morning.

A rapping on the door at her back startled her. "W-who is it?"

"Jason," a low voice responded.

"What do you want?"

"Let me in, Liz. I refuse to have a discussion through a closed door."

She didn't want to have a discussion. She didn't want to let him in, either, but she wasn't sure she had a choice. She eased the door open slightly. "I'm already dressed for bed."

A large hand pushed the door against her. "Since I've seen you in the bathtub, I really don't think a robe and gown will be a problem," he explained dryly.

Liz backed away and he followed.

"I'm just fine."

"Let me see."

"Mamie doctored my middle. She said there's no infection," Liz assured him.

"I just want to be sure," Jason answered in a reasonable voice.

But Liz wasn't prepared to give in. "Jason, I'll go to the doctor in the morning if you want, but I'm not going to show you my middle tonight."

"I don't know why that bothers you," he muttered, his hands on his trim hips.

Liz ignored his words. She was feeling cornered

and wanted to end the charade of the interview. "I think I should leave tomorrow."

Jason's head snapped up, and Liz looked away from his burning stare. "Why?" he demanded.

"I have quite a lot of information, and I know you're not interested in continuing the interview. I'll just work from what I have."

"So you're still going to write the article?"

Liz sighed. "Jason, please, I don't have a choice."

"Everyone has a choice. If it's money—"

"Try not to insult me any more than you already have," Liz said stiffly.

Jason jerked away from her accusing eyes. "You don't understand! I have to protect my children."

"Do you really think I would do anything to hurt Rosie and Robbie?"

Jason swung back around. "Not intentionally, Liz, but just bringing them to public attention may make some nut decide to kidnap them."

"I promise not to give any specific information about the kids, or where your ranch is located, Jason. But I have to write the article."

He didn't respond to her challenge, turning away from her again. Liz closed her eyes, swaying slightly from exhaustion. When masculine hands seized her shoulders, her eyes popped open.

"I thought you were going to faint," Jason muttered in explanation.

A hint of his aftershave drifted by her and Liz could feel her muscles tensing at his closeness. "I'm fine." She waited for him to remove his hands, but instead his fingers stroked her arms through the silky material of the robe. Chills shivered down her spine.

Unable to bear his touch because of the desire he provoked, Liz stepped away.

"I think I'll turn in now," she said, avoiding his eyes as she moved to open her door.

Unfortunately for Liz's peace of mind, and what little reputation she had left after dinner, Roseann and Robbie were in the hallway, accompanied by Mamie.

Three pairs of eyes stared at her and then Jason as he appeared in the doorway beside her. Liz attempted no explanations. As soon as Jason was through the door, she murmured good night and closed it.

Wasting no time, she turned off the light, removed her robe, and slid into bed. The contrast between a sleeping bag on the ground and the silky sheets and comforter on a well-sprung mattress occupied her senses momentarily, but the surprised faces in the hallway chased away such pleasantness.

Disasters had been occurring ever since she took on this assignment. Tonight's events fit right in. She would just have to forget about what these people thought of her. After all, she would probably never see them again. Somehow that thought didn't soothe her. But what her mind could not do, her body could. Sleep eliminated worry . . . for the moment, at least.

A pounding noise interrupted her dreams. When it faded away and Liz was snuggling down again, a cheerful voice in her ear forced her eyes open.

"Good morning, Liz."

Groggily, she lifted a heavy eyelid and found herself staring at Mamie's cheerful face behind a bedtray. She struggled to an upright position, protesting even as she did so. "Mamie, you didn't need to bring me breakfast in bed."

"I reckon you deserved it, saving Robbie's life. And even if you didn't deserve it, I wanted to." She beamed down at Liz, unconsciously wiping her hands on the white apron she wore over her flowered housedress.

After a sip of black coffee, Liz smiled gratefully at the woman. "I really needed that. What time is it?" She could see the sun shining through the windows, glinting off the white snow.

"It's almost eleven o'clock. I was going to let you sleep, but Jason said he needs to leave at eleven-thirty if you're going to make it to Doc's office before he closes."

"Eleven-thirty?" Liz gasped. "I'll have to hurry," she muttered, bringing the coffee mug to her lips once more.

"Don't you worry about it. I called Doc and told him you might be a little late. He said he'd wait."

"Thanks, Mamie. That's one of the nice things about living in a small town. But I'll hurry."

Mamie turned to leave, but she said over her shoulder, "You just be sure and eat a good breakfast. It's the most important meal of the day, you know."

Liz smiled. She could almost hear her own mother saying that. She had avoided thinking of her mother since she moved to Los Angeles, but lately she had come to mind more and more. Her death Liz's senior year in college had been unexpected and her anger toward her stepfather had made leaving home easy.

Shaking her head, Liz turned her attention to the scrambled eggs and bacon, along with toast and jelly,

Mamie had brought her. If she kept eating such mountainous meals, she wouldn't fit into any of her clothes.

When Liz came down the stairs, she discovered Jason prowling the entry hall. He'd exchanged his jeans for gray flannel trousers and a sweater over his shirt. Liz wished just once he'd look average instead of knock-your-socks-off handsome.

"It took you long enough. Let's go."

"And a good morning to you, too," she said sweetly, and swept out in front of him.

He said nothing more until they were driving down the long drive in a fire-engine-red Blazer. Seen from the perspective of a warm vehicle, the snow was beautiful. It hadn't seemed quite so wonderful when they were sliding down the mountain.

"I didn't mean to snap at you."

Jason's words surprised Liz. "Is something wrong?"

"Nothing other than both my children promoting our marriage."

Liz choked, coughing for several minutes.

Before she could respond, he added, "Seconded by Mamie, Matt, and Jesse. Al and Archie haven't indicated their preference yet, but I feel sure they will."

"What . . . what an interesting morning. All I did was sleep."

"I wish I had."

There was nothing to say, Liz decided, and she turned back to the picture-book scenery.

"Don't you have anything to say?"

"No, I don't."

"You didn't have anything to do with putting them up to it, particularly Rosie?"

That accusation caught Liz's attention. She stared at the man beside her in exasperation. "You've got to be kidding. All I did was come here to do an interview. I'm not the one who grabbed me and kissed me at the airport, or attempted to seduce me in the limo!"

"That was a long time ago and Rosie wasn't there."

"And what about last night? Your daughter finds you in my bathroom while I'm bathing. Was that a long time ago?"

"I should've let you drown?" he demanded in righteous tones.

"No, but you shouldn't have stayed around to chat, either. I didn't exactly invite you." Liz stared straight ahead.

"What I saw was inviting," he murmured.

She was surprised to see a smile peeping at the corners of his firm lips. She looked away again. "You shouldn't say things like that."

"Why not? It's the truth. And I don't want you to get a complex because I'm not proposing marriage to you. I find you very attractive." There was a pause before he added under his breath, "Too much so."

Liz's cheeks flamed. This conversation was making her decidedly uncomfortable.

"And I think you could say the same."

She pressed her soft lips together, refusing to say anything.

"But I'm just not looking for a wife."

As if she had been setting traps for a husband! Liz thought indignantly. Anger forced her to say, "I'm not looking for a husband, either, so consider yourself safe, Mr. Harmon!''

"Good. I'm glad we got that cleared up.''

Their conversation seemed to have put him in a much happier frame of mind. He snapped on the radio and whistled along with a popular tune Liz had heard several times in Los Angeles. Liz, however, experienced no such relaxation. She was more tense than ever before. It was definitely time to return to Los Angeles. His next question assured her her decision was the best one she ever made.

"How do you feel about an affair?''

TWELVE

Liz gulped. She wanted to appear sophisticated and blasé to his suggestion. But the thought brought back those moments beside the lake when she had discovered just how much she could want this particular man.

"Don't tell me you're not attracted to me, Liz. We both know the attraction is mutual."

There was an impatience in his voice that caught her attention. Because he was wealthy and attractive, did he expect her to throw herself into his arms?

"No, thank you," she said primly, as if she were declining a cup of coffee.

"No thank you?" he repeated. "You mean you're not attracted to me, or you're not interested in an affair."

"I'm not interested in . . . in an affair," she mumbled.

"Why?"

Of course he would want to know why. Why couldn't he just accept her refusal? She searched frantically for a reasonable response. "I have to return to Los Angeles."

"All the better. I couldn't carry on an affair here without everyone knowing about it. But I visit Los Angeles several times a month."

Liz's fingers were trembling as she smoothed down the crease in the navy wool pants she wore. What could she say now? Fortunately she was saved by their arrival at a large log cabin that had a small sign on it, announcing the location of Dr. Caleb Martin. She grasped her door handle like a drowning man would a life raft and swung open her door as soon as the car came to a stop.

Fortunately for Liz there was no wait once they were inside. The doctor was standing next to a very pretty woman dressed in a nurse's uniform, chatting.

"Sorry to keep you waiting, Caleb," Jason said from behind Liz.

"No problem. Liz, I'd like you to meet my wife, Sylvia. Syl, this is Liz . . . I'm afraid I don't know your last name."

"Broadhurst, Mrs. Martin," Liz said with a smile.

"Right. She's Jason's houseguest."

"Actually, I'm here to—"

"Visit Mamie. She's an old friend of Mamie's," Jason said, cutting off Liz's explanation.

"She can't be too old a friend," Sylvia remarked, her smile showing dimples.

Liz smiled in response. She liked both the doctor and his wife.

"Come on in, Liz, and let me check your wounds. Syl, you want to come help?"

"You mean I'm going to be left out here all alone?" Jason protested.

"Yes!" Liz exclaimed before either the doctor or his wife could answer.

After sending a smile to Jason, Caleb Martin indicated a door with his hand. "This way, Liz."

As Liz had suspected, her wounds were all surface ones, healing nicely. Dr. Martin suggested she continue to use a salve such as the one Mamie had put on them last night, but he thought they would heal in a short time without leaving scars.

Driving home, Liz sat tensely, afraid Jason would resume their conversation. When he did just that, she gnawed her bottom lip, at a loss for an answer.

"You didn't answer my question."

Finally, she said, "What question?"

"Come on, Liz. You know what question."

"Yes, I did answer it. You just didn't like the answer," she pointed out indignantly.

He slowed for a turn out of the small town before he responded. "No, I didn't like the answer. And I'd like an explanation."

Liz sat stubbornly silent. She didn't owe him any explanation, she assured herself.

"Is there someone else?"

When she didn't respond, he added, "If you're living with someone else, just tell me."

"Yes, I am." She crossed the fingers on her right hand, hiding them from his sight.

His response was silence, and Liz had no complaint about that. It was much better than his questions. Unfortunately, she congratulated herself too soon.

"Tell me about him."

"No."

"Why not? Are you going to marry?"

When she didn't answer, he said, "I hope you're not letting yourself be taken advantage of."

"Only by you," she muttered.

The sharp look he sent her didn't settle the butterflies in her stomach.

"I think you're lying."

"W-what do you mean?"

Jason swung the Blazer over to the side of the deserted road and cut the motor.

"What are you doing?" she demanded, panic rising.

"I'm stopping the car."

"I want to go back to the ranch."

Jason smiled. "I don't intend to set up camp, Liz. Just calm down. We won't be able to talk once we get home."

"I don't want to talk." She felt her voice rising but couldn't bring it under control.

His hand reached out to caress her shoulder, and she jerked away. With one eyebrow rising, he commented, "That wasn't your reaction up in the mountains."

"It must've been the altitude."

"Look, Liz, you said you weren't looking for a husband. Why not enjoy each other? It wouldn't hurt anyone."

"Yes, it would," she whispered, before turning to stare fiercely at him. "It would hurt me! I want to leave, to never see you again!"

He stared at her uncomprehendingly. Unable to bear another moment in his exasperating, exciting company, Liz wrenched open the Blazer door and slipped out into the cold, snowy world.

"What are you doing? Come back here!" Jason exclaimed as he, too, got out of the car.

Liz panicked. She didn't want him touching her. With a hurried look over her shoulder, she began to run.

"Liz! Watch out—"

His warning came too late. The leather soles of Liz's boots slid on the snow and she lost her balance, falling in a heap, one leg twisted beneath her.

Tears of pain filled her eyes. Jason bent over her, concern on his face. "Are you all right?"

"No," she whispered, biting her lip to keep from crying.

"Let me help you up," he insisted, grabbing her arms.

"No!" she shrieked. "No," she repeated as he stopped. "I think I've broken something."

So much for her plans for an immediate departure. Liz stared at her offending ankle, encased in a temporary brace to immobilize it until the swelling went down. The past two hours had been painful and frustrating. Jason had brought her straight back to the ranch after getting her into the Blazer. Once she was carried up to her bed, he had cut off her lovely boot while Mamie called Dr. Martin.

"I'm beginning to think you have a crush on me, young lady," the doctor had teased as he examined her ankle.

"She's just a blithering idiot!" Jason growled. He had insisted on staying in the room while the doctor examined her.

Even though she had winced at his words, she hadn't bothered to respond.

When the doctor told her she would have to remain in bed until the swelling went down, she wanted to cry. Instead she kept her features as immobile as her ankle and merely nodded.

After escorting the doctor to his car, Jason returned to her bedroom.

She turned her face away.

"Not feeling friendly?"

"Please leave."

A large hand seized her chin and pulled her face around to him. "Don't you think you're being rather juvenile?"

She squeezed her eyes shut, hoping to hide the tears that filled them, but she could feel several seeping down into her hair.

"There's no need for tears, Liz. You've broken your ankle, but it's not the end of the world. If you hadn't been so silly, you wouldn't be lying here like this."

That remark brought her eyes wide open. She ignored her tears and almost screamed her answer. "Me? Me? It's not my fault I broke my ankle! It's your fault!"

With an indulgent smile that sent her blood pressure soaring, he said, "Don't be ridiculous, Liz. I can't be responsible for your panic."

Irrational anger seized her, and she sought a way to pierce his arrogance. "Why not? You said those reporters were responsible for your wife's death just because she panicked!"

Contrition was immediate, but it couldn't erase her

words. She watched as Jason's face paled and he rose unsteadily from the chair beside her bed.

"Jason, I—" she began, reaching out a hand, but his furious stare silenced her.

After a moment that seemed like hours, he turned and strode from the room, leaving Liz a miserable heap of regret and tears.

She had no idea how much time passed before Mamie appeared in her room. The concerned look on her face was a comment on Liz's tear-stained cheeks and red-rimmed eyes. "Are you all right, child?"

Liz ignored her concern. "Mamie, have you seen Jason?"

"He blew through the kitchen a few minutes ago. That's why I thought I should check on you. You two cross ways again?"

The tears started again. "Oh, Mamie, I said something terrible. I didn't mean to. He just made me so angry!"

"What did you say?"

Liz hated to confess to Mamie. She had come to count on her as a friend, and she felt sure the woman would hate her for hurting Jason. "I . . . I said he was to blame for my breaking my ankle." She gulped and then continued. "When he laughed, I said he was as much to blame as those two reporters."

Instead of the anger and disgust Liz expected, Mamie appeared thoughtful. "Mercy. You really gave it to him between the eyes, didn't you?"

"I swear I didn't mean to, Mamie," she pleaded, clutching Mamie's wrinkled hand. "He just . . . just acted so . . ." She couldn't think of the word to describe his behavior. Finally she gave up and covered her face with her hands, sobs wracking her body.

"Now, now, child, don't you fret so," Mamie said, reaching her arms around Liz's woeful frame.

The wonderful comfort in that motherly figure soothed the ache in Liz's heart. As her sobs turned into occasional hiccups, Mamie released her and sat back in the chair.

"T-thank you, Mamie. I don't deserve your being so kind to me."

"Quit lashin' yourself, Liz. I think you may have done Jason a world of good."

"What do you mean?"

"That boy has been punishing himself for Marty's death for about ten years. He may say it's the reporters who were responsible, but he really blames himself. No matter who told him he wasn't responsible for Marty's panic, he wouldn't listen."

"But I told him he *was* responsible," Liz cried.

"Don't you see? He didn't agree with you. Now he's either got to think it's his fault you broke your leg or he's got to admit it was Marty's fault she had that accident."

Unable to make sense of Mamie's logic in her highly emotional state, Liz just shook her head. Mamie seemed to realize rational thought was beyond her. She pulled the cover up over Liz.

"Never mind, child. Everything is going to be just fine. But right now, you need to rest. You've had a tough afternoon."

Closing her eyes, Liz had one clear thought before nature gave her release from the strain. Truer words had never been spoken.

* * *

When Liz awoke, the moon had replaced the sun and a ribbon of silver ran over the snow. She rubbed her eyes, gritty from her earlier tears. A noise in the hallway caught her attention. That must have been what awakened her. She tensed as a knock came at her door. Please, God, she couldn't deal with Jason Harmon again today.

The door swung open, and Mamie entered with a laden bed tray followed by the two children. Before Liz could speak, the twins passed the housekeeper and rushed to her bedside.

"Poor Liz," Rosie commiserated, patting her arm. "Does it hurt?"

" 'Course it does," Robbie assured his sister. "I broke my arm once," he explained to Liz.

Liz smiled but said nothing.

"Stand back now and let me set this down," Mamie ordered, and the twins backed away from the bed. Liz struggled to sit up, but the pain in her ankle caused her to sink back against the pillows.

"Don't fret, Liz. We'll plump up the pillows behind you."

"Thanks, Mamie, kids. I didn't intend to sleep so long."

"Well, it's a good thing you did. Of course, I had trouble keeping these two from camping out on your doorsill," Mamie said with a teasing look at the children.

"We just wanted to be sure she's okay," Robbie protested.

"It's sweet of you to be concerned," Liz assured them, a smile on her face. "I'm doing just fine. But I have to stay in bed for a couple of days."

"We'll read to you and play cards and do puzzles,'' Rosie assured her. ''That way you won't mind so much.''

''Thanks, Rosie, but won't you have to go back to school?''

The child's face fell. ''Oh, yeah, I forgot. Daddy said we have to go back tomorrow.''

''Robbie, is your ankle okay?''

''Yeah, I only twisted mine,'' he explained, looking at Liz's swollen ankle.

''I'm glad you won't miss any more school.''

Their faces didn't reflect any agreement.

''We'd rather stay here with you,'' Rosie protested.

''I'll be here waiting for you when you get home. And you can tell me all about your day. I might even be able to help you with your homework.''

''Wow,'' Robbie replied, a hint of awe in his voice, ''just like a real mom.''

Liz flashed panicked eyes to Mamie, who rescued her.

''Well, now that you've seen that Liz is okay, it's time you two were off to have your baths. I've laid out fresh clothes for school tomorrow, but you'd better see if you approve of them.''

''Okay,'' they chorused before Rosie turned back to Liz.

''May I kiss you good night, Liz?''

In spite of her intention not to encourage the children in their hopes, Liz could not refuse the request. She held out her arms to the little girl and gave her kiss for kiss. To her surprise, Robbie followed his sister without any embarrassment.

''Thank you for coming to see me. I'll look forward to tomorrow afternoon,'' she assured the two as they left her room. Once they had gone, she looked at the housekeeper, a question in her eyes.

"He's downstairs eating his dinner. He drove off shortly after he left your room without a word to anyone."

"But he's all right?"

"Well, he didn't break anything, if that's what you mean," Mamie said, her lips pursed. "Matt came in as the kids and I were coming up. Maybe he'll talk to him. They're real close."

"I feel so guilty, Mamie," Liz confessed.

"Nonsense. I told you it was a good thing. Now, let's get you propped up so you can eat your dinner."

Liz didn't have much interest in food, but she couldn't tell Mamie that after all her efforts. She managed a fair amount of the delicious homemade tomato soup but put only a small dent in the roast beef and vegetables.

Mamie sat beside her, chatting about everyday things, perhaps knowing Liz wouldn't have made the effort without her. When her patient gave up, she pushed forward a bowl. "Now, this here is my famous banana pudding. I sent Archie to the store special for fresh bananas. You'll try some of it, won't you?"

Put that way, Liz had no choice. She took her first bite and smiled at Mamie. "I see why it's famous. It's delicious, Mamie.

The woman smiled contentedly, her hands folded in her lap. "Archie feels the same way. We've been married some forty years, and when he gets crotchety, I know it's time to make banana pudding."

"And it works? He feels better?"

"Every time, child. I'll make my recipe your wedding present," she added conspiratorially. "Every bride could use something to tame her man."

Liz put down her spoon, her appetite wiped away. "I don't think I'll have need of your recipe, Mamie, but thanks anyway."

"Why, whatever do you mean, Liz? A pretty girl like you? I bet you've had a lot of offers."

Liz gave her a twisted smile. "I don't intend to marry, Mamie. I'm a career woman."

"Nonsense! You're a perfect mother. I've watched you with the twins."

"That's practice. I had a lot of younger brothers and sisters."

"I still think—"

"Good evening."

Liz's body jerked in response to that deep-timbered voice. Her eyes flew to the door, hungry for the sight of him, and yet afraid of what she would see.

"Has Liz finished her dinner yet, Mamie?"

"Well, I believe she's had all she wants, Jason. She hasn't eaten enough to fill a bird, but then she's been lying here, not doing much."

"Then, if you don't mind, I'd like to speak to her alone."

His even tones may have reassured Mamie, who stood up to leave, but Liz wasn't fooled. "No! Mamie, I don't think—"

"Hush, child. Jason's not going to do anything to upset you. He knows you've had a difficult time of it. Right, Jason?"

With glittering eyes and a slight smile that caused Liz to tremble, he said, "Right, Mamie."

"Please, Mamie—"

"I'll be back up in a few minutes to tuck you in

for the night,'' Mamie assured her. Without another word, the housekeeper left the two of them alone.

"What's the matter, Liz?'' Jason asked, his smile widening but not growing any warmer. "Afraid?''

"Yes,'' she whispered.

He walked over to the bed and grasped her chin, holding her face still as he studied it. "You should be. That was a low blow.''

"I didn't intend to hurt you, Jason.''

Surprisingly, his hand left her chin and caressed her cheek. "I know.''

"You do?'' Liz gasped.

"Yes. I've done a lot of thinking this afternoon. I may even owe you a debt of gratitude for finally making me see some things clearly.'' He paused, but Liz had nothing to say. "Anyway, I've given a lot of thought to us, and I've come to a conclusion.''

Liz's eyes widened and her lips trembled. He surprised her by bending over to kiss her briefly.

"We're going to get married.''

THIRTEEN

His hand remained against her cheek, its warmth the only assurance Liz had that she was awake. Surely he could not have said what she thought she heard. She stared up at him, her eyes wide with confusion and fatigue.

"Don't worry, honey," he assured her, warmth entering his voice. "I know you've had a long day. We'll discuss everything tomorrow. I just wanted you to know what I decided."

"No! No, Jason, you're wrong."

"I'm wrong about what?"

"I'm not going to marry you."

His hand stroked her cheek. "Didn't I say you were too tired? You don't know what you're saying. Just go to sleep now, sweetheart." He bent to kiss her again, and she jerked her head aside.

He stood back up and stared at her. "You know, Liz, your attitude is beginning to wear on me."

With clenched teeth, she muttered, "Not half as much as yours is on me."

There was a flicker of anger in his eyes that gave Liz pause, but she was too panicked to consider her words carefully.

"Just get out and leave me alone!"

Her words should have angered him, and, she hoped, sent him off in a huff. Instead, he considered her with pensive blue eyes. "You're scared, aren't you? It happened today in the truck. That's why you ran. Not because I frightened you, but because you're scared of something."

She closed her eyes and turned away.

Suddenly she felt his lips moving on hers, coaxing a response. She raised her hands to shove against him, but he drew them up around his neck. Before she could free herself, his lips made her a willing prisoner. A fire that built inside her engulfed all reason as she opened her mouth to his and welcomed him to her arms.

She was barely conscious of his lowering himself to the bed, the twinges of pain from her ankle arousing her momentarily from his embrace. But his hands caressing her shoulders and moving steadily lower to her throbbing breasts distracted her.

He pushed down the straps of her gown and bared her flesh to his touch. His lips left hers and followed his hands, and Liz gasped in pleasure. As if she had called for his return, his lips sought hers again.

"Well, now, I guess you two made up," a satisfied voice said from the doorway.

"Go away, Mamie," Jason said without rising from the bed or looking back at his housekeeper.

"Now, Jason, I can't do that. Liz is too tired. You'll have plenty of time for all that tomorrow."

Having pulled her nightgown up with Jason's assistance, Liz kept her eyes closed. She didn't want to face either of the people in her room.

She heard Jason sigh and then the mattress rise as he stood up. There was another brief caress on her swollen lips. As his mouth left hers, she opened her eyes to find him staring at her. "I'll see you in the morning, sweetheart." She made no response and he added, "I meant what I said."

Though she stared at him until he was no longer in sight, she said nothing else. What could she say? She couldn't marry him, in spite of what her body told her. And she didn't want to explain why.

Tears seeped from her eyes as she lay in the bed, and Mamie took her hand. "Here now, child. You've got to turn off the water works. Jason is a fine man. You should be shouting hallelujah instead of crying."

When Liz presented her with a tragic face, Mamie gave up. "Never mind. Let me help you to the bathroom so's you can get ready for bed. What you need is a good night's rest."

What she needed, Liz decided a few minutes later after Mamie had tucked her in and turned out the light, was a magic carpet that could waft her back to the dirty, teeming city of Los Angeles. The cold, clean air of the Rockies was bad for her health.

Liz woke up periodically during the night, any movement bringing pain to her swollen ankle. Each time she gained consciousness, Jason's words seemed to be hanging in the air above her, taunting her. When she finally awoke to discover sunshine in place of darkness, Liz was relieved. She was exhausted from her attempts to rest.

As she lay in her comfortable bed, her mind filled with the events of the past twenty-four hours, her bedroom door opened slowly and Mamie crept into the room. In her hands, she carried a large crystal vase filled with a dozen red roses. When she discovered Liz watching her, she broke into a smile and came over to the bed.

"Well, now, you're awake, are you? And looking better for the rest, too."

"I hope so," Liz said, though she doubted Mamie's words.

"Good. Look what I have for you. Archie drove all the way to Denver early this morning to pick these up."

"H-how sweet of him, Mamie, but, truly, he shouldn't have bothered."

"You think these are from Archie?" Mamie giggled. "He'd never get my banana pudding again if I caught him sending red roses to another woman."

"But . . . Oh." Liz frowned. "They're from Jason, aren't they?"

"Why, of course. Don't you like roses, child?"

"Yes, they're lovely."

Mamie set them down on the bedside table and their rich velvety scent encircled Liz. "Here's the card. You read it while I go down and get your breakfast tray."

Liz took the white envelope between her thumb and forefinger and stared at it. She wasn't even aware of Mamie's departure so engrossed was she in the message she was afraid to read. Finally, she slipped a finger beneath the gold seal and extracted a card with Jason's bold black writing.

American Beauties for an American Beauty
Love,
Jason

Not original, but a nice thought, Liz thought, relief filling her. She had feared he would repeat his crazy declaration of the night before.

When Mamie reappeared with the breakfast tray, she helped Liz to the bathroom for a quick toilette. After a sponge bath while she sat on the edge of the bathtub, Mamie handed her a beautiful long blue nightgown.

"This isn't mine," she protested.

"Jason thought you might could use a few spares. When you have to live in a nightgown, it makes you feel better to have a pretty new one."

The silky material had already warned Liz the gown was expensive, but when she saw Christian Dior on the tag, she knew Jason had spent more on the nightgown than she paid for an entire outfit.

"Mamie, I can't accept this gown. It's much too expensive, and besides, Jason can't buy my . . . my undergarments."

"Pooh! You saved his son's life. That's worth a lot more than any old nightgown."

Liz stared at the older woman curiously. Mamie was a romantic, but she was being very careful this morning not to mention any romance between her and Jason. Had Jason warned her not to? A shiver distracted Liz from her thoughts.

"You get that gown on before you catch your death of cold," Mamie warned.

Liz gave up and slipped the silky garment over her head. She couldn't help enjoying the elegant feeling the gown gave her. She had often admired the Dior gowns, but she couldn't justify spending her limited resources for such a frivolous reason.

"Now, how shall I fix your hair?"

"Oh, if you could just brush it and braid it, Mamie, I'd appreciate it." Liz was already tiring from her time out of bed.

Minutes later, Mamie was tucking Liz in again, only pausing a brief moment in front of the mirror so she could admire her new nightgown.

Mamie had put fresh sheets on the bed while Liz washed, and she settled into the newly made bed with a sigh of relief. "Thanks, Mamie. I feel much better, but that short trip really exhausted me."

"That happens when you have to stay in bed a long time, child. Don't worry your head over it. Doc said he'd be out to see you around lunchtime."

It wasn't the doctor's visit Liz dreaded. But she refused to ask about Jason. Mamie might interpret her question as a desire to see the man, and she didn't want that . . . did she?

Mamie sat down beside the bed to keep Liz company while she ate. At least it kept her from thinking. By the time Mamie removed the tray, Liz was ready to try sleeping again.

When next she awoke, Dr. Martin was standing beside the bed. "How are you, young lady?"

"Fine, Dr. Martin."

"Hmm, sleep well last night?"

"Fine."

"I should've prescribed some pain pills for you. I'll give a prescription to Jason. That will ensure you a better night's rest."

So much for Mamie's lie about looking better this morning, Liz thought.

"May I look at your ankle now?"

"Yes, of course," Liz agreed as the door to her room opened again and Jason and Mamie entered.

Her eyes darted from the man who occupied her thoughts back to the doctor as he lifted the sheet from her ankle.

"Well, the swelling has gone down a little, but it's going to be several more days before we can put a permanent cast on it."

"Could I travel like this? I hate to impose on . . . on Jason's hospitality for so long." She avoided looking at the other two people in the room, staring up at the doctor.

"I'm afraid not, but I'm sure Jason is glad to have such a pretty houseguest." Dr. Martin smiled down at Liz before turning to Jason. "Right?"

"We're delighted to have Liz stay as long as she'd like," Jason replied, his eyes focused on her.

When Liz said nothing, her gaze falling to the pattern her finger was drawing on the cover, the doctor excused himself with the cheerfulness all doctors invoke around their patients.

"I'll be back tomorrow, Liz. And I'll give Jason the prescription for the pain pills."

Mamie escorted the doctor downstairs, leaving Jason standing at the foot of the bed. Liz refused to look up, nibbling on her bottom lip while she waited for him to break the silence.

"I hope you like the nightgown."

"Oh. I'm sorry. I should have thanked you for it at once. It's beautiful."

"I'm glad you like it. Could you stand a little company? I thought I'd have my lunch up here with you." Before she could reply, he added, "Mamie doesn't have time to keep you company, and she's afraid you won't eat properly if someone doesn't stay with you."

How could she refuse him now? Mamie would insist on coming up when she had too much to do. "It's really not necessary," Liz insisted, but his eyes warned her differently. "But if Mamie feels that way, of course you may join me."

Contrary to Liz's fears, she enjoyed her lunch. Jason brought up trays for both of them and teased her into eating more than she really wanted. He kept her off guard, telling funny stories about his youth that even drew forth chuckles on occasion.

Later, Liz realized he had interspersed questions about her own childhood among those stories. It wasn't that she wanted to be secretive, but she tried to be selective about what she told other people. Her stepfather was a subject she avoided at all costs.

Jason never mentioned his crazy proposal, if it could be called that, of the night before. Liz tried to dismiss the entire subject from her mind. The brief kiss Jason gave her when he removed the trays and encouraged her to go back to sleep seemed part and parcel of their comfortable lunch. A friendly kiss, she told herself.

When the kids returned from school, they came immediately to Liz's bedroom.

"Liz? Are you doing better?" Rosie asked as she

came through the door. Robbie was right on her heels.

"I'm fine. How was your first day back at school?"

"Okay," Robbie said, "but you wouldn't believe all the homework we've got to make up. And we did lots of extra before we went," he protested indignantly.

"But it's important to keep up with your schoolwork. If you get right to it, it will probably go faster than you think."

"Mamie said if it's okay with you, we can have our snack here, and then maybe you'd supervise our homework. Would you mind?" Rosie asked.

"I'd love to. It'll remind me of home."

"You mean Los Angeles?" Robbie asked.

"No, my home in Texas. I helped my brothers and sisters with their homework."

Mamie's entrance centered their attention on the snack, and shortly thereafter, the homework was begun.

When Jason came in an hour later, he stood at the doorway watching his children. Rosie was sitting beside Liz reading to her, while Robbie was lying across the foot of the bed doing his math. Liz said nothing, waiting for the kids to realize their father had come.

When they did, both of them rushed to his side for a hug, and stories came pouring out of them. Just for a moment, Liz contrasted that entrance with the one her stepfather would make whenever he bothered to come home before bedtime. With a shudder, she looked back at the others.

"You okay, Liz? These brats haven't worn you out?"

"I'm fine. It's been a lot of fun."

"Yeah, Daddy. It was just like having a real mo—"

"I think you should go to your rooms and finish up now," Jason said hurriedly. "Let's give Liz a chance to rest before dinner."

"I'm not tired, Jason, honest," she protested as the kids gathered their books.

Jason didn't answer her as he shepherded his children from the room, but then he closed the door and came to her side.

Her eyes grew larger as he sat down on the edge of the bed, his hand reaching for her cheek.

"Your skin is so soft." As his lips followed his hand, trailing down the side of her face, she opened her mouth to protest, but his lips covered hers in a sweet kiss that she never thought to object to.

When he raised his head, he asked matter-of-factly, "Do you need some help getting to the bathroom? I'll carry you in and then wait outside until you're ready to come back to bed."

"All right," she agreed, staring at him uneasily. He reached for the cover, pulling it back, and then scooped her up into his arms. She grimaced as her ankle protested the movement and he kissed her forehead.

"Sorry if it hurts. I brought your pain pills. Caleb said you should take one at bedtime."

"Thank you."

He opened the door promptly a few minutes later when she called out to him. Taking her in his arms again, he strolled over to the window on the west side.

"What are you doing?"

"I thought you might like to take a little walk before going back to bed. You know, a change of scenery. Want to go downstairs?"

"Oh, no, thank you. I'm wearing a nightgown. I don't think—"

"Liz, when you're sick, it's okay to wear a nightgown. It's not as if it's sheer," he said, staring down at her. "Though, come to think of it, it is pretty sexy . . . on you."

"Jason, I don't think—"

"You keep saying the same thing, young lady. Has your mind stalled?"

The grin on his face made him look years younger. Liz gave up her protests and grinned back. "Probably. Some of Robbie's math was beyond me."

"Don't feel like the Lone Ranger," he said ruefully. "I can get the answer, but if I don't do it exactly the way the teacher does, he has a fit."

"Aren't your arms getting tired?" she asked, feeling ill at ease.

"A little, but it's well worth it. I could get used to holding you."

"I think I'd like to . . . to return to bed," Liz whispered.

"Yes, ma'am. One bed, coming up. By the way, the guys wondered if they could come up to see you before dinner this evening?"

"The guys?"

"Jesse, Matt, Al, and even Archie. They want to pay their respects."

"That's very thoughtful of them."

"Great. I'll bring them up in a few minutes." He lowered her to the bed, arranged the covers for her, and dropped another kiss on her lips before striding from the room.

Liz lay back against her pillow, a bemused expression on her face. She certainly couldn't complain about the care she was receiving. Mamie was wonderful, and she loved the children. Jason . . . Jason was everything a host should be . . . and more. It was the more that occupied her mind until dinner.

FOURTEEN

The parade of visitors before dinner was fun. Mamie shooed the men out after half an hour, but before she did, Liz was brought up to date on the events that had occurred since their return from the camping trip.

Matt promised to show her twin heifers born the night before, and Jesse offered to cook a special Mexican dish sure to have her on her feet in no time. Al's intention of giving her riding lessons she declined with a knowing grin that the cowboy acknowledged. Even shy Archie suggested he take her for rides in the limo when she tired of staying in bed. Touched by their thoughtfulness, Liz scarcely noticed Jason remained when the others filed downstairs for dinner until his hand covered hers as it rested on the coverlet.

Her eyes flashed up to his and then away. "Aren't you going to have dinner?"

"Sure am. It'll be right up."

"Jason, you don't have to eat up here with me. I promise I'll eat a proper dinner."

He squeezed her hand and whispered, "I know. That's just an excuse to be alone with you." He finished with a cackling laugh and a twist to an imaginary mustache.

"Well, at least if you go broke, you can earn a living on the stage," Liz said in a pretended satisfaction.

"I don't think so. I'm a very private person."

Liz couldn't hold back the laughter that bubbled up in her. When he raised an eyebrow, she muttered, "I think I'm the last person you need to tell that."

Mamie's entry followed by Al with a second tray halted their conversation. Liz was surprised to discover her appetite had returned, and she had no objection to digging into the delicious meal once they were alone again.

After dinner, it was the children's turn to visit the invalid. Jason remained as well, and the four of them played a game of Scrabble. Robbie spent a lot of time studying his options, but Rosie slapped her tiles down to form the most ridiculous words imaginable. Frustrated, Robbie would challenge his sister and she would lose her turn. But it didn't seem to affect Rosie's enjoyment of the game.

"All right, you two. You've got school tomorrow, so it's time you were in bed," Jason finally said, interrupting the game.

"But, Dad, we're almost through," Robbie protested.

"I can't play, Robbie," Liz said. "I have a W, an X, two O's and the Z."

"Boy! Were you unlucky!" Rosie exclaimed.

"I guess so."

"You just haven't thought about it, Liz. After

these two are in bed, I'll show you how to use those letters to your advantage,'' Jason promised, a smile on his face that left Liz uneasy.

Rosie looked at her father and then covered her mouth to hide her giggles.

"What are you laughing at, young lady?"

"I know what you're going to show Liz,'' she bragged.

"What?" Robbie wanted to know.

"I think the both of you had best be off to bed,'' their father warned.

The two children slid from the bed and gave both adults a night kiss. When they got to the door, Rosie turned back around. "Liz, X's and O's mean kisses and hugs!'' With another giggle she disappeared down the hallway.

Jason shook his head. "I think I'd better supervise that young lady more closely.''

"Oh, I think she's about the age that little girls begin to think about boys.''

He rubbed the back of his neck, a look of confusion on his face. "But Robbie hasn't shown any signs of it.''

"Robbie's a boy.''

"Boys do think about girls,'' Jason assured her dryly.

"Of course they do, but not until later.''

"And I suppose I should've already had a talk with Rosie about the facts of life?''

Liz grinned. "Only about four or five years ago. And not only with Rosie.''

"You sound more like a parent than I do.''

"I helped raise my brothers and sisters,'' Liz said abruptly, losing her relaxed air.

"What about your mom and dad?"

"What about them?"

"Were they both around?" Jason probed, his eyes fixed on her.

"Hadn't you better check on the kids?"

Jason didn't fall for her red herring. He sat back down in his chair and took her hand again. "Why won't you answer me?"

"I will. It's no big deal. I just thought you might need to see if the kids were getting in bed. My brothers and sisters always used to find a jillion excuses to avoid it."

"Did your parents get a divorce?"

Liz laughed bitterly. Several times she had urged her mother to do so, but she had refused, pointing out that she couldn't raise six children on what she could earn. "No. No divorce."

"Explain, Liz."

"My father died when I was a year old."

"Then your mother remarried?"

"Yes."

He cradled her hand in both of his, a thoughtful look on his face. "Not happily, I take it?"

Liz tried to remove her hand, but he wouldn't let go. She looked away. "I don't know. I don't see how she could've been, but . . . sometimes I'd hear her laugh, see her smile. I couldn't understand it."

"You were a child, Liz. There were probably a lot of moments you didn't see."

Liz swung back around, her eyes flashing. "I saw more than enough to know that he mistreated my mother."

She looked away again, and they sat silently, Jason still holding her hand. Finally, he asked, "Is that why you don't want to talk about marriage?"

Liz refused to look at him or answer. She had said more than she intended already.

"Because if it is, it's just as dumb as me shutting myself off from marriage because I thought it was my fault my wife died."

Liz turned and stared at him. His eyes met hers with no hesitation, their warmth mirrored in the understanding smile on his face.

"When did you decide that?" she whispered.

"Yesterday, when a certain young lady pointed out the absurdity of my ways."

Liz bit her bottom lip. "Jason, I didn't mean to—"

"Yes, you did, because you were angry with me. And I appreciate what you said. I had refused to even think about my wife's death because secretly I blamed myself. When I forced myself to think about the past ten years, I saw what a fool I've been." He shook his head, grinning. "I don't want you to think you can have full responsibility for opening my eyes, though. I spent the rest of the afternoon with Caleb, talking out my problem."

She couldn't face him anymore. The happiness in his face disturbed her more than any words. She felt like a child pressing her face to the candy store window. "I . . . I'm glad you're happy, Jason."

Firm fingers took her chin and pulled her face back around to his. "I'm very happy, Liz," he said quietly, "because I've awakened in time to find a new love."

"No!" she sobbed, wrenching away from his hand and burying her face in one of the pillows.

"Don't you care for me?"

"How can I? I've only known you a few days!"

She felt the side of the bed lower as he transferred to it from his chair. Then his arms went around her and he pulled her against him. "Do you really think any more time would make a difference? If I'd admitted it, I was attracted to you from the very beginning. You scared me half to death when I kissed you at the airport."

Liz couldn't help listening to his words, though she warned herself not to.

"Then I discovered the sophisticated blonde also had a mind of her own and she turned the tables on me. I don't think I would've been so angry if I hadn't already realized you'd be trouble."

"Jason—"

"That night by the lake." His words stopped her at once. She didn't want to talk about that night. "I lost my head completely. If Matt hadn't interrupted us—"

"Nothing would've happened! I would've stopped you!"

"Maybe," he conceded, a smile on his lips that drew Liz's eyes. His arms tightened around her and she realized they were stretched out on her bed like lovers. She tried to sit up, but he held her against him.

"Jason, we can't . . ."

"Can't what?"

"I can't marry you!" she exclaimed, pushing against him.

"You're already married?"

"No! You know I'm not. But that doesn't mean I'll agree to marry you."

"Why not?"

His reasonable voice drove her insane.

As his lips caressed her temple, he murmured, "I'm not your stepfather, sweetheart. Can't you trust me?"

The agony of rejecting him forced an honest answer from Liz. "I can't trust *me*!"

Jason turned on his side so he could face her. "What do you mean?"

"Can't you just leave it alone, Jason?" she pleaded.

"No, I can't. I love you, and I'm going to fight for you, Liz. So spill the beans."

"I'm just like my mother!" she said, sobbing. Somehow, to herself, she had explained everything with those words. But Jason frowned, waiting for more.

"Oh, when I went to L.A., I was a naive dreamer. I believed in true love. I thought it could never happen to me. I could never be taken in like my mother. Well, I was wrong! This man . . . this man said he l-loved me, and he moved into my apartment. We were going to marry." Tears were running down her face and she rubbed her cheeks with the back of her hand. "Then, after he'd taken all my savings, I found out he was spending *my* money on another woman!"

He cradled her against him, whispering comforting words as his hands and lips caressed her.

Liz could stand it no longer. She shoved mightily against him and rolled away, only to scream as pain shot up her leg.

"Are you all right, sweetheart?"

Exhausted, Liz lay with her back to him, her eyes closed. She had fought her body and her heart, and she had no energy left. "Please, Jason," she whispered, "just let go."

"Never," he whispered in return. "We belong together, Liz—you, me, the kids. We're already a family in our hearts. Couldn't you feel it tonight? I can't let you go."

"But, Jason—"

"Look, I don't know anything about this other guy. But you don't have to trust your own judgment. Talk to Mamie, to Matt, or any of the others. They've known me forever. Talk to Caleb. I promise not to rush you into anything. But don't give up on us."

He sensed her weakening and drew her back into his arms, shifting his body so he wouldn't disturb her ankle. "Just try," he whispered as his lips brushed hers, leaving Liz hungering for his kiss. His lips sought out her neck while his hands caressed her body through the silky nightgown. Then his mouth returned to hers, and Liz gave up thought completely. She drowned in the sensations Jason stirred in her.

She was rudely awakened from his intoxicating embrace when he pulled back.

"I'd like to stay," he explained with a grin, "but I'm not going to persuade you that way. Even though it'd be a lot of fun." He dropped a quick kiss on her lips. "But I want you to make your decision with a clear head. And if I don't go now, I won't be able to keep my honorable intentions."

Liz stared at him, her eyes wide with fatigue but colored by a hint of arousal. He groaned and hugged her close to him.

"I'll see you in the morning, sweetheart. Dream of me," he advised, and Liz felt sure she would follow his directions.

*   *   *

Jason was wrong. Liz didn't see him the next morning. Before she awoke, her sleeping prolonged by the pain pill Mamie had given her after Jason went downstairs, Jason was gone. Mamie brought up her breakfast tray with the news that Jason had been called to England because of a strike at one of his new acquisitions, an appliance firm in Manchester.

"When will he return?" she asked, and hated herself for sounding so forlorn.

"He wasn't sure, Liz, but he made me promise to take good care of you."

Liz gave Mamie an awkward smile as she wondered just what Jason had told his housekeeper. Mamie's next words drove that thought out of her mind.

"He left a note for you. It's on your tray."

Any thought of food was forgotten as Liz searched for the precious piece of paper. Once she found it, she was afraid to open it. What if he'd changed his mind? Last night she had begun to believe, just maybe believe, that Jason was right. Had she been an idiot, shutting herself away? Was it possible she could have a happy marriage? With Jason, her heart assured her. What if he had now changed his mind?

When she finally read his note, she could've wept with joy. His loving words gave her no more information about his schedule than Mamie, but they filled her heart in a way Mamie never could.

"Well, I hope whatever he wrote restored your appetite."

"Hmm?" Liz asked, looking up reluctantly from her note to the housekeeper.

"Jason said you were to eat your breakfast."

Liz sat up and began eating, her heart and her mind with the man on his way to another country.

That night as the children and Liz kept one another company, Jason called from England. He talked to each of his children and then spoke to Liz.

"Are you trying?"

Her mind flew back to the previous night and his admonition to try to trust him. Her heart had been working overtime, she knew, to convince her mind, and she thought the battle was almost won, but she was afraid to admit it. Jason tended to move too fast.

"Yes" was all she answered in return.

He sighed gustily. "I hated having to leave. I came in and kissed you good-bye. Do you remember?"

"No."

"Hmm, I must be losing my technique."

"Just make sure you don't do any practicing over there," Liz warned him.

"Aha! Do I detect a note of jealousy?"

Embarrassed, Liz mumbled, "Maybe."

"Good. Listen, sweetheart, I've got to go, but keep dreaming."

"I will."

Liz's next telephone call, after awakening in the morning, was not nearly as wonderful. As if from another world, Joe, her editor, called.

"Well, how did the camping trip go?"

"Oh, Joe. Um, fine, except I broke my ankle."

"What?"

"It's okay. But I have to stay in bed until the swelling goes down."

"Have you gotten anything written on the article?"

Liz's heart sank. She knew there had been something troubling her dreams, but the euphoria created
by Jason's love had buried the remembrance of the
article deep within her.

"Joe . . . Joe, what if I can't do the article?"

"You're joking, right, Liz? You know how important this article is to me. The owner's been on my
back the last couple of days wanting to know if you
had it ready. If it's not here by the deadline, I'm
gone."

When Liz said nothing, she could hear the panic
rising in his voice. "Liz? Are you there?"

"Yes, Joe, I'm here."

"Listen, Liz, I've got to have that article. I can't
make it if I lose this job."

The quaver in his voice tore at Liz's insides. "It's
all right, Joe. I told you I'd do the article and I
will."

"That's my Liz," he gushed in relief. "I knew I
could count on you. When will you be back?"

"I . . . I don't know exactly. Is the deadline still
the fifth?"

"Sure, but that's only ten days away, and we'll
have to get Harmon's approval by then. You can do
it, can't you?"

"Yes, Joe, I can do it." Liz's voice was emotion-
less as she realized what she was promising. The one
thing Jason would never forgive was a breach of his
privacy.

She hung up the phone and lay back against the
pillows. Her heart cried out against the irony. The
article that had brought her to Jason Harmon would
now force her away. To have been given a glimpse

of the happiness she wanted, craved, only to have it snatched away, was torture.

Mamie, entering her room, stopped and stared before hurrying over to the bed. "Gracious, Liz, what's the matter?"

Liz hadn't even realized she was crying until Mamie handed her a tissue. She wiped her face and tried to erase the wobble in her voice. "Nothing, Mamie. That was my editor."

"Everything all right?"

"Yes, of course. Could you call Dr. Martin? I'd like to get the cast put on my ankle today."

"What is it, Liz?" Mamie asked, cutting through her formality.

The warm concern blasted away what little control Liz had maintained, and she collapsed in Mamie's arms. "I have to go away, Mamie. And Jason will never speak to me again."

"Why, child, what are you talking about? You know he's crazy about you!"

"Don't you see, Mamie? He forgot all about the article. So did I. But I have to write it. I gave my word."

Unfortunately for Liz's morale, Mamie's face revealed her own fears. "Oh, dear," the housekeeper murmured.

Liz sat up and wiped her eyes again. She was ashamed of her collapse.

"You're sure you have to write the article?"

"Yes, I'm sure. I gave my word. And if I don't, the new owner will fire my editor. He doesn't deserve that, Mamie."

"Maybe Jason will understand."

Liz gave Mamie a brief smile, but neither lady felt confident of his reaction.

"Would you call Dr. Martin?" Liz asked again. "I need to return to L.A. as soon as possible."

"But you'll come back?"

"I don't know, Mamie. Jason may not want me back."

FIFTEEN

Five days later, Liz sat on pins and needles waiting for Joe to finish reading the article she had labored over. Torn between her love for Jason and her need for objectivity, her duty to reveal him to her readers and her need to protect his privacy, Liz felt she was teetering on a tightwire.

Joe looked up from the last page and stared at Liz.

"Well?" she demanded impatiently.

"A nice job, Liz, but it has a different tone from your other work."

"What do you mean?"

"If I didn't know better, I'd think you have personal feelings toward Jason Harmon."

Liz looked away from his shrewd eyes. "Is the article okay, Joe?"

"Sure. Mr. Parks will be pleased. And you skirted any personal details enough that I think it will get by Harmon. We'll send it to his L.A. office at once."

"No, don't do that. I'll get his approval."

That comment drew another sharp look. "You're sure?"

"Yes."

"And you're determined to leave me?"

Liz stood up, smiling down at her former editor. "I've already turned in my resignation, Joe."

He rose and came around the desk. "How about a hug, then? I hope you'll keep in touch. Maybe send in a free-lance article occasionally?"

Liz hugged the only man who had dominated her life the past few years. "Maybe. You never know."

"You'll let us know when you have Harmon's approval? We'll need it in writing. Pick up a release form from the legal department." Joe's thoughts had already returned to business.

"Yes, I'll let you know. He's still in England at the moment, but they expect him back anytime."

She hobbled back to her desk for the last time. She had already picked up the release form and cleaned out her desk. Only Joe's approval of the article had remained. Now she could get back to more important matters.

Leaving the ranch, she had asked Mamie just to tell Jason she had had to return to Los Angeles when he called. Each day she had talked to the housekeeper and then the children. Leaving them had been difficult. She couldn't explain all the ramifications of her departure, nor could she promise them she'd come back. Everything depended on Jason.

After talking to Mamie last night, however, Liz had changed her mind. Jason had left messages at her office, and her telephone had rung every night since she'd been back in Los Angeles, but she had refused to take any calls.

She didn't want to tell Jason about the article. Now that it was written, she wanted him to read it and then they'd talk about the future.

It was his own words that made her decide to return to the ranch and await him there. When she resisted him that last night at the ranch, he had refused to give up. He said he'd fight for them to be together. She could do no less. And her position of strength was at the ranch, surrounded by his children and his housekeeper, his friends. It was unfair, but she had discovered the love she had for Jason Harmon and his children was the most important thing in the world.

Archie met her at the airport. Her arrival wasn't as exciting this time, but she had a lot more to look forward to. The kids were waiting on the porch, bundled up against the cold, watching for her. They had the door of the limo opened before Archie could come around to her side.

Liz hugged them both tightly. "I've missed you so," she assured them, bringing beaming smiles to their faces.

"Wait until we tell you what happened at school the other day," Robbie said.

"But Daddy's more important. He asks if we've heard from you every day, but Mamie always says no."

"Yeah. Why are we lying to Daddy?" Robbie asked, a worried look on his face.

Liz's heart sank. Was she doing the right thing? When she tried to explain, Archie and Mamie interrupted, hustling all of them into the house.

Later that evening, Liz asked Mamie to help her explain to the kids as they sat around the large kitchen table, cleaned off after their dinner.

"You see, your Daddy and I . . . care about each other—"

"Wow! Does that mean you'll be our mother?" Rosie demanded, a smile wreathing her face.

"No! Wait!" Liz protested. As the child's face fell, she amended her answer. "I don't know. That's why I didn't tell you before. Because there are problems."

Robbie, in a move so like his father that it tore at Liz's heart, reached out his hand to her. "We don't care about anything else. We want you to be our mother."

"Oh, Robbie," Liz sighed, tears in her eyes. "I want to be your mother, and Rosie's. But, you see, I had to write the article about your daddy. And . . . and I'm afraid he will be angry."

"Why?" Rosie demanded. "That's why you came, isn't it?"

"Yes, but . . . well, your dad doesn't like publicity. It's a complicated thing, honey," she rushed on as the little girl opened her mouth. She couldn't explain any more. "Anyway, I asked Mamie to just tell Jason that I had left because . . . because I wanted him to read the finished article before we talked again. And that's why I wanted you not to tell your father you'd talked to me, Robbie."

"But I think Daddy's really hurt that you went away," Robbie muttered.

Liz squeezed his hand. "I know, Robbie, but until I know he can forgive me for writing the article, I don't know what else to do."

The phone interrupted them, and Mamie moved across the kitchen to answer it.

"Jason? Where are you?" Mamie asked. The three people at the table riveted their attention on her. "I see. Yes, I'll tell them." Her eyes flew to Liz as she said, "No, I haven't." Liz closed her eyes, praying she was doing the right thing. "Yes. You be careful."

When Mamie came back to the table, three pairs of eyes demanded information without saying a word. "That was your father. He's in Los Angeles," she said, her eyes seeking out Liz's. "But he's coming home now. He won't be here until after your bedtime. He said for you to go on to sleep and he'd see you in the morning."

Robbie opened his mouth to protest but changed his mind as he looked at Liz. "You'll talk to Daddy tonight?"

The child's concern for his father was touching. "I promise, Robbie. This hasn't been easy for me, either. I love your father. But I promised to write the article. I couldn't break a promise."

"I know," he agreed solemnly before giving Liz a hug. "In the morning, will you know if you're going to marry Daddy?"

"I hope so," Liz said fervently. She gave Rosie a hug also, relishing their warmth. She hadn't felt warm since she left Jason's arms.

Mamie took the children up to bed. When she returned to the kitchen, Liz was still sitting at the table. "When will Jason get here?" she asked.

"Well, he's coming in on the 10:45 plane and it's about forty-five minutes from the airport, so I'd guess about eleven-thirty or so."

Liz nodded, wishing it were already that time. She didn't think she could bear the waiting.

"It's a good thing you're here. He's planning on flying out again tomorrow for Texas."

"For me?" Liz asked hopefully.

"I don't know any other reason he'd fly to Amarillo after spending six days in England." Mamie's grin gave Liz a little more confidence. "I've got to tell Archie he needs to go to the airport."

Liz considered going with Archie. It would mean she'd see Jason almost an hour earlier. She fantasized about greeting him as he had first greeted her, but as much as that thought gave her pleasure, she couldn't do it. She had to show him the article first. Then, if he still wanted her . . .

"Archie's getting dressed," Mamie said, coming back into the kitchen. "I'll put on a pot of coffee." After the coffee was perking, Liz noticed Mamie getting down a mixing bowl.

"What are you making, Mamie?"

"Banana pudding. I'm not taking any chances. If you have any problems with Jason, you just feed him this banana pudding." Winking, Mamie added, "And don't forget to stir in a few kisses."

Liz laughed and went over to give Mamie a hug. "Thanks for being such a good friend. I'm going to go upstairs and get ready."

"Good. Put on some more of that fancy perfume, too. Let's not give that man a chance to make a fool of himself."

Liz waited anxiously on the leather couch in Jason's office. Pacing the floor was out of the question, but it might have eased her stress. It was past time for Archie and Jason to arrive, and she didn't think she could wait another minute.

The quiet hum of the limo's motor reached her, and Liz gulped. Now she wasn't sure she was ready. She pushed back her freshly shampooed hair and stood, leaning on her crutches. The simple navy slacks and patterned sweater had disappointed Mamie, who had expected some Mata Hari outfit to sway Jason's decision. But just as he had refused to seduce her to aid his cause, Liz didn't intend to take that route, either. If their love had a chance, it must be based on truth, not lust.

In her hand, she clutched a copy of her article, along with the legal release.

She heard Mamie opening the front door, greeting Jason. As footsteps moved down the hall, Mamie said clearly, "I know you're tired, Jason, but there's an emergency waiting in your office."

"Hell, Mamie, it'll have to wait. I've spent most of the day trying to track down Liz, and I've got jet lag so badly, I couldn't make a decision if my life depended on it."

"It won't take long," Mamie assured him, and Liz tensed as the housekeeper swung open the door.

"It can't be . . ." Jason halted in his tracks when he saw his guest.

Liz trembled at the sight of him. *Oh, please, God, let him forgive me,* she prayed silently as her eyes devoured him.

Jason stared at her before turning back to Mamie. "Thanks, I'll take care of this," he said stiffly before shutting the door. When he turned back around, Liz waited for the angry blast she could see in his eyes.

Instead, he said, "I see you finally got the cast on your ankle."

"Jason . . ."

"Won't you sit down, Miss Broadhurst. I'm sure you must be uncomfortable standing."

Liz's heart sank at his formal tones. She collapsed on the sofa, misery filling her.

"Why are you here?"

If he would only yell at her, shake her, turn his anger loose on her, but his cold formality was killing her. Mutely, she extended the article and release form.

"What's that?" he demanded, not moving any closer.

"The . . . the article," she whispered.

His eyes never left her face, but he took one step closer. "Why wasn't it sent to my Los Angeles office?"

"I wanted to give it to you personally."

"Why?"

Liz gulped. She reminded herself she came to fight for her happiness. Struggling to her feet again under his silent watch, she had to clear her throat before she could say, "I had to write the article, Jason. I gave my word."

"So?"

He wasn't making this easy for her. Nothing had been easy since she met Jason Harmon. She bowed her head to gather her courage. She stared back at him. "I tried, Jason, and you were right. I can trust you. But I forgot about the article. I couldn't tell you how . . . how much I love you until . . ."

She never got any further because the silent, unmoving Jason had swept her into his arms, his lips sealing hers. Her crutches and the pages of the article fell unheeded to the floor as Liz held on tightly, her hands grasping his broad shoulders.

When next she surfaced, they were seated on the couch, wrapped in each other's arms. "Jason," she whispered in his ear as his lips sought the soft skin on her neck. "Jason, don't you want to read the article?"

"Hell and damnation, woman! I couldn't care less about the article. I've almost gone crazy thinking I'd lost you." Jason's lips returned to hers and Liz took several minutes to assure him he hadn't lost her.

"But, Jason, I have to give them the article . . . with your approval. I promised."

"Fine," Jason said unconcernedly as he nibbled at her ear.

"But, Jason . . ."

"Liz," he said plaintively, "if I sign whatever right now, could we get on with more important things? Like making love, or setting a wedding date? And telling the kids?"

"But you were so concerned earlier about the publicity, I thought . . ."

"It will be inconvenient if they put my face in front of half of America, dear heart, but I've learned it's not the end of the world. As long as I have you, I can put up with a little inconvenience."

"No problem," Liz assured him, her arms pulling him closer, ready to address his list of important details.